nnon

and THE LAKE SEASON

"Hannah McKinnon's *The Lake Season* is a pure delight. Iris Standish is such an appealing woman, handling an overload of family calamities with good sense and good will, not to mention a few really good times. It's a bonus that the setting on Lake Hampstead is as enticing and refreshing as McKinnon's voice."

—Nancy Thayer, *New York Times* bestselling author of *Nantucket Sisters*

"Two sisters, a glittering New England lake, and one desperate, last-chance summer set the stage for Hannah McKinnon's emotionally affecting new novel, *The Lake Season*. The story features the complex Iris and her unpredictable sister Leah but its power extends well beyond the beautiful, heartbreaking bond between these two women. A memorable rumination on life, loss, and how to find a path home."

Michelle Gable, nationally bestselling author of *A Paris Apartment*

"This is a beautiful tale of sisters, a heartfelt journey of truth and choices that will leave you deeply satisfied."

—Linda Francis Lee, bestselling author of *The Glass Kitchen*

"Hannah McKinnon's lyrical debut tells the story of a pair of very different sisters, both at a crossroads in life. McKinnon's great strength lies in her ability to reveal the many ways the two women wound—and ultimately heal—each other as only sisters can."

—Sarah Pekkanen, *New York Times* bestselling author

"Charming and heartfelt! Hannah McKinnon's *The Lake Season* proves that you can go home again; you just can't control what you find when you get there."

—Wendy Wax, nationally bestselling author

"Charming, absorbing, and perfectly paced, *The Lake Season* is as full of warmth as summer itself. Don't blame Hannah McKinnon if this cinematic tale has you glued to a beach chair until it's finished."

—Chloe Benjamin, author of *The Anatomy of Dreams*

"Sometimes funny, sometimes sad—but always bursting with compassion and sly humor. *The Lake Season* is a joy to read for anyone who cherishes the complexity and richness of family dynamics. Impossible not to be swept along by the characters. The perfect book to spread out with luxuriously on the beach."

—Saira Shah, author of *The Mouse-Proof Kitchen*

"Here is sisterhood in all its complexity, rich with tenderness, resentments and shared jokes, disappointment, admiration, and profound love. Those who have a sister will read this book and pass it on to them; those who do not, will wish more than ever that they did."

—Gabrielle Donnelly, author of *The Little Women Letters*

"An emotionally charged story about returning to yourself."

—K. A. Tucker, *USA Today* bestselling author

"A delicious tale of sisters and secrets. Hannah McKinnon's writing style is as breezy as a weekend at the lake, yet her insights into the murkiness of family interactions run deep. The takeaway of this compelling read is clear: you can know someone your whole life and not know them at all."

—Mary Hogan, award-winning author of *Two Sisters*

The Lake Season

◆ a novel ◆

Hannah McKinnon

EMILY BESTLER BOOKS
—
ATRIA

NEW YORK   LONDON   TORONTO   SYDNEY   NEW DELHI

ATRIA PAPERBACK
An Imprint of Simon & Schuster, Inc.
1230 Avenue of the Americas
New York, NY 10020

First Emily Bestler Books/Atria Paperback edition June 2015

EMILY BESTLER BOOKS / ATRIA PAPERBACK and colophons are trademarks of Simon & Schuster, Inc.

For information about special discounts for bulk purchases, please contact Simon & Schuster Special Sales at 1-866-506-1949 or business@simonandschuster.com.

The Simon & Schuster Speakers Bureau can bring authors to your live event. For more information or to book an event contact the Simon & Schuster Speakers Bureau at 1-866-248-3049 or visit our website at www.simonspeakers.com.

Interior design by Kyoko Watanabe

Manufactured in the United States of America

10 9 8 7 6 5 4 3 2 1

Library of Congress Cataloging-in-Publication Data is available.

ISBN 978-1-4767-7764-1
ISBN 978-1-4767-7766-5 (ebook)

To my parents, Marlene and Barry Roberts, who first put a book in my hands. And who allowed me to fill my childhood with stray pets, finger paint, ponies, wildlife, and what not . . . all the messy ingredients that make up a good story. And a great life.

The Lake Season

One

Iris should've had her nervous breakdown that morning. But there just wasn't time.

Instead she found herself bent over the ironing board in the laundry room, one puffy eye fixed on the driveway, where Jack, Sadie, and Lily awaited the bus, and the other fixed on the miniature Girl Scout badge she was attempting to iron onto Lily's uniform. Today was Thursday: Girl Scout day. And there was Lily standing uniform-less, once again, at the mailbox, while her mother frantically willed the iron to heat up.

"Damn it!" Iris singed her finger and stuck it in her mouth. She examined the Girl Scout patch, a small green circle containing a lone sheep. Had it been for farming? Or spinning wool? She couldn't remember. Nor had she remembered to iron it onto the uniform when Lily earned it, well over three months ago. Lily had refused to wear her sheep-less uniform to school one more day.

"It's embarrassing, Mom. All the other kids have their sheep."

Iris didn't blame her. The troop leader, Mrs. Crum, a sturdy woman with thick knees, had noticed, too. In fact, she'd asked Iris at the last meeting if perhaps the patch had been lost. Had gone so far to suggest, in a concerned tone, that Iris could indeed buy a replacement at the local hardware store that carried the badges, for cases like these. But Iris had no trouble deciphering the Mother-to-Mother Code: *Your kid was the only one to hand in her cookie sales proceeds late this year. And that was after you lost thirteen boxes of Do-Si-Dos. Are you going to screw this up, too?*

After singeing her finger twice more, Iris angrily flipped the patch over. She cringed at the melted brown plastic oozing from the underside. Of course: she'd forgotten to remove the sticker covering. Which she would have known to do if perhaps she'd read the directions in the first place.

"Crap!" She yanked the iron's cord from the wall. "Krazy Glue," she decided aloud, rummaging through the laundry room's overstuffed drawers. "Mrs. Crum will never know."

No sooner had she affixed the damaged badge than the kids and the dog stomped back into the mudroom.

"I did it!" Iris exclaimed, holding up the sash victoriously, careful to conceal the half-melted sheep with one finger.

"We missed the bus," Sadie announced, glaring accusingly at her mother.

Jack shrugged. Samson whined.

"Again?" Iris groaned.

As if in reply, there was a deep wretching sound at her feet. Iris looked down just as Samson threw up all over her fuzzy slippers.

❖ ❖ ❖

"If you hadn't made me change . . ." Sadie muttered, staring pointedly out the passenger window.

It was too early in the day, and besides, Iris's head pounded from sleep deprivation. She fumbled with her hot coffee as they pulled out of the driveway, choosing her words carefully. She'd learned this.

"That skirt was too short, Sadie. How about I take you to the mall this weekend for something new? Something that fits."

"It *fits* just fine," Sadie said.

Iris bit her lip, keeping her response to herself. *Not if your underpants flash every time you sit down.*

Ding, ding, ding. The car chimed, and she glanced quickly at the dashboard. Was a door open?

"Besides," Sadie went on. "Amy's mother bought her the same skirt. In three *different* colors."

Iris sighed, three tiny skirts dancing across her mind: pink, red, blue. Each the size of a napkin. She turned to Lily in the backseat. "Here, honey. Put your Girl Scout sash on."

Lily pulled it over her head and peered down at her chest. "Mom, why is the sheep brown?"

The chiming continued, loudly. Absently Iris pushed the nearest button on the dash. The window went down, then up. She swiped at another. The radio crackled.

Ding, ding, ding.

"Mom. *Seat belt*," Jack reminded her gently.

Ah.

Behind Iris, Lily's shoes tapped the floor in rhythm to the music. Iris reached toward the backseat, grasping her seven-year-old's purple Mary Jane and giving her toes a grateful squeeze.

Sadie riffled through her book bag and pulled out a lip gloss Iris didn't recognize. "I have talent-show tryouts today. Remember?"

Iris hadn't, of course. She had not slept in weeks. But at Sadie's mention of it, she recalled her daughter and her friends strutting around the bonus room to the tunes of Lady Gaga. Where had they learned to sway their hips like that? she'd wondered.

"I remember," she lied. "I'll pick you up at four."

"No way!" Sadie snapped the lip gloss shut. "Everyone's walking to the diner afterward. I already told you."

Iris turned, careful not to stare at her vampire-red lips. *Pick your battles.* "And your dad and I told *you*, we don't want you leaving school property and walking down a main road." She paused, considering her footing. "I could drop you and Amy off at the diner."

"Like some nursery school carpool? Are you insane?"

Clearly, yes. "Then I'll see you in the auditorium at four." She'd tried. Secretly Iris hated the other parents for so blithely turning their heads as their teenagers traipsed all over town, or stayed until closing at the mall, always unsupervised. Where the hell were these mothers, anyway?

"Mom?" In the rearview mirror Jack peered earnestly at her. "We need lunch money."

"But I packed chicken salad. Your favorite."

Sadie snorted. "Yeah. *Yesterday.*"

Iris scanned the car, eyes roving over the seats, across the floor, before a fuzzy image of three lunch bags flashed through her mind. All sitting on the kitchen counter, empty, three miles behind them.

"I could have sworn . . ."

Lily had already retrieved Iris's wallet from her purse. She and Jack counted out five dollars—they were short. "It's okay, Mom. I can borrow some lunch money from Mike," Jack said.

Iris wasn't sure which was worse: her eldest child's relentless disgust with her, or her younger children's tireless empathy. To be honest, she didn't feel she quite deserved either. And, resentfully, she couldn't help but think it was another one of those things their father somehow managed to evade.

As they turned onto the main road toward school, the car bumped over a pothole. The coffee mug lurched, drenching her lap in a ribbon of tawny liquid.

Sadie scowled at her mother's stained sweatpants.

Was *this* Iris's fault, too? She blinked, cursing the tears that threatened to leap from the corners of her eyes. Damn, Paul. She was coming undone in front of the kids.

But she was overcome with gratitude when Sadie didn't comment, and instead rummaged through the glove box for a napkin. Finally she pressed a wadded bunch in her mother's outstretched hand.

For a second their eyes met, and Iris smiled hopefully, blinking.

Sadie pursed her red lips. "For God's sake," she muttered. "Doesn't this car have a gas pedal?"

◆ ◆ ◆

She hadn't told the kids. Not yet. Despite the fact that it had been two weeks since Paul had dumped the news on her. He'd sat on the edge of the bed with his back to her, fiddling with the TV remote, when he'd said it.

"This isn't working, Iris."

She'd kept reading, stifling a yawn. "I think there are batteries in the drawer," she'd said.

"Not the remote, damn it. *Us*."

She set her book down.

Paul wanted a separation. No, a divorce, he'd said at first. But he'd withdrawn the jagged word when he saw the look on her face. As her whole body crumpled against the pillows, weakened suddenly by the suffocating air in their bedroom.

"A separation, then," he'd offered, backpedaling, as if it were somehow kinder to ease her into a dismal room for a time, before ushering her down an eternal tunnel of darkness.

She'd put her hand to her mouth, as if reaching for words. But for once she hadn't any.

And so he'd filled the space with his own. Paul was good at that. Litigation attorneys usually were.

"Come on, Iris," he'd said impatiently. "This can't be news to you. It's been dead for a while. Right?"

It had been, of course. But she'd refused to agree. She wouldn't give him that. Not after hanging on to the fabric of their family so determinedly for so long. If Paul was quick with the scissors, then Iris was deft with the glue.

With each rift, each disappointment over the years, she'd felt him pull away. Looking back now, she caught fleeting glimpses of it; a decline that crept from the shadows of their shared life. The threat was present, but always retreating, brushing up against them every now and then like an ominous black cat. If she forced herself to reconstruct the last few years like a jigsaw puzzle, she could see it in the background. A whisker here, a flicked tail there, until she couldn't deny the full feline form.

Ever since that night two weeks ago, Paul's demand had consumed her. Immobilized, she'd spent each morning in her bathrobe staring out the living room window at the magnolia tree in the front yard, trying to come to terms with the vibrant pink buds that somehow managed to thrust themselves into her now disjointed world. She wandered through the house entranced, only pulling herself together at three o'clock, right before the bus delivered her children home.

If she were honest, she supposed she could see it coming. They were very comfortable now in their Newton Victorian, but they hadn't always been. In the early years, things were tight. Paul was a junior associate in his firm, logging painfully long days, even weekends, for the senior partners. And when there was a big case, which there always seemed to be, he'd be called on day and night to research and file. Surely, Paul had felt those pressures. But what about hers? Staying home alone, year after year, resigned to a uniform of spit-up-stained tees and nursing bras. She remembered those early milk-drunk months viscerally, where she'd barely untangle herself from the bedsheets to nurse at all hours of the night, only to roll herself out again each morning to face yet another full dishwasher, another basket of laundry, and the seemingly eternal trail of toys that coiled from room to room no matter how many times she bent to retrieve them from the unmopped floor. The late-night coughs, followed by long waits at the doctor's, where equally weary parents comforted runny-nosed tots in an overheated waiting room. Friends had warned her about the fatigue. About the mood swings, and the monotony. But they'd also warned her about the fierce love that would pull her through.

Besides, there was such irreplaceable, seeping-into-your-bones joy that came with the sacrifices they'd made. The smell of a baby's downy head, warm with sleep, and Iris's own grateful tears in those middle-of-the-night rocking-chair moments. The raw hormonal surge of a love so urgent as she pulled her newborn to her breast, the silent reverberations of love coursing as steadily as her milk.

"Don't you miss your colleagues?" Paul asked once, somewhat incredulously, when her maternity leave from Sadie was up and she'd declined to go back. "Wouldn't it be nice to go in on the ski condo with the other guys from the firm this season?" She had enjoyed her work of course, but not in the way he meant. She did not long like he did for the fancy vacations or the sleek thirty-foot Hatteras that gleamed at the end of the neighbor's driveway. Perhaps Paul missed her old life more than she.

To appease him, once the kids were in school Iris had gone back to work. Sort of. She took on a few private writing clients of her own, and carved a small office space out of a corner in the upstairs hallway where she reviewed manuscripts and contacted publishers as a freelance agent. But while she initially relished the foray back into work, and the opportunity to prove herself to Paul, Iris often felt she was straddling a perilously sharp picket fence. On one side her family shouted her name, holding up empty dinner plates and feverishly waving incomplete homework assignments. On the other side loomed her clients, a less boisterous, but equally needy, crew. New writers expected scrupulous feedback, and established authors awaited overdue royalty statements. With one foot in each world, Iris teetered unnervingly in midair, never quite feeling like she fulfilled the demands of any of her flock. And in the rare instance that she even considered her own well-being, she found herself in jeopardy of landing hard on the pickets in an oh-so-private place.

But all of her efforts had gone unappreciated anyway, because once he made partner, Paul pulled a 180 on her and insisted she quit work altogether. By then she'd gotten into the swing of working from home. She enjoyed the creative outlet; she needed it. They'd argued about it for months. But the point was lost on Paul. He insisted they did not need her income, especially given how small it was. It was a kind of old-fashioned machismo Iris detested, and she further detested the creeping sense that she was a kept woman.

Then there was sex. Or the lack of it, truth be told. Admittedly, there were nights when Paul reached for her in the darkness and she'd roll away, mouth ajar in a rehearsed snore. But there were also nights she asked him to set down his BlackBerry, pressing suggestively against him, and he'd wave her away, blaming an early meeting.

But for all the challenges of raising a young family, Iris had muddled forward each year. Strode, even. Sure, there were days when Paul arrived home to find her weeping quietly at the kitchen table, face in her hands as the kids crawled through the spilled contents of the pantry that sprinkled the floor, tiny floury-white handprints inviting him into the living room; smashed chocolate chips that caulked the cracks of the antique wooden floors rather nicely.

"What on earth?" he'd asked, mouth agape in the doorway.

To which she'd wiped her eyes and replied evenly, "They wanted to bake."

That was the rarity. Most days Paul had arrived home, his own hair askew, flinging his briefcase onto the table with barely a hello to Iris, sinking into the toy-filled recesses of the couch as the kids clambered across him.

But in the end, Iris figured they'd made it. Just look at what they'd accomplished! The kids were healthy. They did the ski trips to Utah, and they joined the tennis club. The house was finally renovated. For her fortieth birthday Paul had shocked her with a Range Rover, a car she was embarrassed to drive, but secretly loved. He was a partner now, he reminded her. By both of their definitions, they'd made it.

Which is why she was so shocked when Paul came to her late that night two weeks ago with his decision, after she'd tucked the last child into bed. Laid out. Bowled over. This was their family. It was not perfect, but it was the way they'd done it for so long, in such silent seeming agreement, that she'd never seen it coming.

"There's someone else, isn't there?" she'd howled. It was the only answer that made sense.

Paul had denied it, and in a way that made her feel small. "Come on, Iris. Don't be so cliché."

Now, waiting in the long drop-off line at the school entrance, Iris watched her children hurry through the school doors, her heart in her chest. The driver behind her laid on the horn, jolting her.

She needed a plan. A lawyer. Something. Back at the empty house, Iris tossed her keys on the antique table by the door and took the stairs two at a time. She contemplated Paul's golf shorts on the bedroom rug. Out of habit, she bent to retrieve them, along with a dirty pair of balled-up socks, but then changed her mind and kicked them across the wood floor. Let him wash his own damn clothes. What she needed was a shower. Had she even had one yesterday?

At the sink Iris caught her reflection in the mirror. The creased eyes, the pallid complexion. Paul had spent two weeks sleeping on the couch, while she stared numbly at the bedroom ceiling overhead, willing him back upstairs. She teetered unnervingly between the urge to either throttle him or pull him under the covers and press herself against him. But he never came. Each morning the blankets would be folded neatly in the hall closet, the throw pillows politely replaced on the sofa. She knew it was to protect the kids, but the practiced ease with which he went about this new ritual stunned her and infuriated her, too. And now, after keeping a silent front for the last two weeks, she wasn't sure if it was him or herself that she was more disgusted with.

Despite the steady stream of the shower, Iris walked past it fully clothed. As the windows of the bathroom filled with steam, she climbed into the claw-foot tub in the corner, sank into its cold embrace, and wept.

Two

To Iris's dismay, Ainsley Perry was manning the soccer team's refreshment table. *Patrolling* would be more accurate. As parents approached, Ainsley lurched from behind her post, arms outstretched, not so much to accept their offering but to deflect the parents themselves. With a fixed smile, she steered them away from her potluck domain and redirected them to distant lands: the bleachers, perhaps, or the sidelines to cheer on the team. But Iris knew better. Backdrop to the congregants at this Saturday-morning ritual, the soccer field symbolized a sort of suburban pilgrimage: cramming the parking lot with their Volvo wagons and hybrid SUVs (a glaring oxymoron, in Iris's opinion), families paid weekly homage to gawk, gossip, and draw comparisons among their unwitting children's skills and, more often, one another. Pious attendance was casually noted, but lack of was nothing short of sacrilege. Iris knew: she had made that shameful mistake already this season. And so today, while stacks of unrevised manuscripts lay neglected on her office desk, Iris emerged from her car and began her maiden trek to the refreshment table, closing the perilous chasm between working mother and penitence. But she was not unarmed.

She had risen early, rolling out small circles of homemade dough for the occasion. Discarding the ones that landed on the floor, pulling stray dog hairs from the ones that did not. She'd pinched and shaped and sprinkled powdered sugar, traces of which still coated her furrowed brow. Because beneath the twinkling tinfoil on her antique ironware platter radiated the promise of deliverance in the form of two dozen almond crescents. Hastily, she tucked a stray hair behind her ear (oh no, was that her old scrunchie securing her ponytail?) and forced a smile. Today Iris would attempt to fit in, like the other moms who regularly graced the playground, hovered in the cafeteria, and clogged the school driveway at dismissal, while Iris's own offspring suffered the snail-trail route of the school bus. These mothers were everywhere.

It was in that same spirit that Ainsley Perry committed herself to her role as refreshment manager.

Ahead, a group of mothers hovered around the table, sleek heads bowed, inspecting the goods. Iris would do this to win over Sadie, whose adolescent good graces she had inexplicably fallen away from since the first day of middle school. For Jack, whose easygoing personality made him grateful for any cookie, period. And for Lily, still her baby, who'd throw her arms around her mother in that blessed unself-conscious way of the preadolescent. And lastly, for Paul, to prove to him that she could juggle it all, that there was a place for her at the refreshment table, should she wish to claim it. If only she'd remembered to change out her filthy running shoes for a cute pair of ballet flats! No matter.

"Well, Iris Standish, I haven't seen you *in ages!*" Ainsley said, but somehow her mouth remained conspicuously pursed. Collagen.

Iris tried not to stare at Ainsley's lips. "Good morning. I brought treats."

Ainsley peered beneath the foil, a look of alarm coming over her. "Are those cookies?"

Iris smiled. "Almond crescents. Homemade this morning."

"Well." Ainsley's smile shrank. She turned to a brunette woman Iris did not recognize, who blinked several times. The two immediately launched into some eye-fluttering dialect that Iris could not interpret.

"Gluten free?" Ainsley asked finally.

Iris shook her head.

"Non-GMO?" the other pressed hopefully.

Iris shrugged. "Um, I'm not sure."

"Huh. How about I put these over *here*," the other woman replied, relieving Ainsley of the platter and turning to a second table that Iris noted was void of all refreshments.

Ainsley's brow unfurrowed. "Perfect."

Iris was confused. Her eyes moved over the plates before her, each carefully unwrapped and uncovered for easy access: carrot sticks, kale chips, hummus, orange wedges, edamame. Were those grapes *peeled*? Then at her own platter, alone on the other table, whose foil remained sealed, obscuring the loveliness that was her batch of crescent cookies.

"Why don't I help?" she asked, peeling back the foil.

Ainsley and the other woman bumped against each other as they lurched in choreographed unison. "No!" the brunette cried, her smile faltering. "No, *thank you*, we've got it." Her fingers danced across the foil, curling it back over the cookies, covering them in darkness once more.

Ainsley nodded vigorously, playing with the top button on her cashmere cardigan. Iris made note of her manicured nails, a tasteful shade of colorless pink.

Iris swiped at her frayed ponytail. "Well, it's just that these are Sadie's favorites. And some of her friends', too," she added hastily, though truthfully Iris had no idea if any of Sadie's friends liked almond crescents.

"I'm sure they are," Ainsley said. "But this is the healthy food table. That one's for . . . *others*."

Iris looked again at the table before her, mountainous in its elevations of varied nutritional terrain. As if these mothers sliced their snack profiles right out of the government's Recommended Dietary Allowances poster, with one of those handy little Williams-Sonoma vegetable clippers.

And then she glanced at the other table. The table where her contribution lay. It was empty, an open plain of Formica surface, save for a lone keg of illicit Kool-Aid that some other unenlightened mother erringly brought. Poor soul.

It was more than Iris could stand. Suddenly the predawn hours she'd spent in her ratty bathrobe bent over the kitchen island surged up in her throat: the whirring of the beaters, the powdering of the crescents. How her back ached bending over each tray as she formed individual half-moons, imagining the cheerful squeal the kids would emit upon seeing the cookies.

Behind her the air horn blew. Now she'd missed the damn game.

"Well, since it's the *only* dessert on the dessert table, let's unwrap it." Hastily, Iris removed the foil again. She could hear the kids thundering toward the table.

"Really, you needn't trouble yourself." The brunette covered the cookies once more, with a flourish.

"No trouble at all," Iris said flatly. She reached for the tray, this time whisking the foil right off the platter and crumpling it quickly into a tiny, silver ball, which she clenched triumphantly in her closed fist. "Ta-da!"

The two women regarded her with a look of cool contempt, just as the players rose up around them like a uniformed tide.

"Children, children!" Ainsley Perry cried, trying to gain control. "Fruits and veggies, over here!"

Obediently, the children lined up. Quickly the mothers went to work, doling out carrot sticks like Civil War nurses tending to battlefield soldiers.

But Iris was not to be excluded. "Cookies! Who wants COOKIES?" Yes, she was sabotaging Ainsley's order. But she could not help it.

"Cookies?"

"Come and get them!" Iris was yelling now. But it felt great. The children surrounded her like a mob, and she whisked the cookies off the tray. Onto plates, into the hands of those with no plates. One right into a little boy's mouth. She looked up, unable to contain her laughter. Now, *where* was Sadie?

A small hand tugged her shirt.

"Jack! Want a cookie?"

Jack's brow wrinkled. "Coach says no sweets at games."

And then reality hit. Beyond the crowd of cheering children, there was another. A stunned group. Parents with arms crossed. A coach blowing his whistle in an attempt to restore order. And one distressed face in particular: Sadie's.

Sadie was in the fruit-and-vegetable line. Not in Iris's.

"I made your favorite!" Iris sputtered, holding the tray overhead as she waded toward Sadie.

When had it gotten so quiet?

"Want one?"

Sadie glared at the smashed crumbs scattering the platter. Then at her mother. "What are you *doing*?"

And before Iris could respond, she was gone.

Paul appeared at Iris's elbow. "What's gotten into you?" At least he whispered it, relieving her of her tray, guiding her away from the table and the wondrous expressions of those surrounding it.

Lily and Jack followed behind them, all the way to the car. Iris did not resist.

It was only after Paul had closed her driver door, leaving her alone in the Rover, that Iris realized what a scene she'd made. "Meet you at home," he'd mumbled, before stalking off.

The kids had gone with their father, of course. The sensible one.

Iris gripped the steering wheel and rested her head on its cool surface. What was happening to her?

There was a gentle tap on the window. *Lily.* Chewing one of her forsaken cookies.

Iris unrolled it.

"Don't worry, Mom. These are really good."

◆　◆　◆

The orange postcard came in the mail that morning. Iris hadn't noticed it at first, tucked as it was amid the bills. She separated them from the newspaper, which she tossed directly into the recycling: there was enough sadness in her house at the moment—she hadn't any room left for wars or failing economies. Iris was halfway through making the kids lunch when she saw the glimmer of orange from behind the electric bill on the counter. She plucked it out. Immediately she recognized the scene.

Hampstead, New Hampshire. A red canoe tethered to a dock. It was one of the old lake postcards that Hawley's Market used to sell when they were kids. She and Leah liked to collect them and hide them for each other under rocks or on the back porch, like secret messages. She hadn't seen one like this in years. Where had Millie found it? Iris flipped the card over. But right away, she saw it was not Millie's handwriting. The loose cursive was as dreamy and breathless as Leah's voice.

"Please Come."

No signature, no date. Iris shook her head, reading the two words over and over. *Come where?* she wondered impatiently. Leah was all the way out in Seattle, where she had recently moved with her new fiancé, and the last Iris had heard, she wasn't scheduled to fly in until just before her wedding. The same wedding she hadn't even bothered to call her sister about, after not bothering to inform her that she'd become engaged to a man Iris had never even met. Maybe the postcard was an overdue attempt to reach out, an apology of sorts. It wasn't as if the postcard was the wedding invitation itself. Iris had already received that lavish statement, an ecru (whatever that meant) card embossed with hand-gilded gold. She couldn't help but wonder at the cost. Her parents had money, yes, but they were conservative. Modest. This invitation was all about excess.

Iris tossed the postcard back on the pile of bills. How like Leah to pen something cryptic and leave her struggling to decipher it. As though she had nothing better to do. Iris wasn't having it. If anyone should be sending off warning flares or writing messages in the sand, it was her. She called the kids inside for lunch. She cleared the dishes when they were done, took Samson for a long walk, and drove Lily across town to a playdate. But as with everything Leah touched, the orange postcard demanded attention, nagging at Iris's thoughts throughout the day, and when she came home later that afternoon she sheepishly retrieved it from the mail pile and tucked it in her jeans pocket. As much as it annoyed her, the postcard represented something beyond Leah's furtive message. It was a sort of final push. One that Iris accepted with both dread and relief.

Three

"Ernesto! Ernesto, is that you?" Her mother's voice was distant, muffled, followed by a *clunk* and sharp barking. "Hello? Are you there?"

Iris sighed. "Mom. It's me."

"Oh, hello, dear. I thought you were Ernesto. I sent him to the nursery and I can't imagine what is keeping him."

Iris pictured Millie standing amid the well-tended plants in her vegetable garden, a cultivated wake of lettuce leaf and tomato vine trailing behind her. No doubt she was clad in her collared linen shirt and khaki shorts, a wide-brimmed hat set elegantly on her gray hair, as one of her rat terriers raced around the garden borders, in its usual crazed orbit.

"What's wrong, Mom?"

Her mother's pinched expression was vivid through her voice alone. "Blight!"

"You got a bite?"

"No, Iris. *Blight!* The tomatoes have blight. I'll have to tear out the whole lot!" Her voice was shrill now, and Iris imagined the blighty vines cowering in the shadow of her mother's Wellington boots.

Millie Standish was not an avid gardener. She was a champion, a commanding presence in her local garden club and a force to be reckoned with in her own backyard. Throughout her county, Millie gave seasonal lectures about preparing spring beds, cultivating summer soil, and putting perennials to sleep for the hard New England winter. Practices that gave the cozy, if false, impression that she was a nurturing woman. Her expertise in all things growing was well known and respected in the community, though Iris could hardly call her ministrations tender. Millie Standish did not coax flowers into bloom so much as she forced them. Her lush lakeside property may have evoked English countryside images of tea among the roses to the unknowing visitor. Big mistake. Millie Standish was an evolutionist, hard bent toward survival of the fittest. There was no pity for the delicate. She plucked and pruned with a vengeance, armed with various primitive tools to clip, hedge, and deadhead. What did not thrive was ripped from its roots and discarded without thought. Iris always pitied the seasonal work staff Millie hired. Like the meeker species in the garden, most didn't survive the summer. Except for Ernesto, who for some reason returned year after year, as robust as the hedges that swelled around the family house's foundation.

"Mom, can we talk?"

There was a pause, followed by another thud. Iris imagined the tomatoes screaming. "Isn't that what we're doing?"

Iris did not bother rolling her eyes. She was used to her mother's impatient efficiency. "Well, yes. I suppose. Anyway, I was thinking the kids and I would come up there. For a couple of weeks."

"Of course you're coming. The wedding's the first week of August. If we all survive until then."

Iris ignored her mother's invitation to indulge her complaints. She had bigger problems than bridal favors. "Actually, Mom, I was thinking sooner. And that we might stay a bit longer. If that's okay with you and Dad."

"Sooner? Longer?" Millie did not sound pleased by the idea. But then, she did not like surprises, even when they involved grandchildren. "What's going on?" Millie Standish's nose was sharper than her rat terriers'. She was onto Iris.

After two weeks of passing each other in their own halls like strangers, Iris had had enough with her and Paul's détente. She'd not spoken to anyone about it, except her childhood friend Trish, who'd told her to come home for a while. And soon. But after summoning the courage to call her mother, Iris could see that wouldn't be easily accomplished.

"Is something wrong, Iris?"

Iris began circling the kitchen island, picking up the leftover breakfast dishes, then setting them down again. "Not really. Paul has a law conference coming up, and he'll be busy, so I thought it would be good for the kids to come up early."

Silence. "Good for the kids?" Millie was sniffing the air, picking up the scent. "What about Sadie's cheerleading camp? And isn't Jack going to lacrosse?"

Iris groaned inwardly. Leave it to Millie to remember. Not that Iris had forgotten. Not entirely. She'd just neglected to realize how soon next week was.

"Well, yes. But they can go to camp, and then join Lily and me later."

"But doesn't Lily have swim team?" Suddenly Iris hated her mother's good memory. It's not like she wished full-blown dementia on the woman, but couldn't her mind wobble just a little, like so many of her friends' aging parents? She was not ready to let the cat out of the bag. Not yet.

"Mom. Yes, the kids have camp, and I'll see that they get to them."

"So this is really about you."

The cat was out. "Yes. Yes, I suppose it is."

Silence. "What about Paul?"

Iris chewed her lip. "What about him?"

"What does he think about this plan?" Once more Millie sounded disappointed. Her daughter, who could not seem to remember her own kids' camp schedules, or manage a happy marriage, had been caught running away like an adolescent summer camper herself.

"Paul's especially busy at the firm this summer." And covering his tracks, whatever he was up to.

On the other line Millie took an audible breath. "I *see*."

The cat was dead.

"Well, the farm stand just opened last weekend. And of course, there's Leah's wedding . . ." Her voice trailed off.

Leah. Iris's sister, younger only in years, who was more seasoned and sophisticated in all ways. Leah, who'd effortlessly gotten into every top-tier college to which she applied, but ended up transferring three times anyway before going overseas for a semester in Greece, which turned into two years of spotty communication from abroad. Leah, who'd charmed every eligible, good-looking athlete their high school proffered up and also several ineligible ones; who'd had the luxury of both never being on the receiving end of a breakup as well as cultivating a handsome crowd of competent replacements on the sidelines. Who had sworn on the very morning of Iris's own wedding day, in fact, that the choice to dedicate herself to one man was not for her, nor would it ever be, as she methodically adjusted her older sister's veil and looked deeply into her eyes and whispered, "I'm just not like you." As if there were ever any doubt.

As teenagers Iris had covered for her sister, fabricating grand explanations for Leah's empty bed in the middle of the night, or the dented fender on their father's BMW, which had been discovered parked at a hazardous angle in the front lawn after a graduation party. Iris tired of it—not so much of the covering up, but of the good luck that followed Leah through their shared adolescent world. Iris was left to struggle in her wake: the one with metal braces, poorly complexioned boyfriends, and the dull social life. How could two people who grew up under the same cedar-shingled roof, who shared not only the same genealogical blueprint but also its idiosyncrasies, be so different? As evidenced in some of the more bitter diary entries that she'd later stumbled across, Iris had envied Leah. Hated her, even. The writing was on the wall, or in this case, in the pink floral journal, penned in harried, angry sentences. *"She's going to senior prom with Thad Turner. And she's only a freshman!"*

The only explanation for her enduring efforts to protect her younger sibling, which provided no real consolation, was that Iris was also in awe of her little sister. She was no more indifferent to Leah's charm than any other unsuspecting fool lured by her sister's charisma, as much as she was burdened by it. Popular, lovely Leah needed her, and the fact of it filled her simultaneously with dread and excitement. In the least, it provided Iris with a sense of purpose. As high school wore on, she took some solace as Leah's ally, believing herself the creative mind behind the more impressive of Leah's adolescent schemes. And that fleeting sense of belonging, however intrinsic by the fact of their sisterhood, was as fundamental to Iris's own teenhood sense of identity as any other relationship she'd forged. The magnetism of Leah's easy laughter, the captivating flicker in her eyes, the air that shifted with every graceful gesture. Sure, there was the homecoming weekend when Iris took her to a party at the Cove, where Leah drank so much grain alcohol punch that she spent the night vomiting puddles of red all over the backseat of a friend's new VW, staining the pristine white leather a nauseating pink. And there was the time that some of the more popular senior girls on the varsity field hockey team spent weeks spreading hateful gossip because Leah had attracted the attention of some of their senior boyfriends. But eventually even that petered out, because Leah was a star on the JV squad and she never really cared about those boys anyway. Besides, soon most of the senior girls had included her in their tight inner circle. Something unheard-of to Iris, who was herself a largely anonymous junior at the time.

Even in college Leah had kept her family on their toes, calling home from Mexico to inform them that not only had she used Bill's credit card to sneak off on spring break but she'd been kicked out of the hotel she'd been staying in because the group she'd gone with had partied too loudly. And could he please send money? While predictable Iris was home, seated at her child-hood desk dutifully studying for spring exams.

But in the end, in spite of her wrongdoings, Leah was always forgiven. And now that she'd come to her senses in adulthood, "straightened out" (or however Millie chose to explain away the facts), Leah was finally fulfilling all of their hopes and wishes. She'd found a good man and was settling down, like a good WASP daughter.

"You have spoken with Leah, right?" Millie's tone implied accusation more than inquiry.

"We've been playing phone tag," Iris lied. The truth was, aside from the quick formal cheer over a long-distance Christmas phone call, she and her sister hadn't really talked in a couple of years.

Now, with Leah's wedding ahead, and her own marriage pos-sibly behind, Iris swallowed hard and chose her words carefully. "Let me help with the wedding," she offered. "Or put me to work at the vegetable stand."

Millie's tone was impatient. "It's not as simple as selling a few ears of corn, Iris. The farm business has taken off, if you'd both-ered to come see."

"I'll figure it out, Mom. Tell me what to do, and I'll do it." Iris cringed as she said it.

There was a painful pause, during which Iris repeated silently, *I will not beg. I will not beg.*

"All right, I'll fix up your old room."

There was a distant roaring over the phone, followed by the tinny barking of at least a thousand small dogs. "Ernesto, finally! Park the truck over there."

Iris collapsed against the kitchen counter, relieved. She'd done it. No need to wait for her mother to come back on the line. The conversation was over.

Four

"You *left*?" Trish, her high school best friend, sounded almost gleeful on the other line.

"No, Trish, I didn't *leave*. I'm just getting away for a little while." Iris exited the highway and headed down the ramp toward a sea of tufted pines. She took a deep breath.

"Yep, you left."

Though leaving, if that's what it really was, had been almost impossible.

"What do you mean you're going to Grandma's?" Sadie had asked Iris the night before.

She'd cornered Iris in her closet, surrounded by piles of unfolded clothes. Iris had looked up at her daughter's willowy frame in the doorway. When did she get so beautiful?

"Honey, we're all going to Grandma's. I'm just going up a few weeks early."

Sadie's green eyes had narrowed. "Why?"

Iris tossed one last pair of jeans into the suitcase and zipped it closed. Wait—toothpaste! Whenever she traveled she always forgot the toothpaste. It drove Paul crazy.

"Aunty Leah's wedding is just a few weeks away, and they need help. Besides, you'll be at cheer camp, and Jack and Lily will be busy, too. You won't even miss me."

But Iris had worried that they would. Certainly, she would miss them. That very morning as she said her good-byes in the driveway Jack had good-naturedly kissed her good-bye. "Have a great time, Mom. Make sure you bring a good book to read." He frowned. "You did pack a book, right?" Jack. Always thinking of his mother, wishing her the best right down to the detail of reading material. She ruffled his hair and kissed him again, hard. Lily had placed her hands on either side of Iris's face and looked at her for a long time. She said nothing, her face serene and open, as if memorizing her mother. And then just as quickly she darted off, yelling, "I'm going to Olivia's. She got a new trampoline!"

Sadie had leaned one hip against the car, her expression accusing. Guilt inspiring. "Lily's going to cry for you, you know that, right?" The child was masterful.

"No, she won't," Jack said from across the driveway. He bounced the basketball against the garage door. "You're just trying to make Mom stay."

"Am not." Sadie glared at him.

Iris reached for Sadie, pressing her hand against her cheek. "She'll be fine. And so will you."

Sadie allowed her mother to hold her for just a moment before pulling away. "Whatever. Besides, Daddy's taking us to Chow Mein's for dinner."

And there it was. A tiny, perfectly aimed teenage blow.

Iris didn't do Chinese. It sent her thundering to the ladies' room every time, and the family joke was that whenever Iris had a PTA meeting or appointment, Paul and the kids could sneak out for a greasy meal without her.

It was no big deal. But standing in the morning heat, notwithstanding Sadie's scowl, the mention of a family dinner without her was more than Iris could swallow. She could hear Paul now: *Really, Iris, since when is takeout food a personal affront?* But she couldn't help it. Sadie announced their dinner plans as if she were suddenly liberated from the burden of her mother's fragile digestive system.

They'd be fine without Iris. They'd eat Chinese nightly, glee-fully toasting her absence with the plastic click of their chop-sticks. *Thank goodness she's gone. Pass the wontons!*

Ridiculous, Iris knew. But here they were, already going on without her.

"Have fun," Iris said, swallowing hard. "I'll call you tonight."

"Whatever." Iris sat in the car, listening to the angry *thwack, thwack, thwack* of Sadie's flip-flops on the walkway, her heart aching in her chest as they grew fainter.

She knows, Iris thought as she backed out of the driveway. *She knows, even if she doesn't know the details.*

Now Trish's voice was firm in her ear as she drove. "This trip is exactly what you need. I'm proud of you."

Iris wasn't sure though. Already, the guilt was grinding her down. It wasn't fair. Fathers left all the time, it seemed. For work, for golf trips, let alone for the most indulgent of male reasons: the generic midlife crisis.

"It's just for a few weeks." Iris said the words for herself as much as for Trish. "The kids will join me at the end of July. And then, well, I don't know."

Silence. "I wouldn't count on Paul. Forget him. Forget the details. What you need is to breathe in some of our murky lake air you love so much. And eat some of your mother's hydroponic tomatoes."

"Hydro-what?"

Trish chuckled. "The tomatoes. They're *hydroponic.*"

"See? That's exactly what I'm talking about. Even *you* know more about my mother's farm than I do."

"Which is exactly why you need to get your rear end up here. Come eat the damn fruit, and forget the details."

For fourteen years Iris's whole life was consumed by details: homework, playdates, soccer games, Girl Scouts. Feed the dog at four, the kids at six. What would happen if she forgot all of that? It was the worst kind of plan!

As if Trish were reading Iris's mind, her voice coursed through the static airwaves. "Whatever you do, don't even think of turning around."

Iris laughed. "Would you drag me back to Hampstead if I bailed?"

"Worse. I'd drag you to the Jersey Shore for our annual trip with my mother-in-law, and make you sit through backgammon on the boardwalk with Aunty Ro. With all twenty of Wayne's relatives packed into that two-bedroom shanty. Two bedrooms!"

Honestly, Iris didn't think it sounded so bad. Right now she wouldn't mind someone named Aunty Ro feeding her home-made cannoli. The woman was probably soft as a pillow, and would cluck her tongue sympathetically while administering Iris copious glasses of Chianti.

Their connection began to break up, but there was one more thing. Iris twisted the wedding band on her finger as she asked it. "Tell the truth, Trish. Do you think I'm a bad mom?"

Trish didn't hesitate. "Even the best moms deserve a break. Especially in your shoes."

Iris would have liked very much to step out of her shoes. She'd like to kick them off, throw them out, and traipse around in someone else's for a while. Maybe in a pair of hot-pink Manolos. She still had great legs. But suddenly she was tired and hungry, and she didn't want to think anymore about shoes or weddings or any of it. She just needed to get there.

It always amazed Iris how quickly the lake infused her senses. Just north of the highway, the hills began to rise before her. Surrounded by thick woodlands, the lake region of New Hampshire was a welcome reprieve for any urban dweller, especially a separated single mother on the run. Where water suffused everything, from damp beach towels hung on the brass hooks in her mother's paneled mudroom to the cool dew that dressed the wicker rockers on the stately wraparound porch. The lake was everywhere: in the air, between your toes. It even found you in sleep, rippling through your dreams, its gentle wake a soothing balm to all that ailed you. And this summer, Iris had lost track of all her ailments.

◆   ◆   ◆

Trish's last words were still fresh in her head as she approached the turnoff for the farm: *Embrace the dirt.* Iris wasn't sure if she'd meant the dirt in the garden or the dirt in her life. But either way, she was determined to do both. Just ahead, her parents' drive was marked by a "Standish Farm" sign. Iris had plans to roll down the driveway, relishing the familiar crunch of pea gravel beneath her tires, past the old barns, and up to the farmhouse, where she could unfold herself from the car and relax on the porch overlooking the lake that wrapped around the formidable New England saltbox. But instead, Iris found the driveway cordoned off with a yellow rope. She had to park the Range Rover along the road with the rest of the traffic. Was this all for the farm stand?

Millie emerged through the crowd as if on cue, trailed by a short sea of frenetic terriers whose stumpy tails kept time to their owner's hurried step.

"Where have you *been*?" Her steel-gray hair was neatly swept beneath a smart straw hat, her collared shirt crisp and elegant against her brown skin. There was no warmth to the welcome. That was left to the dogs, who yapped and snipped at Iris's feet. "Hurry, Iris. This is rush hour."

"Hi, Mom." To herself, she thought, *Nice to see you, too!* Iris navigated the canine wave precariously and checked her watch. It was barely ten o'clock, still a reasonable morning hour to a rational person.

"What are you doing?" Millie asked impatiently, as Iris stopped at the little umbrella stand to inspect some vegetables. "This way!"

And for the first time Iris looked up the length of the stone driveway. The red barn that led to the fields had been renovated. No longer was it the sagging old building Iris used to drive past on her way to the main house. It looked brand-new. Trailing Millie, Iris took in the clapboard siding and the cedar-shingled roof, the lush flower beds and shrubs tucked around it. Neatly arranged wooden barrels teemed with produce. Not to mention the crowd of customers milling about them.

"*This* is the farm stand?" Iris sputtered. Inside, the barn housed a counter and cash register, a half dozen tables of produce, and kitschy country decorations that lined the weathered barn-board shelves. Indeed, it'd been turned into a full-blown seasonal store.

"What were you expecting?" Millie asked over her shoulder.

"It's just so . . . big."

"Your sister spent the last two seasons getting this up and running. Isn't it grand?" She directed Iris inside, where rows of late-season strawberries lined the homemade displays like rubies tucked into little green jewelry boxes.

Stunned, Iris ran her fingers across the fruit. So this was what her mother had been badgering her to come see last summer. "It's incredible. It's so much more than the little umbrella stand you used to run at the end of the driveway." She spun around, taking in the crowd, the store, the sweet fragrance of summer fruit. "You and Leah did all this?"

For the first time since her arrival, Millie smiled. "And your father, of course."

Bill Standish must have already sensed her arrival. "There's my girl!" The door to the back room creaked and Iris's father filled its frame, still formidable in both height and charm. "How are we, darling?" He held her back for a better look through his tortoiseshell glasses and grinned. It was their standard greeting that had not wavered over time, and the "we" always made Iris feel like a little girl again, in the best sense.

"We're good, Daddy." Iris hated that she had to lie.

But there was no time to elaborate. Millie directed her away. "We need to get back to the customers. Iris, I'm putting you on strawberry duty with Naomi."

Naomi turned out to be an intern from UNH with short, spiky hair. And a nose ring, Iris noted with bemusement—someone whose look her mother normally wouldn't tolerate, let alone employ. She was thrilled to see that the tips of the girl's hair were dyed purple. All morning Iris did her best to shadow Naomi as the customers came; she filled bags, counted change, and struggled to keep up. Before she knew it her stomach was growling and her head felt light. Couldn't she just sneak down to the house for a quick shower? She was relieved when her mother finally called for a break and handed her a bagged lunch.

"Your sister loved working the stand," Naomi said, taking a seat beside Iris in the shade. "We've missed her this season."

Iris turned. "You know Leah?"

"Sure. Leah took me under her wing last summer when I first got here. Was a hoot to work with."

Iris stared into her sandwich, wondering how much of a hoot she'd been to work with so far. Probably not much. And as far as wings went, hers stretched in the opposite direction, from here to Massachusetts.

"Last year was our fledgling summer, but your mom and Leah got the farm up and running. They taught me a lot." She took a swig from her thermos. "I'm happy for Leah, but I still can't believe she moved out to Seattle with Stephen. This farm was her baby."

"I can't believe she's getting married," Iris allowed now, wondering if Naomi knew much about Stephen. Hoping the girl would offer up some information.

"Yeah," Naomi said. "It isn't the same around here without her. But Stephen's good for her." She paused, contemplating her iced tea. "She's better now."

It struck Iris as a strange choice of words. "Better?"

Naomi shrugged. "He balances her, you know?"

Iris did not know. She wanted to ask more. But then Millie pulled up in the truck and beeped.

"Picking time," Naomi said, hopping up. "Got to replenish before the afternoon crowd."

Iris shoved the last bit of sandwich into her mouth. Naomi eyed her as she held open the truck door. "You've picked before, right?"

"Plenty," Iris said, climbing into the cab. Iris had picked vegetables in her mother's small backyard plot when she and Leah were kids. How hard could it be?

◆ ◆ ◆

Two hours later, squatting beside a row of hydroponic tomato containers, Iris had her answer. Millie regarded her warily. "You look awfully red, dear. Did you put on any sunscreen?"

Iris had. But only about an hour before, when her shoulders started to sting with exposure. Now, under a tattered straw hat that Naomi had insisted she wear, she wiped the salty trails of perspiration that ran down either side of her nose. She was pretty sure her mascara had melted. At best, she probably resembled a rabid raccoon.

"Why don't you take a break," Millie said.

"No, no," Iris protested. "I'm fine." She sensed, hopefully, that Millie appreciated her effort, however rusty her gardening skills. And that wasn't something Iris was about to surrender.

When they finally climbed back into the air-conditioned cab of the truck, it was all she could do not to cry out "Shotgun!" and press her forehead to the dashboard vents.

"Can I go up to the house and shower now?" Iris asked hopefully.

In reply, Millie turned the truck back to the stand. "You didn't forget about the afternoon shift, did you?"

It was more than she'd bargained for. Back at the stand, as the customers approached with their cloth bags, Iris glared at Ernesto's and Naomi's tanned skin—thick, seemingly impervious to the heat—and at her mother's own dark complexion. Not the sickly red that Iris imagined her own to be. As Iris weighed boxes of berries, she tried not to hate the steady stream of cars that pulled up by the farm's "Welcome!" sign. Oh, if only Iris had a brush in hand. Black would be her color of choice. In just a few fell strokes she'd paint a little message of her own: "Closed for the Day!" Or better yet, "Pick Your Own Damn Fruit!" The heat was getting to her, she knew. Right now the kids would be home from camp, with Paul, relaxing in the cool shade of their backyard.

"Hey, how much for the lettuce?" a woman with a thick Long Island accent asked. Iris couldn't help but notice her tacky gold sandals. Heels, no less.

Iris pointed to the sign and forced a smile.

"Three fifty?" The woman chucked the lettuce back into its bin.

"It's organic."

"It's outrageous," the woman replied. She laughed too loudly to her friend, and coughed. Probably a smoker as well. "We pay half that in the city. Where there aren't even any farms!"

Iris swiped at her sticky brow. "Because it's probably shipped a thousand miles from South America shellacked with pesticide. And tastes like cardboard."

The woman scowled. "Screw you, lady."

In an instant Millie was beside her.

"What are you *doing*?" she hissed. Iris closed her eyes. It was happening all over again. Just like the day at the soccer field with Sadie.

"I'm sorry," she grumbled, yanking the straw hat off her matted hair.

"Why don't you work the register." It wasn't a request.

Iris slumped on the stool behind the ancient register and eyed the tip bucket with loathing. One more hour, she told herself. She opened the till and began counting the bills inside, summoning the cool slap of lake water on her bare feet. Yes, she'd focus on that image. Not the pressing crowd or the suffocating smell of exhaust emanating from the blacktop. Or the faces that loomed too close as they thrust bills at her. Like the man beside her, who she now realized was studying her, and not the baskets of tomatoes. What was the matter with him anyway?

"May I *help* you?" she snapped, turning to face him.

"Iris Standish?"

Cooper Woods flashed the very same smile of his high school yearbook photo, the one in which he stood in the back row of the lacrosse team with the other tall, broad-shouldered boys. His skin was browned by summer and his handsome features had sharpened at the edges by the years, but his eyes still crinkled with boyish laughter.

"Cooper?" And before she could bring a hand to her melted mascara or wipe away another trickle of sweat, she closed her eyes, slipped off her stool, and slid indecorously into a display of Better Boy tomatoes.

♦　♦　♦

Iris blinked, pushing herself up onto her elbows. "The light . . . make it stop."

Bill Standish straddled his daughter, brandishing a large black Maglite, which he aimed directly into Iris's pupils. "They're not dilated!" he exclaimed to the small crowd of onlookers.

Then came her mother's firm hands, pressing her back down against the cold dirt floor. "For goodness' sake, lie down," Millie commanded. "Or you'll faint again."

Was that what had happened? Iris opened her eyes and found herself wedged between the shelves of fruit, the smell of crushed tomato acrid in her nose. The loud voices disoriented her.

"I need to sit up," she mumbled, feeling her head. It seemed intact, though her hair was all sticky.

"Oh, not my Better Boys!" Millie clucked as Iris pulled a clump of crushed tomato from her hair.

Before she could object, a bottle of water was thrust against her lips, and a rush flooded Iris's mouth, choking her.

"You must rehydrate," Millie said.

Iris sputtered.

And then, suddenly, there was another set of hands pulling her up onto her feet. Large, warm hands that squeezed her own.

"Let's get you up."

It was him.

"Cooper." Iris stood shakily, gazing up at the last thing she remembered.

"You okay?"

From the unfamiliar safety of Cooper Woods's grasp Iris surveyed the view. Her father, still clutching his flashlight like a misguided paramedic; her mother, whose crossed arms left no mistaking her exasperation; and the small group of produce-wielding strangers who'd congregated for a better look. As it all came into painful focus, Iris wanted nothing more than to turn and run.

Cooper leaned in. "Figured I'd better get you up before they drowned you, next," he whispered.

"I knew you'd do this," Millie said, wagging her head. "I kept telling you to take a rest."

Do this. As though heatstroke were a choice.

"Mom, I just got a little overheated," Iris groaned, swiping tomato bits from her hair.

Naomi appeared with a chair, and to her embarrassment, they guided her to a shady corner and made her sit.

"I'm okay," Iris insisted. But she wasn't. Not by a long shot. Propped up like a rag doll in a plastic chair, she didn't dare to think what her face looked like, all blotchy and melted. Her rear end was soaked in tomato juice.

"Well," Millie said, "back to work, then." She clapped her hands, dispersing the onlookers like a ringmaster sending off the clowns, before turning abruptly to Cooper. "Thank you," she said warmly. "I'm surprised to see you on your day off."

Day off?

Cooper shook his head. "I was driving down to the lake, so I figured I'd drop off some lumber on my way."

Iris stole a peek out of the corner of her eye, allowing her gaze to roam over his navy-blue polo shirt, his beach-tousled brown hair. Cooper's lanky teenage frame had filled out into that of a man's, but he'd maintained his athletic carriage.

Millie placed her hand on his arm. "What can I get for you? The Swiss chard is lovely this summer."

"I'll let the expert choose," Cooper replied with an appreciative smile, his gaze returning to Iris, who suddenly wished her plastic chair would fly her away.

"So how are you, Iris?"

Iris would have blushed if her face hadn't already been a deep shade of heatstroke red. "Great," she said, then laughed at the ridiculousness of it. "Well, up until the last five minutes." Or the last five months, she thought. She forced herself to meet his gaze.

Cooper's eyes were a calming blue, like the deeper shoals of the lake, and for a moment Iris felt her insides stilling. "So, you're back in Hampstead now?"

Cooper nodded, stuffing his hands into his khaki shorts. "Came back last year," he said, shifting in his flip-flops. He did not elaborate.

"That's great. I just got up here myself, actually."

"You picked the best season. How long are you staying?"

Iris touched her forehead. Her head pounded, though she wasn't sure it was just the heat anymore. "For the summer, actually."

"Your family here, too?"

Iris paused. Cooper knew she had a family? She'd never spoken this many words to him in all of her high school years. "No. Not yet. My kids are coming up in a few weeks. And my sister, too," she added hastily. Surely he'd remember Leah.

Cooper nodded. Had he guessed about Paul by her omission? Or was it pathetically obvious already: the forlorn single woman returning to her hometown, husband-less, homeless, and flailing around in her mother's perfectly good tomatoes. Oh, why had she come back here, anyway?

"Yeah, your mom mentioned something about a family reunion. You must be excited."

"Thrilled," Iris said, smoothing her rumpled shirt. "So, you're working here?"

"Didn't your mom tell you?"

Iris shook her head, confused. What was the lacrosse captain doing on her parents' farm?

"Your folks hired me to work on their barns. I do historic preservation." He looked up at the wooden rafters overhead. "I restored this for them last spring, when the farm opened."

Iris followed his gaze. "You did this? It's stunning. I barely recognized it."

Cooper flushed. "Thanks. Your dad asked me to come back and restore the roof on the old horse barn by the main house."

"Wow." It was all Iris could manage. Of all the tedious things her mother peppered their rare phone conversations with, you'd think she could've shared that tidbit. Cooper had been working for them all year.

Millie returned with a large bag. "I added some rhubarb. Splendid with vanilla ice cream."

"Thanks, Mrs. Standish." Cooper tried to hand her a twenty-dollar bill, which Millie refused.

"You've done enough already," she insisted, throwing Iris an accusing look. "Feel free to drop off any materials at the barn. It's open."

He nodded, glancing over his shoulder at Iris once more, and she wished suddenly that her mother would disappear to the register, or the scene of the crushed tomatoes, anywhere else.

"Well, I'd better get down to the barn," Cooper said finally. "Feel better, Iris. Good to see you."

"You, too." Iris stood, unsure if she should shake his hand or give him one of those quick hugs between old friends. But she didn't get the chance to do either. Instead, Millie placed her hands firmly on Iris's shoulders, pushing her right back into her seat.

"Sit down, dear. We don't want you fainting on us again."

As if any of them had forgotten.

Fuming, Iris allowed herself to be chaired, watching help-lessly as Cooper headed down the drive. He was already climbing into his truck when Iris realized she hadn't even thanked him.

Millie interrupted the thought. "A shower would do you good, Iris. You need to pull yourself together for dinner."

Iris turned. "Dinner?"

"Didn't I tell you? Leah and Stephen changed their plans. Their plane lands tonight."

Five

It's the runaway!" The tiny bell over the bakery door had barely chimed, and Trish was already flying out from behind her counter, untying her floury apron.

"Please stop saying that," Iris groaned. But she allowed herself to be hugged and sank gratefully against her old friend. Even nearing forty, the girl was still a knockout, her long, dark hair swept up behind her. Iris breathed deeply. Trish smelled like baked apple and something else; coffee, maybe.

"I'm teasing. You're not a runway so much as a stray. Now come sit." She placed a miniature tart in front of Iris. "Key lime. I want your honest opinion."

Iris sank her teeth into the pale green cream and rolled her eyes. "You're killing me," she said, running her tongue over the graham cracker crumbs on her lips.

Trish grinned, handing her friend a napkin. "You look good."

"Liar." She'd eaten poorly for weeks. She hadn't slept more than an hour or two a night either, for that matter. She ran a hand over her ponytail. At least she'd finally managed to wash the tomatoes out of her hair.

"No, you do. Thinner, but good."

"Well, that'll change pretty quick if I come here each day."

Trish laughed. "How's the farm?"

"It just about killed me."

Trish smiled. "So Millie put you right to work, huh?"

Iris couldn't reply. The shower she'd finally gotten, and now the key lime dessert, were both too intoxicating to be spoiled with any further explanation.

"So how are those kids?"

"Fine, I think. I called them on the way over. Lily and Jack told me camp is great. Sadie mumbled a few syllables before hanging up."

"What about Paul? You guys aren't talking?"

"No, we are." But they weren't really. Aside from discussing the machinations of the day: who was on carpool, how much the new cheer uniform would cost, what to heat up for dinner. Paul had sounded distant and vaguely bored. Not missing her. Not sorry she'd gone. Iris could hear Millie's take: *Well, what do you expect? You abandoned him!* But she liked Trish's take better. "Let the bastard figure it out. Have another tart."

"So does this wedding stuff make you want to jump off a cliff?" Trish had always harbored love-hate feelings for Leah.

"Not for the reasons you'd think." According to Millie, Leah had chosen a wide expanse of pasture at the far end of the lake for the ceremony and reception. *An intimate affair amid a rustic setting*, Millie had informed Iris, which conjured images of hauling wooden tables and chairs across sweltering fields.

"I just can't believe she's settling down. You and me, yeah. But Leah?"

The fact that Leah had suddenly settled on one man, after a string of loves that stretched from one end of the country to the other, had come as a surprise to them all. Since college, she'd remained on the go—backpacking through Europe, landing briefly for a spell in New York, then heading out west to work in the national parks. And with each new destination there appeared a heavy new relationship that inevitably crumbled when Leah moved on. Iris never thought she'd settle down.

"So what do you know about the fiancé?" asked Trish.

Iris threw up her hands. "Nothing. But I'll find out soon." She checked her watch. "They're coming in tonight."

Trish shook her head. "Just like the old Leah. Never a dull moment. Whatever you do, don't go crying through your old wedding album when she asks you to pick out bridal flowers or write out seating cards."

"More like locate misplaced relatives at the airport," Iris muttered. "Or pick tomatoes." Wait till she told Trish about *that* incident. She was dying to find out more about Cooper Woods.

But Trish interrupted the thought. "Isn't the farm great? We've expanded our summer catering menu, thanks to all of their organic produce. Leah got a bunch of the local restaurants on board."

"What? I didn't know you did business with the farm." Iris stared into her mug. It was still happening. From a thousand miles away, Leah was already taking her seat at the table with them. Reminding her of her special spot within the family. Even in Iris's best friend's life, too, it now seemed.

"The local news channel ran a big feature on them this spring. But you probably saw that already," Trish added.

Iris nodded. But she hadn't seen the segment. She'd heard about it, had even gotten the CD her mother had mailed her with the seven-minute recording on it. But she'd never actually taken the time to sit down and watch it. She had a fuzzy recollection of seeing it stuffed in a junk drawer in the family room. Or was it the laundry?

"I didn't realize how big the 'farm stand' had gotten," Iris admitted sheepishly. "I knew Leah was working with Mom when she came home last summer, but I thought it was more like Mom giving her a little charity work." The truth was, Iris hadn't given it much thought when she heard that Leah had left her job at Yellowstone and was stealing back to New Hampshire. If anything, it had annoyed Iris that her parents still tolerated her sister's flippant approach to life.

Iris changed the subject. "Enough about my crazy family. Look at you. And this place!" The bakery was just as she'd imagined it. A cluster of vintage tables lined the picture window that looked out onto the cobblestone village street. The café walls were a rich butterscotch yellow. "Even the color is cozy!" Iris exclaimed.

"Yellow makes people hungry," Trish confided.

"I'm so proud of you," Iris said, peering longingly at the tidy arrangement of pastries and cakes in the bakery case.

Iris had marveled at her friend's gumption when Trish left her nursing job and threw open the doors to the Chat 'n' Chew. Been jealous of it, even. But secretly, she'd worried. After all, Wayne's dental practice was still relatively new. And the economy was a mess. Shouldn't Trish stick with her RN position? Wasn't that the more sensible thing to do?

But Trish had plowed ahead. She could make her own hours to be home for the kids, Josh and Michael, who were both working as counselors up in Maine for the summer. And besides, with all the sugary confections she'd sell, she'd be cultivating a slew of new patients for Wayne's practice. Iris couldn't argue with that, as she bit into another key lime tart.

"Oh, and look at that!" Trish said suddenly. She pointed to the sidewalk outside. "The view's not bad, either."

Iris turned. Across the street, stepping out of his truck, was Cooper Woods.

Instinctively Iris ducked.

"What?" Trish asked. "It's just Cooper Woods."

"Exactly!" Iris hissed, burying her nose in her coffee mug. "He's not coming in here, is he?"

Trish glanced out the window. "Unfortunately, no. He's headed for the post office." She looked questioningly at Iris. "What's going on?"

"We sort of had a run-in," Iris explained sheepishly.

"Ah," Trish said, eyebrows rising. "So you've crossed paths."

"You could say that." With a friend like Trish, there was no choice but to spill, sharing every detail, however humiliating.

"You mean your mom never told you Cooper worked for them?"

Iris shook her head emphatically. For all her long-distance, one-sided conversations about soil and fertilizer, couldn't her mother have thought to mention *that*?

Trish snorted. "Well, I guess he knows you're back in town."

"That's one way of putting it. What's he doing back here anyway? Last I heard he'd moved out to Colorado after high school."

"He's been back for about a year now. Runs a restoration business, preserving local buildings and that sort of thing. He comes in sometimes for a coffee. And he looks pretty damn good."

Iris couldn't disagree. Unlike Cooper and Leah, Iris had been one of those kids who was friends with everyone and with no one in particular at the same time. The kind of girl who was pretty enough and smart enough. But also quiet enough to be overlooked, certainly by the group that Cooper hung out with. Cooper was one of those enigmatic kids who was charming enough to smooth the disapproval from even the strictest teachers' foreheads when he made excuses for lost homework, but also nice enough to tell the other lacrosse players to lay off the freshmen, whom they routinely shoved into lockers. Iris could remember one incident when Cooper had whispered her name in chemistry class, asking to borrow a pencil. She'd been stunned that he knew her name. But Cooper dated the popular girls. Girls who roared up to keg parties in their Jeep Wranglers, a bevy of backup blondes packed in the backseat. Not red-faced girls who stupidly surrendered their only pencil and spent the rest of class gawking at the back of his head.

Trish grinned wickedly. "Maybe we've found you a date for Leah's wedding after all."

"Don't be ridiculous. Besides, I'm still *married*, remember?"

"A technicality. What's a spin on the dance floor, even if it is twenty years late?"

On her way out the door, with a loaf of warm sourdough bread tucked under her arm, Iris gazed over her shoulder. Trish belonged here. Concocting sweet confections, nourishing neighbors. Iris licked the crumbs from her fingers, wondering where exactly she belonged.

◆ ◆ ◆

Back in her bedroom at the farm, Iris pulled the linen shift dress over her head and turned in front of the mirror. Not terrible. Even after a second long shower, her hair still held a faintly acrid scent of tomato. There was a rap at the door. Millie poked her head inside.

"What do you think?" Iris asked, turning left then right in her dress.

"Nice, but what are you still doing here?"

"Doing here?"

"In this room. Why is all your stuff still here?"

Iris glanced around. Her bags had long since been unpacked, her shirts folded in the armoire, her jeans tucked into the antique dresser drawers.

Millie pointed across the hall. "Didn't your father tell you? I'm putting Stephen and Leah in here."

"But this is my room."

"This room has a queen. And there are *two* of them."

Iris knew her mother didn't intend it that way, but the reference to her singleness caused her to bristle.

"So I'm being moved out?"

Millie scowled. "It's not personal."

Across the hall, Leah's bed was a single canopy, fairylike and girlish under its lace overhang. Iris couldn't help but notice that little had changed in her sister's room since childhood. While Iris's old room had been stripped of its boy-band posters and rearranged to accommodate guests, Leah's remained the same old teenage living space, a sort of high school mausoleum. She caught herself looking up at the doorway as if a young uniformed Leah might stride through at any moment with a gaggle of friends and her field hockey stick.

Iris dumped her suitcase on the bed and allowed herself a good sulk, indulged by the adolescent decor around her.

Outside, the farm rolled out in front of her, a sight that caused Iris's chest to suddenly ache. It wasn't just the rural beauty of the barns and garden plots, but the thought of all that life within; each plant carefully tended and nurtured. Attention Iris feared she herself might never feel again.

As she stood looking out, a silver truck rolled up the drive. It stopped in front of the large red barn.

Iris pressed her forehead against the cool glass. Cooper Woods exited the cab. She watched him lower the tailgate and pull lumber from the bed of the truck. How strange time was: in high school she'd dreamed of stealing a single moment with Cooper Woods. Now, twenty years later, here he was in her own backyard. She admired the competent ease with which he carried the materials, the swift pace at which he worked. And then, just as quickly, to her dismay, he drove away.

Downstairs, Iris sought relief on the porch, joining her father for drinks.

"Feeling better, my dear?"

It was a relief to see Bill fretting over olives, rather than her pupils. He handed her a gin martini, another love the two shared, which she gratefully took a deep sip of. The cool liquid slipped easily down her throat, and she sank into a wicker chair. "I am now."

From out front came the crunch of gravel in the drive.

"They're here!" Millie shrieked.

Without warning, Iris's stomach filled with dread.

"Come," called Bill excitedly as he strode to greet them.

Iris stood. But she couldn't bring herself to follow. Instead she slipped into the dark privacy of the back hall, pressing her back against the cool plaster wall.

Iris took another sip of her martini, imagining the scene unfolding in the driveway. Her mother's air kisses, the exclamations over the happy couple's arrival. Her father would shake hands with Stephen, and the two would playfully argue over who would carry in the bags. Iris was exhausted by the mere thought of it all.

The voices grew louder, followed by the thump of footsteps ascending the porch stairs.

"Dinner will be ready in half an hour!" Millie's voice carried down the hall, and Iris sank a little lower against the wall.

"I'll bring the bags up," Leah answered, and suddenly, hearing her sister's voice filled Iris with a soft and familiar guilt.

Around the corner, in the butler's pantry, came her father's lighthearted whistle, followed by the clink of bottles; he was probably searching for the champagne he'd stowed earlier. And then the slap of the screen door, which meant they'd gone back out to the porch for drinks. Iris pressed a hand to her temple. She really should go out there. She stood, just as the patter of light footsteps approached.

"Hand it over!" Leah swept around the corner and flattened herself against the wall, beside her older sister. She reached for Iris's martini, tipped her elegant chin, and downed the remains. "Much better." She closed her eyes dreamily.

Leah's dark hair fell across her shoulders, and her skin was warm and brown against Iris's bare arm.

"What are you doing?" Iris whispered, feeling the sudden rise of girlhood laughter in her throat.

Leah grinned and raised the empty glass. Her engagement ring flashed between them. "Same as you, my dear. Now, go and get us another."

Six

The early morning was Iris's favorite time on the lake. The dew lay dense across the grass blades as she strode barefoot from the porch to the shoreline, savoring the spongy carpet beneath her.

She'd found one of her old swim tanks in the mudroom closet tucked in a faded L.L.Bean bag where Millie stored all the beach towels and forgotten swimsuits from previous seasons, along with a few errant pairs of goggles. The suit, once bright red, had been sun bleached to an orangey hue, which Iris preferred, and she pressed it to her nose, intoxicated by the heady scent of lake water, sunscreen, and sand.

Iris paused at the shore, peering over her shoulder at the shadowy house. The curtains to her room were still drawn, and she imagined Leah and Stephen asleep behind them, their legs entwined, safely ensconced in darkness.

Iris stuck her big toe in the water and resisted the urge to tug it back out. The water was penetratingly cold this early in the season, not reaching its warmest temperatures until mid-September, which any lakeside resident knew was the best time to swim. Nevertheless, the invigoration she felt surprised her, and she welcomed it as she waded in. She began a slow paddle toward the center of the lake, but quickly realized that she hadn't the stamina. So she turned onto her back to float. The night before had been fun. But despite the easy candor, Iris had been unable to concentrate on the content, distracted instead by her sister's fiancé, Stephen.

Stephen had ignored her outstretched hand when Leah introduced them, opting instead to pull Iris into a firm hug. Which had made her blush; the guy was ridiculously good-looking— dark haired and strong jawed. But what had she expected? Look at Leah.

Iris marveled at the couple's shared ease, something she and Paul had never mastered in all their years. Paul just never seemed invested in forging relationships beyond casual banter, business talk, and the polite consumption of beverages. While her parents had always gotten along with Paul, she couldn't say for sure if they'd ever actually *liked* him. But Stephen was different. Immediately he'd slid open his coat pocket and pulled a Cuban cigar out for her father, then offered one playfully to Millie. Iris had been rendered speechless when Millie shooed him with a dainty hand and laughed, a completely uncharacteristic gesture of "Oh, go ahead" acquiescence. Iris was impressed; Stephen knew not only what Bill Standish liked but also how to navigate Millie Standish to make it happen, something the man himself had been unable to do in all the years of his marriage.

But despite the abundant flow of chatter and wine on the patio, Iris found herself stealing curious glances at her sister throughout the long evening, remembering Naomi's words that morning. *She's better now.* It made her wonder again about Leah's cryptic postcard. But on the surface, she detected nothing. Leah shone in her pale blue crepe dress, and Iris couldn't help but note the enviable flush of her cheeks, dewy with both her youth and excitement. She'd never been more radiant.

By dessert, Naomi and Ernesto joined them, along with a few of the neighbors Millie had called and invited to stop by to welcome the soon-to-be-wedded couple.

"It's you!" Naomi squealed, darting across the patio. Iris couldn't help but notice that it was the kind of hug reserved for old friends.

"In the flesh." Leah laughed. "Didn't think you could get rid of me that fast, did you?" Leah gave Ernesto a hearty high five, and Iris could've sworn the shy man blushed.

By ten o'clock they were all heady with celebration, and Bill set up his phonograph by the open window in his library, so that the music flowed onto the patio and across the sloping green lawns. It lent an old-fashioned elegance of an era gone by, like something out of *The Great Gatsby*. The stars were out, and Iris found herself slumped on the stone wall of the patio watching as her parents took a spin. When Bill whispered something in her mother's ear, Millie laughed, and for a moment Iris was sure her heart would break. At the song's end Stephen dipped Leah dramatically, and the others clapped.

"You must be so glad to see your sister," Naomi said, sitting beside Iris on the wall. "This place just isn't the same without her."

Iris had already had too much to drink, but she helped herself to another glass of champagne from the table. "Nothing ever is," she mused. And then she excused herself abruptly. Iris hadn't meant to be rude, but it was suddenly too much. The music, the star-strewn sky, the couples moving in harmony before her. And herself: forever the forgettable older sister.

She'd stumbled up the narrow back stairs to her room—Leah's room—and fumbled through her purse for her phone. *No messages*. It was twelve thirty. If she called home now, she'd wake the kids. And she didn't want to talk to Paul, she really did not. But she was suddenly sick with the excess of the night: the wine and whipped cream, the rich lobster that turned in her stomach, and the deafening loneliness that filled the empty room.

At some point she'd passed out on the bed, only to wake hours later in the predawn light, heady with nausea and exhaustion. And anger. Why had Leah asked her here? It was the worst kind of escape.

Now, safely stretched across the surface of the lake, she floated, concentrating on the cool water that supplanted the rocking in her stomach, blinking at the cloudless sky.

"Is this spot taken?"

Iris lifted her head from the water, startled. On the shore, Stephen stood grinning in a pair of Hawaiian swim trunks. The dark hair on his chest was curly, and Iris looked quickly away from his taut physique, embarrassed. Why did he have to be so nice?

"It's all yours," she said, slipping through the water to the shore.

Stephen nodded toward the house. "Though, I think we have dangerous company."

Leah sat on the steps, dangling her legs like a child. She waved vigorously.

Up on the porch Leah planted a kiss on Iris's damp cheek. "You smell like a lake rat," she teased, pressing a warm cup of coffee into Iris's wet hands.

And before Iris could respond, Leah was racing down the porch steps, streaking away from her.

Stephen had already swum back to shore. Iris watched as Leah met him on the sand. Arms outstretched, she leaped, wrapping her legs gracefully around Stephen's wet waist, and he staggered backward into the water, laughing.

Stephen carried her all the way up the yard, the two giggling and carousing, as Iris stood awkwardly on the porch, unsure if she should turn away from their rush of affection.

"Your sister's a wild one," Stephen puffed as he mounted the stairs. He deposited Leah at the top step and smacked her playfully on her bottom.

Iris suppressed a twinge of envy. "Always has been," she mused.

He shook his head playfully, like a wet dog, and trotted through the patio door.

"Watch it! Millie will have your tail if you track sand on her hardwood floors," Leah called after him.

Reclaiming her coffee from Iris, she sighed girlishly. "Isn't he a catch?"

Iris winced. "Sure. Though I might have been able to figure that out for myself if you'd told me about him earlier. You know, before the wedding announcements went out."

Leah just grinned over the rim of her cup. "Oh, come on, Iris. It's not like Mom didn't invite you up here."

She handed her back the empty mug. The tables' sudden turn stung.

"Leah, what am I doing up here? Why did you even ask me?"

Leah frowned. "I didn't ask you."

"The postcard? 'Please come.' It sounded urgent."

"Oh, that." She lifted one tanned shoulder casually.

"Yeah, that. I took off and left everything at home, thinking something was wrong. That maybe you needed me. But everything's fine. *You're* fine. Perfect, in fact."

Leah's lips pursed. "What made you think something was wrong?"

Iris stood. "Oh, I don't know. Outside of a Christmas phone call, I don't hear from you for years. You're in Yellowstone, then suddenly you're back home, farming with Mom. Then, *whoosh,* you're in Seattle with a new guy. *Engaged.*"

Leah rose from the porch step. "Don't the phone lines work in Massachusetts?"

"It's not like I can just drop everything and take off every time you start a new project. Come on, Leah, the farm wasn't exactly your first whim."

"What's that supposed to mean?"

"It means I can't hold my breath every time you turn left instead of right. That while you hop in and out of our lives, the rest of us have been raising families, paying bills. You know, growing up." The words tingled on her lips, but it was a relief to finally air them. And one more thing. "We're in different chapters, Leah." She held her breath, awaiting the response, and then a small noise escaped Leah.

Iris reached out. "Please don't cry . . ."

And then she realized Leah wasn't crying at all. No, her sister was in fact suppressing her laughter.

"This is funny?" Iris sputtered.

"Just sit down," Leah said, wiping her eyes. She looked at Iris. "Chapters? Seriously?"

Iris was too offended. "Forget I said anything."

"No, you're right." Leah leaned in closer. "We both dropped the ball in the communication department. Maybe we have been in different *chapters*. But now I'm about to be joining yours."

"Joining mine?" Iris couldn't keep the sarcasm from her voice.

"You know, marriage. The old ball and chain."

But Iris didn't laugh.

"Look, I've made some mistakes," Leah said softly, "but so have you." She grabbed Iris's hand and squeezed it in her own. "*I'm getting married.* And I need my big sister." Her voice trembled a little when she said it, and Iris felt herself bending.

"Fine," Iris said reluctantly. "You've lured me up here after all."

"Good! Then, let's catch up. Ask me anything," Leah said, eyes flashing. "Anything at all."

Iris stared back at Leah's childish optimism. And just like that the pendulum swung back, reminding Iris of the globe-spinning game they used to play in Bill's den. *Where in the world are you going to live?* But she went along with it. "Fine. Where'd you two meet?"

"Here, at the farm. Didn't you know?"

Iris withdrew her hands and wrapped her towel more tightly across her waist, piqued again.

"It happened last summer. He'd come up with some friends from New York. They rented the Thayer place."

The Thayer place was a formidable summerhouse, one of the oldest and handsomest in Hampstead. The Thayer family spent most of the season residing in it themselves, but on occasion they loaned it to close friends from the city.

"Stephen knows the Thayers?"

"His parents do. Anyway, he came by the stand one day when I was working. He bought a pound of strawberries. Then he came back the next day, and the day after that. By the end of the week, I told him that I didn't have a strawberry left on the farm. And he laughed and asked me out." Leah's eyes sparkled as she related the story. "It was funny. There I was, in a crumpled sun hat, covered in dirt and sweat. And he just kept coming back. Said he'd never seen anything like me."

Coming from anybody else, the comment would sound smug. But Leah was simply relating a fact, still as perplexed by her charm as she'd been since they were kids. "Amazing, huh?"

"Amazing." Iris hoped she sounded sincere. She was, mostly.

"So what does he do?" From the Breitling on his wrist to the Brooks Brothers shirt he'd worn at dinner, Iris knew Stephen was successful. But she was more interested in what he did.

"He's a CPA. Used to work for a firm in New York."

Iris contemplated this; Stephen seemed a far cry from the outdoorsy, ponytailed national parks guys Leah used to hang out with.

"But he left all that recently to manage his family's foundation. His grandmother started it thirty years ago, for the Special Olympics."

This seemed more in line with the Leah Iris knew. "So, what do you do out in Seattle?"

Leah frowned. "Do? Well, I've been decorating our new apartment. It's right by the Needle, you must come visit! And I handle the schedule. That sort of thing."

"The schedule?"

"You know, planning charity events, trips . . ."

Iris blinked. It was the exact sort of thing she could not picture her sister doing. Leah was a doer, not a planner. The girl had never worn a watch, let alone followed a schedule. And certainly not someone else's.

Leah jumped up. "Speaking of schedules! You're coming to the dress fitting today, right?"

Iris ran a hand through her hair, which was now mostly dried, and sufficiently tangled. No one had mentioned anything about a fitting. Truthfully, Iris had looked forward to a day alone in the hammock. Especially before she sat her family down for the Paul Talk. The other reason she was here.

But the look on her sister's face left no room for begging off. "Can't wait to meet the dress."

Leah pointed a finger at Iris. "Don't forget about yours," she said coyly. "The bridesmaid dresses won't be in for another week, so it'll be a surprise. But it's to die for!"

Iris winced. She had forgotten about the bridesmaid dress. Back at home, in her attic, at least twelve bridesmaid dresses rested in various states of disuse, each tucked away into weepy cardboard boxes, no matter the fact that many had been chosen by some of her dearest friends, bestowed with the grave promise that *this dress* could be worn again. But Iris knew the cold, hard truth. No such dress existed.

Seven

Patty's Bridal Boutique was nestled at the south end of Main Street, in one of the historic brick shop fronts between Sprinkles Ice Cream and Tate's Pub. Appropriately so, Iris thought to herself. The nervous bride could throw back a shot of tequila while two doors down her maids consoled themselves with a double scoop of cookies and cream. Which is exactly what Iris planned to do, as soon as this fitting was over.

Honestly, Iris was surprised that Leah had purchased her gown at Patty's. The boutique was elegant, as were most of the shops in Hampstead village, but it catered to a traditional New England set. She'd been sure Leah would have flown home with an haute couture dress bag flung over her shoulder, having long ago secured a gown from one of the trendier fashion houses on the West Coast.

Now, she found herself thrust into one of those overly stuffed ornate chairs outside Miss Patty's stately dressing room, balancing a tray of coffees in her lap, each one a sound representative for its intended recipient: a double espresso for Millie, an iced caramel latte for Iris (with extra whipped cream, which would have to be the last if her dress measurements were to be taken), and a suspect swampy liquid that Leah swore was a rejuvenating green tea.

"Soothes the complexion," Millie informed Iris, regarding the tea. Though Iris seriously doubted Millie Standish had ever consumed one of the shimmering concoctions herself.

"Put those beverages down," Millie said now, holding up a veil from the display rack in the corner. "I need your opinion."

Iris trudged over. It was a far cry from home, where in Sadie's case, everything Iris attempted to assert her opinion on, from fashion to pizza toppings, was met with a dubious glare, or in Paul's case, a dismissive tsk of disapproval. At least here she was being consulted.

"So, what do you think?" Millie held up a simple veil with an appliquéd headband.

Iris shrugged. "It's nice. But I haven't seen the dress yet."

"Trust me, this will work." Millie thrust the veil at Iris, just as another stole her attention. "Oh, my. Look at this!"

One after another, Millie plucked veils from the rack, piling them into Iris's outstretched arms until she could no longer see over the cloud of tulle.

"Um, Mom."

"Hush. Put this on," Millie said, handing her yet another.

"Me?"

"Yes, you. We need to help your sister narrow her choices."

"*Whose* choices?" Iris mumbled.

"Excuse me?"

"Nothing." Iris dumped the pile of veils onto a nearby settee.

"Here, now isn't this lovely?" Millie tossed a fingertip veil over Iris's head, where it promptly snagged on her ponytail. "Dear, what is going on with your hair?"

"Mom."

"Fine, just turn around." Millie pursed her lips. "Yes, that's a possibility." She shoved another in her hand, this one dotted in pearls. "Next."

"Shouldn't this be up to Leah?"

"Leah doesn't know what she wants," Millie replied, fussing with the edges. Iris glanced sideways at her mother. She'd always thought herself the sole possessor of such an opinion. Now she wasn't sure whether to rejoice in a newfound teammate or abandon the field given the company.

While her mother sorted through the remaining pile of veils on the settee, Iris lifted the blusher to check her phone.

No messages.

"What about this one?" Millie set a French birdcage veil on her own head, turning admiringly in the mirror.

"Mom!"

"Well, what else am I supposed to do? You're hardly cooperating."

Iris plopped down on the couch.

"Isn't Stephen wonderful?" Millie asked, taking the veil off her head. She patted the sides of her hair into place, not waiting for Iris's response. "We're so fortunate to have him joining the family."

As opposed to Paul? Iris wondered. Though she could hardly argue that point now.

"Yeah, he seems great. But isn't this all happening sort of fast?"

Millie turned to face her. "What do you mean?"

"Well, she's only known the guy for less than a year, right?"

Millie frowned. "A year is a long time, Iris. I knew your own father for less before we became engaged."

"I know. But it was different then. Besides, they haven't been together for all that time. He's been in Seattle, and she's been living here up until a few months ago."

Millie shook her head. "Stephen travels a lot for his foundation, so it wouldn't have made any difference where Leah lived. They made great use of the time they had."

"Yeah, in places like Vail. And Capri. *Vacations*, Mom. And never for more than a week at a time. What do they know about their compatibility when it comes to the mundane stuff? Like who takes out the trash, or who pays the bills? Have they even had their first argument yet?"

Millie crossed her arms. "Iris, I know you seem to be going through a difficult time right now, but I really don't think you should be displacing your personal issues on your sister."

Iris wanted to disagree, but they were interrupted.

"La-dies!" Miss Patty rounded the corner in a flowing tent of a dress. "Your bride is ready."

Iris found it ridiculous the way Miss Patty detained them outside the dressing room, but when the peach curtains parted, she couldn't contain her gasp. There on a carpeted riser, like the tiny ballerina in a childhood music box, perched Leah.

"Oh, sis." Any misgivings Iris had had were tossed aside. "You look—"

"Striking," Millie interjected, and Iris couldn't disagree.

"Do you like it?" Leah turned before the mirror in exactly the sort of gown Trish had predicted. It was a silk organza sheath, perfectly fitted to Leah's trim physique, highlighting every elegant curve of her figure.

"It's lovely. *You're* lovely," Iris choked, swiping at a stray tear.

Millie nodded, dabbing her own eyes.

Miss Patty extended a box of tissues to the women. "I figured these would be in order."

Iris grabbed a wad, wondering if Miss Patty swept through her shop with a tissue box in hand every day. Probably, she decided. Though the sight of Leah in her dress was enough to give even Miss Patty due pause.

"So what do we think?" Patty asked, lifting the modest train and spreading it elegantly across the carpeted floor. "The alterations girl did a wonderful job, didn't she?"

Leah turned left, then right, her brow knitting.

"I don't know," she said quietly.

"What's not to know?" Millie asked.

Leah lifted one shoulder. "There's just something about it . . ." Her voice trailed off.

The four women pressed into the confines of the mirror, studying Leah's reflection. The creamy organza. The strapless bodice. The fitted waist void of any glittery distraction from the design's impeccable lines. Iris had to agree with Millie; it was striking. In short, it was Leah.

"I think it's the waistline," Leah said, and before she could continue, Miss Patty summoned a tiny Italian seamstress named Vera who lost no time kneeling beside the bride and tugging expertly at the fabric.

"There's enough room to breathe," Vera said. "If it's any tighter it will crease."

Leah sighed. "What about this?" She pulled on the bodice. "Do you see this gap?"

The women craned their necks, peering down Leah's bust.

Vera tucked two discreet fingers beneath the fabric. "No gap here," she announced to the group.

Deflated, Leah turned to scrutinize the view from behind. "These pearl buttons, they need to come off."

Vera made a small noise in her throat, which made Iris wonder just how many perfectly good pearl buttons she'd been asked to sacrifice in her career at the mercy of an edgy bride.

This time Miss Patty stepped forward to place her hands on Leah's. She spoke softly. "The pearls line the seam. Exactly where you said you wanted them at the last fitting. Remember, dear?"

Iris could feel the collective holding of breath in the tiny dressing room. She herself was feeling like she needed air.

Millie broke the heavy silence. "You're going to worry Miss Patty. The dress is perfect, dear." Iris recognized the frustration in her mother's tone, even if the others didn't. It was a warning that Millie's already thin brand of patience had worn. From here on out there would be no more hand-holding.

But still Leah balked.

Iris drew Miss Patty aside and whispered to her. "Maybe we should go through the racks one last time?"

"The *racks*?" Miss Patty clasped her large bosom. "This gown is custom. And even if she wanted something in-store, the wedding is in three weeks. There's no time to order and fit another."

Iris wavered, the tensions of Miss Patty and Millie pressing against her temples like bookends.

Four sets of eyes fell on Leah again, whom Iris suddenly

feared might bolt. Millie began fiddling with her purse straps, and Miss Patty squatted at Leah's feet, frantically adjusting the train, as if this might somehow transform the bride's angst.

Leah turned to face them. "Iris? Tell me what to do."

Iris stiffened. Was Leah really placing all bets on her? Because Iris didn't think that was such a great wager. While her bright, beautiful sister was about to embark on a brand-spanking-new marriage, her own was in shambles two hundred miles south.

"Come on, Iris. Truth."

Iris felt the other women's strained expressions shift in her direction.

The truth. Oh, there were plenty of truths Iris could have shared, even more colorfully if, say, a chilled bottle of Grey Goose had been handy. Where to begin? The part about "till death do us part"? Or the part about the thousand little deaths you suffer, even in the marriages that last? And what about sisterhood, that ever-shifting bond that Iris's sisterless friends seemed to believe held some female magic they'd missed out on? *Best friend for life. Keeper of your deepest secrets.* Iris couldn't remember the last time she'd told Leah a secret. Or the last time that her sister had kept one. As Iris stood beside her in the mirror, a million little truths swirled between them. *Don't expect too much. Don't let your ass go. Or your dreams, for that matter.*

But it was Leah's pleading expression that sliced through them all.

Iris cleared her throat. "You'd probably look beautiful in any dress," she said, ignoring her mother's imploring look. "But this is the one." There. She'd said it.

And with that small offering, the air shifted. Millie's face crumpled with relief, and Miss Patty clapped her hands together. The sisters' eyes remained locked in the mirror.

"*Please Come,*" the postcard had said. This wasn't about a dress.

◆ ◆ ◆

As children, Millie had taken Iris and Leah shopping for back-to-school clothes each August. Iris had dreaded those visits, not only because they drew her out of the lake on a perfectly good summer morning, but because of the inevitable suffering in the dressing room. Pleated plaid kilts with brass buckles at the waist that felt scratchy against Iris's bare skin and caused her to reach under the wool to itch her mosquito-bitten legs. But there was one summer excursion that had been particularly dreadful. That year they had taken separate dressing rooms, each emerging from their private quarters to model the clothes. The outfits still matched; but the similarities screeched to an abrupt halt there. The same angora sweater that looked lumpy and unformed on Iris draped elegantly at Leah's tiny waist. The corduroy painter's pants that gaped unflatteringly on Iris hugged the curve of Leah's back, the back pockets showcasing her rear end in a way that was both girlish and alarmingly sexy, much to Leah's delight. From acid-washed denim jeans to the painful floral Laura Ashley dresses that delighted only the elderly saleswoman and Millie, everything looked good on Leah. It was Iris's earliest memory of any dissatisfaction with her own body. The sisters were not just growing up, but apart.

Leah noticed it, too. Iris could tell, from the way Leah admired her own reflection, then allowed her green eyes to travel briefly over her sister's. And from the way she slumped a little in the mirror afterward, undressing quickly, as if to spare Iris the humiliation of further comparison. And though Iris couldn't explain the reasons for their differences at the time (her sharp knees and pale complexion, her wiry hair and strong nose), it was a pivotal discovery for both sisters, a joint realization that for the first time drew an imaginary line between them.

◆　◆　◆

Now Millie stood at the cash register, checkbook in hand, while Iris waited outside the dressing room, ready to help Leah out of her gown.

"Are you sure I made the right decision?" Leah called out.

Iris swallowed. "You mean about the dress?"

"Of course the dress. What else would I be talking about?"

"It's stunning. Don't you think so?"

"I guess."

"So, are you nervous?" Iris asked. It was the first time they were alone together.

"About what?"

Iris suppressed a laugh. "About all of it: the wedding, the dress, the marriage. You've got to admit, it's all happening pretty fast."

Leah didn't answer.

"Do you need help getting the gown off?" From behind the curtain came the swishing sound of fabric. "I can hang it for you," Iris offered.

"I've got it."

Iris couldn't shake the look on Leah's face, standing before them in her gown. "Because if you are nervous, it's totally normal."

Leah peeked from behind the curtain. "Can I borrow some lip balm?" Either she hadn't heard Iris, or she wasn't interested in discussing it.

"Um, let me check." Iris rummaged in her purse, but she only managed to find an uncapped cherry ChapStick that belonged to Lily. "Here. Just don't get any on your dress." When she pressed it into Leah's palm, she felt Leah's fingers shaking. Iris gave her hand a squeeze. "Are you okay?"

Leah withdrew her hand quickly. "I just need a minute."

Millie beckoned to her from the front of the store. After several moments, when Leah still hadn't joined her, Iris peeked behind the curtain. The dress had slid off the chair into an unattended heap on the carpet. Leah stood exactly as Iris had left her, in her underwear. Unaware her sister was watching her, she stared hollowly in the mirror drawing the ChapStick back and forth, back and forth, across her smeared red mouth.

Eight

So, how's Paul?" Stephen asked. The family was huddled around the kitchen island making lunch. "Is he joining you soon?"

Iris drew the paring knife down sharply through the cantaloupe, narrowly missing her finger. "Not this weekend." Iris was going to have to tell them soon.

Iris had always been the family's pleaser: the "plaster," as Leah used to tease. It was a sort of sacrifice she had long acknowledged with a certain level of pride. But now she realized it hadn't served her so well. She felt unbalanced, worrying already about the reactions her news would cause, when really, she knew she shouldn't have been concerned about anyone beyond herself and her kids.

They sat down to eat and Leah filled the men in on her dress fitting, which she described with a joy more embellished than actual, until Stephen cleared his throat and smiled at her. "Honey, I'm afraid we're achieving wedding domination at the table." He turned politely to Iris. "So, Iris, I hear you're a literary agent."

Iris considered the lack of sales she'd made that year. Winter was a slow time. "Trying to be, anyway."

Stephen grinned at her. "That's great. Any woman who is able to hold down a career and raise a family sounds successful to me. What are you working on now?"

Encouraged, Iris told them about her latest pitch. It was the one project she'd felt most excited about that spring. Before Paul had brought her world to a screeching halt. "One of my lifestyle writers and I have been working on a cookbook concept. I've spent most of the spring shopping it around, but we're still trying to get an editor on board."

Bill perked up. "What kind of cookbook was it?"

"The concept is to do a family cookbook using local farm-to-table ingredients."

"Well, that's right up our alley," Millie said approvingly.

Leah agreed. "That's what we're pushing here at the farm. Mom and I have been talking about turning it into a CSA."

Iris brightened. "Exactly. One of my favorite cookbook editors, Joan, loves the idea. But she wants to take it back to her marketing team for final approval. I'm hoping to hear from her any day."

"Well, that sounds promising," Leah said.

Iris wished that were true. But Joan usually gave her a decision right away. The wavering left room for doubt. "I hope so. My writer is great, but I'm a little worried about her lack of cooking experience." Honestly, Iris was worried for herself, too. She needed a project now more than ever.

"Fingers crossed," Stephen said. "Maybe they'll think she's got the culinary chops to get if off the ground and you'll get your offer."

Iris smiled. "Maybe."

It had been a while since anyone had shown interest in her work, and she welcomed the spark of hope she felt. "What about you, Stephen? I'd love to hear more about your foundation." As Stephen spoke, Iris was surprised to hear just how much he traveled, giving presentations to corporations and schmoozing executives in his fund-raising efforts.

"Really, I'd love to say I get to spend more time with the kids," he admitted. "But I'm afraid I'm knee-deep in the business end of things."

"Fund-raising allows those kids to have all of those opportunities," Bill reassured him. The admiration in her father's voice was evident.

And her own was beginning to form. Besides his clear friendliness, the evidence was irrefutable: Stephen pausing to refill Leah's glass before it was empty, gently touching her arm between lulls in the conversation. Not to mention the look on his face every time she entered a room. The guy was smitten.

"I just hope I can convince this beauty to join me," he said, grinning at Leah.

But it was clearly a subject she did not want to pursue. "Enough about work," Leah said, tossing her napkin on her plate. "What are those kiddos up to?"

Despite the distance between the two sisters, Leah had always adored Iris's children. Elaborate packages arrived in the mail for birthdays and holidays, and letters from exotic places appeared in the mailbox regularly, the kids' names scrolled across the blue airmail envelopes in sparkly ink. In fact, the distance had worked to Leah's advantage, shrouding their young aunt in mystery, a light far more intriguing than that of their predictable suburban mother.

"They're great," Iris said, wondering how they really were. The table quieted as Iris struggled to summarize Sadie's year in middle school, leaving out the parts she really would have liked to talk about, like how emotionally draining her teen had become. She mentioned Jack's second prize in the art show, and the first story Lily'd ever written, things that caused Iris's heart to swell and tears to press the corners of her eyelids.

"What about soccer? Are they still playing?"

Iris nodded that yes, they were. But her throat grew tight, and she reached so quickly for her iced tea that she almost toppled her glass.

She could feel Stephen's concern from across the table.

"I'll never forget that right foot Lily had as a toddler," Leah went on. "What was she, like two? And she kept kicking goal after goal!"

They all laughed, recalling how Leah had fussed over the kids, spending whole afternoons teaching them to kick the ball into a net she'd fashioned from one of Millie's bedsheets hanging from the clothesline.

"I miss the kids," Bill said, his voice rich with fondness.

To her horror, Iris's eyes suddenly spilled.

"Honey, what is it?" her father asked, reaching to touch her hand. Which only made the tears fall faster. He pulled a handkerchief from his pocket.

"It must be hard to be away from them," Stephen said. He turned to Leah. "I can't wait to have some of our own."

Even through her tears, Iris was sure of what she saw: Leah pulling her hand swiftly away from Stephen. The startled look on her face.

"Will you look at all these dishes?" Leah said, standing abruptly. "Let's get these cleared." Was she giving Iris a moment to compose herself? Or was this about something else?

"You know, maybe I'll call the kids now," Iris said, standing with the rest of them.

"Good idea." Leah tapped Stephen's arm, her silver bracelets jangling on her wrist. "Honey, give her your cell."

He fumbled in his shirt pocket.

"That's okay. Mine's upstairs. I need something from my room, anyway." But Iris didn't go inside. Instead she headed across the backyard, taking deep and desperate breaths. By the time she'd rounded the house and walked up the grassy rise to the barns, her scalp began to prickle with perspiration. The talk at the table had been too close to home: weddings, babies. The way Stephen reached for Leah, the way she lit up beside him.

Feeling as if she might be sick, Iris sought refuge in the red barn, stumbling into its cool, dusty recess. "Oh, God," she cried, sinking onto an old bale of hay by a horse stall. Then, more urgently, "Damn him. God damn him to hell." Standing, she swiped furiously at the hot tears that sprang from her eyes. Paul had sent her here, tearing her summer and her family apart.

Without thought, she grabbed the first thing she saw, a dented old shovel in the corner. And she swung.

Again and again, Iris swung the shovel. First overhead, then, when she tired, sideways like a bat. She hit the door of the horse stall over and over, the metal clattering against wood. It sent a splintering vibration down her arm and into her spine, and it was a relief as welcome as it was painful. In her mind the slights flashed with each blow: the soaked heap of bathroom towels Paul left for her to pick up from the tile floor each morning. The impatient way he clicked his tongue whenever she joined in the conversation at a dinner party, and how he'd shamelessly correct her in front of their friends and embarrass her. But most of all, the curve of his spine away from her in bed each night. As if he could not stand to be near her. Which only flamed her suspicions about his fidelity. With each image, the shovel struck the wooden door with a resplendent shudder. *Slob*. Thud. *Arrogant*. Thud. *Liar*. Thud.

Iris was bent over the shovel, heaving, when she heard a shuffle in the doorway behind her. She spun around.

"That's quite a swing." Cooper Woods set down a large red cooler and flicked the lights on.

Iris closed her eyes, willing herself a million light-years away. "Oh, God. I . . ."

"Did you bring your tool belt?"

"What?"

Cooper looked directly at her. "Because it'd be a shame to waste an arm like that." Before Iris could explain, he filled the awkward silence. "Why don't you go outside and pick out a hammer. My tools are in the back of my truck."

Iris set down the shovel. "Excuse me?"

"Well, as much as I'm sure you'd like to talk about it, we can't just stand around chatting all day." He pointed to the roof.

Iris shook her head, paralyzed somewhere between humiliation and curiosity. "But I don't know anything about building." Besides, couldn't he see that she was in the middle of a nervous breakdown?

Cooper held up his hammer. "Know what this is?"

Iris rolled her eyes. "Duh."

He flexed his arm. "Got any muscle left?" He glanced at the dented stall door behind her.

She crossed hers self-consciously. "Enough."

Cooper tossed her a pair of gloves. "Good. Then stop gawking and get to work."

For the next two hours Cooper showed Iris how to support an overhead beam with two-by-fours. He didn't ask one question about the scene he'd witnessed, and she didn't offer any explanation. The work was too focused, and soon she'd forgotten herself and settled into a rhythm, passing materials up the ladder and listening to his careful explanations as he worked above her.

They only broke once, for iced coffee, which Cooper shared with her from his thermos. "Go on, have some." It was sweet and icy, and Iris found herself opening up a little. Asking questions about the barn. The materials. The job he was doing for her parents. Anything was a welcome refuge from all the pent-up stuff in her head.

Cooper seemed pleased to share. At one point he rested one hand on her shoulder, directing her gaze overhead with the other. "These old beams are still solid," he explained, pointing to massive columns that crossed overhead. "But they just need a little support. Which is why we pair a new beam beside it, and link them together." He paused. "It's called 'sistering.'"

Iris followed his gaze, making note of the younger, narrower beams buttressed beside the older, and sucked in her breath. "That's beautiful."

Cooper glanced at her appreciatively. "I think so."

By the time the sun began to hover above the hills, they'd finished buttressing a wide stretch of the center beam. Iris was completely out of her element. It was intimidating and wildly liberating. When they finished, Iris flushed as she stood back to survey the work.

"Well, look at that," Cooper said, standing beside her. "Iris Standish has tool skills beyond her beloved shovel."

Iris winced. "I'd better get back down to the house. They're probably wondering what's happened to me."

"Wouldn't want to take you away."

"Oh, believe me. I wish you would." She blushed again. "I mean . . ."

Cooper shook his head. "You always were a funny girl."

Iris followed him back to the truck. "What's that supposed to mean?"

"The stuff you say." He looked at her, smiling. "I sat behind you and Penny Middleton in chemistry class, remember?"

Iris nodded, her eyes narrowing.

"You girls whispered back and forth the whole class. And the more you talked, the faster your ponytail swished back and forth on my desk." He laughed. "I could barely take notes."

"You were eavesdropping on my private conversations?"

"It was kind of hard not to. For such a quiet girl, you talked nonstop."

Iris laughed self-consciously. "No, I did not."

Cooper grinned. "Still do. Especially after a thermos of coffee."

Iris pushed him lightly on the arm. "Well, that's the last time I share coffee with you." But she was secretly touched. Cooper remembered her from chemistry class? And that she wore ponytails, no less?

◆ ◆ ◆

Before leaving, she helped him carry the tools back out to his truck. When they finished, Cooper hopped in the cab. "Hey," he said. "Thanks for today."

Iris blushed, thinking back to the way he'd first walked in on her. "Look, about before . . ."

Cooper held up his hand, silencing her. "You did great." He smiled. "Besides, next time I have a demo project, I'll know who to call."

Iris pulled off her gloves and handed them to him. "Very funny."

She watched as he rolled down the drive, a new sense of fullness in her belly.

Cooper braked suddenly and leaned out the window. "You know, I could always use another set of hands," he shouted back to her. "I'm here almost each day."

Iris shielded her eyes. "I may take you up on that."

Iris stood in the driveway, watching him go. For the first time all day—in weeks, come to think of it—she couldn't stop smiling.

"Here you are!"

Iris turned, pulled from her reverie. Leah was making her way up the hill from the house. "Mom sent me to find you." She stilled, noticing the truck. "Who was that?"

"Remember Cooper Woods? Mom and Dad hired him to work on the barn."

Leah followed the truck with narrow eyes. "Yeah, I know."

Iris glanced at her watch and gasped. "Is that what time it is?"

"You've been gone a while." Leah chewed on her lower lip, something Iris knew was a sign of her sister's agitation.

But Iris was already heading back into the barn, admiring her work one last time. She smiled up at the ceiling. "Didn't realize how late it was. I helped Cooper support one of the beams."

Leah glanced at the barn floor, bending to scoop up a pile of shavings. She sifted them through her fingers, letting them fall like snowflakes. "You've been up here with Cooper the whole time?"

"What's the matter? Was I supposed to help out with dinner or something?"

Leah turned on her heel, not waiting for Iris to follow as she headed back to the house.

"Hang on." The heavy door creaked, dragging on its rusty wheels, as Iris pulled it closed. She caught up to Leah halfway down the grassy hillside.

Leah halted. Her eyes flashed as she turned, and in them Iris saw the color of the lake. And something else. "What were you two doing out here?"

The question stretched between them. "Nothing. Just working. Why?"

Leah looked out on the water, her lips pursed as if there was more she had to say. But she didn't speak.

"Dinner's waiting," she said finally.

Together they walked down the hill, but Iris felt a shift in the air around them. It was more than just the chill from the shadows. And it filled the recesses between them where moments earlier so much sunlight had spilled.

Nine

They still hold the fireworks show at the lake?"

"Every summer, Iris." Millie bustled about the kitchen, filling containers with summer favorites: kale-and-strawberry salad, barbecued chicken, and corn on the cob that she'd grilled earlier. "Grab the lemonade," she said, pointing to the large blue thermos that Iris recognized from her childhood, scratched from too many summers at the beach.

Iris fingered the plastic cup affixed to the top. "I can't believe you still have this old thing." If Iris closed her eyes, it might be any other Fourth of July she'd celebrated as a girl, and she could almost feel the pull of her pigtails that her mother used to tie tight with red, white, and blue bows.

"Don't forget this!" Leah leaned over and stuck a cold bottle of Grey Goose deep into the cooler.

There was no sign of her odd mood from the day before, Iris noted, as Leah swirled through the kitchen, helping their mother pack food. She sent Stephen out to the garage for folding chairs and returned with a checkered red-and-white blanket, her eyes lit with excitement.

"Iris, go find Dad! We're going to be late."

◆ ◆ ◆

The town beach parking lot was crowded with both locals and weekenders, and Bill had to circle several times before finding them a spot. They'd all squished into one car, and in the backseat Leah pinched Iris's knee. "This is going to be great. Just like when we were kids."

They found a spot on a grassy slope above the sandy spit of beach, which was already crowded with kids tossing Frisbees and young mothers plucking toddlers from the water's edge. Iris smiled.

"Is this a family tradition?" Stephen asked.

Bill and Millie had settled into folding chairs, leaving the blanket for the rest of them to lounge on. Stephen passed Bill a beer.

"Every year," Bill replied, with what Iris thought was a hint of nostalgia. "It marked the official start to summer." He pointed out to the water, where a convoy of boats had anchored. "They set off the fireworks from a small barge on the lake. The same family has been doing it for years."

"The Havens," Iris said fondly, remembering their youngest daughter, who'd been a good school friend. It was funny how the mere fact of something staying the same could bring such deep-seated comfort.

"Well, I don't know about the rest of you, but I'm starving." Leah riffled through the picnic basket and arranged the containers of food in the middle of the blanket. When she passed Iris one of their mother's frayed stars-and-stripes cloth napkins, Iris gasped.

"Mom, you kept these all these years?"

Millie examined her own napkin. "They're pretty ratty now, aren't they?"

"No, they're perfect." Iris had forgotten what summer at the lake felt like. Back at home, she and Paul usually took the kids downtown to the annual Fourth of July parade, which was overcrowded and smelled of hot pavement, or to a neighbor's backyard barbecue. Neither could compete with a picnic feast on the beach, homemade lemonade, and fireworks over the water. The kids would've loved this. "Dad, do you guys still come every year?" she asked hopefully.

Bill shook his head. "It's for the young people," he said, chuckling. Though Iris was pretty sure from the look on his face that he would've liked to.

As they picnicked, old friends stopped by to visit: women from Millie's gardening club, neighbors, and a few of the regular summer people Iris recognized from years ago. Iris polished off a buttery cob of corn and reached for another. She felt almost giddy as dusk fell over the beach and the crowd hushed.

Beside her, Leah leaned contentedly against Stephen. "I wish you didn't have to fly back to Seattle tomorrow," she said, reaching up to stroke his hair.

He kissed her hand.

Iris pulled her sweater around her shoulders, wishing she, too, had someone to curl up on the blanket with. But her thoughts were interrupted with the first crack and whistle of the show. A collective hush fell over the beach.

Overhead, red-and-gold pyrotechnics popped and sizzled against the sky, sending a lazy blue cloud of smoke out over the water. Faces glowed in the surrounding light, and children shrieked and pointed. Iris lay back on the blanket, gazing up at the sky. She felt a twinge of loneliness. As a giant pink bloom exploded overhead, she felt a hand encircle her own.

"It's just like when we were little." Leah had scooted beside her, and her breath was warm and close in Iris's ear. They lay together, shoulder to shoulder, watching.

When the fireworks ended, people lingered. Some of the children ran down to the water's edge as the adults stood to stretch their legs, savoring the last moments of the annual celebration.

Iris scanned the crowd for Trish's family, knowing they'd be there somewhere. "I'll be right back," she said.

At the shore Iris stuck her toe in. The lake felt warm against the cooler air of evening, and she swirled her foot around. It was harder to see by the water and she realized the crowd was beginning to disperse.

"Glad you made it."

Iris turned around, squinting in the darkness.

"Up here."

She recognized the voice. Cooper Woods sat atop the wooden lifeguard chair, just yards away in the sand. Surprised, she smiled and raised a hand in greeting. "I didn't see you up there."

He leaned down and extended his hand.

Iris hoisted herself up and sat beside him. She hadn't remembered the seat being so snug. "Did you watch the show from up here?"

He chuckled. "Best seat in the house. But no. It was full of teenagers well before I got here."

She nodded, remembering fondly. "I'll bet."

He glanced over their shoulders, at the thinning crowd behind them. "You here with your family?"

"Just like old times." She, too, looked across the beach toward the grassy hill. "They're over there somewhere."

And as if on cue, Iris spotted Stephen and Leah. They were gathering up the picnic blanket. Meaning they were all probably planning to go. Which she realized she suddenly did not want to do.

"Are you here alone?" she asked.

Cooper shifted and the wooden seat creaked beneath them. A group of children ran past, and in the glow of their sparklers she saw his white smile. "Not anymore."

◆　◆　◆

Monday morning found them in the driveway, exchanging good-bye hugs. Stephen had to catch a flight back to Seattle for work. Leah was staying behind to work on the wedding.

"Just like the old days!" Bill declared wistfully. "Both my girls back home."

Millie eyed Iris evenly, her expression more strategic than emotional. "It will give you kids a chance to finally catch up."

Iris wasn't so sure. This was her time to sort through her own issues, not flower arrangements.

But it was Stephen who had finally cajoled her. "Keep an eye on this one for me, will you? She's a troublemaker," he said, pulling Iris into a firm hug. His hair was still damp from his shower, his polo shirt crisp. Iris breathed in. How lucky Leah was.

As Bill's BMW pulled away, Leah was the last one standing in the driveway, waving tearfully. Just as she had when they were little and their parents left them home with a babysitter.

"Does she always get this upset when he travels?" Iris asked. She and Millie stood watching from the porch.

"They're in love, Iris."

But it was more than that. Leah's heightened responses to all things had always confused Iris: the boundless hysteria when Leah found out she got her favorite teacher for an upcoming school year, followed by her bedridden week of uninterrupted weeping the time Bill found a dead baby bird along the driveway. Responses that initially left the family exchanging loaded glances, but soon after swept them along unwittingly, each mimicking Leah's brand of reply: finding Millie, herself, foolishly dancing around the kitchen as Leah brandished the back-to-school letter. Or Bill hovering outside her bedroom door, with a little stuffed toy bird in his palm. Had it been Iris languishing in bed, she was pretty sure her mother would have pulled her out, brushed her teeth, and marched her right down to the bus stop, telling her to get on with things.

Now Millie fingered her pearl necklace, watching her younger daughter uneasily. "Which is why we'll need to keep her busy. With the wedding, the farm, that sort of stuff."

"Or else, what?" Iris wondered aloud.

"She's sensitive, Iris," Millie said. "You know that."

Iris stiffened. Then, with an impending divorce, what did that make her? Leah was approaching them now. Millie rearranged her expression and called to her cheerfully, "I'm sure he'll call you from the airport, dear. Why don't we have some tea on the patio and go over the seating charts?"

Leah nodded glumly, looking more crushed than she should have for a bride who'd be seeing her groom in another week. Stephen traveled all the time, after all. And besides, they were about to be *married*.

When Bill returned from the airport, Leah's mood hadn't improved. She'd taken a tearful call from Stephen in the locked den and emerged with red eyes. She even refused Millie's offer to go check on the farm stand, something she'd claimed to be looking forward to all weekend. Instead, for the remainder of the cloudless summer day, Leah took to her room.

"She's probably just tired," Millie sympathized. But still, the family hovered, wandering the farmhouse like some misguided fleet who'd fallen off course, circling from room to room, the energy not unlike that of a coming summer storm. Iris felt aimless, too. Cooper had mentioned the evening before that he'd be working on another project across town. As she eyed the barn outside, she wondered if she was craving more the work in the barn or the company. Even her mother was fidgety, riffling through kitchen cabinets in search of a zucchini bread recipe she could not find, leaving a wake of ingredients strewn across the kitchen island that she never bothered to put away.

After an uncomfortably quiet dinner, for which Leah did not join them, Iris gave in to her concern and went upstairs to check on her sister. She was halfway down the hall when she heard the weeping, muffled at first.

"Leah?" Iris knocked on her door. "Are you all right?"

After a heavy pause, there was movement on the other side of the door.

"Just taking a nap," she replied hoarsely.

Iris pressed her forehead against the door. "You've been napping all day. Come down and eat something."

When there was no reply, Iris tried the door handle. It was locked.

"Can I come in?"

"No!" Leah answered firmly. Then, "Wait."

Iris heard the scrape of furniture. Finally, the lock clicked and Leah filled the doorway.

"What are you doing up here?" Iris asked. "The day's over."

The shades were drawn, casting the room in shadows. Iris took in Leah's swollen eyes.

"You're crying?"

"No, just tired." She did not move aside to let Iris in.

It was then Iris saw the pill bottles, a cluster of orange plastic, on the bedside table behind her.

"What is all that?"

Leah followed Iris's gaze and quickly stepped back, blocking her view of the nightstand.

"They're Stephen's. He has allergies. And trouble sleeping sometimes." Before Iris could ask anything else, she turned away, tugged open the table drawer, and swept the bottles into its depths.

"Well, Mom has a plate for you in the fridge," Iris said, her eyes fixed on the drawer.

"I'm not hungry," Leah whispered, shutting the door between them.

◆　◆　◆

Downstairs Iris found Millie reclining on the couch with a book. She plucked the book from Millie's hands, standing over her. "Is she sick?"

Millie rose up, her jaw flexed. "What are you talking about?" Then, "Why would you say such a thing?"

"Mom, she's practically running her own damn pharmacy up there. Did you know that?"

"Watch your language," Millie said, as if any of that mattered. Her mother glanced out at the kitchen, where Bill was now puttering around, looking for dinner leftovers. She lowered her voice. "Your sister has trouble sleeping. It's no big deal."

"Then why'd she say it was for Stephen? Come on, Mom. There are enough bottles on her nightstand to put an elephant under."

Millie shook her head. "Iris. Leah is under a lot of stress right now. And Stephen just left."

"At least *he's* coming back." She tossed the book on the couch.

"Iris, I didn't mean . . ."

Iris spun around to face her mother. "Things are not exactly easy for me right now, either."

Millie stood. "Iris. I don't know exactly what is going on with you, but I'm sorry."

Her words caught Iris off guard. There was no tender gesture, no hug, but it was at least an acknowledgment. And that was more than she'd gotten in the past.

"And just the same, there are some things you don't understand around here," Millie added quietly.

"Meaning what?"

Millie wagged her head, as if shaking the thought away. Having said too much already, she turned for the stairs. "I'll try to get her to eat something."

"Mom. I'm sorry." She threw up her hands and sat on the couch. "Make me understand. Tell me what's going on with Leah."

But Millie was already halfway up the stairs. "She just needs our patience, Iris. It's nothing to worry about."

"Mom."

But Millie did not answer.

Iris watched her move away from her. For sixty-five, her mother maintainted a lean and strong physique, equal to her zest. Unlike other women her age, Millie wasn't fading into the recesses of a floral couch or settling into the earth like an old farm relic. Iris should have been more proud of that fact, she knew. But as Millie reached Leah's door at the top of the landing, she stopped. Iris couldn't help but notice the sag of her posture, the way she shrank as her hand touched the door handle. As if sensing Iris's concern, Millie glanced sharply over her shoulder and down at Iris, as though she were summoning a measure of help across the carpeted expanse between them.

Ten

I ris had always known she would be a mother. It wasn't that the role of motherhood was an expectation thrust on her by society, or anyone else, for that matter. Rather, it was an intuitive desire, a puzzle piece of her identity that she did not question. But putting those pieces together to make her little family did not come easily.

It had taken Iris and Paul three years to conceive Sadie, something that Iris still had not recovered completely from. As newlyweds, she and Paul had entered marriage with the same naive smugness as their peers, focused on the starter home, the career, the weekend getaways. A few years into their marriage, as photos of newborns began popping up in Christmas cards, and a few of Iris's close friends disappeared into the thick haze that is new motherhood, she began to ache for a peach-complexioned baby of her own. And so they'd started trying. When a few months went by with no results, Iris began to worry. Paul, on the other hand, took it in stride, reminding her that it would happen when it was supposed to. But a year later Iris had reached full-blown panic, and they'd scheduled an appointment at a fertility clinic. And that's really when the unraveling began. The IVF treatments. The daily injections. The scrutinized calculation of cycles. Until one bright winter day, finally, a double line on the plastic tester! An occasion that caused Iris to interrupt a case, calling Paul from the courtroom to share the big news. For the first time they were on the same page again, curling up on the couch, reading baby books, and talking late into the night. Until one afternoon, in early spring, when Iris went to the bathroom and began to bleed. Hours later in the doctor's office, they learned that the pregnancy was lost. And with it all those hopes and expectations, and to some extent, herself.

But Iris did not give up. Finally, after another round of IVF, there was Sadie. Followed quickly by Jack. And three years later, to their surprise, Lily! Iris was so smitten, so grateful, that she did not question the bumps, or hiccups, or the growing distance between herself and Paul. The children would provide the strings to bind them back together. Now, twelve years later, Iris wasn't sure where those strings were anchored. She felt more bound to her children than to her spouse.

When she awoke to the smell of pancakes the next morning, Iris had the urge to find her children and pull them into bed with her. Disoriented by her fitful sleep, she thought she was back home in Massachusetts. "Lily?" she called, hearing the pitter-patter of feet in the hall.

But it was Templeton, who poked the door ajar with his nose and, seeing her, barked loudly. Iris jolted upright in bed.

Downstairs, Millie was manning the stove. Iris had just plunked into a kitchen chair when Naomi knocked on the mud-room door.

Millie waved her in. "Join us. I made pancakes."

Naomi greeted Iris and took a seat across from her at the table. "It's gorgeous out there today. Just wanted to update you guys on the baby peas. They're ready for picking."

"Ah!" Millie looked pleased as she heaped a plate full of pancakes for Naomi.

"Leah will be glad to hear that. Maybe it'll get her out in the garden."

Naomi looked up. "She's still here? I thought they went back to Seattle."

Iris watched the looks pass between the two women. It was a subtle exchange that needed no translation.

"So, he's traveling again," Naomi concluded, and Millie nod-ded solemnly.

Iris sipped her coffee, perplexed. How had Naomi inferred that?

Switching the subject, Naomi turned to her. "How's it going? You enjoying being back at home?"

Enjoying wasn't exactly the word for it; *surviving* was more fitting. "Pretty good," Iris said. Hopefully about to get better. According to her father, Cooper was expected back at the barn that morning, and Iris was prepared to take him up on his offer. So what if she didn't know much about construction? He'd asked her to help, and she'd figure it out.

"Morning," came a soft voice in the hall. They all looked up.

"Well, here she is!" Millie pulled out a chair. "Naomi has good news, dear. The peas are in!"

Iris checked Leah's expression to see just how this piece of information would register, but clearly it did not have the hoped-for effect. Leah nodded glumly and poured herself a cup of black coffee. "Hey, Naomi," she mumbled.

"I could use your help out there," Naomi said, stealing an-other quick glance at Millie. "Those new trellises you put in last season were magic. You can't believe how thick the vines are."

"Great." Leah dumped a spoonful of sugar in her cup.

"Well," Iris said, standing quickly, "I'd better get going."

"Where are you off to?" Millie asked.

"The barn. I'm helping Cooper Woods with the ceiling."

"You're what?" Millie's expression couldn't have relayed more shock.

This got Leah's attention, too. "Again?"

Iris looked at the upturned faces, awash in disbelief. "Yes. Again," she informed them. "Cooper said he could use a little help."

Millie cocked her head. "I thought you'd be working on that cookbook deal. Or something."

Or something. "Not today. I want to work in the barn."

With that, Leah stood and tossed back the rest of her coffee like it was a shot.

"And where are you going?" Millie asked, turning in surprise.

"To get dressed," Leah announced. "Maybe I will go check on those peas, after all."

"Wonderful!" Millie turned to Iris with relief. "You come, too. You've got to see what Leah's done in the garden. It will boost her spirits."

"But I told Cooper . . ."

Now Naomi was giving her the same look as Millie. As though *she* had some say in the matter.

Iris glanced at the kitchen door, her escape route. *Damn the peas.*

"It's not a big deal," Leah said, setting her cup in the sink.

But Iris could tell it was. "I'll come check out your peas." She wanted Leah to know she was interested in the farm. And after yesterday, she was determined to be a little softer around them all.

Minutes later they were climbing the hill behind the house, struggling to keep up with Leah.

"Let's get some picked before the stand opens," she said brightly.

The previous fall Leah and Ernesto had installed several rows of small wooden trellises along a fence line, and the narrow vines clung in lengthy, vivid tangles. Iris knelt beside a plant and plucked a pod, running her finger over the small pea bumps within.

"Try one," Leah urged, kneeling beside her. "They're heaven."

The work felt good, despite the fact that her arms were still sore from her episode in the barn two days ago. But working with Leah made Iris forget. Leah worked fast, her small hands moving expertly over the plants, picking and pruning, just as Iris had seen their mother do each summer when the family garden was just a small plot of overturned earth behind the house. But there was nothing laborious about Leah's efforts. Unlike Millie, who moved somberly among the rows, Leah made the work appear artful, much like the close-up cooking shots on Iris's favorite Food Network show, when the camera zoomed in on Giada De Laurentiis's manicured fingers as they seductively peeled a juicy orange. Iris paused to watch as Leah stooped among vines, taking the time to touch and taste the fledgling plants, her eyes closing as she considered a sampling. Leah infused the rows Iris had loathed until now with a quiet beauty and Iris realized with a sudden pang that her sister was new to her here. Surrounded by the carefully tilled lengths, Leah's usual roaming limbs and quick tongue were stilled, her hands busied. Leah belonged there.

"See?" Millie whispered approvingly. "She just needed to get out, is all."

In spite of herself, Iris stole glances at the driveway, wondering where Cooper was. Twice the sound of tires on gravel caused her to stand up in anticipation. But it was just Bill coming back from the grocery store. And Ernesto, with a truckload of mulch. Maybe just as well, Iris told herself.

They picked a few baskets of peas. "Let's wash these and get them to the farm stand," Millie suggested when they'd finished.

"You coming?" Leah asked.

To Iris's dismay, Cooper still hadn't arrived. She forced a smile. "You bet."

Back at the house, Iris submerged her dirty hands in the mudroom slop sink. She scrubbed with the cracked bar of castile soap, right up to her elbows, and then splashed her face. The calluses from her afternoon with Cooper were no longer so raw, and it gave her pleasure to feel the worn skin on her hand growing tough.

"You did good out there," Leah said, joining her at the sink. As though Iris had been the one in need of a boost, and not the other way around. Despite the work and the heat, Leah's spirits were still high, nothing like those of the sullen girl who'd taken to her room the day before.

Iris moved over to make room for her and passed the milky bar of soap. "That's being generous. I don't really think it's my thing."

Leah groaned contentedly as she scrubbed up. "I forgot how good it feels to get my hands in the ground."

"I didn't realize just how much you and Mom had going out here," Iris said, glancing over at her. She'd not taken the chance to credit Leah, until now. "The farm is incredible."

"Yeah. It's hard to believe we started out with just a few raised beds and Mom's old umbrella stand. When I first came back last year, I was aching to do something meaningful, you know?" Her eyes sparkled.

"So don't you miss it, being out in Seattle? Excuse the pun, but you just seem so rooted here."

Leah's expression changed. "Sure, but it's different in the city. We're busy renovating the new apartment. We've got tons of restaurants, and theater. Shopping!" She winked at Iris. "Besides, Stephen's arranged for this great rooftop deck to be constructed. I'll get a container garden going in no time."

"A container garden." Iris frowned. "Will that do it for you?"

"Why not? It's not like we cook; we eat out most nights."

"Oh. Right." But that didn't sound anything like the Leah Iris knew. "It's just that you seem so happy here."

Leah blinked. "I'm happy in Seattle, too."

"So you like decorating the new place? Shopping?" As soon as it came out, Iris regretted it. She hadn't meant to trivialize Leah's life out there.

"Yes. Since you're finally asking, I do like those things. But that's not all I do out there. Stephen travels a lot. Sometimes I get to accompany him to exotic places: like Saudi Arabia. Dubai."

Iris adjusted her tone, patting her raw fingers with the damp towel. "From what Stephen said at lunch the other day, it sounds like there's some expectation for you to join his family foundation. What was that all about?"

Leah paused, looking down at her glimmering engagement ring. "Nothing, really. That's just something his parents want."

Iris considered this, though the hopeful look on Stephen's face at lunch the other day had said otherwise. "Sounds like it meant something to him."

"Stephen knows how I feel. He's not going to push me to do something I don't want to. He's just passionate about his family business," Leah added defensively.

"But what about *your* family business? This thing you and Mom have going isn't just a dinky little vegetable stand. I see the way you are out on the farm, and the way everyone responds to you. Are you sure you want to give all of that up?"

Leah turned and tugged the hand towel from Iris's grip. "What exactly are you trying to say, Iris? Because I could be asking you the very same questions. I know the kids are away at camp, but why did you come suddenly home? You haven't been up here in years. You didn't even know we'd gotten the business off the ground, which you've made painfully clear is not your thing. So what's going on that finally sent you scrambling back here?"

Iris was stunned. But not deterred. "Look, I'm sorry," she sputtered. "It just seems like everything is happening so fast. The move to Seattle, the fiancé, the wedding. I guess I haven't seen you in a while."

Leah thrust the hand towel at Iris. "No. I guess you haven't."

◆ ◆ ◆

The kitchen simmered with tension, and as soon as the peas were washed, Iris was relieved to see the silver truck pulled up beside the barn.

"Gotta go," she told them.

Millie stood, checking her watch. "Ready for the farm stand?" she asked Leah.

But Leah declined. "Actually, I'm pretty hot," she said, standing in front of the open refrigerator. "I think I'll take a quick dip and meet you up there. Okay?"

Millie frowned. "Well, don't be long. The afternoon crowd is a doozy."

Iris hurried upstairs to change her shirt. Sure, she'd be working in the dusty barn. But still . . .

By the time she'd changed and smoothed her hair into a fresh ponytail, the house was empty. She filled a thermos with fresh iced tea and grabbed two apples. Just in case.

Outside the afternoon sun was high and bright. The shade of the barn would be welcome. The thermos sloshed under her arm and Iris smiled. Finally, the day belonged to her.

She was halfway up the hill when she heard laughter. Iris halted. There, leaning against the side of his truck, was Cooper. He was not alone.

Leah, in a red bikini top, was seated on the tailgate of Cooper's truck. She wore a pair of denim shorts, ones Iris recognized from high school, if she wasn't mistaken. Ones that probably would've fit Lily. Apparently she'd taken a detour from her quick dip in the lake. The two did not see her approaching.

"So you stayed on in Hampstead," Leah was saying.

"After Dad recovered from his heart attack, it just made sense. My restoration business had grown by then," he said. And then something Iris couldn't hear.

Leah arched her back, laughing openly again. What was she doing? And that bikini top: it was so . . . red. Iris slowed, her heart pounding.

Leah noticed her first. "Oh. Look who I bumped into." As if she'd had no idea Cooper was working that day. Or that Iris had been waiting all morning to join him.

Cooper turned. "Oh, hi, Iris."

Iris couldn't quite read his expression. For an awkward moment she stood, feeling as though she'd interrupted something. Then she thrust the apples at Cooper. "Here."

"Isn't Iris the greatest?" Leah said. She snatched one playfully from Cooper's hands and bit into it, rolling the fruit on her tongue.

Iris shot her a look. She didn't need Leah's flimsy accolades.

"Thanks," Cooper said, tossing the other apple in one hand, his eyes fixed on Leah. "So, what're you up to today, Iris?"

Suddenly Iris felt like an idiot. Yes, Cooper had asked her to help him out the other day. But she realized now that it'd been a gesture. As in, "I'll see you around." Not an invitation. Beside her, the tailgate jiggled as Leah slid off.

"Well, I'd better leave you two to your work," she said, stretching her brown arms overhead and turning her face slowly toward the sun. "The lake's calling." Her voice was as rich and thick as the afternoon heat. Or was Iris imagining it?

But Cooper seemed to hear it as well. He gazed at her retreating figure in that way that left men slow to recover their words. "Good to see you again, Leah," he called.

Leah turned to face him and, walking backward, raised the bitten apple. In one graceful motion she tossed it his way, and he leaped to catch it. "You too, Coop."

Coop. The heat prickled Iris's neck. *If you take a bite of that, too, I will throw up right here*, she thought. But worse, he just stood there shaking his head. It was high school all over again. Iris had to get out of there.

"You going for a swim, too?" Cooper asked.

Iris held out her hands, and for the first time he noticed, bashfully, her denim jeans and work boots.

"Oh. Wait, did you come up here to help me?"

Here was her chance. But she didn't want it anymore.

"Actually, no." She shoved the thermos into Cooper's free hand. "Just brought you some iced tea."

Cooper looked confused.

"Maybe it'll cool you off," she said over her shoulder. And though it was the last place she wanted to go, she headed across the lawn for the farm stand.

Eleven

Lily? Is that you?"

"Mama!" Lily's voice trilled through the phone.

Iris closed her eyes and leaned back against the bed pillows. It was early in the morning, but she couldn't wait a moment longer to hear her kids' voices. The confrontation with Leah in the mudroom, combined with the uncomfortable scene at the barn the day before, had weighed on her all night, and she'd slept poorly.

"How are you, honey? How's camp? Tell me everything."

And she did. Lily spoke at a breakneck speed that caused Iris to hold her breath for fear of missing a syllable. Her words jumbled into a jubilant account detailing swim lessons, playdates, camp, and, most recently, her lemonade stand.

"You started a lemonade stand?" Iris sat up, picturing Lily with a homemade sign. She could almost hear the clink of quarters in a mason jar.

"Daddy helped. We made pink lemonade and cookies. Well, not exactly. We bought the cookies. But everyone came, and we made sixteen dollars! I'm donating it to the Humane Society."

Tears pressed at the corners of her eyes as Iris forced her voice to remain steady. "That's wonderful, honey. I'm so proud of you. Did you take lots of pictures?"

"Daddy did."

Daddy did. Iris swiped at a tear. "Can't wait to see them."

Before she could ask anything more, Lily was passing the phone. "Here's Jack."

"I love you!" Iris said quickly, wondering if Lily had waited long enough to hear it. She grinned when Lily shouted back a distant "You, too!"

The phone clunked, and Iris strained to hear what was happening on the other end, picturing the kids at the kitchen island in their pajamas. Paul was probably hunched over a cup of coffee, his brow as creased as the morning paper. She hoped he'd remembered to let the dog out.

"Hey, Mom. What's up?"

Iris smiled at Jack's casual ease. Her fingers ached to tousle his chestnut hair.

"How are you, buddy? This mom sure misses her boy. Tell me about camp."

"It's cool. Ryan and Aiden are there. Did you hear about Aiden's tooth?"

She grimaced as she listened to Jack's gruesome account of his friend's dental mishap with the lacrosse stick, feeling simultaneously bad for Aiden and relieved that it wasn't her own child.

"You're wearing your mask every practice, right?" she asked.

"Mom. You missed the point. He's getting a fake tooth! How cool is that?"

"Very," Iris relented.

Then the phone was passed again, and she held her breath waiting for Sadie.

"Iris?" Paul's voice startled her.

"Oh . . . hi." Reflexively, she sat up straight and tucked her hair back. As if he could see her. As if she should care. "Is everything okay?"

"Good. Fine. Listen, where's the cortisone cream for Lily?"

Iris's mind flashed: it was in the kids' bathroom closet. But why did he need it? "Is she okay? Is her eczema flaring up?"

He cleared his throat impatiently. "She's fine. Just a little dry skin from the pool water."

"Oh." Immediately Iris's maternal radar went off. Lily's eczema bouts could get pretty bad if they weren't treated—something Paul probably wouldn't remember. "You know, that prescription may be expired. Why don't I call the doctor and—"

"It's fine, Iris. She just needs a little."

"Well, how bad is the eczema? Because—"

"Iris," Paul interrupted again. "It's a tiny spot on her leg. I've got it under control."

"Which leg?" Iris couldn't help it. She felt so far away all of a sudden.

"Does it matter?" Paul's tone was his usual one of exasperation. Which infuriated her. She was their mother. A mother who was two hundred miles away. If she wanted to ask about eczema, he should answer. Hell, he should take a picture of it and message it to her.

"I'm her mother, remember?"

"Yes, Iris. How could we forget?"

Finally, Sadie came to the phone.

"Hey." Sadie's morning voice was gravelly.

"How are you, honey?"

"Fine."

Iris waited for her older daughter to elaborate, as she attempted to switch gears from separated spouse to sullen teenager. It was like learning to drive stick shift all over again, only in one of those touchy European sports cars, the ones that never failed to stall in a long line of traffic.

"So, what's new at home? Is cheerleading going okay?"

"Yeah. It's going." Sadie yawned audibly.

"Did you just wake up?"

"Nope."

Iris covered her sigh with her hand. No use letting Sadie hear her struggle two hundred miles away.

"I can't wait 'til you guys come up to the farm. We've got corn, tomatoes, peas. Maybe you could work at the stand? I'm sure you'd be better at the cash register than I am."

"Maybe. Is Aunt Leah there?"

Iris swallowed. "Yes. But I'm not sure if she's awake yet."

Instantly Sadie brightened. "Can you check?"

"Well, sure, but why don't you tell me a little more about what you've been up to first?"

Sadie grew impatient. "I'm fine, I already told you."

"Okay, then how about Samson?" The dog was a pathetic last resort. But he was also the sole topic everyone in the family could agree on.

"Samson rolled in something dead the other morning. Lily and Dad had to give him a bath in the backyard. He still stinks, though."

"No, he does not!" Lily disagreed loudly in the background. Iris smiled. They sounded so close, her chest fluttered.

"So, can I talk to Leah?" Sadie asked again.

Iris gave up. The fermenting smell of Samson's coat was the most she'd gotten from Sadie since she'd left. "Hang on."

She handed the phone to Leah, whom she located downstairs at the kitchen table with a cup of tea. "For you," she said.

Iris plopped down across from her, trying to hide how hard she was listening, as Millie scrambled eggs at the stove. The two sisters had not spoken since the day before, but now, chatting with Sadie, Leah was her old cheerful self. Iris listened to the description of her wedding dress. Sadie's excitement was audible on the line as she fired questions at her aunt, causing Iris to scrape irritably at her eggs. Why couldn't she speak to her own daughter like that?

"How're the kids?" Millie asked her, setting a glass of juice before her.

"Good. I miss them."

"Are they enjoying their summer camps?"

"Seem to be."

"And Paul?"

When Iris didn't answer, Millie turned, her arched eyebrows raising the question again.

"I don't know, Mom. We didn't talk much," Iris mumbled, surprised by the annoyance in her voice. And a wave of shame rose up in her throat, as it occurred to her right then that her conversation with her own mother was not that unlike the one she'd just had with Sadie.

Millie turned back to the stove. "Eat up, Iris. You need to stay nourished."

Iris forced herself to take a few bites as Leah held court on the phone. By this point, she'd lost track of which girl she was talking to; it appeared the phone had been handed back and forth as the topics jumped from swimming to movies, and more details about the now famed lemonade stand. Perhaps Leah should take over the daily phone calls; she'd garnered more information in one sitting than Iris had since leaving home.

"Miss you," Leah said, rising from the table.

Iris motioned to her to pass the phone. "Leah!"

But Leah had moved to the window. "Give your brother a big raspberry for me." A pause, followed by a laugh. "Yeah, love you, too, Sades!"

Iris bit her bottom lip. *Love you, too.* Meaning Sadie said it first.

"They're so grown-up," Leah said, returning to the table. She set the phone down between them and Iris reached for it, but the line was already dead. "Can you believe Sadie made junior varsity?" Leah asked.

"She what?"

Leah cocked her head. "Didn't she tell you? She made the JV cheer squad. And she's just a freshman!"

Iris stood and stalked to the sink, where she dumped her breakfast plate.

"You barely ate," Millie observed.

"I'm not hungry." She was torn; desperately wanting to stay and hear more about her kids, and furious that she'd gotten so little from them herself. Not to mention Paul; he'd barely spoken to her. They were still parents, after all. He should've told her about the junior varsity squad.

Upstairs her bedroom was already sticky with humidity, the morning haze having risen off the lake to fill the upstairs chambers of the house. Iris tugged her blankets back into place in a makeshift attempt to tidy up, then stripped them off the bed altogether. She spun around to the window, raking her hands through her hair. What was she doing here? It had only been a week, but already it seemed she was missing the kids' whole summer. If she packed quickly, she could be on the road and home in three hours. But the thought of that filled her with an emptiness so acute, she had to force herself to breathe. It would only make things worse. As much as she missed the kids, she didn't want to see Paul. She didn't want to drag the kids into the mess she was sure would erupt if she were to return home unannounced. And so, like a refugee, she was forced to sit tight where she was. The farm was hardly neutral territory, but there really wasn't any place else for her to go.

There were two new messages on her cell, but she had to walk back downstairs and out onto the patio to get any reception. The first was from Joan Myer, the cookbook editor. "Hello, Iris. I wanted to get back to you with a final decision about the proposal." Joan paused, and Iris held her breath. "I'm sorry, but as much as I love the concept, I can't get my team on board with this writer. She's not a chef. And what we need is an actual chef." Iris closed her eyes. She'd known it was coming, but as with all rejections, it was like a punch to the gut. Now she'd have to call her author and share the bad news.

In the next message Trish's voice boomed into her ear, grounding her instantly. Good old Trish, who wanted to know if she was free to grab a drink. Was the pope Catholic?

Quickly Iris punched in Trish's home number. It didn't matter that it was eight o'clock on a Wednesday morning. A drink was exactly what she needed.

◆　◆　◆

Wednesday night was ladies' night at the Hampstead Brewery. Iris paused outside the pub doors, glancing down at her baggy mom jeans. She hadn't brought anything terribly trendy to the lake, not that she owned anything terribly trendy these days. Since she'd arrived Trish had already ordered her to go shopping, and fast, before marital assets were divided.

"What?" Trish had said, looking at her with exasperation. "You need to wake up, Iris. A separation is the last set of doors before a divorce." She'd looked Iris over as she said it. "Besides, it might not hurt to get Mama a new look."

But shopping for her new self would have to wait. For now, her dark jeans and white T-shirt would have to do. She fingered her chunky silver bracelet nervously as she peeked inside the pub window. The bracelet was a gift from the kids for her last birthday, something Sadie had picked out. The girl had great taste, and had recently begun to troll Iris's closet, borrowing little things here and there. Iris suspected that was part of the reason for the fashionable gift. But it didn't matter. At that moment, it felt like her kids were wrapped around her wrist.

Inside the pub the music was loud. "Jack & Diane" played on an old jukebox in the corner, and a row of young men lined the stools at the mahogany-paneled bar, glued to the ball game on the TV screen. Not much had changed since Iris had been a regular here, during her college summers, except perhaps for more tourists in madras shorts. She made her way through the small dining area to the rear, where Trish waved from a corner table overlooking the lake.

"Sit that bottom down," she ordered Iris, giving her a quick peck on the cheek. "I already ordered you a drink."

Iris took a deep sip of the icy lemon martini.

"So tell me everything," Trish said, leaning in.

Iris laughed. Trish had known the ins and outs of the Standish family since childhood, and the recent reunion was, therefore, ripe for analysis. "Shall I just whet your appetite for the wedding, or sate it altogether?"

Trish didn't hesitate. "By all means, sate it!"

For the next hour, Iris did just that, filling in every tidbit from the weekend, from Leah's dress fitting to Stephen, who as far as she could tell was pretty damn near perfect. Go figure.

"Sounds like quite the guy," Trish said.

"Which we should be happy about." Iris paused. "Except for the fact that—"

"He's nothing like the other guys she accumulated over the years," Trish said, finishing her best friend's thought.

"Exactly! And that should be a good thing, right?"

Trish shrugged. "I'm sure in Millie's book it is. Boy, she had some real winners back in college, didn't she? I used to be so jealous, listening to her stories when she came home during semester breaks." Trish laughed, recalling some of the stories Iris had tried to forget. "Well, now that she's finally found 'the one,' things are gonna be boring. No more dashing off to the Himalayas with . . . what was his name again? The guy from her senior year that she left school for?"

Iris rolled her eyes. "Martin the mountain climber."

"Right. And no more midnight rescue missions to Portland police to bail Leah out. She was dating some activist at the time. What protest group was she involved with?"

"PETA, I think?"

Trish threw up her hands. "My point exactly. This guy seems rooted. A necessary change, if you ask me."

Iris couldn't disagree. "Let me ask you something. How was Leah last year when she moved back here? Did you see much of her?"

"A little. She came by the café every once in a while. Why?"

"Did she seem happy?"

"Yeah, I guess. She always is, though, don't you think?"

"Something's different about her."

Trish narrowed her eyes. "Spill."

"Something's off," Iris admitted. "She's getting married to this great guy, and she's finally settling down, but she's not . . . herself. When Stephen left for Seattle, she basically took to her bed."

"Maybe she missed him."

"For two days! And it's more than that. She's taking pills."

"What kind of pills?"

Iris paused, wondering if she sounded like an alarmist. Maybe, as Millie had insisted, it really was no big deal. "I saw a bunch of prescription bottles up in her room. She says they're for sleeping."

Trish shook her head. "Christ, it seems like everyone I know is taking something for something. But let's be honest. How sane were you before your wedding?"

Iris laughed. "You know I was a wreck. But this is different. One minute we're trying to lure Leah out of the house like an injured animal. And the next thing I know, she's bouncing on Cooper Woods's tailgate sporting a bikini."

"Ah."

"Don't 'ah' me. It's just that she's all over the place."

"Like Cooper's tailgate?"

Iris sipped her drink. "Yeah, yeah, laugh all you want. But she seems either really high or really low. Does that sound like depression?"

Trish leaned back in her seat and regarded Iris coolly. "Sounds like good ol' Standish sibling rivalry, if you ask me. Are you sure this isn't more about you?"

"Give me a break. It's just that she and my mom have this *thing* going with the farm. Sure, Millie has been nagging me to come back up here forever. But it's not like you can just drop your kids on their heads and take off. And besides, Leah is famous for all these 'great big ideas.' How was I to know this one would turn out?"

Trish nodded sympathetically.

"And I'm happy for her, really. But now everything's changed at home with Paul, and I thought maybe I could come back here and feel, I don't know . . . *normal*. But it feels like I've been gone too long to be myself. I don't have a place here anymore."

"You know that saying 'You can't go home'? Well, it's bullshit. That's the one good thing about family. They *have* to take you."

"Yeah, but now that I'm here, it's like I'm this big fat disappointment."

Trish looked into the bottom of her empty martini glass. "Well, on that point, I'm afraid I'm siding with Millie."

Iris's face fell. "You think I'm a disappointment?"

"No, not the disappointment part. But I think you stayed away long enough to *make* it hard to come back."

"Like I did it on purpose? Why would I do that?"

Trish shrugged. "I was going to ask you the same thing."

Iris hailed the waitress, who brought them another round. "I'm going to need another drink for this, aren't I?"

Trish reached across the table. "Look, I don't mean to put you on the spot, but you can't give them all the blame for your estrangement. Outside of a hot toddy three Christmases ago, I haven't seen you in years. It's like you fell off the map or something. What happened?"

Iris stared at her lap. It was a soft blow, one that she knew Trish hadn't intended to sting. But the delivery was deserved. Each summer Iris had promised to come back with the kids. But when they were little it'd been hard; there were playpens and baby equipment to tote, cribs to set up; Millie's dogs were too loud, the house too close to the water. They'd seemed like good reasons at the time. And Paul had never been one for the outdoors. Boats and lakes meant mosquitoes and mud. Why risk West Nile virus when you could sip iced drinks with umbrellas by a perfectly chlorinated hotel pool? Though Iris couldn't totally lay the blame on him. Hampstead was her home, where her friends and family resided. She should've been more insistent about returning. More independent. More something.

"I've pretty much sucked in the friend department, huh?"

Trish shook her head softly. "No. But you missed a lot of birthdays. I wished you'd been here for more of that stuff."

It was Iris's turn to reach across the table. "Me, too. I'm sorry about that."

Still holding her friend's hand, Iris looked out at the lake, which was turning a rich shade of purple under the setting sun. Trish was right—she should've come home sooner.

Trish clinked her glass against Iris's, interrupting her thoughts. "So. Speaking of people who suck, tell me about Paul."

Iris laughed, genuinely, for the first time in days, but a wave of hurt followed close on its heels. "You know those women you see on the news, the ones who go to the hospital with what they think is a bad stomachache, and then they pop out an eight-pound baby? And you think to yourself, 'That's ridiculous. How could she not know she was pregnant?' Well, that's me."

Trish coughed. "You're pregnant?"

"No! I mean I never saw this coming. I know I've been living in this dead relationship for years. And yet when Paul mentioned separation, it was like I'd been hit by a Mack Truck."

"How do you feel now?" Trish asked.

"Out of control. Like someone is making this massive life-wrecking decision for me, and all I can do is sit on the sidelines and watch."

Trish made a small noise of empathy. "I can't imagine. I just don't get how men can do this."

"But it's not all him."

Trish raised her eyebrows in disbelief. "Are you kidding?"

"Don't get me wrong, if I were to see him standing in the rearview mirror, I'd still throw the car in reverse. But on some level Paul is right. We are horrible together, and we have been for a long time. I guess I figured we'd survived this long, why pull the plug now?"

Trish shifted in her seat. "Look, there's no easy way to ask this. Do you think he's having an affair?"

The word caused Iris's throat to tighten.

"I'm not an idiot."

"And?"

"I've asked. I've looked. But there's nothing there I can find." When he'd asked her for the separation, she'd lost no time going through Paul's stuff—emptying his pockets, checking his email, even going so far as to peruse the credit card statements. As sure as she felt it in her gut that there had to be someone else, she came up empty-handed.

She cleared her throat. "You've no idea what it does to you, having to skulk around like that. You go from feeling suspicious to guilty. And wondering all the while if you're the one who's crazy."

"You're not crazy. It happens."

"Well, I can't seem to find any proof. But I still have this horrible feeling."

Trish nodded sympathetically. "I'm sorry, kiddo."

"There's one thing I do know. Once we had kids, he started looking at me differently."

Trish was a firm believer in embracing the full female experience, saggy post-nursing breasts and all. "You mean, like you'd turned into someone's mother, instead of a sexual partner?" She scoffed. And she held no tolerance for men who traded up—or more accurately, down—in the age department when all their partner had done was age gracefully in the natural order of things.

"No, really. I could see it when I stood next to him brushing my teeth in the morning. Or whenever I walked in the door. It's like he'd look up expecting someone else, but it was just me."

"*Just you?* Don't even go there. Not after you supported him through law school and raised those kids." Trish's voice rose, and the couple beside them glanced over.

"Paul always pushed me to go back to work at the agency in Boston. Maybe I should've. Maybe it would've taken the strain off him. Or made me, I don't know, more interesting. That's one thing our therapist suggested."

"Therapists are idiots," Trish said.

"That's what everyone who's happily married says."

"No, really. I mean, look at you. You are a sharp, accomplished woman."

Iris scowled.

"Stop it, you are. Sure, as women we go underground with our kids and work sometimes. And yes, we get caught up in stuff like planning birthdays and packing school lunches. But that's what good mothers do. And instead of giving you a high five, the guy decides he's feeling ignored, you're looking dull, and so he cries crisis. When what Paul really needs is a good kick in the ass and a mirror. 'Look at you, buddy! Look at that potbelly. That receding hairline. When was the last time you gave the dog a bath, or painted the planetary system for a fourth-grade science fair?'"

Iris sat back in her chair.

"I'm just saying you made the right choice to be home with the kids. It's one of the best jobs a woman could have, if not the hardest. If Paul finds that uninteresting then he's a horse's ass."

"You sound so June Cleaver. What would Gloria Steinem say?"

Trish sniffed. "I'm not saying anything Gloria doesn't know herself. We can do it all, just not all at once. Or you end up accomplishing nothing. And look like shit." She fluffed her hair for emphasis.

Outside, the night was a fluid mix of shadows, leaving no separation between water and sky. Iris glanced around the pub, at the couples finishing late dinners, and the regulars settling in at the bar.

"I just feel so unbalanced," Iris whispered.

Trish grabbed her hand. "Balance is bullshit."

Iris couldn't help it, the tears were starting. "So what's it about then?"

"I don't know. Maybe time."

"Time?" Iris raised her eyebrows. "Like we have *so much* of that."

"Humor me, okay? Picture a clock. The hands are never on more than two numbers at the same time, right?"

Iris nodded.

"And you've only got two hands."

"Go on."

"But they're always moving, Iris. Think about it. Every number gets touched, every day, by those two hands."

Iris glanced out at the dark water, picturing her hands moving. Through Lily's blond hair as she braided it for school. Across Sadie's back as she headed out the door. Always reaching, touching, holding on.

"Forget balance," Trish said.

Iris's eyes welled, blurring her reflection in the window's glass. Time was the one thing she'd never shorted her kids on. She forced a small laugh and looked back at her friend. "So unbalanced is a good thing, huh?"

"Honey, love is the most unbalanced thing there is."

Twelve

When Iris pulled into the farm drive that night, she noticed the lights on in the big barn. Had her father forgotten to turn them off? She parked down at the house and stood listening. Her heart leaped when she heard the sound of a saw.

Inside the barn, Cooper Woods was bent over a board laid across two sawhorses. He didn't see her leaning against the open doorway, and she reveled in the stolen moment, watching him work.

"Psst . . ."

Cooper jerked his head up, the board in his hand wobbling. "Geez, you startled me. What are you doing out here this late?"

"Sorry. I was going to ask you the same thing." Feeling braver, she stepped into the light. "Burning the midnight oil?"

Cooper smiled. "Something like that. Hope I didn't wake you."

"No, I'm just getting home actually."

He eyed her more carefully, and she blushed in the dim light, suddenly aware of how made-up and out of place she must look in the barn.

"You look nice." Another compliment Iris stored away, with a smile.

"So, do you always work this late?"

"Nah, I'm just not a great sleeper. Plus I like working when it's dark out. There's something peaceful about it."

Iris nodded, an image of Trish kneading bread dough in the back of her café in the early morning floating through her head. "I'm not much of a sleeper these days, either."

Cooper looked at her. "No?'" It was a one-word question, but it veiled a hundred more. Suddenly, Iris wanted to answer them all.

She wrapped her arms around herself, though the night was warm, and sat down on her old tack box. Fireflies were flickering in the distance.

"I used to come out here to be alone, when I was a teenager," she said, watching the lights bob in the spaces between the fir trees. "When I needed to think. There's something about a barn at night."

Cooper looked around appreciatively, his eyes moving over the empty stalls, the hayloft, and finally, her, and she knew he understood. "You must miss your family," he said softly. He'd returned to the sawhorse, and Iris admired his competent hands. They were comforting.

"Yes." She paused before admitting, "It's complicated."

He glanced back at her curiously.

And without hesitating, Iris told him. In the dim light of the barn, surrounded by the deep-throated chirrup of tree frogs, she told Cooper everything about her recent separation. That she missed not just her family but the dream of what she'd held for them. And now . . . well, now all of that had changed. And no matter how desperately she tried to imagine them getting through this, she couldn't help but hang on to what was supposed to be: that basket of happy endings that every woman tries to fill for her children. No matter how exhausting it became to haul around.

For the first time Iris held out her basket, with all its broken pieces, and allowed someone to look inside. To touch and examine, to turn over in his callused hands all the jagged hurts. The fears of what would come. And the feeling that she'd somehow failed.

Not once did Cooper interrupt. Nor did he offer up any platitudes, telling her it was going to be okay. Instead he leaned thoughtfully against the sawhorse and let her finish.

"I'm sorry," she said finally, wiping her nose on her sleeve.

Cooper stood and pulled a bandanna from his back pocket. She accepted it gratefully.

"You're not alone," he said finally. "It happens to the best of us."

Us. And yet it was a team she wasn't sure she wanted to be on.

"But you're home now," he added.

Iris laughed uncertainly. "Yeah, I guess."

"Believe me, I never planned on moving back to Hampstead. I loved being out in Colorado. Thought I had it all figured out."

"What happened?"

Cooper shrugged. "Things changed. I finally realized I had to change with them. When my dad got sick, it made sense to come home. I just didn't plan on staying."

"So, you're glad to be back?"

"Yeah, it's been good for me. Funny how things work out."

Iris looked around the barn. Cooper had everything he needed here. The lake, his work. His history. "I wish it were that simple."

Cooper cocked his head. "A girl like you with so much going for her? Look at all you've already accomplished, Iris. Give yourself a chance."

A girl? Whom Cooper viewed as accomplished? Iris smiled softly, accepting the gesture.

"You'll figure out what you need. I can tell."

Iris stood, suddenly sure of what she needed at that very moment.

"You going?" Cooper asked.

She handed him back his bandanna. "It's funny, but I think I can sleep now."

"Well, sweet dreams, then." Cooper stepped aside, and Iris imagined him allowing a wide berth for her and all of her troubles. But his expression was gentle.

In the doorway, she paused. "Thanks," she said. And then she placed her hands on the wooden door and pulled, rolling it across its rusty runner. The wheels squeaked in protest. Cooper watched, holding her gaze as she slid the creaky door between them.

◆ ◆ ◆

Back at the house, Iris slipped from her clothes and lay naked on the bed. Her eyes rested on the barn windows outside, which still glowed up on the rise. When they finally went out, she rose and pulled on her nightgown. Downstairs the kitchen floorboards creaked in all her favorite spots: by the large farm table; in front of the granite island, where her mother was so often stationed. And loudest at the refrigerator, where Iris stood now, surveying its contents. As she debated between basil biscuits and a leftover drumstick (though what she really wanted was to grab a stick of butter and eat it right out of the wrapper), she imagined what she must look like from behind. A rumpled figure illuminated by the lone yellow bulb of the fridge, alone in a dark kitchen. Not even her own kitchen, but her mother's. And before she knew it she was weeping. She imagined the kids tucked into their beds, some two hundred miles away. If she left now, she could be home before breakfast. How surprised they'd be to awaken and see her at the stove, flipping pancakes! Reminding Lily to feed her hamster, Jack to park his smelly sneakers in the garage, Sadie to remove her conspicuously applied makeup. They'd sit down together and get ready for a brand-new day.

But no. She could see it now. Lily would be confused by her sudden return. Jack would be concerned. Sadie would take one look at her straggly hair and the circles beneath her eyes: "What are you *doing*?"

And Paul. His exasperation, his head-shaking sympathy. No, she wanted none of that.

Instead, she sat at the old farmhouse table with one of her mother's drumsticks and ate, wiping tears between bites, until the bone was clean and her face dry. Hungrily, Iris licked the grease from her fingers. She poured herself a glass of milk and drank it; then another. She wandered the rooms, sipping milk and drying her eyes with the hem of her nightgown. Stopping in the den to run her fingers over a bronze figure of a dragon her father had brought back from China one year. Touching the globe by his desk, as she used to when she was a little girl— spinning the orb like a game-show contestant, she'd hold her breath to see where her finger pointed when it finally came to rest: the purported place she'd spend the rest of her life. But it was never anyplace exotic. Her sister, Leah, always got those. Hawaii, Tibet. Once Egypt. Iris always ended up in forlorn or mundane locations: Alabama. North Dakota. And the place that Leah laughed the hardest over: Siberia.

At the living room piano, she paused. It was where she'd endured long summer lessons with Mrs. Hamilton, the local music teacher. And in the end she'd only ever mastered "Mary Had a Little Lamb." She wondered if she could still play it. Briefly, her fingers fumbled on the keys, and she realized she had forgotten the notes. Another rush of tears pricked her eyes.

Finally, she stopped in the hallway. Rows of framed pictures lined the walls, each stately and carefully polished, as if their inhabitants were expecting her. The crackled black-and-white images of her great-grandparents, formally posed. There were her parents on their wedding day, her father's easy smile unchanged from youth. Baby pictures of her and Leah, their bald heads capped in lace hats, feet adorned in little white leather booties. Followed by graduation photos, and later, the shots of her wedding. And finally the framed faces of her own children. As she moved down the hall in her bare feet, the images peered back at her, beckoning her forward through the years and depositing her once more at the end of the hall, in the present.

Iris drained the milk glass. She was not alone. Even in the creaking old house of her childhood, with her aging parents overhead, while her own family slumbered two hundred miles away. Cooper Woods was right.

The subtle pull of sleep washed over her with a suddenness that made her limbs heavy. Uncertainly, she made her way back to bed and pulled the sheets up over her head. The curtains stirred as the lake's scent filled the room, rising up over the rocking chair, wafting over her pillows.

For the first time in many weeks, she slept soundly.

Thirteen

Cooper Woods's silver truck rolled up the farm's driveway by eight o'clock each day. And for the next few mornings, Iris's bed was empty well before it did.

After an early swim, she towel-dried her hair and dressed in worn jeans and a T-shirt, her new uniform. She applied mascara carefully, and a swipe of lip balm. But nothing more. She was working, after all.

She ignored the curious looks that Millie and Bill exchanged as she hurriedly buttered pieces of toast, heaping them with homemade jam. Sometimes she fried eggs, nestling them between warm slices of Millie's bread. She'd head out the door with a bagged breakfast for two, and a thermos of coffee in the crook of her arm.

"See you at lunch," she'd call, and before anyone was able to question or comment, she was already heading up the grassy slope to the barn. And why not? She was doing exactly what Trish had suggested: giving time. Only now it was to herself.

The morning after she'd told Cooper everything was the only day she'd awakened late. The kitchen had been empty, Leah and Millie long since gone for the garden. With a copy of the *Boston Globe* in hand, she'd wandered out to the patio. Bill was down at the water's edge, retying the dinghy to the dock. She watched him climb the yard toward her with his fishing rod, a look of contentment on his face.

"So, look what the cat dragged in," he'd said fondly, reaching the edge of the patio.

"Catch anything?"

He smiled. "Not a bite today, though I usually throw them back anyway. The bass are small this year."

He joined her at the table, where they sat gazing at the water.

"You know, you can take the boat out anytime you want. You're a big girl now."

She smiled. "I know, Dad. Thanks."

"Have you spoken to the kids?" he asked, glancing over at her.

"Yes, last night. They're having fun at camp."

He nodded, resting his chin in his hand. "That's good. Your mother and I can't wait to see them."

Iris let the silence settle, but it wasn't with the usual ease. Questions, however wordless, pressed the humid space between them, and she closed her eyes, wondering where to begin. Or how.

"Daddy, I'm in trouble," she whispered.

Bill Standish fixed his gaze on the dock. "I'm listening."

Iris cleared her throat. "Paul and I, we're not doing so well."

Bill Standish leaned back in his chair and let out a breath. "I'm sorry to hear that, honey. Is there anything I can do?"

Iris shook her head. "We've been in therapy for a while. A long time, actually." She glanced at her father. "I think it's really over."

"Is that what you want?"

Iris shrugged helplessly. "I don't know. We're not good together. But I don't want my kids to come from a broken home." Her voice cracked, and Iris covered her face with her hand.

Bill stood. Just as he had when she was a child, he held her as the sobs racked her rib cage, until the stifled tears slowed.

"Maybe if you give it some time," he said. "Marriage is no different than this farm." He looked around them. "It's hard work."

"You make it look easy."

Bill shook his head and chuckled. "Your mother is a complicated woman. Sometimes I have to remember to duck my head. Fly low."

"But what about you? Don't you mind that?"

Bill looked her evenly in the eyes. "I love your mother. You learn to adapt in ways that let you both get on with things. Besides, I'm a bit of an old bear myself."

"Come on, Dad. You're always so patient. Sometimes I get mad at her, for being so, I don't know, strong. So pushy. It's like she can't see us for what we are sometimes, she's so focused on what she wants all of us to be."

Bill nodded. "That's love, my dear. In just one of its mysterious forms."

"But she's so hard on me. And you, too." Iris glanced at her father, hoping she hadn't offended him. It wasn't her place to remind him of his marriage's shortcomings. Certainly not now.

But he shrugged good-naturedly. "It's the only way your mother knows how to love. I know how it can feel sometimes, but I've learned that I can't change that about her." He laughed. "And I'd be taking my life into my own hands if I tried." Which made Iris laugh, too. "You have to remember, her own mother was tough on her growing up, so it's not like your mom knew much else. And I think she's come a long way, considering."

Iris recalled Grandmama Whitmore—never to be referred to as "Grandma"—only in snapshots. There were her gloved hands, crossed chastely in her lap. They were not hands that dug in sandboxes or wiped tears. Not even hands that held her own, at any time that she could remember. Her grandmother had died when Iris was just five, and the few memories she had were of her face from across a hemstitched tablecloth, probably at a holiday dinner, their interactions formal and distant.

Bill shifted in his chair, drawing her back to the patio. "Honey, I wish there was something I could say to you. I hope you two are able to work through this." He took her hand tightly in his own, and Iris looked down at his large knuckles, gnarled with age. "But even if you don't, you will be all right."

She looked away, pressing the fingers of her free hand to her eyes.

"That's one thing about you kids," Bill added. "You were the one I always knew would be all right."

◆ ◆ ◆

After that morning on the patio, there'd been no need to say more.

But Iris had a sudden, restless urge to *do*. So she'd climbed the hill to the barn. If he'd been surprised to see her return, Cooper didn't say so. Instead, he accepted the thermos of coffee with a grin, and her presence without question. He instructed her matter-of-factly: *Hold the board at this angle, aim the nail gun like this, watch your fingers.* Surprisingly, it wasn't as backbreaking as the garden work had been, much to Iris's relief. But it was hard work nonetheless, and it required her concentration and her strength, two things that batted away her worries that bobbed like moths, incessant against the light.

At first, Iris had felt in the way, stepping gingerly around equipment that terrified her; nail guns, circular saws, and the like. More important, she wondered if Cooper thought she was in the way. Like the morning she grabbed a two-by-four, catching her finger on a jagged edge.

"Shit!"

"Let me see." Cooper came over to where she stood holding her index finger.

Iris groaned. "I'm an idiot. I shouldn't be here to begin with."

"Nonsense." He took her hand, turning her finger over toward the light.

Iris looked away. "Is it bad?"

"It's still attached," he said, chuckling. "It's a sliver."

"A sliver?" Iris withdrew her hand and examined it herself. "That's all?"

"Yup, it's a good one. Let me get it out for you."

Without thinking, Iris tucked her hand behind her back.

"Don't worry," he teased. "I promise, I'll be gentle."

And he was. She cringed as he squeezed her fingertip, but within seconds the sliver was withdrawn. He held it to the light for her to see. "Brave girl," he said, still holding her hand. "You should probably wash it."

She looked up at him. "Thanks," she said, withdrawing her hand slowly.

"The first injury on a site is sort of like a badge," Cooper told her.

"Of what, stupidity?" Iris lifted the handle of the pump in the corner, letting the cold water rush over both hands.

"Of hard work," Cooper said. "Don't be so hard on yourself. You're learning."

Iris pushed the pump handle back down and wiped her hands on her jeans. "Be honest. Am I completely in your way out here?"

"Are you kidding? I like the company. Besides, nobody's brought me breakfast in years."

Iris laughed. "Well, I guess I'm good for something." And so she returned to the barn the next morning, and the morning after that. By the third day she'd figured out how to use the table saw and rip a board. She actually felt useful.

Besides, Cooper was so easy to be around. And patient: like the time he drove into town to the hardware store and returned to find her stranded straddling a high beam, white in the face, having attempted to finish some buttressing work in the hope of proving herself. But her embarrassment did not last, and he'd merely shaken his head as he helped her down.

And it wasn't just the barn roof she was learning to repair. If Cooper Woods was quiet, it also made him a good listener. Suddenly Iris was letting a few of her worries trickle out. Worries about raising well-rounded kids. And mending her relationships. And staying true to herself, whoever that was.

"What about Paul?" Cooper surprised her with the outright question one morning. "Is he a pretty handy guy?"

The hammer in her hand stilled as Iris struggled to put words together. "Not really," she said carefully. Then, "He's more of a hands-off kind of guy."

"Ah." And that was all.

Cooper asked more about the kids, and what sorts of things they were interested in. Delighted, she'd gushed about them, finally catching herself when she looked up breathlessly and saw him staring back at her, wordless. "Oh, God. I'm doing it again, aren't I?" She made a mouth with her hand. "Talk, talk, talk."

But he'd just grinned. "I already told you, I like that about you. Besides, you're a great mom." Which had been an instant balm to a bruise within that she'd thus far been unable to soothe.

By the end of their first week working together she was feeling braver. They were working at different ends of the barn, backs to each other, which allowed her to voice the questions she'd been keeping.

"So, how about you? Did you ever marry?" She squeezed the handful of nails she held in her palm the second the words were out.

"Yeah, actually. I was married for about five years."

Iris braved a quick look over her shoulder. Cooper was measuring another board, his eyes trained on his work. "It ended badly," he admitted.

So. Iris's thoughts raced, teetering between the pressing desire for more information and the fear that that very information could alter the careful image she had constructed of him. And something else . . . hope? *He's just like you*, she reminded herself firmly. Just a person, with bones and blood, and flaws. And, good God, those blue eyes.

"I'm sorry," she said quickly. Then, "I didn't mean to pry."

Cooper shrugged. "It was my fault I didn't see it sooner. Sherry wasn't happy. Wanted things I couldn't give her."

Which made Iris's thoughts race faster. What sort of things? A beach house? Kids?

Instead she asked, "Is she still in Colorado?"

"Last I heard." He looked at Iris. "But I'm here."

Iris was getting to know Cooper Woods. The real, grown-up Cooper Woods, who was not just an older or more experienced version of the boy in the yearbook. Which frightened her.

And in return for his divulgences, she did something spontaneous. She invited Cooper to the house. "My mother had a loaf of homemade bread in the oven this morning," Iris said, looking at him out of the corner of her eye. "Why don't you join us for lunch?"

Cooper eyed his cooler in the corner.

"I think she's making BLTs," Iris added, pushing any warning thoughts aside. Her parents loved his work, and he seemed genuinely fond of Millie, which Iris found both perplexing and admirable. Besides, what man could say no to a slab of bacon on homemade bread?

Confirming her suspicions, he tossed his hammer in the tool kit. "Done."

◆　◆　◆

Millie welcomed Cooper politely, though Iris could feel the weight of her curiosity.

Leah was no better. "Oh, hi, Cooper," she stammered, looking a little rattled.

Millie broke the silence at the table first. "Leah, Tika called this morning. She wants to know the final head count for the caterer."

"Oh, she did?" Leah glanced quickly over at Cooper, then back at Millie.

"You'd better call her back. We've only got a couple of weeks until the wedding."

"I will," Leah replied, her voice barely a whisper.

In the beat of silence that followed, Cooper looked from Millie to Leah. "Is someone getting married?"

Millie beamed. "Didn't you know? Leah's engaged!"

Iris watched Leah duck her head.

"Congratulations. When's the big day?"

Leah smiled uncertainly, crossing her brown arms delicately in front of her. "August tenth," she said in a hushed voice.

"It'll be the event of the summer," Millie said, raising her chin proudly. But Iris's attention was focused on Cooper, trying to read his expression as he learned the news. He seemed surprised. But she couldn't tell if this mattered to him or not.

"Who's the lucky guy?" Cooper asked.

Was it her imagination, or did Leah look sheepish? "He's not from around here," she said. Then added, "His name's Stephen."

"Stephen Willets the third," Millie said, filling in the gaps. "He was just here, but he had to return to Seattle for business. The city they will call home after the wedding," she added meaningfully.

What was going on? Iris wondered. The wedding was all Leah talked about to anyone who'd listen. And the fact that Cooper hadn't known about any of it? All of it left Iris feeling suddenly not so hungry anymore.

But then Bill joined the table, seeming quite pleased to find Cooper sitting across from him. "So, how are you doing up there?" he asked, gesturing up the hill toward the barns.

"It's coming along faster than I thought," Cooper said. "Now that I've got help." He nodded toward Iris, and Millie and Leah both glanced her way, as if surprised to see her still there. She smiled back at them tightly.

"I had no idea you were so interested in carpentry," Leah said flatly.

"The beams look marvelous," Bill continued. "I'm glad you talked me into those salvaged pieces from Vermont. Made all the difference."

Iris watched the care Cooper took to arrange his sandwich. For a man who worked carpentry, his hands looked soft, his nails spotless. "That barn's almost two hundred years old. It needs history, to go along with its own."

"Well said." Bill chewed thoughtfully. "I think I'll walk up with you after lunch. I want to start thinking about doing the smokehouse next."

Iris smiled. So, Bill had more restoration work in mind. Cooper would be staying on longer. Millie looked firmly at Bill. "But I thought we were saving the smokehouse for next year."

Bill shook his head. "If Cooper can get the materials from that site in Vermont, we need to move forward. Do you think you can get your hands on more chestnut?"

Again, Iris could feel her mother's gaze. "But we're so busy at the moment," Millie interjected. "With the wedding and all . . ." Her voice trailed, and she looked to Leah, who hadn't even touched her lunch.

"I'm going up there next week," Cooper told him. "I'll check the inventory if you'd like." He turned to Iris. "I've got a little cabin in Stowe."

"Really? Sounds like a nice getaway spot." How fitting; woodsy Cooper living on the lake in New Hampshire, traveling to Vermont for rustic weekend getaways. The images unfolded in Iris's mind like a glossy travel brochure.

"Get an estimate and let me know," Bill said, standing. "I'd love to finish these renovations."

When Bill and Millie finally excused themselves to clear the table, the three were left alone.

"That's great news about your wedding," Cooper said.

"You should come," Leah said quickly. She ran her hand through her hair and looked at him sideways. "You'll know a lot of the guests from town. Plus, we've got a great band." And there it was again, her flirtatious ease.

Iris held her tongue. Why was Leah acting as if the wedding were just a casual barbecue? Even a man would know that the invitations must have gone out weeks ago, and that the table settings would be finalized. What was Leah doing?

Cooper must've realized it, too. "It's real nice of you to offer, but you don't have to. In fact, I may be up at the cabin that weekend."

But Leah either didn't notice the look on Iris's face, or ignored it. "I'm the bride. I insist."

"Well, in that case, thank you. I'll dust off one of my suits."
He glanced at his watch. "I'd best get back to work. Can I help
clean up here?"

"Go ahead," Iris urged. "I'll meet you back at the barn."

No sooner had he left than Leah cornered Iris in the kitchen.
"What are you doing?"

"What do you mean?"

Millie stood behind them at the sink, scraping plates. Iris
knew she was listening.

"It's just weird. You're spending all this time in the barn with
the hired help."

Iris met her gaze. "Hired help? What, are you an aristocrat
now?"

"You know what I mean."

Iris had never heard Leah make such an unflattering reference. Sure, their family was accustomed to a certain lifestyle. But
this was about something else.

Iris glanced at her mother, who was making no attempt to
hide the fact that she was hanging on every word.

Leah strode to the mudroom and pulled on her boots, tightening the laces with quick, angry tugs.

Why should Leah care how she spent her time?

Leah stood abruptly. "Mom, I'm heading back to the farm
stand. Naomi's going to need more berry containers. Did you
unpack that order yet?"

Millie nodded solemnly from her post at the counter. "I'll
bring some up."

Iris watched Leah pause at the washroom sink. She pulled a
small bottle from her jeans pocket and tipped two yellow pills
into her palm. "What are those?" she asked as Leah scooped a
handful of water into her mouth.

"Vitamins," Leah snapped.

Vitamins, my ass, Iris thought. The mudroom door slammed
loudly, and Leah was gone.

"What is her problem?" Iris asked, tossing the dish towel

she'd been holding onto the counter. There was nothing wrong about helping Cooper with the barn. It was no different from the work Leah herself was doing in the fields. Would they rather she sulked around the house, or lay in bed all day?

Through the kitchen window she could see Cooper getting something out of his truck in the distance. "I'm going back up to the barn."

Millie kept her eyes trained on the dishes.

Iris was halfway out the door when her mother's voice stopped her. It was soft, and Iris hesitated a moment before she was sure she'd heard right.

"Be careful, dear."

Fourteen

There was nothing careful about the way she looked.

It was Friday night, and Iris had called Trish and asked her for a drink. Demanded was more like it. Beforehand, she'd hurried into town, hitting a few of the trendier boutiques on Railroad Street before she found what she was looking for. A black one-shouldered top, simple and sexy at once. While she was there she figured she might as well splurge on a new pair of jeans. Her old ones were baggy in the rear now, and she was finished with the drab, shapeless items she'd hurriedly packed from home, which she now referred to as her mourning clothes. Which meant, of course, that she needed a new pair of shoes— in a style decidedly unsensible. She'd found them, in a pair of strappy black sandals that made her toes throb but her calf muscles flash. And a pair of open-toed cream wedges that added at least three inches to her height. She'd charged all of it, tossing a coral scarf on the counter at the last second. Let Paul worry about the bill.

When she came downstairs that night, Bill looked up from his wing chair and smiled. "Well, look at you."

Leah, who was curled up on the couch with the TV remote, narrowed her eyes suspiciously. "Where are you going?"

"Down to the Dock, with Trish. Want to come?" She was determined not to argue with her sister. But Iris bit her lip the second the words came out. This was her night.

Leah shook her head, sinking back into the cushions. "Stephen's supposed to call. And I'm tired, anyway."

Relieved, Iris checked her reflection in the hall mirror. A quick coat of lipstick, and she was ready. As she sailed through the kitchen, she almost ran into her mother.

"Iris?"

Millie blinked several times in the bright light, trying to reconcile the outfit, the styled hair, and the makeup with her eldest daughter. "It's late. Where are you going?"

But Iris wasn't about to get bogged down by questions. She was forty years old, for God's sake. "Out. See you later!" she called as the door slammed matter-of-factly behind her.

◆　◆　◆

At nine o'clock the Dock was already crowded, a mixed group of post-college kids and middle-aged patrons, the latter of whom, Iris realized with dread, she now belonged to. The lakeside restaurant housed an outdoor patio bar and was a popular seasonal spot. She eyed the younger women warily, their tanned brows unfurrowed by sleepless nights, their slender physiques unmarked by motherhood. Funny how her age never really occurred to her, until she was confronted by twentysomethings with bare midriffs. But the boisterous atmosphere had not changed, and as she and Trish took a deck table by the water, she soon felt young enough again. "You look hot tonight," Trish said.

"Thanks." Iris crossed her legs and admired the way her polished toes peeked from her wedge heels. "I took your advice and went shopping."

Trish lifted her beer. "See what a little retail therapy can do?" She ran a hand through her hair. "Wish I'd had the energy to dress up a bit more. I still have cake batter in my hair."

Iris laughed. "Rough day at work?"

Trish forced a smile. "One of the ovens broke, so we were behind on the baking. And on a day when we had a large order from a local caterer. I had to talk her into changing the menu."

Iris winced sympathetically. "You always throw together the best food at the last minute. I don't know how you do it."

Trish shrugged. "It worked out."

Which gave Iris a wild idea, one that she couldn't believe she hadn't thought of before. "Hey, have you ever thought of doing a cookbook?"

Trish took a swig from her beer. "We put out a holiday book each year, for the chamber of commerce."

Iris shook her head. "No, I mean a published cookbook that's all your own."

"Are you kidding? I own a café; I'm not a chef."

"But you are, in the most real sense. You're a working mom and a business owner. Your schedule is crazy, so you have to come up with good food fast. Believe me, I'd kill for some of your ideas on a Wednesday night after soccer practice."

Trish laughed, shaking her head. "Well, thanks for the vote of confidence. But I can't imagine anybody buying a book of recipes that ordinary."

"That's exactly why they'd buy it! Who has time for hand-made ravioli? Bread salad with garden vegetables is exactly what we need. With some of that sesame chicken you do." The more Iris thought about it, the more excited she got. Here was the culinary talent she needed for her cookbook idea. And in the same package as an old friend!

"I don't know," Trish said, rolling the idea around in her head. "I've never considered it, to be honest."

"Well, you should. We both should. Seriously, we could write this thing, together."

Iris ordered them another round. It took some convincing, but whether it was the beer or Iris's persistence, she could tell Trish was warming up to the idea. Iris had just begun explaining how they could propose their ideas to a publisher when Trish reached across the table.

"Don't look now, but somebody just sauntered in."

Iris glanced over her shoulder at the growing crowd on the upper deck.

"At the bar." Trish pointed.

It was Leah in a short white dress, her brown legs dazzling in a pair of strappy black sandals. Hardly a staying-in-for-the-night outfit.

"Hey, those are my new shoes!" Iris sputtered.

"Hate to say it, but she's doing them justice."

Iris scowled. "It's a bit much for the Dock, wouldn't you say?"

They watched as Leah ordered a drink, laughing animatedly at something the young bartender said. When she turned in their direction Iris motioned her over. But instead of joining them, Leah threw Iris a coy wink before disappearing quickly into the crowd.

"That brat. Did she just ditch us?" Iris asked.

Trish stood, scanning the crowd for a better look. "More important, who is she here with?"

Iris scoffed. "This is so like her. Moping at home in sweatpants, then popping up like Cinderella. Did I tell you about the other day with Cooper?"

Trish brightened. "What about him?"

"Well, I've sort of been helping him out. You know, with the barn."

Now Trish covered her mouth in a poor attempt to conceal her surprise. "You? Working in a barn?"

Iris rolled her eyes. "Yeah, yeah, who knew that clumsy Iris could manage a hammer? Can we get on with it now?"

Trish nodded, suppressing her laughter.

"So, I went up to the barn one day, and we sort of got to talking. He showed me what he was working on, and I don't know . . . I just felt like I belonged there."

Trish raised her eyebrows. "In the barn. Or with Cooper?"

Iris grinned sheepishly. "Maybe both?"

"Ah. Now we're talking."

"No, no, it's not like that, I swear. It's something about the work. Something about waking up early and knowing what I'm going to do with myself. Knowing that someone is depending on me." She looked up. "And that I can do it."

Trish's expression softened. She nodded knowingly. "Like I feel in my kitchen."

"Exactly." Iris was relieved. She'd feared saying it out loud, but Trish understood.

"Though the company doesn't exactly hurt," Trish added.

Iris grinned. "I'm not blind."

"So what's the problem, then?"

"Leah. I asked Cooper to come down to the house for lunch yesterday. No big deal, right? And she sort of freaked out. She accused me of 'fraternizing with the help.' Like I'm doing something wrong."

"Wrong in regard to your marriage?"

Iris shook her head. "To her."

Trish considered this. "You know, I didn't see much of Leah outside of the farm last summer. But there was one time, I saw them at the lake together."

Iris felt her body stiffen. "You mean Leah and Cooper?"

Trish nodded. "Down at the town pier. It must've been the Fourth of July, because we'd gone down to see the fireworks. And they were there, getting out of his boat."

"Just the two of them?"

Trish grimaced. "Yeah, I think so."

Iris pressed a hand to her temple. "As in together." She knew it shouldn't bother her. But it did.

"I don't know that for sure. But I remember it got my attention; they just seemed sort of close."

"Huh." Iris sat back, suddenly deflated. If that's how it was, it certainly explained things.

"It was over a year ago," Trish said hurriedly. "And it may have been nothing. Besides, you know how my memory is. Mommy mush."

"No, no, it's no big deal. It's not like I'm interested in Cooper Woods."

"And Leah's got Stephen now," Trish added quickly, as though Leah were all that stood between Iris and a high school crush, leaving out Paul, and her kids, and the glaring black question mark of her marriage.

Iris waved her hand. "Trish, really. I have no say in what either of them does, or did last year. I'm not in a position to have an opinion anyway." Iris said the words, but she didn't believe them any more than she could tell Trish did. She looked over her shoulder. Where was that waitress?

"It's okay to flirt with the guy, Iris. You're going through a crappy time."

"It's nothing like that. Really. But I guess it explains why Leah was so weird at lunch. I just wonder why Cooper hasn't said anything about it in the barn. I mean, we're side by side for hours."

"Ask him. Maybe there's nothing really there to tell."

Iris swung her leg over the bench. She didn't want to talk about it anymore. "I'm going to get another beer."

Trish held up her empty bottle. "Make it two."

At the bar Iris tried to wrap her head around what Trish had told her. So, Cooper and Leah had hung out together, whatever that meant. And neither had told her about it. Though it wasn't any of her business, she reasoned. Besides, it was over a year ago. Leah was engaged now, and in love with someone else. And Cooper, well, who could tell? He could be out on a date with someone else right now, for all Iris knew.

She threw down a ten-dollar bill for the bartender and grabbed their beers just as the band started up. It was a local group that she suddenly recognized from years ago, and she paused to let the music wash over her. But there was Leah on the dance floor, turning and laughing in Iris's new heels. Iris watched as Leah and Naomi secured their places in the center. Off the farm Naomi was nearly unrecognizable, her skirt twirling about her knees, her arms glittery with bangle bracelets. But it was Leah who stole the attention, swaying her hips.

And there was that nagging feeling again, climbing in Iris's throat. That dual sense of being left out and awed at the same time. Muttering to herself, Iris turned back for her table when someone touched her arm.

"I was going to shout you a drink, but I see you already have one." Cooper Woods stood before her in the crowd in a pressed button-down shirt. Iris couldn't help but notice the way his collar opened at the neck, and she fought the sudden urge to touch the tan skin of his collarbone.

"Hi," she managed.

He leaned in closer. "This is a great band. You remember these guys from back in the day?"

She nodded. But she was distracted by the smell of his cologne, spicy and fresh, like new-cut grass. Something he never wore in the barn. Which only made her thoughts race: *Who is it meant for?* Followed by, *Of course the guy has a life outside the farm.* And it wasn't hers to worry about.

"I'm here with Trish," she shouted over the music, motioning over her shoulder.

But something else had stolen his attention.

"And Leah," she added quietly.

As Cooper's eyes rested firmly on her sister, Iris turned to go. "Guess I'll catch you later, then." Clearly, whatever they'd had going on last summer was still permeating this one. And Iris certainly wasn't about to stand around and watch.

But when she pushed her way back to her table, Cooper was right behind her.

Struggling to contain her surprise, Trish spoke first. "Hey, Coop! Have a seat."

Iris held her breath as he slid onto the bench beside her.

As Cooper and Trish chatted, she pretended to listen. *He followed me.* She smoothed her hair and tried to look interested in the conversation, but their knees had touched under the table, and she couldn't think straight, wondering instead if he noticed. What did it mean that he hadn't pulled his knee away?

Cooper ordered another beer, and Iris felt her limbs loosening. They talked about high school, and work. Cooper didn't laugh when he told Trish that Iris was helping him in the barn. Iris had almost forgotten that Leah was there, too, but eventually the worried-older-sister urge surfaced, and she turned to scan the dance floor.

Leah was still there, only now she wasn't dancing with just Naomi. The two were surrounded by a few younger men, and Leah was getting particular attention from one who was dancing a little too closely.

"Someone's having a good time," Trish said, and Iris watched Cooper's blue-eyed gaze move back to the dance floor.

Trish excused herself. "I'd better check in with poor Wayne. Make sure the kids haven't launched a coup." She laughed, holding up her phone.

The relaxed ease Iris had felt left right along with Trish.

She cleared her throat. "So, no hot date tonight?"

Cooper smiled shyly. "Nah, not tonight." And Iris raised her drink to her lips to stop herself from asking when the last one had been.

"I've been meaning to ask you something," he said, resting his elbows on the table. "How would you like to come with me to Vermont?"

"Vermont?" She swallowed hard, trying not to choke on her beer.

"I was thinking of going up tomorrow afternoon," he said. Which made Iris's heart leap wildly against her ribs. Until he explained that he was driving up for a lumber order for her father. "I could use the help, if you're up for it."

"Oh, right. The lumber," she said, feeling foolish and determinedly stamping out all images of leaf-strewn trails and cozy bed-and-breakfasts. *What is wrong with me?* But she recovered quickly. "Sure, I'd love to come with you. To help."

He smiled. "Good. There's a great little roadside bistro in Stowe where I always stop to eat. I thought maybe we could have dinner on the way home."

Iris brightened. So it was sort of a date. Maybe.

"Sounds great."

Their smiles were interrupted by some loud whoops from the dance floor.

"Is she okay?" Cooper asked. And Iris knew he hadn't forgotten about Leah any more than she had.

Leah was still dancing with the stocky guy in the plaid shirt. He spun her around. Iris winced, watching her new shoes wobble, imagining the scuffs and dings.

"She's had too much to drink," Iris said. It had been a while, but the years hadn't changed the signs. When Leah drank, her volume and animation climbed, matching the intake. According to her current display, she'd had plenty. "And Plaid Shirt Guy isn't helping."

Suddenly Plaid Shirt pulled her into a rough embrace, and Leah stumbled up against him, nose to nose.

Cooper jumped up.

"What are you going to do?" But he was already heading for the dance floor. Iris rushed after him, a mixture of relief and worry in her chest: Was he jealous?

Leah spotted him first. "Coo-per!" she cried out, extricating herself from Plaid Shirt's clutch and throwing her arms around Cooper.

"What's the deal?" Plaid Shirt asked, stepping back.

Cooper held up his hand. "She's had a little too much," he said.

"What the hell do you care?" the guy blustered. Apparently he had, too.

"Want to dance?" she slurred, looking up at Cooper.

Two other guys came to stand behind Plaid Shirt. Iris touched Cooper's arm. "Let's get her home."

Leah broke away. "Who's leaving?" she sputtered, weaving grotesquely between them. "Not me!"

Plaid Shirt grinned hungrily. "No one's gonna make you, sweetheart."

Iris could feel Cooper inhale slowly. "Look, buddy, we're just looking out for our friend."

"Your friend is fine," Plaid Shirt hissed. "Fuck off."

At that, Leah spun around and slapped him.

"Leah!" Iris shouted.

Cooper reached for her arm, bringing it calmly but firmly down. "Easy there."

But Plaid Shirt reversed, turning on Cooper. "Hey, don't touch my girl!"

And then everything erupted. Iris felt herself being shoved backward, and instinctively she shielded her face.

Iris watched, stunned, as one guy grabbed Cooper's arm and the other took a swing.

Cooper's head snapped to the left, and Iris let out a shriek. But in an instant, Cooper shoved the guy who was holding him to the side and returned one clean hit to the other. Both men stumbled away from him as the bar staff descended to break up the fight.

There was the scraping of chairs and feet, and finally the men parted. Cooper stood in the center of the floor, still holding his jaw.

Iris went to him. "Are you all right?"

Cooper winced. His hair was askew, but there was no blood. "Shit," he mumbled.

"Let me see." Gingerly she touched his chin, already an angry shade of red.

"Should've seen it coming," he muttered.

They found Leah slumped in the doorway, one arm draped around Naomi, who seemed sober enough, and, Iris noted, not terribly surprised by what had just unfolded.

"Are you all right?" Iris asked them.

"Yeah," Naomi said, brushing the hair out of Leah's face as she propped her up. "But I think this one's done for the night." She exchanged a knowing look with Cooper. "Just like old times," she said, shaking her head.

"You're gonna break a leg in these," Cooper said, bending to unbuckle one of her shoes. Iris observed the way he took Leah's feet in hand and carefully slid the heels off. The gesture was almost too intimate, and she looked away.

"Geez," Trish said, coming up behind them. "I swear, you call home for a second and you miss all the good stuff. What just happened?"

Iris shook her head. "Leah."

"Well, if you can get Miss Dancing Feet in my car, I'll drive you kids home," Trish said. Before Iris could answer, Cooper scooped Leah up in his arms like a small child.

Outside in the parking lot, Trish held the car door open and Naomi and Cooper settled Leah onto the backseat. "I'm getting too old for this," Naomi joked.

Iris leaned into the backseat, cupping Leah's chin. "What the hell were you thinking?"

"Cooper doesn't mind." Which only confirmed that old feeling creeping up on Iris from the past. She was still the older sister, the more sensible one. But not necessarily the more desirable one.

Cooper was waiting by his truck. "You girls okay to get home?"

"Listen, I'm sorry about all that," Iris said, feeling awkward. Under the street lamp she could see that his hair was rumpled. She wondered for a fleeting second if he looked that good in the morning.

"It's not your fault," Cooper said. "I didn't want it to go that way. I didn't realize the guy would be such a jerk." He gave the others a quick wave before climbing in his truck. "Drive home safely."

Iris watched in dismay as he pulled away, the distance growing between them.

◆ ◆ ◆

Back home in her bed, she replayed the night again and again. The warmth of Cooper's knee pressed against her own beneath the picnic table. The speed with which he stood and approached the dance floor and walked away from her. All of it swirling in her head, until she thought she'd never sleep. Which was probably just as well. She couldn't wait until tomorrow, when she and Cooper would climb into his truck and head to Vermont. When she could put words to the questions that stirred inside her. She just hoped she had the stomach for the answers, whatever they might be.

Fifteen

The damn bridesmaid dresses were in. Which meant Iris had to give up her much-anticipated morning in the barn.

"Honestly, Iris, you'd think we were dragging you off by your hair to be tortured. It won't take long," Millie said. Iris barely touched her food, but Leah miraculously managed to shovel in large mouthfuls of eggs. With ketchup. Eyes bright and cheeks flushed, she showed no residue of the excesses of the night before, and Iris wondered at her sister's speedy recovery, and waited to see if an explanation, or at least an apology, might be offered. Neither was.

Walking into Miss Patty's dress shop was like déjà vu, only in reverse. This time Leah plopped herself on the peach settee to await the great unveiling, and Iris was sequestered to the fitting room.

Iris sighed as the salesgirl hung up a plastic garment bag. She wondered what time Cooper would be arriving at the farm. The hairs on her arms lifted, just imagining herself seated beside him in the cab of the truck. She'd left a note for him in the barn, just in case she was late.

"Here you go," the salesgirl said. She unzipped the bag with a dramatic *whoosh*.

Iris, who'd kicked off her jeans, turned reluctantly to survey the damage. The dress was a deep shade of purple. *Eggplant*, Leah had called it.

"Arms up," the girl ordered, and Iris obeyed as the dress was slipped over her head, thinking that "Stick 'em up" might be more appropriate.

Purple was not her friend. In Iris's experience purple was the color sure to bring out the blotchiness in her fair complexion, or illuminate the tired shadows beneath her blue eyes. She turned left, then right, allowing herself to be tugged and fitted in the slippery fabric. *Whoosh* went the zipper again.

"There you go!"

Iris opened her eyes. She'd been right about the color. But so wrong about the effect.

"My, my," the salesgirl said.

Iris took a deep breath. Who was this woman in the mirror? Somehow Iris hadn't noticed the new caramel color of her skin, from all the hours outdoors. Or the golden highlights in her hair. She grinned, noting for the first time the toned muscles of her upper arms. How had all of this escaped her?

"Well?" Millie breathed audibly on the other side of the curtain, and for once, it was Iris who eagerly swept it aside for the revelation. "Iris. Look at you!"

Miss Patty and Millie launched forward for inspection.

Leah, who was deep in conversation on her cell, peered around them to see what the fuss was about. Her eyes roamed up and down Iris. "Well."

"I know!" Iris beamed. She couldn't help it. She'd not felt this good in a long time. Ever, perhaps. She turned to the mirror, admiring the low-cut drape in the back.

Patty grabbed a fistful of fabric at the waist. "This'll have to be taken in. You're clearly not a size six. Maybe a four. Maybe even a two?"

"Two?" Iris shrieked.

"The magic of farmwork," Millie said, as if she'd been awaiting this transformation all along. But there was genuine pleasure in her voice. "Do you like it, dear?"

I'm never taking it off, Iris wanted to cry out. But behind them all, something about Leah's expression reined her in. "You chose great," Iris told her sister. "I love it."

As Vera, the seamstress, was summoned once more, Iris inspected herself shamelessly. She'd known she'd slimmed down. But initially it had been a loss of more than just weight, leaving her pale and loose with sadness. Now, the sun and lake had worked within her. There was nothing shrunken or defeated about the woman in the mirror, and something inside her stirred with that bright realization.

Returning them all to business, Leah was brusque in her directions. "The other bridesmaids will be arriving next week," she told Patty, ticking through the list on her phone. "I'll call to schedule fittings." She turned to Iris, impatience furrowing her brow. "And don't forget to schedule your makeup and hair consult. I asked you to do that last week."

But Iris was preoccupied. She didn't even flinch when Vera's needle poked right through the fabric and into her thigh. She had an electrifying urge to try on a pair of skinny jeans. But Leah interrupted it.

"Please don't dawdle," she told them, throwing her purse over her shoulder and glancing briskly at her watch. "I'll wait for you at the café."

"What's the hurry?" Millie inquired. But Leah was already striding toward the door.

"Grump," Iris muttered loud enough for her mother to hear.

Who surprisingly did not argue, for once.

Back in the dressing room, Iris reluctantly shed her dress. Who knew self-confidence came in eggplant? And just in time for her trip to Vermont with Cooper. She couldn't wipe the smile from her face.

Outside, despite the early morning hour, the streets were already clogged with weekenders flocking into town. "Shall we hit a few shops?" Iris asked. Cooper had said they'd be leaving sometime after lunch. There was still time.

Millie raised her eyebrows. It was an invitation neither had extended to the other all summer, until now. And shopping had always been her sport, not Iris's. "Why, I'd love to!" She glanced around. "But we should probably find your sister first."

Leah was at a small outdoor table in front of Trish's café, staring glumly into a coffee cup. She made a point of looking at her watch as they approached. "Finally. Let's go home."

"But we just got here. Besides, I want to say hi to Trish."

"She's not in today."

Iris narrowed her eyes. "She's probably still recovering from last night."

"I'm going to grab a quick tea," Millie said, oblivious to the glares exchanged between her daughters. "Iris, tell her about our shopping plans. This'll be such fun!"

The second the café door shut, Iris plunked herself in the chair across from Leah. Enough was enough. "What's your problem?"

"Nothing. I just want to get back to the farm."

"For what?"

Leah drummed her fingers noisily on the café table, her nails clicking as quickly as her words. "For final head counts. And menu changes. Not that it applies to you," she added curtly. "Since you're so occupied with the barn these days."

Iris reached across the table, covering Leah's nervous fingers with her own. "Why are you so mad?"

"I'm not." Leah lifted one shoulder. "I'm just edgy."

"Is that what we're going to call last night? *Edgy?*"

"Look, I was just blowing off some steam. No big deal."

"Oh, really? Dancing with strange guys, starting drunken fights. Would Stephen call that 'no big deal'?"

Leah blanched. "Last night had nothing to do with Stephen."

"Good. Then tell me what it was about. Because I'm dying here, trying to figure all this out."

The door to the café opened, and Millie emerged with two cups of tea. "So are we ready to hit the shops?"

When neither girl answered, she set the cups down, glancing from face to face. "Did I miss something?"

"I need to get back home," Leah said, standing quickly.

"And I need to get back to the barn," Iris added. She was too annoyed to shop now.

Millie deflated like a balloon. "But I thought we were shopping."

Before Iris could think of an excuse, Leah's phone rang.

Her face fell as soon as she took the call. "Oh my God."

Millie placed a hand over her chest. "What is it, dear? Is everything okay?"

Leah shook her head gravely. "When did this happen?" she cried into her phone. "Are you sure?"

"What?" Millie pressed. "Is it Stephen?"

Leah waved her away. "I can't believe this."

Iris and Millie stood frozen. Finally Leah set down her phone, tears in her eyes. "That was Tika," she informed them gravely. "The linen rentals are all messed up. And now there's an issue with the flowers."

Millie exhaled with relief.

But Iris was not having it; she slapped a hand on the table. "Seriously? All that was just about wedding arrangements?"

Leah scowled. "*Just?* Do you realize the flower arrangements aren't confirmed? And I just found out that the silk tablecloths don't come in persimmon. Only in cranberry!" At that, she burst into tears.

Which only made Millie look like she might do the same. "Oh, honey."

Iris coughed into her hand. *Persimmon?*

But Leah was not letting up. "Everything's ruined." She was crying openly now. People at adjacent tables began to stare.

"Calm down, darling, we'll figure it out," Millie promised.

She did not object as Leah reached into her purse and produced a bottle of pills.

Here we go, Iris thought. But as Leah popped one pill, then another, and threw them back with a sip of their mother's tea, Iris realized Leah's affected response was real. Over the top, but real nonetheless.

"Look, let me help," Iris offered. "I can make those calls for you. Find pomegranate tablecloths, whatever you need."

"Persimmon," Leah corrected her.

Millie beamed. "You'd do that?"

Iris shrugged. "Why not?" How long could it take to locate a persimmon tablecloth?

By the time Millie drove them home, Leah's mood had transformed. She'd scrolled through copious wedding lists on her iPhone. Unfazed, she unloaded all of it on Iris, who'd given up, eventually handing over her own phone for Leah to sync.

"But isn't Tika taking care of these things?" Millie asked, echoing Iris's silent SOS calls from the backseat.

"Well, technically," Leah allowed. "But I'm not trusting every detail to a stranger." She said this last word as if Tika were a denizen of the streets, and not the Jimmy Choo–wearing, manicured event planner she'd negotiated around a six-month waiting list to retain.

Back at the house, Leah led Iris to her room, where she loaded her arms with folders, a few books, and several dog-eared magazines. "Is this required reading?" Iris joked.

Leah did not smile. "The linen information is in the red folder."

"You mean persimmon," Iris quipped.

Leah ignored this. "Along with the favors, which are in the green folder." She paused, thinking. "Oh, and if you could also confirm the wedding party bouquets with the florist, that'd be great." She pointed a manicured finger at a purple folder.

"Great," Iris echoed, wondering suddenly why on earth she'd offered to help.

Iris had just staggered out the door with her armload when Leah suddenly halted her. "Wait. This is your room. Why don't you leave that stuff here, and I'll move back across the hall to my old room?"

"Really?" Iris brightened. She'd been pining for her own bedroom with its view of the lake, and her childhood cabbage-rose wallpaper. Her little haven.

"Why not? Stephen's back in Seattle. Besides, it'll be just like when we were little." Leah hugged Iris hard. "I can't tell you how much this means to me. Having you here, doing all this." And there it was again: the surge of light in Leah's expression that filled the room, making Iris feel guilty for ever complaining.

◆　◆　◆

But it didn't last. By lunchtime, any trace of sisterly guilt was long eradicated. Iris lay her throbbing head on the cool marble surface of the kitchen island, surrounded by Leah's stacks of binders and hand-scrawled notes. Where was Cooper?

"Everything all right?" Millie asked. She'd been out with the dogs, whom she now closed off in the mudroom. Templeton, the only one allowed free range of the house, trotted in at her heels and made a beeline for Iris.

Iris groaned. "Did you know that Tika has already confirmed all of these appointments? The hair salon, the nail parlor, the bridesmaid breakfast? All of it has already been done. Twice!" Tika, Leah's wedding planner. The *real* wedding planner, whose flustered assistant had just called Iris to tell her with strained politeness that she was very nice to be making all of these calls. But to please *stop*.

"Well, maybe Leah just wanted to be thorough. You know how she is."

Iris eyed Millie, who bent to scratch Templeton's wiry tummy. The little dog closed his eyes in a contended stupor. "Are we talking about the same person?"

"She's nervous, Iris. It's her big day."

"Uh-huh. Well, I'm done for today. And for the record, they've already filled her linen order in persimmon. So, what was all *that* about?"

Millie shrugged. "Just an oversight, I guess."

Iris cleared her throat. "Among many. Perhaps I should check in with Her Highness, and give her the official update. Where is she, anyway?"

Millie glanced out the window. "Oh, she won't be back until later tonight."

"Where'd she go?"

Millie hesitated. "Didn't you know? She went to Vermont."

"Vermont?" A coppery taste rose up in Iris's mouth, and she swallowed hard, trying to squelch it.

"Yes. With Cooper." Millie picked up Templeton. "You remember the lumber run he had to make? Your father's out on the lake with Morris, from next door. And I couldn't very well leave the farm stand unattended. So Leah volunteered to go along with Cooper."

"Oh, she volunteered, did she?" Iris slapped the wedding binder shut.

Just then, the mudroom door flung open. Bill strolled in with a bucket of fish, which he set down abruptly upon seeing their faces.

"What's wrong?"

But Millie had her own questions. "What are you so upset about, Iris?" Her voice was high, suspicious.

"*I* was supposed to go to Vermont."

Millie studied her. "Well, I don't see what the big deal is. We can drive up there any weekend."

"No, Mom. This is about Leah."

"What about Leah? Considering all she has on her plate, it was nice of her to offer to make the lumber run."

Iris was flabbergasted. "Mom, don't you see what she's doing? She loves the dress, then she hates the dress. She sulks for Stephen, then runs off with Cooper. The scales are always tipping in the wrong direction. Leah lives life according to these crazy whims. Nothing's changed!" Iris could feel the heat in her cheeks.

"Iris, your sister is doing the best she can. Besides, you were busy."

"Busy with *her* wedding. Which she dumped on me. And besides, she doesn't even like long car rides; they make her throw up!"

Millie stood very still, listening. But Iris could see the wheels turning. "I didn't realize you felt so strongly about *Vermont*."

"What is all this about Vermont?" Bill asked.

Iris stood quickly, her chair scraping across the hardwood. "Fine, let's get this out. You and Leah don't want me to go to *Vermont*, because I should be focused on *Massachusetts*. Isn't that right?"

Millie's lips tightened.

"Are you going somewhere?" Bill interjected.

"For the record, I've given my life to Massachusetts. For sixteen years! But Massachusetts doesn't want me anymore. Which brings me here. Where everyone's so preoccupied with weeds and weddings, I don't belong here, either."

Millie flinched. She'd taken a step back against Templeton, who let out a low growl.

"I'm afraid you've lost me," Bill said. But Iris was on a roll.

"No time for a nervous breakdown; there's farmwork to be done! But as it turns out, I'm no good at that, either. Even the tomatoes aren't safe in my presence." Iris was shouting now. "And now that I've finally found something to do with myself, something I'm actually good at, you all think I'm moving to *Vermont*. Well, I'm not. *Vermont* is just a place to go. A nice place to visit. That's all!"

The kitchen fell silent. Like wayward civilians who'd innocently stumbled into a minefield, her parents remained frozen, wary of the next detonation.

Iris gathered herself. "And besides, you can all rest easy. Because I'm sure *Vermont* has no interest in me!"

Millie blinked several times.

"Who's going to Vermont?" Bill whispered.

"No one!" Iris stormed out of the kitchen. "*No one* is going to *Vermont*."

Outside, Iris raked her hands through her hair. Leah had guilted her into helping out with wedding plans that were already planned. Burying her beneath files, all so she could get Iris out of the barn and slide into the seat next to Cooper in the truck. *Iris's* seat.

And yet, as murky as Leah's motives appeared, there was a vivid truth to be extracted. The uncomfortable smile on Leah's face whenever Stephen wrapped his arm around her and talked about their future little family together. The pained expression when she watched Cooper's truck drive away that first evening when she'd found Iris working with him in the barn. The unhappiness over the bridal gown. Over Stephen's departure. And Iris's work in the barn.

Millie had blamed it all on wedding jitters and the stress of family reunions. Iris could appreciate that. After all, here she was, the estranged big sister, all grown up with a family of her own, returning home empty-handed and on the brink of divorce. What new bride would welcome that? She was like a black cat crossing the path of Leah's happily wedded future. But it was more than that.

And what of Iris, anyway? Iris felt as if she'd just found her own footing. Sure, she wasn't stupid enough to think this summer escape bore any resemblance to reality. *That* would still be waiting for her, in all its painful glory, when summer ended and she returned home. There were facts to face. The fact of Paul. And their ugly next steps. But here, if only for a moment, she'd felt the familiar flutter beneath her skin. The old Iris. She was here: in the water, balanced on a ladder in the barn, in the waking moment before sleep surrendered to the truth each morning. She was not barren of her old self as she'd feared. She was just beginning to reunite with her, like a ghost, from a much-missed past.

Sluggishly, Iris climbed the grassy hill, her cumbersome thoughts slowing her pace until she needed to sit. And so she did. Right in the middle of the hill, she sank down and allowed herself to unfold against the landscape, her head pillowed by the dense green blades around her. Iris closed her eyes. The smell of summer was strong in the sun-bleached grass. It felt good. She knew she should worry about ticks or bugs. But she didn't move. Not when the peepers began their twilight chirrup around her. Not when Millie called her name from the back door, over and over, finally giving up. Not even when dusk fell like a gauzy blanket, suffusing the sky and her worries in twinkling darkness.

◆   ◆   ◆

The next morning they were still not back. Millie watched Iris from across the kitchen as one watches a rabid animal: keeping her in her sights, but at a safe distance.

"So, no sign of Leah?" Iris slammed the sugar bowl back down on the table.

Millie paused, choosing her words carefully. As if they might be her last. "No. It seems they had to stay overnight." Then she rushed to add, "Leah said they had some kind of car trouble."

"You mean truck."

"Excuse me?"

The coffee sloshed onto the table as Iris stirred her cup roughly. "They were driving Cooper's *truck*. Not car."

Millie gripped her own mug more tightly. "Fine, then. Truck."

Iris was acutely aware of the looks her parents exchanged. She was beyond caring.

"Not to worry," Bill chimed in. "They'll be home sometime this morning."

"There, you see," Millie said brightly, as though that wrapped everything up with a neat bow.

"Perfect," Iris muttered. The coffee rose up in her throat with a new bitterness. She had to get out of there. She felt like a certain measure of power, power she'd worked so hard to gather for herself, had been taken away. But most of all it was the image of the two side by side in the cab of Cooper's truck that she couldn't shake. She'd waited up, determined to confront Leah. But when they still hadn't shown up by midnight, she'd decided to hell with both of them. Unable to sleep, she'd spent a long night flipping absently through magazines and, later, TV channels. Aside from the crow's-feet around her eyes, she might as well have been in high school again, sitting home alone on the couch with a *Seventeen* magazine while Leah was out on a date with a cute boy Iris secretly coveted.

She rose abruptly from the table.

"Now, where are you going?" Millie asked.

"To the lake."

Outside the day was bright. Her morning swim took her farther into the center of the lake than ever before, a sardonic nod to one of the few benefits of anger. Limbs limp with exhaustion, Iris pulled herself out of the water and headed back up the lawn to the house. The truck had still not returned.

She showered quickly and phoned Trish at the café. "Can I come over?"

"What's wrong?"

"Nothing," Iris lied. "I just thought we could get a head start on the cookbook."

There was a clattering of pots and pans in the background. "It's still morning rush hour here," Trish puffed.

Iris winced. She couldn't stay at the farm another moment. She certainly didn't want to be there when the truck returned. "I don't mind waiting. Consider me another customer."

Downstairs, both of her parents were still loitering in the kitchen, sentinel to the door.

"Now, where are you going?" Millie asked.

Iris ducked into the mudroom. "Into town."

She'd just slipped her feet into a pair of sandals when she heard the crunch of gravel outside. All three of them looked up at once.

"They're back!" Millie announced.

Iris froze. She did not want to be caught here, trapped in the mudroom with her still-wet hair and puffy eyes. She spun back toward the kitchen, but Millie was already blocking the doorway, coming through it herself.

"Iris, really," Millie grunted as Iris bumped against her. The two women shuffled left, then right, trying to get out of each other's way.

"Mom, can you just . . ."

But the mudroom door swung open behind them before Iris could escape. And it was not Leah who filled the doorway.

"Stephen!" Millie gasped. "What a surprise."

Iris's jaw dropped. What was he doing here?

"Come in, come in!" Millie welcomed him.

Stephen, in a linen shirt and holding a dozen yellow roses, stood in the door with a sheepish grin. The poster boy of chivalry.

"I know I'm two days early, and I apologize for not calling ahead. But I wanted to surprise Leah." His eyes twinkled in anticipation. Instantly Iris felt bad for the guy.

"Nonsense," Millie said, leading the way. "It's a wonderful idea. Bill, look who's here!"

More coffee was poured, and chairs were pulled out around the kitchen table. Mute, Iris found herself seated once again, derailed from her escape to the café.

"So," Stephen said, looking at the three faces smiling nervously back at him.

"So," Bill repeated.

In the awkward silence that followed, Iris held her breath, waiting for it.

Stephen cleared his throat and looked around. "So, where's Leah?"

♦ ♦ ♦

"What did they *say*?" Trish asked. She grabbed Iris's hand across the café booth, squeezing too hard.

"Ow!"

"Sorry. I just can't believe this. I mean, this is awful, right? For you, of course. But for Stephen, too . . . the poor schmuck."

"Yeah, well." Iris dumped the contents of her bag on the table. She was too numb to discuss it anymore. "Can we get to work now?"

Trish shook her head. "No way! Finish the story."

"There's no ending yet. Leah and Cooper are still gone."

"Did you try calling them?"

Iris held up her hands. "Not me. Though Millie just about set the phone lines on fire. The woman literally closed herself off in the pantry with the phone, pretending to hunt down some alleged baked goods, when what she was really doing was hitting redial over and over. All while Dad poured Stephen cup after cup of coffee, just a few feet away. She kept shouting, 'Still looking for those cookies. Can't imagine where I put them.' As if we couldn't see the long yellow phone cord shut in the pantry door."

Trish's head wagged back and forth. "Good lord. What was their explanation? And did he buy it?"

Iris shrugged. "They just said she'd driven to Vermont for a lumber order."

Trish's eyes widened. "No mention of Cooper? Or an overnight stay?"

"Nada."

"I'm sorry," Trish said, lowering her voice.

"For what?"

Trish appraised her old friend knowingly. "The whole thing stinks. I mean, I'm not saying anything happened between Leah and Cooper—I'm sure there really was a problem with the truck. But, I don't know . . . things just seemed to be going somewhere with you two."

Iris held up her hands. "Whoa, let's not get ahead of ourselves. There is nothing going on with Cooper and me." She opened a notebook and started flipping through it irritably. "Let's just get to work, okay?"

Trish eyed the files and notebooks strewn across the table

between them, and let out an ominous breath. "So we're really going to do this cookbook?"

"We are," Iris informed her firmly. She bit into a chocolate-dipped croissant, willing the confection to eradicate her ill will. She needed to focus on something good.

But Trish could not let it alone. "Can I ask just one more teeny question?" She had a cheeky expression on her face, one that usually got her what she wanted.

"Not getting into it," Iris warned her, tearing off another piece of croissant. "These are killer, by the way. They have to make it into the cookbook."

"Sure thing." Trish crossed her arms. "But it'll cost you."

Iris looked up, licking a stray dab of chocolate from her upper lip.

"One chocolate croissant recipe for a straight answer. Hell, I'll even throw in some cream filling."

Iris narrowed her eyes. "You wouldn't."

"Start talking."

"Trish." Iris set the last bite of croissant down on her plate. "You get three questions. That's it."

"*Three?* What are you, a genie now?"

"We've got work to do." Iris smacked the large binder of recipes on the table for emphasis.

"Party pooper. All right, then. Is Leah on the top of your hit list?"

"I am, if you really want to know. That's one."

Trish rolled her eyes. "None of this is your fault, Iris. Stop being such a masochist. So, what are you going to say to Leah when she gets back?"

Iris clucked her tongue. "Tsk, tsk, tsk. They have to be yes-or-no questions. You know the rules!"

"No fair. If it's just three questions, then I need more elaborate answers."

"Uh-uh. Make it work."

"Question two: Are you going to confront her?"

"I don't know."

"What do you mean, you don't know? Surely you've got something to say?"

Iris popped the last bite of croissant determinedly into her mouth. "That's three."

"Strike that one," Trish decided. "Last question. Forget about Leah. What about Cooper?"

"What about him?"

"We both know you have feelings for him."

"Are you asking me or telling me?"

Trish narrowed her eyes. "Tell you what, you don't even have to answer that last one. I already know."

Iris ignored her friend's smug grin and slid the notebook roughly across the table. "Good for you. Moving on. Here are some notes I worked on last night. I think we should start with a table of contents, you know, to give ourselves some sort of outline for recipes."

Trish flipped open the notebook, but her detectivelike gaze remained locked on Iris. It was going to be a long morning.

An hour later the lunch-shift kids arrived, bleary-eyed and in matching pink flip-flops. "Rise and shine!" Trish greeted them loudly, with a boisterous clap of her hands. "Shoot an espresso, ladies. Lunch starts in five."

Iris watched as the college-aged girls shuffled past, frowning. "Looks like someone had a good Saturday night last night."

"Every night's a good night when you're twenty-one," Trish muttered. "Want another coffee?"

"No, thanks. I'll let you get back to work. I've got plenty here to get started on."

"When do you want to meet again?" Trish asked. "I'm free tonight, after the boys' swim practice."

Iris winced, thinking of Sadie and Lily, at their own practices miles away. "Maybe we can get together Friday?"

"Friday, it is."

"Oh, wait." Iris slapped her forehead. "Tell you what. Come

by for dinner Friday night, and we can go over recipes afterward."

Trish eyed her suspiciously. "What's going on Friday?"

Iris lifted one shoulder, trying to look casual. She needed Trish to agree to this. "It's just a little gathering. With Stephen's family."

"*This* is the weekend they're flying in to meet your family?"

Iris didn't answer, but instead feigned focus on the notebooks she was stuffing into her bag.

"Oh no. Don't get me wrong, I love to hear about the family drama. But I'm not sure I need to witness it."

"Come on," Iris pleaded. "It's just one little dinner. And I really need someone in my corner. We can sit at the end of the table, away from the crazies."

Trish shook her head.

"Near the bar!" Iris added, slipping toward the door. "It'll be like front-row seats."

And with an audible sigh, Trish caved. "Oh, all right. But you owe me more information!"

"It's a running tab," Iris shouted, hurrying out the door.

Sixteen

The farmhouse was quiet when she got home, the driveway by the barns empty. Iris strode through the kitchen, relieved. She grabbed a peach from the bowl on the kitchen table and headed upstairs to hole up in her room. She would not try to guess where Leah was right now. Or Cooper. She would not care.

Trish's notes were fanned out around her: fish-and-avocado tacos, cucumber chicken wraps, soba noodles. A culinary circling of the wagons, with Iris protected in its calorie-rich core. Relaxing into a rhythm, Iris began to put together a theme for different sections of the book, starting with a chapter of grab-and-go family dinners. But first, she'd need a name. "Busy Moms On the Go"? Too dull. "Moms on Wheels"? Sounded more like a Dr. Seuss book. Besides, wasn't this for fathers, too? Let the damn men fret over what to make and how to get the kids to practice, for a change. She had finally decided on "Carpool Creations" when she heard the screen door slap shut below.

Gathering her knees to her chest, Iris listened. There were no voices. But a moment later, footsteps sounded on the stairs. Iris held her breath. There was a knock on her door.

"Can I come in?"

Without waiting for an answer, Leah pushed the door ajar. She blushed. "Hi there."

Iris opened her mouth, then shut it. She had no idea where to begin.

"I'm back." Then, when Iris didn't answer, "I guess you heard what happened."

Iris looked away. She would not look at Leah's innocent smile. Or her dangly turquoise earrings that swayed girlishly as she cocked her head and waited for Iris's reply. Briefly Iris wondered if she'd worn those purposely, knowing how green they made her eyes look. Or if she'd selected that particular pair of denim shorts to wear on the ride to Vermont, seated beside Cooper in the cab, her brown limbs stretched up on the dashboard. She'd gone too far this time. "Frankly, Leah, I don't want to talk about it."

"Can you believe we were stranded overnight?"

Iris held up a hand. "Or hear about it. About you or Stephen or whatever happened in Vermont." For the first time Iris looked her directly in the eye. "But don't worry, your wedding bookings are perfect. Just as they were *to begin with*."

Leah blinked. "Thanks. I guess I overreacted . . ."

Iris cleared her throat loudly, turning back to her notes on the bed. "Is there anything else? Because I'm sort of busy here."

Leah turned to go. "It wasn't anyone's fault, you know."

So that was it: no apology; no honest explanation. Typical Leah. It was all Iris needed to let the floodgates open. "Really? Aren't you the one who dumped all her wedding crap on me? Who took my spot to Vermont? Who disappeared overnight, without even a phone call? And what about your poor fiancé, who showed up in the doorway with roses, and couldn't understand why none of us knew where the hell you were?" Iris realized her hands were shaking now.

"Why are you so upset?"

"I'm upset because you never take responsibility for anything. Somehow it never occurs to you that maybe you've made a mistake. Or that maybe you've hurt someone's feelings, or taken something away from them."

Leah scoffed. "What did I ever take from you?"

Furious, Iris began shoving her notes into her bag, a list of ready-to-air grievances flashing through her head. Childhood Barbies, favorite jeans, boyfriends. "I've got work to do. I'm not playing this game with you anymore."

Iris pushed past her in the doorway and stormed down the hall. She needed air.

"Iris, wait, I just want to explain something . . ."

Iris held up her hand. "Save it."

But Leah was not giving up. She shouted down to Iris from the top of the stairs. "Is this about Cooper? Because *nothing* happened."

Iris froze on the last step. "Who said anything about Cooper?"

"Oh, come on. Since when are you interested in construction, Iris? It's pretty transparent what's been going on." She paused, backpedaling. "Look, I didn't mean it like that."

But it was too late. Iris turned to look back at her. "No, of course you didn't. Just like you don't mean to drink too much, or drop out of college, or wander off to Europe for a few years."

"What has any of that got to do with you?"

"Everything! I'm the one who cleans up your messes, Leah. I drive you home when you're too tanked. I make calls to get you jobs that you quit without a second thought. I'm the one who remembers Dad's birthday every year. And yet you just keep taking!"

Leah stuck her chin out, indignant. "Name one thing I've taken from you."

Iris's eyes flashed. It was all flooding back. "Jake Tanner. The *day* before senior prom!"

"The kid from the fro-yo shop? That was high school, Iris. Grow up!"

"Exactly! So why are you still pulling this crap now? You didn't want Jake Tanner back then. I don't think you want Cooper now. But you have to remind the rest of us that you can have them. You're worse than Templeton, pissing on everything like a dog just to mark your territory!"

Leah coughed back a laugh. "That's pathetic."

"You want to know what's pathetic? You're about to marry this great guy, and you're going to blow it. You're going to lose *everything*."

Leah raced down the steps toward Iris, her cheeks burning. "Me, lose everything? What about you? Remember Paul? Besides, it's not like Cooper would . . ." She stopped and put a hand to her mouth.

Iris sucked in her breath. "Go on. I dare you to say it."

Leah shook her head.

But Iris was not letting this one go. "Let me guess. It's not like Cooper would be interested in someone like me?"

"That's not what I said!"

Iris leaned in, her voice low and trembling. "But it's what you meant, isn't it?" She spun away from Leah.

"Iris, please . . ."

Iris waved her away, a sob catching in her throat. At the patio doors, she fumbled with the handle, jiggling it once, then twice, but the door wouldn't budge.

Leah trailed close behind. "Let me help."

"Leave me alone!" Iris roared. She popped the lock on the patio doors and threw them open. The doors flung back on their hinges as she burst through, gulping at the humid air. She collapsed onto a lounge chair.

For an hour she sat, the sun on her face drying her tears into salty trails. But Iris did not wipe them. Her thoughts were fixed on the lake, the birds, the sun's heat on her raw cheeks. Surrounded by them, she willed the numbness to dissipate. Just feel, she told herself. Just feel, and hear, and breathe.

◆ ◆ ◆

She must have fallen asleep, because the ringtone on her phone startled her. Iris opened her eyes to see the sun lower on the horizon, and the shade shifted over the patio. She scanned her phone's screen. *Home.* Relief flooded her. She needed to hear the kids' voices.

"Sadie? Is that you, honey?"

"It's me," Paul said.

Immediately Iris stood up. Paul hadn't called once since she'd arrived, and her stomach flip-flopped. "Are the kids okay?"

"The kids are fine," he said. "They're outside playing."

Relieved, Iris glanced back at the house, which remained dark and quiet. "That's good." She hesitated, waiting for Paul to continue.

"So, how are things up there?"

The question irritated her. Paul didn't care one iota how things were up there. There was something else. "Fine. What's going on, Paul?"

He hesitated. "Listen, I need to tell you something."

"What?"

"I'm sending some papers up for you to review. I wanted to let you know in advance."

Iris stiffened. "What kind of papers?"

"Just some papers from the office. We need to start thinking about things."

"Your law office?" Iris moved off the patio and onto the grass. She strode across the lawn, the phone crackling in her ear.

"You still there?" Paul asked, his voice fading.

"What are you talking about, Paul? Tell me what you're sending."

Paul paused.

Across the lake the jagged shore rose up and away from the water, a jumble of craggy rock and wild spruce. Sunlight slipped in and out among the trees, and Iris longed to duck among the cover.

"Paul, are you asking for a divorce?" The words were acrid in her mouth.

"Iris. Please. Just read through them, and call me later."

"Jesus Christ. You are."

"Iris, you had to see this coming."

"Who is she?" Iris screamed into the phone.

Paul did not answer right away. Then, "Does it really matter who she was?"

The ground seemed to rise up beneath her feet, and Iris kneeled to meet it. He had cheated. Even before the separation she'd tried to shake the sinking feeling that he might have. She'd wondered, asked questions, even resorted to snooping, which in the end had only served to make *her* feel guilty. Through all of it Paul had denied it, his denials so firm they'd left Iris wondering if she was crazy, if perhaps she really was making all of it up in her head. And in the end she'd ignored her gut.

"Iris?" She could hear Paul's voice on the phone, which had dropped somewhere nearby, but she did not retrieve it. The lawn began to spin.

And then there was the vibrating rush of footsteps.

"I'm here." It was Leah. She pulled Iris's hair away from her face as she heaved twice, and then vomited in the grass.

Between them, Paul's voice rose from the ground. "Hello? Are you there?"

Leah kicked the phone aside with her bare foot, and Iris watched from the corner of her eye as it tumbled away from her. She pressed her face into the grass, willing herself to feel the dampness. The prickly blades. Anything but the desolate pressure rising in her chest.

Leah's hands moved gently around her middle.

"Please. Don't." But the sobs rose up in her throat anyway.

"I've got you," Leah whispered.

Paul was divorcing her. He'd lied to her. It was really happening, and there was nothing Iris could do to stop it. No time to examine the cracks or mend the fissures.

"Paul told me . . ." Iris sobbed.

"It's okay. I've got you."

Like a small child, Iris went limp.

In the middle of the sprawling lawn they rocked. Leah did not let go. Back and forth, back and forth, until no tears remained, and the lake and the sky stopped spiraling inside Iris's head.

◆ ◆ ◆

On Monday, Iris stayed in bed. She did not know what excuses her sister made, or what words she'd chosen to explain Iris's sudden retreat to the cushioned depths her mattress allowed. Only that Millie knocked lightly on her door midmorning to let her know she'd be at the farm, in case Iris needed her. And that, sometime later, someone left a tray with toast and tea beside her bed. After that, there was silence and darkness. And Iris slept.

When she awoke much later the sky was dark, and she struggled to read the hands of the clock on the bedside table. Ten thirty-five. She reached for the small lamp beside the bed. The tray of toast had been taken away, and in its place was a bowl of fresh fruit, more tea, and a sandwich. Iris drained the teacup, which had gone cold. But the sudden sweetness on her dry tongue surprised her, and without warning she began to sob uncontrollably into her pillow. When she'd cried herself out once more, she took a bite of melon, which also made her cry. The fruit caught in her throat as she struggled to swallow, but the deep pitted nausea in her stomach subsided, and she forced herself to eat some more. She tried a bite of the sandwich, then lay back down and fell into a deep and uninterrupted sleep. The next time she awoke it was Tuesday.

"Iris?" Leah lingered in the doorway. "Are you up?"

Iris rolled onto her back, staring at the white ceiling. The wrenching colorlessness of it echoed her sadness, and she squeezed her eyes shut.

"You need to get up and eat something," Leah said, lowering herself gently onto the bed. She settled a plate onto the nightstand, and the smell of fresh eggs caused Iris's stomach to turn. She shook her head.

"Really," Leah said, placing a hand on her wrist. "You'll feel better."

Iris pulled herself up on her elbows and surveyed the room. The brightness of the scrambled eggs was too much, Leah's touch too strong. She protested as her sister moved to the window and parted the curtains.

"I'm sorry, but this is for your own good," Leah insisted.

Sunlight flooded the room, and Iris imagined her corneas bursting into flames. After twenty-four hours of uninterrupted tears and darkness, her eyes felt papery, her lids swollen shut. She did not care that she couldn't see. It was better that way.

Leah pressed her cool palm to Iris's forehead. "Mom is starting to worry," she said.

Iris's voice was rough and unused in her throat. She swallowed. "What did you tell her?"

"Just that Paul had called." Leah looked at her gently. "They know."

"He cheated."

Leah pressed her cool palm to Iris's cheek. "I'm sorry. He never deserved you."

Iris turned away, pulling the sheet tight under her chin. All summer she'd focused on surviving the separation. But that was nothing compared to the wrenching finality she was feeling now. Separation was a mere shove; divorce, a caving blow.

"How can I help?" Leah asked. "Do you want me to run the shower?"

Iris shook her head, tears springing to her eyes once more. The salt stung her swollen lids. "I want my kids," she cried, covering her face with her hands.

"They'll be here soon. But I think it's better you have this time to yourself, don't you?" When Iris didn't answer, Leah reached over and began to rub her back in slow circles, the way Iris had with each of her babies.

Iris heaved against it. The images washed through her like a poisonous wave: Paul's mouse-brown hair, going a handsome gray just above his ears. The small cleft in his chin that disappeared when he smiled. How long had it been since she'd witnessed that? The particular way he folded his newspaper each morning, at the kitchen counter, the ends tucked neatly behind the headlines of the article he was reading. Oh, if only she could tuck this suffering away like that. When Iris's cries finally softened and her breathing returned to its normal cadence, Leah rolled the blankets back.

"Come," she said gently.

Iris did not resist as Leah pulled her wrist, lightly at first, then more firmly. She allowed her sister to lead her away from the bed. Silently, she followed her into the bathroom, where Leah rolled up her sleeves and leaned into the shower to turn on the faucet. When Leah tugged Iris's wrinkled nightgown over her head, Iris did not protest. Instead she stood, naked and obedient, under the steady stream of hot water, and allowed herself to be soaped. As Leah massaged her scalp with shampoo Iris opened her eyes. Outside the bathroom window, the tree leaves stirred. A bird took flight from a branch.

Seventeen

For the next few days, Iris escaped to the Hampstead library, where she secured a quiet table in a dark corner, a cave of sorts, where she could lick her wounds. The library was a historic brick building that had been added onto over the years, and she relished its dark, air-conditioned recesses. Coming out of her bedroom was just a first step, she knew. Though she had purged some of the initial grief, the gut-wrenching shock of it all remained stubbornly, like a dull ache in her head. And there were moments she welled up, unexpectedly. Picturing Lily's pink room at home: Would she keep the house? Or Jack's patient expression: How would they ever deliver the news to the kids? She could not imagine she had the capacity for the grief that would follow. She'd wake up at night, remembering the cardboard boxes of baby clothes she'd carefully tucked into the attic, wondering who would get them. As if the divorce was finally forcing her to riffle through all their shared past, both the sentiments and the belongings. But one question haunted her most. Who owned the memories—that sacred ground of a shared past? If the family split, how would she uphold them for the kids at holidays, at weddings, at the births of their own children, without the bleak surge of guilt corrupting them?

To block it out, Iris tried to focus on the next moment, the next hour, the next meal. It was inevitable now, this course she could not alter. And finally, one that she found she did not entirely care to.

On Tuesday, a carrier had delivered a flat manila package to the farm, addressed to Iris. She'd left it unopened on the kitchen table. Her family observed the offering of her once-secret wound in quiet reverence. It remained there until breakfast the next morning, when Bill stood suddenly from his chair and removed it to his office. "When you're ready," he told Iris, returning to the table. And gratefully, she had nodded.

Trish had checked in several times since Iris told her the news over the phone. She'd been furious and worried and pressed Iris to come by. But Iris wasn't ready to see anyone. Finally Trish had relented, as long as Iris answered her hourly texts, which Iris found both madly irritating and deeply comforting.

Millie was the one who kept a grave distance, instead watching Iris with worried eyes, placing small offerings in front of her: a cup of coffee, a warm muffin, a worn scrapbook of old family photos. All tidings of comfort, yet tendered at arm's length, as if she might break apart, or say something regrettable, should she make actual contact. It did not surprise Iris; she was used to such restrained demonstrations. But she was thankful that her mother had not yet intruded with her own concerns and advice, which she knew would come later. Probably regarding the kids. Or counseling. Millie was not a religious person, but vows were vows. And family—well, it was everything.

Iris had allowed herself one brief call to Paul since that afternoon. He hadn't answered, for which she was relieved. There was just one thing she had to say. She waited, heart in her throat, as his voice mail picked up. "Paul," she said, straining to keep her voice even. "Whatever you do, don't you dare tell the kids. One word to them before I get home, and I'll tear you to shreds. I swear to God I will." That was one matter she would not surrender; she would make him break the news, but she would control the way it was broken. And she would be there, to pick up the pieces.

By four o'clock on Friday, Iris was slumped over the library desk. She'd long ago finished the chapter on "Carpool Creations" and was now almost done with a section on family breakfasts, which quite frankly made her sick.

She checked her watch. Surely Stephen's parents had landed and would have driven in from the airport by now? Their anticipated arrival was something that had occupied the family since Paul's phone call, a nerve-racking if not welcome distraction for all, allowing Iris to disappear with her cookbook pages, and propelling Millie and Leah from one room of the house to the next, as they fussed over the welcome dinner and readied the guest room. Stephen and Bill made regular escapes to the golf course, when allowed, but more often were dispatched on errands or to the farm stand, to fill in, while the women contended with menus and table charts. The Willetses' arrival was a sort of mini-wedding in itself, bringing together the two families for the first time, and it left the Standishes fluttering about their own farm like nervous fowl.

Iris collected her things and hurried down the library steps toward her car. Though she still had strong doubts about Leah's impending wedding, there was a dinner tonight to worry about. Millie would be wondering where she was. Iris dreaded the evening ahead. At least she'd had the sense to invite Trish along.

Back at home Iris showered quickly and changed into a pale pink blouse and creamy linen pants. Shaking her head as she strapped on the black sandals that Leah had "borrowed," she tried to smooth the scuffs from the heels. Below, the gentle vibrations of music were making their way up from the patio. Peering outside, she caught a glimpse of Leah in a smart little black A-line. Stephen stood beside her, pressed and fresh as always, his hand resting protectively on her lower back. Iris had been so caught up in her own sufferings, she hadn't given any real thought to his surprise arrival days earlier. But somehow, as usual, Leah had seemingly wiggled her way out of the Vermont debacle. Honestly, Iris couldn't imagine what on earth Leah had told Stephen, but apparently no ill will had been suffered. It figured.

Downstairs, Millie had outdone herself, and as she walked through the house Iris felt a momentary pang of guilt for not having stayed home that afternoon to help her mother. Everything was understated yet elegant, just the way Millie Standish liked things. Huge bouquets of lilies and hydrangea adorned the antique tables in the living room in stately silver pitchers. Simple white platters lined the kitchen island, taped with Post-it notes that assigned each to a menu of her summer favorites: lavender chicken fillets, roasted garden vegetables, and colorful mesclun salads. For the first time in days, Iris's mouth watered.

She was about to head outside when she heard the clink of glassware in the butler's pantry. Leah was bent over the bar counter. Iris watched as she poured herself a shot of amber liquid—their father's whiskey?—and threw back a shot. Unaware that Iris was there, Leah pressed a wadded tissue to her eyes.

"Are you crying?" Iris asked.

Leah spun and forced a smile. "Oh, you made it down. Are you sure you're up for this tonight?"

"I'm fine," Iris said hesitantly. "Are you?"

"Yes, of course. Just a little tired."

"Listen, I wanted to thank you for the last few days. You were really there for me."

Before she could go on, Leah pulled her into a quick hug. "Oh, stop, you're going to make us both cry. Of course I was there for you."

"About that," Iris began. She pulled away and looked at Leah sincerely. "I just want you to know that I want to be there for you, too."

Leah cocked her head. "Meaning?"

"Meaning that sometimes you seem a bit overwhelmed."

Leah's expression shifted uncomfortably.

But Iris was determined to get it out. "When Paul said he wanted a divorce I thought it would undo me. But it won't. I have you and Mom and Dad. And the kids. I don't need to rely on Paul. Or any other man."

"That's good, Iris. I'm glad to hear you say that." She glanced over her shoulder at the guests outside the French doors.

"And you don't need to rely on anyone else either."

Leah blinked. "What are you saying?"

Iris indicated the twinkling lights outside, the guests, the flowers. "All of this. It's great. Stephen's great. And I'm happy for you. But . . . I'm not convinced you are."

"I'm *very* happy, Iris."

"Okay, maybe you are happy. But it doesn't mean you need to jump into this marriage and walk away from everything here that you've worked so hard for. I know that's not what you want. I can see you struggling with that."

Leah shook her head. "Are you kidding? Are you really saying this to me now?"

"Look, I know the timing sucks, but just hear me out. Rushing into this marriage doesn't have to be the answer. I've got your back, whatever you decide."

"Decide? What are you talking about, Iris? How dare you say these things to me, tonight of all nights."

Iris reached for her hand. "Leah, these past few weeks I've been watching you. The pill popping, the mood swings. I know what I'm seeing."

Leah yanked her hand away. "You don't know anything." And with that she tugged open the patio doors, leaving Iris alone in the living room.

"There you are!" Behind her, Millie's voice was high and practiced, and Iris recognized it instantly as her formal-company tone. "Come out with me to the patio, dear. Everyone's here!"

Indeed they were. No sooner had Iris stepped warily outside than Bill handed her a gin and tonic. "Take a long, hard sip. I'm about to toast," he warned her with a wink. A handful of close friends had joined the two families for the evening. The patio was resplendent in bridal tones. Pink and white hydrangea arched gracefully from glass urns down the center of the table, which was dressed in creamy linens, allowing the greenery to pop. Tiny votive candles were interspersed among fluted glasses, and the whole picture conjured the gauzy romance of something right out of *A Midsummer Night's Dream* set.

"Iris, I'd like to introduce you to my family." Stephen came forward, his arm looped boyishly through his mother's. "This is my mother, Adele. And my father, Lance."

Stephen's mother had the same impossibly white smile as her son. "We've heard so much about all of you and this wonderful farm," she said. Iris smiled, sneaking a glance at Leah, who stood waifishly to the side, avoiding eye contact.

"Is this your first time to the farm?" Iris asked politely.

"Yes. And our first time meeting your family," Adele added pointedly. "We were beginning to wonder." Everyone laughed uncomfortably.

Iris took a deep swig of her gin. No posturing here, she thought. Despite her tiny frame, Adele Willets emanated strength.

"Last month we were finally able to lure these two lovebirds west to our little cottage on the peninsula. At least it gave us the chance to get to know Leah a little better."

Iris wondered just how "little" their cottage on Grose Point was, knowing full well from Leah's descriptions of their Washington peninsula that it was an exclusive spot, dotted by sprawling estates.

"We're so excited to have your sister join our family," Lance said. "We have big plans for adding her charisma to our foundation."

"Unless, of course, a grandbaby arrives sooner than we expected." Adele tittered coyly.

Leah smiled back at her future in-laws, but it was the tight, false smile Iris knew too well.

"Speaking of that," Leah began, her voice wobbling a little. "I was hoping to talk to you a little more about some ideas I had for the foundation. Since I've been back home, I've been thinking about how I might combine my expertise on the farm with the educational work you do." She looked at them hopefully.

Adele cocked her head. "I'm not sure I follow you, dear."

But Lance was nodding. "Let's hear her out."

Leah took a deep breath. "My mother and I have been toying with the idea of turning our farm into a CSA. You know, a community supported agriculture venture?" She paused. "There are plenty of CSAs outside of the Seattle area. It's a great opportunity to get some of the kids from your foundation some hands-on experience in the community. I was thinking we could look into a work-study program on a farm out there?"

The two exchanged a glance. "But our foundation is the Special Olympics."

Iris knew what Leah was getting at. Despite their confrontation, she silently cheered her sister on.

"I understand. But given my own area of expertise, I was thinking we could start a program for some of the special needs kids. That involves educating them about the local food business, and fosters life skills. Something that goes beyond just the sports aspect of it."

"Interesting," Adele allowed, looking quizzically at her husband.

"I like that you're thinking outside the box," Lance added.

"Though, right now our focus is on fund-raising," Adele said. "As we've already discussed, fund-raising is critical to the programs we offer. And it'd be a good way to get your feet wet."

Stephen, who'd been listening thoughtfully to both sides,

finally weighed in. "Leah has many talents as well as some fresh ideas that I think would really benefit the foundation." He smiled at her reassuringly. "Let's pick a better time to sit down and discuss them."

But Leah wasn't quite through. "I'm in awe of the work you do," she told Stephen's parents. "And I'm honored to be included in it. But I'm more of a people person than an office person."

Lance shook his empty drink glass gently. Iris could sense any interest they may have had in her sister's ideas melting along with the ice in his glass.

"Have you had a chance to tour the farm yet?" Iris interjected, in an attempt to lend a little support. "It's hard to believe that Leah and my mother launched the business just two years ago."

"Huh." Adele, seeming not to have heard, reached past her and touched Leah's hair. "Darling, are you sure you want to wear this flower? It's looking a little wilted around the edges."

Leah put a shaky hand to the lily.

"She looks *beautiful*, Mom," Stephen interjected, stepping forward and drawing Leah's hand away from the lily in question. Iris loved the man for it.

Adele shrugged. "Well, of course she looks beautiful, darling. She's always beautiful. I was just saying . . ."

Just in time there was the gentle chiming of a dinner knife against glassware. Bill Standish had positioned himself formally at the head of the table. "If I may," he began, clearing his throat. "I would like to thank all of you for coming this evening to celebrate Leah and Stephen's union and the joining of our families, most especially. We welcome Stephen, Adele, and Lance wholeheartedly into our home. And into our lives." There was a murmur of approval. "Tonight, my lovely wife has created a feast for us to savor, and I invite everyone to join us. Let it be the first of many family dinners together." Always the gentleman, Bill came forward to kiss Adele and shake hands with Lance.

"And another toast, if I may." Lance lifted his glass heartily. "We are grateful to be merging with the Standish family, a fine New England clan, if I do say." There was a pause as guests chuckled and murmured their approval. "And we have an announcement of our own to make. As many of you know, our family runs the Willets Foundation for Special Olympics. We are thrilled to invite Leah, a promising young woman who we think has a promising future, to join our foundation as head of national fund-raising."

Iris's heart pounded in her chest, drowned only by the eruption of clapping. Across the way, Bill and Millie were poised on the patio's edge, their expressions hovering somewhere between uncertainty and false cheer. Stephen was grinning, looking at Leah expectantly. But Leah's paper smile was answer enough.

Iris waited until Leah was able to break free from the congratulations and well wishes around her. She caught her at the bar.

"How're you doing?" Iris glanced around and lowered her voice. "That was a lot for the Willets to unload on you tonight in front of everyone."

Leah took a glass of champagne and tossed it back. "It's an opportunity," she said flatly.

"You're kidding, right? They basically arm wrestled you into a job in front of your whole family."

Leah set the champagne down on the tray, smiled sweetly at the bartender, and took another.

"Iris, you have to stop."

Iris was genuinely confused. "But I just heard you tell them that you had some farming ideas you wanted to propose, and they didn't even listen. Instead they made you fund-raising chair."

Leah shook her head. "They didn't make me anything. Stephen's family is different than ours, Iris. There are some sacrifices that you have to make when you join a family like that."

Iris stepped back. "I'm sorry. So you're telling me that you really want that job?"

Leah met her gaze. "I'm telling you to butt out." And with that she brushed past Iris.

"Iris!" Trish appeared suddenly at Iris's elbow.

"Thank God you're here. I don't think I'm going to survive this dinner."

"Sure you will." Trish did a quick spin. "Now tell me, how do I look?" Her apricot dress was stunning against her dark curls and tanned skin. "It's new. I figured if we're going to strike it rich with this cookbook, I could splurge on a little treat for the ol' girl." She looked down at her highlighted cleavage. "And these girls, too!"

Iris smiled. "You're stunning." At least some measure of rescue was here. They found their seats at the table, which to her dismay were directly across from Millie, who looked less than celebratory as she flopped down in her seat and glared at the empty plates in front of them.

"Where is the food?" she hissed across the table at Iris.

Iris looked around, flummoxed. "Isn't the kitchen staff on it?"

But the look on Millie's face warned her not to argue. "Come with me. Now."

Once in the kitchen her mother dropped her calm demeanor like a hot plate and began simultaneously directing the staff and interrogating Iris.

"Did you know anything about this fund-raising job? I had no idea your sister was joining the Willetses' foundation."

"No, Mom. I swear. Leah doesn't exactly tell me everything."

"What about her work on the farm?" Millie pulled a pair of mitts right off the server's hands and tugged the oven door open to inspect the chicken herself. "I wish you'd talked her out of it, Iris."

"How could I? She never told me!" But the words were lost on her mother, who was distracted by the food.

"Iris, get the chicken to the table, quick, before it's cold." She draped a towel on Iris's arm and shoved a platter into her hands.

Warily, Iris maneuvered toward the door, holding the juicy platters away from her silk shirt. As soon as this godforsaken dinner was over, she was going back up to her room with a bottle of wine.

"Don't spill!" Millie called behind her.

"I've got it, Mom," Iris snapped, then instantly regretted it as she realized too late that the patio door was latched, and she hadn't a free hand to open it.

"Um, Mom . . ."

There was a clatter of pans behind her. "Oh, for Pete's sake," her mother cried. "The basil biscuits!" A large cloud of smoke filled the kitchen.

Desperate, Iris glanced at the chef, who'd conveniently ducked into the pantry. "Um, can somebody help . . ."

"Let me."

Iris turned and found herself staring up at Cooper Woods. His hair was still damp and he smelled like soap. The platter tipped in her hands. "What are you doing here?"

"Is that how you greet all your guests?" He grinned, then reached quickly to right the platter. "Your father asked me. I hope that's all right."

This was not how Iris had pictured facing Cooper. Not after last weekend's Vermont debacle and her subsequent week in hiding. Certainly not coming to her rescue with a plate of chicken. She'd been so engrossed in just trying to get out of bed each day, and in distracting herself with the cookbook, that she'd pushed Cooper Woods out of her mind.

Or so she thought.

"Iris, get the salads!" Millie shrieked.

Cooper raised his eyebrows playfully. "Go on, Iris. Get the salads."

Reluctantly she surrendered the chicken, and even more reluctantly followed him outside with her mother's salads. Luckily, the guests appeared unaware of the kitchen chaos on the other side of the wall. Iris snuck a glance at Cooper as he settled the chicken platter before her father, greeting him with a clap on the back. She tried not to watch as he returned to her end of the table, taking his seat on the other side of Trish.

"Sorry I'm late," he said, greeting everyone.

Leah's eyes rested on Cooper a moment too long.

"So, Cooper, I didn't realize I'd have the pleasure of seeing you tonight," Trish said, nudging Iris.

Iris nudged back.

"Pleasure's all mine," he said, looking directly at Iris. He lowered his voice. "I missed you in the barn this week. Things okay?"

"I-I wasn't feeling well," she stammered, glancing away. Iris tried to focus on the gorgeous dishes being passed around the table, instead of the swirl of unsettling emotions around her.

Adding to them, Millie set a platter down in front of Iris and leaned in, her voice a sharp whisper. "What is Cooper Woods doing here?"

Leah was watching, her eyebrows also raised in question.

"Dad invited him," Iris whispered back defensively. But even as she said it, Iris realized she was relieved that her father had invited Cooper. Thrilled, in fact.

Millie leaned in again, too close. "I know you've had a rough week, dear, but this isn't the evening to be inviting just anyone."

Iris had had it. It had been all she could do to pull herself together for this dinner. Now, here she was, polished and grinning for the guests like one of those wind-up monkeys with cymbals. While her own marriage was in the toilet. And then Cooper appears, charming and handsome and the rescuer of dinner plates. And finally, Leah, who has an amazing man on her arm, and a rock on her finger, but for whom it still doesn't seem to be enough. And Millie, her own mother, who can't get past her plates of food and heirloom linen to notice the crises rising like a wave around her. Yet, despite it all, Iris had swiped on lipstick and showed up at the table. If it were up to her, she thought, she deserved a fucking Oscar.

Iris bit her lip, trying to temper the fury she felt at all of them in that moment just as Millie reached over and deposited a large spoonful of curried couscous on her plate.

"Mom, no thanks."

"But why not? It's a beautiful dish. I made it myself," she said, a little loudly.

"It is beautiful," Iris said, lowering her voice. "But you know I don't like curry."

Millie scowled. "Oh, just have a few bites, Iris. You'll love it. It's Leah's favorite."

And just like that, Iris lost it. "Fabulous. Then Leah can have mine!" Abruptly, Iris reached across the table through the oversized floral centerpiece and snatched her sister's plate. With one audible scrape she dumped the offending mound of salad onto it and slammed it back on the table before Leah, who jumped in her seat.

The conversations halted. At the head of the table, her father cocked his head tentatively. "Iris?"

"What?" Iris barked. "It's Leah's *favorite!*"

◆   ◆   ◆

In the safety of the bathroom, she turned the faucet on and let it run, bracing the pedestal sink with both hands. There was a gentle rap on the door.

Iris groaned.

Trish poked her head in. "Boy, you weren't kidding," she joked, closing the door behind them. "Dinner at the Standish table hasn't changed a bit."

"You're not helping." Iris patted her cheeks with cold water.

Trish smiled sympathetically as she turned to go. "You'd better get out there. Plus, I think Cooper's wondering where you went."

Cooper. Iris wondered how much he'd seen. And what he could possibly be thinking.

A moment later, there was another knock at the door.

"I'm coming," Iris groaned, pulling the door open.

Millie's face was pinched. "Are you sulking? Because you're missing Leah's special night."

"Mom. I need a minute."

"You've taken plenty already. And for the record, I did not appreciate that scene." Millie spun on her heel.

Iris stared after her mother's departing figure. She closed the door again and pressed her forehead against the mirror. Then banged it.

She realized someone was hovering outside the door again. This time she threw it open.

"Mom, I'm not in the mood . . ."

Cooper Woods leaned against the door frame, hands stuffed in his pockets. "Well, remind me not to make you couscous," he said, breaking into a slow smile.

Iris winced, flushing. "Sorry. My family is driving me crazy."

"Isn't that what family's for?" Before she could answer, he reached around with one hand and gently tucked a stray piece of hair behind Iris's ear. His fingers lingered a moment, touching her cheek.

Iris blushed. "Um, did you need to use the bathroom?"

"No."

Suddenly Iris couldn't avoid it any longer. She'd never been good at playing games, and here was Cooper Woods, touching her hair, in her mother's bathroom no less. "Listen, about Vermont . . ." she began.

"What happened? I thought you'd said you were coming with me."

Iris frowned. "I was. I mean, I wanted to, but then you took Leah."

Cooper's brow wrinkled. "Only because she came up to the barn and said you couldn't make it."

"What? You didn't invite her?"

"No. I figured you'd changed your mind. Leah insisted on coming along instead."

Iris shook her head. It was suddenly too warm in the doorway. And Cooper Woods was standing so close.

"Are you okay?" Cooper asked. He leaned in, searching her expression.

"I just . . ." Her voice trailed off as their eyes met.

"You just what . . . ?"

"I just need . . ."

"This?"

Cooper leaned forward and pressed his lips against hers gently. His mouth was flushed and sweet, like a summer peach. Exactly what she'd imagined. It was the whole summer, coming to a breathless, heady halt between them.

But they were interrupted. "Iris, where are you? Dessert's ready." Leah rounded the corner of the butler's pantry, a stack of delicate ironware dishes in her hands, the ones their mother reserved for special occasions. She halted, and the dishes rattled precariously. "Oh," she said, her eyes moving from Iris to Cooper as they stepped apart.

Iris spoke first. "Let me help with those." She reached for the plates, which Leah surrendered without question. Her gaze had fallen hard on Cooper, who jammed his hands in his pockets and cleared his throat.

"I was just washing up," Iris explained, drawing her sister hastily back out to the patio, where the others were waiting.

Leah said nothing, but as everyone sat around the table, passing tiny plates of impossibly red strawberries, Iris stared at her lap, unable to contain her smile. She would not steal a look at Cooper, two seats away, who she knew was studying her. Nor would she look at her sister, whose curious gaze felt like an intense weight. The moment was hers, and though she wasn't entirely sure how she felt, the unmistakable smile she struggled to contain between her aching cheeks was pretty damn telling.

Eighteen

O h, God. Oh, God. Oh, God. All night Iris tossed and turned in bed like a restless schoolgirl. He'd kissed her. Cooper Woods had kissed *her*.

Her mind shot back to the kiss, again and again. The fullness of his lips. His warm breath, which she'd inhaled as they parted.

But then came the aftershocks. Leah's interruption, and the pained look on her face. Had she once kissed Cooper Woods like this? Was she mourning something that Iris was only tasting for the first time?

But most pressing and terrifying of all was the one question Iris refused to consider, could not consider, until daylight came and brought with it some perspective. Iris was still a wife. A mother. And she took pride in that. It confirmed that, despite all, she had not fallen weak as Paul had. She had not given in to loneliness or doubt or ego at her family's expense. And now this kiss. Of all the questions that swirled through her head as she tossed among the sheets that night, there was one Iris kept returning to. What did this make her now?

◆ ◆ ◆

Iris arose groggily the next morning. In the bathroom she stared at her reflection, touching her face, examining herself for change. She'd half imagined she'd see a different person in the mirror.

Downstairs the Willetses were at the table, sipping coffee with her parents. Leah and Stephen had not yet come down.

"Well, good morning," Bill greeted her.

"Morning, Daddy." Iris bent over her father's chair, shyly, to kiss him. Wondering, as she had as a teenager, if he could tell what had happened to her last night. And what he'd think, if he could.

To her dismay the coffeepot was empty, so she waited by the counter, half listening to the conversation behind her, as she brewed another batch. "Why don't you join us?" Millie asked. It wasn't so much an invitation as an SOS call. "We were just telling Adele and Lance about the farm," Millie said.

"It must have been nice to grow up in such natural environs," Adele said, turning her attention abruptly to Iris. She drank her coffee black, which Iris thought fitting somehow.

"We were lucky," Iris agreed, pouring her cup and sitting down at the table. She was eager to escape outside. "Though I'm sure Leah's told you all about it."

Lance and Adele shook their heads in unison. "Your sister's a quiet one," Adele said. "Quite the little mystery."

Millie interjected. "Leah was a star swimmer, did you know? We had her in the lake at age two! Couldn't keep her out of it."

Lance chuckled fondly, but Adele turned to Iris. "And you? Were you an accomplished swimmer as well?"

Accomplished? Iris gulped her hot coffee, unnerved by the intentness of Adele's gaze, and struggling to put a finger on any one thing she might truly describe herself as accomplished at. "Not quite like Leah," she allowed. "But I loved to swim. Still do."

"And what do you *do*?"

Iris glanced at the clock on the wall. Was this an interrogation? "I'm a literary agent," Iris answered, standing quickly. "But I'm working on my own project now."

"Iris has her first book coming out," Millie lauded. "A cookbook. With farm-to-table recipes, much in the spirit of our family business."

Iris flashed her mother a look, shocked that Millie had paid enough attention to realize what she'd been working on, and just as shocked she was pitching her so hard. There was no mistaking her aim, though—Millie was driving the ball right into the Willetses' net.

"There's no publisher yet, Mom," Iris corrected, leaving out the very real possibility that there might never be. That at present it was little more than a pipe dream between old friends, and therapy for a runaway wife. "It's in the works," she explained to Adele.

"How charming. And I hear you have children. Where are they?" There was a note of appraisal that made Iris bristle. Millie glanced into her lap.

"They're coming up soon," Iris said. "They're at camp for the summer."

"And your husband?"

Iris drained her cup and moved to the sink. "I need to get to work," she said to the group, forcing a smile.

"Iris is very busy," she heard Millie telling the others as Iris hurriedly filled a thermos with coffee. "Did I mention that she's also restoring one of our antique barns this summer?"

"Is that so?" Adele said. "You know one summer, Stephen—"

But Millie's voice rose above Adele's. "That's our girl. Books, barn restoration. Busy, busy, busy." Score two for Millie Standish. For once Iris felt like they were on the same team.

◆ ◆ ◆

Cooper's truck was parked in front of the barn. Iris hesitated outside. What exactly did a soon-to-be-divorced woman on the brink say the morning after a stolen kiss?

Inside Cooper was on a ladder, his back turned, but he had sensed her arrival. "Good morning."

"Morning to you, too." Iris could not bring herself to look up to see what he was doing. She could barely will her body to remain still, suddenly aching as it was with the urge to flee.

Speak, she ordered herself. *Now, while he's too high up on the ladder to get a good look at the wreck that you are.*

But before she could decide what to say, Cooper was climbing back down. Iris busied herself with a nearby broom; a handy prop, she decided, sweeping madly at sawdust shavings. A cloud of dust rose between them, but she kept sweeping. Even as Cooper came to stand beside her. Even as he reached for the handle and gently removed the broom from her grip.

"Iris." He was so close. She had no choice but to return his gaze.

Cooper set the broom against the wall. "About last night . . ."

Iris blinked. "Yes?"

Cooper paused, choosing his words carefully. "I was going to start out by apologizing."

Iris held her breath.

"But I'm not sorry. I kissed you. And I'm glad that I did."

She exhaled.

"But I am sorry if I overstepped my boundaries. I don't know what's going on with you and your husband. But I want you to know that what I did last night is something I've wanted to do for a while. And I hope it didn't offend you, or put you in an awkward place."

Iris couldn't speak. But she found that she could move. She shook her head rapidly from side to side, *No, no, you did not offend me.* While inside her thoughts raced, *Yes, yes, I wanted it, too!*

"So, we're good?" he asked, placing his hands on her upper arms. It was not an embrace, but Iris could feel the warmth of his skin on hers.

"About that." Iris paused. She wanted to tell him. "You already knew I was separated from my husband."

Cooper nodded solemnly.

"We're divorcing." There. It was out.

"Iris, I'm so sorry." He pulled her against him, his chin resting on her head. "You don't have to go into it."

She would some other time. When she was ready. "I just wanted you to know."

Cooper squeezed her gently. "Thank you for trusting me with that."

It was all she needed to hear.

✦　✦　✦

Together they went over the final buttressing work to be done. Cooper reviewed the measurements of wood he'd need cut while Iris turned her attention to the saw and the lengths of lumber. But she could not concentrate.

Instead, she found herself staring up the ladder at Cooper. At his Levi's that fit just right. At his strong shoulders that moved smoothly beneath his faded T-shirt as he worked. Combined with the humidity of the growing day, it left her light-headed.

Now what? she kept wondering. Were they just friends, acknowledging feelings but tucking them responsibly into their back pockets? Or were they more? And was she crazy to want more at this stage in her life? She knew the answer to that one. She yanked the plug out of its outlet. The last thing she needed in her condition was to be operating a power saw.

Cooper glanced down the ladder. "What's up?"

"Just need a break." She slipped outside and flattened herself against the barn siding, which was rough and already growing warm with the sun's heat.

Below, the lake surface stretched green and placid, and Iris yearned to submerge herself. But it seemed someone else had had the same thought.

Leah strode across the grass, to the far edge of the yard where the sand was the only interruption between lawn and water. She paused and glanced over her shoulder. Behind, Stephen followed, his gait slow and measured, as if he was deep in thought.

They were just below the barn, and their voices carried up the rise, allowing Iris to feel somehow like less of a spy.

"I'm sorry," Stephen said, stopping a few feet away from Leah.

"Like I said, I had no idea my parents were going to announce that."

Leah's arms were crossed. She turned away.

"Come on, Leah," Stephen said, reaching out. "Please understand."

"We already talked about this!" Leah cried. "You promised that I could define my own role with the foundation somehow."

"Nothing's been decided!" he insisted. "Listen, we can work this out. I'll talk to them."

Iris glanced toward the house, wondering if any of the others were within earshot. Stephen and Leah may have thought they'd chosen a spot a safe distance away from the house, but the water carried voices across the lake all the time.

Leah spun to face him. "What about my work here on the farm?" she said, and Iris realized she was crying. Instinctively, she stepped toward her sister. "I've grown this business with my own two hands, out of the dirt. Being back here, I realize how much a part of me this is." Leah opened her arms, gesturing to the fields and the barns above them. "I can't just give it up." Her voice fell, to a low and pleading timbre that Iris could barely make out. "Don't ask me to, Stephen."

And then Stephen pulled her against him and she relented. She raised her face to his, kissing him desperately. Breathing a sigh of relief, Iris turned away. She could not watch as Stephen bent to the grass with Leah still in his arms. She wasn't alone in her struggles that morning. But it was no real comfort.

Nineteen

By the end of the day, Iris was exhausted, though it was more from her worries than the work. She'd managed to get through the afternoon with Cooper, who behaved, oddly enough, as if nothing had happened. He was his usual friendly self, but it was precisely the "usual" part that bothered her. Had he changed his mind?

She needn't have worked herself up, however. As they were cleaning up, Cooper leaned against the bed of the truck and regarded her carefully.

"What?" She pushed her hair away from her face, suddenly conscious of how dusty and sweaty she must be. It was a far cry from her carefully constructed appearance the night before. No heels or lipstick today.

"Nothing," he said. But his boyish grin said otherwise. How was it that a thirty-nine-year-old man could still match his yearbook photo so closely? "Want to go for a swim?"

"Here?" Iris glanced nervously down the hill at the house, wondering what the others were doing, and what they'd think if she were to race down to the water's edge and jump in with Cooper. It was exactly what she wanted to do.

"Here. Or over at the cove, if you'd rather."

Iris hadn't been to the cove in years. No more than a sandy spit, the legendary local spot stretched around the corner from the town boatyard and followed the tree-lined shore where the lake was wider and deeper. A favorite teenage hangout, it boasted some of the highest cliffs on the lake and a rope swing that both Iris and Leah had spent plenty of time on as kids.

"The cove," she said, a rush of excitement filling her chest. "Let me run down to the house for my suit."

♦ ♦ ♦

It was just a swim on a hot day, she told herself as she rummaged quickly through her dresser. The faded red swimsuit was not going to work. She had a navy-blue tank she'd brought from home, but standing before the mirror, she wondered what she'd been thinking. It was something Millie would wear. Frantically she tore through her drawer, realizing she had nothing.

Somebody else did, though. Iris ducked across the hall into Leah's room. She tripped over a pair of Stephen's loafers and headed for the closet. This was no different from Leah "borrowing" her new black sandals, right? Two drawers down she hit the jackpot. She pulled out the red bikini top that Leah had worn on Cooper's tailgate that afternoon. Disgusted, she flung it behind her onto the carpet. There was another bikini, a black string, she realized to her dismay. Leah had no kids; her taut belly told a different story than Iris's.

Finally she laid her hands on a chocolate tankini. A toss-up. The bottoms had high openings, which made Iris cringe. She really should've kept up with that damn spinning class back at home. Nonetheless, she tucked the stolen suit under her arm.

The cove seemed smaller. It still surprised Iris how things that had once seemed so big to her, as a child, were actually not. As if reading her mind, Cooper echoed her sentiments. "The rope swing doesn't seem so ominous now, does it?"

Iris glanced down the shoreline at the cliffs that rose suddenly from the water's edge. "No," she lied. "Not nearly as impressive." There was no way she would consider attempting those rocks now. Motherhood had a way of ruining the prospect of anything remotely risky. Horseback riding equaled head injuries. Skiing summoned images of an orthopedics office. Which meant rope swings off thirty-foot ledges promised certain death.

"Let's go," Cooper said before she could calculate the drop from the highest rock.

"Now? We could go for a walk first." But Cooper had already shed his T-shirt and was trotting down to the water. "Wait!" she called after him.

The first steps were colder than the shallow strip of lake near her parents' house, and Iris froze midcalf, which was probably an unfortunate look. She'd hoped to get underwater before Cooper turned around.

"Come on!" he called.

Iris balked. She looked down, sucking in her stomach where the tankini rode up over her belly button. At least her bottom wasn't hanging out of the back end, she was pleased to note.

In one swift dive she went under, feeling strong and sure of her stroke. In no time she caught up. "Good form," Cooper called out. Which gave her another rush of adrenaline that sustained her all the way along the shore to the rope swing area.

Here, they strode out of the water and up the pebbly shore. Cooper reached the base of the boulders first and began climbing, looking back to check on her. The gray rocks were large and smooth, and fairly easy to climb. At the midpoint, Cooper reached a hand out to her. Iris took it, touching him for the first time all day, and allowed him to pull her up. "It's not much farther," he puffed. She shadowed his ascent, watching the muscles of his brown back.

Soon they were at the top, with a cluster of scraggly pine trees behind them, and the wide blue surface of lake and sky stretching out before them. "It's still fairly ominous," she whispered, crouching on the ledge, and Cooper laughed, resting a hand on her shoulder.

"We don't have to jump," he said. "I just thought it'd be nice to take in the view."

Iris sat, pulling her knees to her chest, and Cooper plopped down beside her. His hair stuck up in wet spikes, and he ran his hand through it in a way that made Iris's heart ache. She shivered.

"You cold?"

"No," she said through chattering teeth. The sun was low in the sky and there was a light breeze picking up over the rocks.

"Here." He wrapped his arm around her, loosely, and she leaned into him, tingling at the press of their warm skin beneath the sheen of lake water.

"Better?" he asked, and she nodded, closing her eyes for a moment.

"So, the wedding's coming up soon, huh?"

The wedding. It wasn't what Iris wanted to talk about up here. Not with Cooper, not with all the rest that rolled uneasily in her mind.

"Is Leah nervous?" he asked.

Iris looked at him out of the corner of her eye. At Cooper's strong profile, his nose, which had the tiniest bump in the center, an old sports injury she found handsome. Why was he asking about her sister?

"I don't know," she said honestly. "Probably."

She felt his eyes on her. "You guys aren't that close, are you?"

"No," she admitted. "We used to be, I think, but I can't remember when, to be honest." Here was Leah, up on the rocks with them. But instead of pushing her away, Iris seized the moment.

"What about you guys?" she asked, her stomach flip-flopping as she said it.

"What do you mean?"

Iris swallowed. "You and Leah. You seem close, sometimes. Like you get each other."

She waited while Cooper considered it, wondering if she'd crossed a line. But she'd crossed so many lately.

"I guess we were sort of close," he said finally. "Last summer." Iris tipped her chin back, facing the breeze that had picked up over the rocks. Here it was.

"I came home around the same time she did, and we sort of ran into each other a few times." He looked over at her. "But it was no big deal. Not like we dated or anything."

For the first time Iris turned to face him. "Really?"

He nodded, his eyes as blue as the water and sky around them, and suddenly Iris felt dizzy with relief. He laughed lightly. "Were you worried?" he asked. "That it was more?"

Iris shrugged, suddenly embarrassed. "Not my business," she said quickly. "But you two just seemed to have a connection. The way you talked. And that time at the bar, when she was so drunk and you stepped in."

Cooper nodded. "I guess we do. Or did, at least. When I first came back to town, I was pretty lost. Sherry and I had just divorced. I'd sold my house, and left my business. It was the worst kind of way to come home, you know?"

Iris nodded. Boy, did she.

"And then I saw your sister at the farm stand one day. She was home, like me, and starting up this new business with your folks, and every time I came by she just sort of cheered me up. You know how Leah is."

"Yeah, she has that effect."

"So I invited her out on my dad's boat."

Iris listened as Cooper told her about the outings on the lake with Naomi and some of the other farm help. She'd been right about them hanging out. But it still didn't add up.

"So, if you don't mind me asking, why didn't you guys ever get together?"

Cooper looked out at the water. "It wasn't like that. I was just starting over. Besides, it wasn't long after when things really fell apart."

"What do you mean?"

"You know, the breakdown."

Iris turned sharply. "What breakdown?"

Cooper met her gaze, his eyes narrowing. "You didn't know?"

Iris shook her head, a sense of sudden dread filling her stomach. Had Cooper had some kind of breakdown after his divorce? An instant rush of pity ran through her, followed by a wave of dread. She didn't want to feel pity for Cooper. It was selfish of her, yes. But right now she needed him to be the rock he seemed to be.

"I'm so sorry. I didn't know you went through that."

Cooper shook his head. "Not me. Your sister. Leah."

Iris choked, a small laugh growing in her throat. "Wait. You're telling me that Leah had a nervous breakdown?"

Cooper studied her curiously. "I wouldn't joke about something like that, Iris. It was pretty bad."

Iris shook her head. "Leah can be sort of emotional, you know? She's been all over the map, so to speak, all her life. You just don't know her that well."

Cooper turned to her, his brow furrowed. "Iris, this wasn't any small thing. She was admitted to New Hampshire Hospital. Under an IEA. Didn't you know?"

New Hampshire Hospital was a psych facility. A small throb began at the edge of Iris's brain. "IEA?"

Cooper's voice softened. "Yeah. When someone is admitted against their will for their own protection."

"Are you saying Leah was suicidal?"

"I don't know. But she was in bad shape. She stayed in the hospital for a couple of weeks. I didn't see her again until August."

Despite the cool wind, Iris felt choked for air. "No one told me anything about this." But deep down, Iris had known something was wrong, and the guilt hit her in the stomach. She'd watched Leah pop pills all summer. Hell, she'd even confronted Millie about it. But her mother had blamed it on wedding jitters—no big deal. After all, Leah was prone to anxiety and bouts of mood swings. And, selfishly, Iris had been too distracted with her own troubles to press it further.

Cooper looked at her empathetically. "Well, your mother knows. And Naomi." And with that the pieces began to fit. Naomi's closeness with Leah. The comments she'd made that first morning Iris arrived at the farm: "She's better now." The shared looks of concern between Naomi and Millie at the breakfast table. They'd been through something together. Over Leah. Something Iris had not.

Iris had been kept in the dark. She could've been there for her younger sister. She could've helped. A mix of anger and worry fueled her and she hopped up from the rock. "I have to go."

Cooper leaped up. "Iris, wait."

Quickly she climbed down the rocks, holding on to the edges of the large boulders as she scrambled down. "I need to get home."

"What for?"

She'd reached the bottom, where the water lapped at the rocks, and the stone surfaces were slippery with moss.

"Careful!" Cooper warned as she nearly slid into the lake. But she caught her balance, pulling her arm away just as he reached for it.

"I'm fine," she said angrily.

The sky overhead was rich with purple and orange, dappling the lake like stained glass. She waded out and dove under, her ears ringing as she swam back toward the beach.

Behind her Cooper was saying something she could not hear. Slicing with her arms, she paddled faster, moving away from him. Her only sister had suffered something life changing but the family had kept her out of it. Even Cooper Woods knew. It was a betrayal that cut as viscerally as her body did through the water. The thought consumed her until she caught a mouthful of water and began to choke.

"Iris!" Cooper swam up behind her, reaching out with one hand.

She splashed at him, warning him away. But when she couldn't stop coughing, she panicked and began to flail.

"It's okay, I've got you."

And before she could object, Cooper's arm encircled her waist. She found herself on her back, looking up at the sky as he stroked with his free arm, pulling them both to shore. Overhead the sky burned redder than any Iris had ever seen before.

❖ ❖ ❖

Cooper made a small fire on the beach with some scrap wood from the back of his truck and pine branches from the cedars along the shore. Iris huddled under a blanket he'd found in the cab, staring at the embers. She was too drained to object.

"Thirsty?" he asked, holding out a canteen of water in one hand and a beer in the other. Iris pointed to the beer, then pressed the bottle to her lips, letting the grainy liquid suffuse the bad taste in her mouth.

"Can I get you something else?"

Iris shook her head. She felt sick.

Cooper settled beside her and twisted the top off his own beer. When her bottle was empty she set it on the rocks beside her and turned to him.

"Let me get this straight. Leah had a nervous breakdown last summer. And you've known about it all this time?"

Cooper met her gaze warily. "Only because I happened to be there when it all went down. Iris, I thought you knew."

She shook her head slowly. "Tell me everything."

Cooper let his breath out. Clearly this was uneasy territory for him. "We'd spent a few weekends hanging out last summer, going out on the lake and that sort of thing. But then Leah sort of disappeared. Didn't leave the farm much anymore, didn't return calls."

"That's not that unusual for her," she said flatly. "Her moods change with the wind."

"This was different," Cooper said. "Until, suddenly, she popped up again one weekend, as if nothing happened. A bunch of us went out on the boat that night, and she had too much to drink. She just started getting really silly, dancing around, like she was that night in the bar. And out of the blue she began sobbing, and lay down on the floor of the boat."

"Why?"

"I didn't know. Naomi was there, too. We tried to calm her down. Then before I knew what was happening she jumped off the boat and tried to swim back to shore."

"Jesus."

Cooper winced. "It was so dark that night. We couldn't see her, but we could hear the splashing."

"Then what?"

"I went in after her. When I caught up, I tried to convince her to swim back to the boat, but she fought me. She kept screaming to just let her go. The second I loosened my grip, she went under. It was like she didn't want help."

Iris wrapped the blanket more tightly around her. "What are you saying? She was trying to drown herself?"

Cooper shook his head wearily. "I don't know, Iris. It was scary as hell; I've never seen someone so distraught. I pulled her out and we all got her back in the boat as fast as we could."

"Was she conscious?"

"Yeah, but she was out of it. Naomi and I rushed her home, to your folks' place, and woke them up. Your mom took one look at her and called the ambulance."

"My God." Iris raked her hand through her damp hair. The awful images swirled through her head; her parents, Leah. And, of all people, Cooper Woods.

Cooper recounted the rest of the details gently. How he followed the ambulance to the hospital with Bill, and how erect her father had sat in the front of the truck, saying nothing. How Millie had paced the waiting room of the ER, refusing to speak until the doctors gave them word.

He paused. "I waited a little while with your folks, but it was pretty clear I was in the way. I was just leaving when one of the doctors came out to talk to your parents. I overheard him say that they'd restrained her."

Iris closed her eyes, trying to imagine her mother's face. She already knew intuitively what it had shown. The pain of a mother for her child.

"And yet they told me none of this. Not even to this day, a year later." Iris stared into the small flames, trying to make sense of it. Leah's mood swings and medications. The secrecy of it all. And the unavoidable feeling of being an outsider in her own family. "Instead we're cheerfully planning a wedding, the event of the season, as if nothing ever happened."

Cooper picked up a rock and tossed it into the fire. "After that night, Leah disappeared for a while. I tried calling, but nobody ever answered. Finally, I just drove to the farm stand. Your mom acted like everything was perfectly normal. Thanked me for my concern. Said Leah was fine, just getting over a bad flu. I got the message pretty quick."

"A bad flu?" Iris rested her head in her hands. Typical Millie. Family matters were private. She recalled her mother's tight smile as she handed over the bag of vegetables to Cooper that first day she came home. As if he hadn't been the one to deliver her soaked, distraught daughter safely home that night.

Cooper shook his head. "A few weeks later I was down at the boat launch, and Leah came to see me. She looked pretty thin and worn-out. She thanked me for helping her that night. Said she was sorry to drag me into it, that things had been hard for her, and she'd had to make some rough choices."

"Choices?"

Cooper shrugged. "I still don't know what she meant by that.

Maybe that she'd tried to work things out by herself. Maybe she was too embarrassed to tell you."

"Embarrassed?"

"Well, let's be honest, Iris. Look at you."

Iris turned to him, the fire crackling loudly in the stillness. "What's that supposed to mean?"

"You're the one who made something of herself. You're married. With the family and the house and the picket fence. Christ, Iris. That's everything to most people."

Iris laughed bitterly. Cooper didn't know what the hell he was talking about. "Don't be ridiculous."

"It's true. You had it all. And Leah was kind of floundering around in your wake."

Whether it was the way Cooper was defending Leah or the way in which he portrayed Iris's life that angered her, Iris wasn't sure. But something inside her snapped.

"Leah could've had any of that if she wanted it. She chose herself."

The fire hissed and spit between them, and Cooper held her eyes in the orange glow before turning away. She'd done it again. She'd alienated the only person she'd wanted to keep close.

After a moment, she went to him. "I'm sorry," she said. "This is about my family. You're just an innocent bystander. Who acted pretty heroically, given the circumstances."

He turned to face her, his expression uncertain.

"There's a lot of personal stuff getting unearthed. At a time when my plate is already full, you know?" She looked up at him hopefully.

He nodded. "I understand. Let me bring you home."

Iris stood nearby as Cooper kicked at the remnants of the fire, smothering the last of it with sand. This night was supposed to be theirs; a chance to confide in Cooper about the divorce, the jagged news she'd held close and was finally ready to release. And instead, once more, the night had become Leah's. Her breathy voice wafting across the lake surface, finding them on the beach. Intrusive, suffocating. But, always, alluring.

On the drive home Iris rested her head against the truck window, her temple knocking against the pane with every jostle of the lake road. It was a relief to be feeling something.

Twenty

Monday morning Iris found herself practically sprinting down Main Street to keep up with her mother and sister. Adele was waiting already for them on the sidewalk of Patty's Boutique as they hurried toward her.

"We're here!" Millie announced, as if the woman couldn't see for herself the three harried figures huffing toward her.

Iris had kept silent in the backseat of the car on the drive into town that morning, still smarting from Cooper's revelations.

Now, surrounded by racks of gauzy white dresses, amid all the trappings of happy endings, Iris sat sandwiched between Adele and Millie as Leah stepped out of the dressing room for her last fitting.

"Oh!" Adele gasped in approval as Leah stood before them. "It's lovely, darling. Stephen will be dumbstruck."

And despite the fact that Iris had seen Leah in the dress before, it still gave her pause. Looking rosy and healthy, she showed no sign of the thin or tormented soul from the last summer.

❖   ❖   ❖

When they were done, the older women went to the front display cases to try to find a new handbag to match Adele's wedding suit, leaving Iris alone with Leah in the dressing room.

"Help me out of this thing?" Leah asked.

Iris rose from the couch slowly. She did not feel like helping her sister with anything.

She fumbled with the buttons, which were impossibly small. "Careful," Leah warned. "They're hand-stitched."

"Of course they are," Iris muttered. She was almost done when she felt Leah's skin pinch between her fingernails.

"Ow!" Leah spun around.

"Sorry," Iris snapped. She worked more slowly, ignoring Leah's impatient sighs, and avoiding her gaze in the mirror in front of them.

"What's with you today?"

"Nothing," Iris said. This was not the time to bring things up, though, honestly, she couldn't imagine when that time might be.

"If anyone should be edgy, I'd think it'd be me."

Iris looked at her sister for the first time all day. Before she could change her mind, she said it. "I could have helped you, you know."

Leah stepped out of her gown carefully and placed it on the hanger. "With what?" she asked distractedly.

"With everything. Anything."

"Is this about Vermont again?"

Iris waited as Leah tugged on her seersucker shorts and sat to retrieve her flip-flops from the floor.

"I'm talking about last summer."

Leah froze, staring at the pink flip-flop in her hand.

"Why didn't you tell me, Leah?"

Leah rose from the chair, her voice paper-thin. "What do you mean?"

And suddenly Iris saw it, behind the glossy hair and freckled complexion. The sadness that shimmered, faintly, in her sister's gray-green eyes.

Iris lowered her voice. "I know about last summer. About your . . ." She struggled to find the word. "About your breakdown."

Before Leah could answer, Iris grabbed her hands. "Why didn't you come to me?"

"Iris," Leah whispered. "Please. Don't." Tears spilled from her eyes, as if some small dam had broken inside her. "Not now. There're things you don't understand."

"Make me understand. I want to help you."

Leah's eyes darted around the dressing room. "I wanted to tell you." She paused. "When the time was right."

"Then tell me."

Leah shook her head. "Iris. I can't."

It stung, but she wasn't going to walk away this time. "Because you don't trust me?"

"It's not that. It's complicated."

Iris forced a smile. "Leah, if anyone knows anything about complicated . . ." She searched her sister's gaze hopefully. "Look, we're both at a crossroads here. Right? This is what sisters are for."

When Leah didn't object, Iris felt herself gaining ground. "How about one day this week the two of us escape the family and grab lunch? We can talk. Really talk, like we should've a long time ago."

Leah shook her head. "Look, I appreciate it. But I can't."

Iris could see her sister's walls going back up. Leah wasn't going to let her in.

"Fine." Iris swept the curtains aside and stepped from the dressing room, tears pressing at her own eyes. But there was no place to escape.

From a display case at the front of the store, Millie motioned to her. It took every ounce of strength Iris had to compose herself and join them.

"Iris, what do you think about these purses?"

Millie held up two small clutches against Adele's green silk jacket. Both women were studying them intently, and Iris realized it was the first time she'd seen them aligned on anything. "Do you like the gold or the black better?"

"Remember," Adele chimed in. "The wedding colors are green and ivory."

"Celadon," Millie corrected.

Iris put a hand to her temple and stepped into the small space between the two matriarchs, trying to feign interest. As if all that mattered at that moment was selecting an overpriced jeweled handbag, when in the background, the past and present swirled dangerously together behind a flimsy dressing room curtain.

"The gold," she said softly. "Definitely the gold."

◆　◆　◆

"It's a slippery slope," Trish said, stabbing a piece of butter lettuce with her fork. She didn't seem at all surprised. Which left Iris feeling somewhat offended.

"You mean you saw this coming?"

"Well, didn't you?"

She'd ditched the other women after the fitting and called Trish, insisting that she meet her at the Village Diner for lunch. "Gotta run—it's a book thing," she'd lied to Millie. Iris needed a moment for herself, even if it meant stealing it.

Now, at the diner counter, they were discussing the kiss with Cooper. Something so seemingly superficial given the circumstances. There were plenty more truly important things to discuss with her best friend. But before Trish arrived, Iris had decided against telling her about Leah's breakdown. The news was still too raw to touch. And it wasn't her news to share.

What was hers to share was plentiful enough. Sitting at the diner counter over a salad, she welcomed Trish's interrogation. If Trish wanted to know about her kiss with Cooper, this time Iris was happy to spill. Hell, she'd reenact it with her lunch plate if Trish asked her to, though it was becoming less enjoyable with every question Trish fired at her.

"So, what's your game plan?"

Iris set down her fork. "I need a game plan? I didn't even know I was in the game."

Trish made a smug noise. "Suit up, sister. You're on the field, whether you like it or not."

Iris pushed the Niçoise salad around her plate. "I don't know what to do about Cooper," she admitted. "Everything just sort of happened this summer."

"Oh, no you don't." Trish wagged her finger. "This sort of thing doesn't *just happen*, Iris. You walked into the path of oncoming traffic."

Iris feigned affront. "Cut me some slack." But Trish was right. She'd put herself on this road. Christ, she'd even hailed the car and jumped in the front seat.

"Here's the thing you have to decide," Trish said, talking around a large bite of tuna fish. Iris listened, wondering how her friend could eat such a thing at a time like this. "What do you want to happen?"

Iris shrugged. "If I knew what I wanted I don't think I'd be in this predicament."

"Look at it this way—if there were no repercussions or hurt feelings to deal with, what would *you* want to happen next?"

"You mean if my kids and my family didn't exist? How can you even ask me that?"

"Because, in the end, it's what you have to ask yourself."

It was an awful question, but it was also *the question*, Iris realized. Forgetting Paul and their failed marriage (could she even do that?), setting aside her fear of familial reactions and the implications her choices might have on others (the kids!), what would *she* want? "This is about much more than just me," Iris reminded Trish. "I may be in the throes of divorce proceedings, but I'm still part of a family."

"Hang on, hang on. I'm not suggesting you toss the kids. But I've watched you make every move of your life around what was best for everyone else. It's time you put yourself back into the equation. What does Iris want?"

The waitress appeared at the booth and refilled their waters. Iris stared at her own untouched plate. "I don't know," she said finally. "I'm sorry, but I really don't." Iris couldn't think. She'd run away to Hampstead to escape her family problems in the first place. To clear her head. And now here she was, more confused and in a far deeper mess than before.

"Then you have to stop."

"Stop what?"

Trish gave her a level look. "Until you figure out what you want, you have to put a stop to all of this with Cooper. No more hanging out, no more stolen kisses. And no more working in the barn, or whatever it is you're doing up there. Seriously, Iris. It's too dangerous. This isn't some little fling."

Trish had her. If Iris was going to give this thing with Cooper a real shot, she needed to figure out the rest first. Besides, no matter how awful things got, she was not the kind of person who could shove her kids and family aside and just give in to temptation. No, Iris was not that person.

"You're right," Iris said, setting down her fork. "No more Cooper." But even as she said the words and Trish reached for the dessert menu as if the matter was solved, Iris couldn't ignore the other fact of the matter: none of this would've happened in the first place if Paul hadn't put her in this position. This was his fault, too.

Trish placed a double order for chocolate malts. "My treat."

"So you think chocolate is going to do it for me?" The joke lightened the mood, but still . . . How could Trish expect her to just walk away from Cooper at this stage?

"Look at it this way," Trish said, more gently this time. "It's not fair to you or to Cooper. You don't want to poison a second chance, do you?"

Iris wagged her head.

"Exactly. If this thing with Cooper is real, then he'll still be there in the end. When you've got your head on straight."

Iris sat back into the booth, feeling both deflated and grateful. She'd asked for direction, and now she had it. "I guess you're right. I owe that much to the kids. And to my family, too."

"Iris."

"What?"

"You owe it to yourself."

◆ ◆ ◆

But staying away from Cooper Woods wasn't that easy. Iris needed this little friendship they'd fostered. And a thousand chocolate malts with your best friend were no substitute for the cravings she had.

By the time she drove home, it was almost dinner. She'd missed another day in the barn, but what did that matter now? Hopefully Cooper would've gone home for the day.

Avoidance, as Trish had instructed. It was a necessary operation. She tried to think of it in clinical terms as she pulled into the farm driveway. Her separation from Paul was a questionable growth. A growth that needed treatment and removal. And as ugly as it was probably going to be, until she'd recovered from that operation she couldn't allow herself any distractions.

By the time she neared home, Iris had talked herself into this new role she'd have to adopt. Polite, but at a distance. Friendly, but not flirty. For extra backup, she summoned visions of her parents: Millie's disapproving scowl, Bill's pained expression. That's what she needed, an unforgiving audience looking over her shoulder. She couldn't kiss Cooper Woods with Millie watching. And as for Bill, oh, it'd probably throw the poor man into tachycardia. Iris gripped the steering wheel tightly. She could do this. Even if it meant that she had to wrap the dreaded weight of parental guilt around her shoulders.

But no sooner had she pulled up to the barn than she noticed Cooper's truck. Okay, she told herself calmly: the first test. What would her parents say about this?

Millie pursed her lips.

Iris drove on.

But then Cooper stepped outside. Okay, plan B. She'd allow herself an innocent wave. What was the harm in that? It wasn't like she could go from kissing to cutting off all connection. Especially not after the conversation they'd had last night. In her mind Millie shook her head violently, but Bill shrugged forgivingly. All right, then; she'd wave.

Cooper approached the car, and her heart began to race as she raised one hand. It was a flat-handed wave, like something a pageant girl on a float might give, and so she tried a more enthusiastic one, but her nerves took over and her hand began to flap uncontrollably.

Cooper stared as she approached, a funny look on his face.

Great. He probably thought she was having a seizure. Now she'd have to stop the darn car. Which Iris did, but then she proceeded to sit there, windows rolled up, the engine still running as she argued with herself about what to do next.

Cooper came over and peered in the window. "You okay?" he mouthed.

Well, this wasn't working. Reluctantly, Iris rolled down the window, thought better of it, then rolled it up again. Almost pinching Cooper's hand. Jesus.

"Iris?"

"Hi!" Iris shouted through the glass. There, greeting complete. Now, if she could just get the hell out of there. Because if she stayed, it would only lead to something else. Like a conversation. Which might lead to dinner. And then, of course she'd have to kiss him again. Oh, God.

At that thought, Iris hit the gas pedal. But much harder than she'd intended, and the car rocketed forward.

Cooper leaped to the side. "What the hell?"

She stamped the brake. "Shit!" Iris jumped out of the car. "I'm sorry. Are you all right?"

Cooper threw up his hands. "Are *you*?"

"Yes. No. I don't know. God, I almost killed you, didn't I?"

"Jesus, Iris. What are you doing?"

It was no use. "I didn't mean to stop. I mean, I wanted to say a quick hello, but I've got to get back to the house. Right away." She snuck a look at him, an intense heat rising in her cheeks. "I'm busy today. Crazy busy." Just plain crazy was what she was.

"Okay," Cooper said warily.

"So," she said, stepping awkwardly toward her car. "I guess I'd better go."

Cooper ducked playfully to the side. "Wait, let me take cover first."

"Ha-ha . . ." She opened the door. But she couldn't get in. Not yet.

"You are something," Cooper said, which suddenly made her smile.

"What?"

He shook his head in amusement. "Nothing. Just that you sure keep a guy on his toes."

Iris liked the way it came out. The way his mouth curved up in one corner as he said it. It wasn't just the way he was looking at her. It was the way he saw her.

"Whatever's so important, can it wait for a swim?" he asked.

Iris looked back at her car, still running. She looked down at the house, where she could not see Millie's look of consternation. Or Bill's befuddlement. And back at Cooper, who was dusty and tan, and still smiling at her in the middle of the driveway.

Trish's words echoed loudly in her head, *Stop it, Iris. Stop it. Now!*

"Why not?" she said breathlessly.

◆　◆　◆

They'd descended the hill below the barn, bypassing the house and cutting left across the lawns to the same spot where Stephen and Leah had passionately argued what seemed like years before. A handful of willows lined the shore, and the grasses were taller here, a spot where mallards nested and where Iris had scouted for eggs and ducklings when she was a child.

"Do you think they can hear us?" Cooper asked, glancing sideways at the house in the distance. Tiki torches on the patio flickered, signaling the dinner hour.

Iris shook her head. "They're all too busy talking over one another."

Cooper laughed. "Stephen's parents are a little high maintenance, huh?"

"Makes my mother look like a pussycat," Iris agreed. "And that's no small feat."

"And what does that make you?"

Iris stopped at the water's edge and kicked off her sandals. "I don't know. A dog?"

Cooper made a face. "Are you kidding? Something fiercer."

Fiercer? "A tiger, maybe?"

"I wouldn't go that far."

She splashed him, and Cooper darted away laughing.

"What then?" she demanded.

Cooper sat on the rocky shore and began unlacing his work boots. "An egret."

"A bird? I remind you of some gangly bird?"

He nodded, his voice growing serious. "The best kind of bird. You've seen them growing up around here. Egrets are graceful." He glanced over at her. "Independent. Loyal to their nest."

Iris tilted her head, contemplating this. She'd observed the quiet shorebird all her life. But it was the attributes Cooper listed that caught in her throat. It was perhaps the nicest thing he could've said, and the thought of her own distant nest filled her with a quiet sadness. And, right on its tail, a small flutter of happiness, too. Cooper thought her independent.

He stood, then pulled his T-shirt over his head, and Iris averted her gaze. She could hear him unzip his work pants, and a moment later he stood behind her, in just his navy-blue boxers.

"Come on," he whispered, touching her shoulder.

Iris watched as he waded in, the shadows of the branches overhead falling across his bare back. Cooper's legs flexed as he navigated the rocky shallows, the water rising up to his waist, and he turned to look back at her.

"You all right?"

She nodded, filled with sudden awareness of her clothed self. She'd have to strip down at least to her underwear, which she desperately tried to recall from when she got dressed that morning. An image of tattered grandma underpants flashed in her mind; God, she hoped she wasn't wearing *those*.

The shade of the willows combined with fading sun enveloped them in a golden hue. It wasn't getting any darker. She dropped her pants quickly, kicking them aside with her foot.

Cringing, she closed her eyes. Which was absurd. Cooper's own eyes were not closed, and she could feel the warmth of his gaze traveling across the pebbly shallows as she tugged her T-shirt off and stood in her white bra and panties before him. At least they weren't the ones with holes in them, she thought, stepping gingerly onto the damp sand.

In one slip, she moved into the lake, passing Cooper underwater, and surfaced just beyond him. Behind them a throaty chorus of peepers had started along the shore.

"Feeling better after the other night?" Cooper asked.

Iris smoothed her wet hair back. "I'm working on it." She leaned back into the water, floating. She did not want to talk about Leah or her family right now. "If I could just stay like this . . ." she said, her voice trailing.

"I know. This is why I came back here," Cooper said, sinking into the water.

Down the beach, voices carried and they both turned, watching as distant figures emerged from the house and onto the patio.

"They'll be wondering where I am," Iris whispered, grateful to be where she was instead. She laughed out loud, suddenly giddy, as if they were a couple of kids hiding from the grown-ups and might be discovered at any moment.

"You're a big girl," Cooper allowed.

"Sometimes." Iris laughed again. "Sometimes I just do a really good impression of one."

"Well, you've got me fooled."

Iris turned to him. "Can I ask you something?"

"Why do people always do that?" Cooper mused. "Ask if they can ask you something, instead of just asking the question."

"Probably because they're uncomfortable about the very thing they want to ask you."

"Are you?"

"Well, now I am," Iris said, smiling.

Cooper swam closer. "Ask me anything."

"All right." Iris glanced back at the house. "What was I like in high school?"

Cooper frowned. "Don't you already know the answer to that?"

"No. I mean, everyone has a vague idea of how other people saw them in high school. But it doesn't always match up with how they felt. Or who they were."

"Exactly. So, why would you care what I thought about you in high school?"

"Forgive me, but only you could answer like that."

"What's that supposed to mean?"

"You were popular. And athletic. Everyone knew who you were. I'm sure it never occurred to you to feel anything less than awesome."

Now it was Cooper's turn to splash her. "That's not fair. I was just as self-conscious as anyone else in high school."

Iris scoffed. "Sure. Says the lacrosse team captain." She rolled over onto her stomach. "Wait, weren't you also homecoming king one year?"

Cooper winced.

"Oh, please. Of course you were!"

"Iris, that was so long ago. Who cares about that stuff now?"

"I know, I know. But seriously, this is important to me."

Cooper rolled his eyes. "I can't imagine why. But if you want to play this game, I will." He paused. "Let's see; in high school I remember you as being kind of serious. And smart. Weren't you in all the honors and AP classes?"

"Yeah, but that's not what I mean. How did I *seem* to you?"

He gave her a pleading look. "Tell me again why you're asking me all this?"

"Because you're right—high school *was* so long ago. We've all grown up and turned into such different people. But now that I'm back home, I don't feel different at all. Suddenly I'm unsure of everything. I'm driven by this ridiculous need to please my parents. And I'm completely overshadowed by my sister's life. It's just like high school all over again."

"Iris, it's nothing like high school. As for Leah, you're just looking out for your sister. It may feel overwhelming, but it certainly can't overshadow you."

"But it is!" Iris insisted. "I came back here to sort things out for myself. And yet I'm so afraid to take the next step, *any* next step, really, because what if it's the wrong one? What if I screw up and can't go back and fix it?" She was rambling now, and she could see that Cooper was trying to keep up. "And I'm listening to everyone else: my parents, Trish, you! Why is that? I'm educated, I've got a family and a career, and I'm forty, for God's sake. Haven't I learned anything?"

Cooper swam closer. "Well, haven't you?"

"This isn't funny."

"I don't think it is. You're struggling, Iris. Welcome to the trenches. All I can say is that you've got to take a step, even if it's in the wrong direction. Because you can always circle back."

"Can I really?"

Cooper's voice was soft, and his eyes full of concern. Iris could feel her heart slowing in the water. "Iris, you can do anything you want to. You're still the smart kid from school." He furrowed his brow. "And definitely the serious one."

Iris flicked him.

"But you're so much more than that. Stop analyzing everything so intensely. Go with your instinct."

"Easy for you to say."

"For the record, being the captain of the lacrosse team was great. But being popular wasn't. You know how stressful that was? Everyone's always got one eye on you. You're constantly thinking about what you say or do, or who you're with. I should've focused a lot more on the important stuff. Like you did."

Iris scoffed. "Yeah, look where that got me."

Cooper waited a beat before reminding her, "Right here, with me."

Iris glanced over, but he'd closed his eyes and was floating on his back. Watching Cooper out of the corner of her eye, she could sense how relaxed he was. Stretched out in the water, a look of contentment on his face. If only she could channel some of that for herself.

Above them the first twinkling stars had shown themselves. Staring up at them, Iris floated beside Cooper. Wondering what the kids were doing under those same stars, back at home. "It's beautiful at this time of night," she said finally.

"You're beautiful," Cooper replied. He was looking at her.

Iris righted herself, planting her feet firmly in the sand. How long had he been watching her like that?

Cooper moved closer. Reaching underwater, he found one of her hands and drew it to him, pressing it to his mouth. Iris watched, trembling. As though it were someone else's fingers pressed to his lips.

"What are you afraid of, Iris Standish?" he asked her softly.

"Everything."

Iris knew what was about to happen, but she closed her eyes anyway. Forcing aside her fears, and Trish's voice, and all the hundreds of reasons she should turn away, climb out of the lake, and race back toward the house.

But she did not. As the voices of her family carried across the water, rising in laughter and falling away in hushes, Iris let Cooper Woods press his wet mouth against her own. She did not pull away as he kissed her assiduously, encircling her waist with his arms. She did not flinch as he ran his hands over her slick, wet head. Nor did she cry out when he drew her toward the shore and lay down against her in the shallow waters, their bodies moving with a gentle rhythm as the lake lapped softly at every inch of their skin.

Twenty-One

The wedding planners had landed. With the big day looming, Tika, Leah's coordinator, arrived to confirm the wedding's "launch and design tactics," something that sounded to Iris like a NASA rocket dispatch.

Tika roared up the drive in a tiny silver Audi TT, top down, followed by another car, filled with people whom Iris assumed were her assistants. Polished young women with sleek ponytails and portfolios tucked under their arms, and a twiggy young man in salmon-colored pants, who sprang from the passenger seat of the Audi and shielded his eyes as he took in the house.

"It's an army," Millic murmured, watching them through the kitchen window.

"An underfed, manicured army," Iris corrected.

Leah swept down the porch stairs and greeted Tika with European-style kisses.

"Welcome!" she said, gesturing to the porch, where Millie and Iris stood watching the congregation. The young man in salmon pants issued a perfunctory pageant-style wave.

"This is Devon," Tika said, "our visionary."

"I've heard so much about you," Leah gushed.

"Uh-huh." Devon snapped his head left and right, scrutinizing the property as he chewed one end of his aviator sunglasses impatiently. "So this is it?"

Tika pressed a small clutch to her chest. "No, no, don't worry. The reception site is up that way." She pointed toward the barn, behind the house.

Devon furrowed his pale brow. "I'm not feeling it."

Which apparently was not a good sign. Behind them the minions began to fidget, and Tika whisked open a portfolio of photos that one of the minions nervously had produced, as if on cue. "These are the shots I took last month. Remember the sloping meadow? The oak trees bordering the hill? You'll see the site is perfect."

Devon, swatting at a stray fly, did not look convinced.

"Guess this doesn't involve me," Iris said quickly, already making a getaway for the door.

"Oh, no you don't," Millie said, placing a firm arm around her daughter's waist and drawing her to the porch steps. "Come meet the team. They're very talented."

"You mean affected," Iris whispered.

Iris tried not to roll her eyes as she followed "the team" up the grassy rise behind the house, as the girls puffed and wobbled in their ridiculous heels. Devon led the small band, his stride brisk and impatient. Iris spotted Cooper's truck at the barn ahead of them, and she felt even more silly following this pastel-clad band up the hill.

"This is it?" Devon asked again. They'd paused at the main barn. He put a finger to his mouth and tapped it, clearly baffled by the scenery. He looked to Tika. "You said we were going for *Out of Africa*. Honey, this is decidedly more *Grapes of Wrath*."

"Africa?" Millie piped up.

"Patience," Tika said coolly to Devon. Though she, too, began tapping her clutch.

"It's this way," Leah told them with an accommodating smile. She stepped in front of the planning party to lead the way, looking cool and unruffled in her seersucker tennis skirt and crisp blouse. "Not much farther."

Devon assessed Leah briefly, then, seeming to decide on

something, slipped his arm into hers. "Love the sandals," he said. "Just don't lose me in a cornfield, okay? I've got a treatment at noon."

Iris snorted.

Millie, who did not find any of this funny, exchanged worried looks with Tika. "He'll be fine," Tika assured her. "He's a genius. And look, he adores Leah."

As the planning party forged uncertainly ahead, Iris stole away and ducked into the barn.

"What's all that about?" Cooper met her in the doorway and gestured curiously toward the departing group.

"It's Leah's wedding posse. They're scouting the joint."

"Sounds insidious."

"You've got that right." Their eyes met and held, but despite the shared laugh, Iris felt uncertainty creeping in. One moment she wanted to reach out and touch his cheek; the next she wanted to run.

"I'd better catch up with them," she said reluctantly.

"What for?"

"Moral support. Millie's about due for a heart attack," she added. "There's talk of Africa . . ."

Cooper reached for Iris's hand, ignoring her nervous chatter. "C'mere."

It was all the invitation she needed. In the cool shadows of the barn, Iris wrapped her arm around Cooper's neck and kissed him on the mouth. A rise of yearning rose up inside her, and she pressed her nose into the curve of his neck, already moist with the heat of the morning. Iris inhaled his smell. A scent already familiar and comforting. Something she ached to lose herself in.

♦ ♦ ♦

For the next several days, Iris did just that. As the Willetses and Stephen took off for a quick pre-wedding visit to Maine, and as Leah and the planners hovered around the kitchen island with charts, Iris trusted herself to get lost. She stole away to the barn.

And to the lake. And once to the shaded bed of his truck, parked in the far fields by the woods—wherever Cooper was. The rafter work in the large barn was finally complete, and with the new supply of Vermont lumber, he had moved on to the old smokehouse.

Cooper issued Iris a special invitation to work with him. She'd risen early and headed to the lake for her usual swim one morning when she noticed something glimmering on the rock wall by the dock. It was a tool belt, with her name stitched in red across the nylon. She lifted it, appreciating the weight of the tools within. Her very own hammer. Wrench. Shears. Each sleek instrument she pulled from its pocket felt right in her hand. A small note was tucked in the largest pocket, alongside a box of nails. *"For Iris, to rebuild. Love, Cooper."* It was the best gift she could ever remember being given.

But Cooper wasn't her only distraction. The cookbook had taken shape and it was time to put out some feelers in the publishing world. Iris put in another call to Joan Myer. Joan was not just one of her favorite editors at Wordsmith Press in Manhattan. Joan was *the* publisher in cookbooks. Even before the Food Network channel had besieged the publishing industry with celebrity cookbooks, Joan had predicted the wave and made her own mark with distinguished lesser-known chefs. She was also game to take on a new author, something not every editor was willing to jump at. The question was, what if that author was Iris?

Iris put in the call to Joan's assistant and was surprised when Joan picked up on the first ring. "Yes, it's Joan."

"Hi there, Joan. This is Iris Standish."

"Iris, hello. Whatever happened to your author's piece on family farm cuisine? Did she ever find a chef to collaborate with?"

"Well, unfortunately, it was just a little too far out of her area of expertise."

Joan clicked her tongue. "Too bad. So, what else have you got for me?"

"Well, it's interesting you ask, actually." Iris paused, gathering herself. "I have this friend who is an amazing cook. Top-notch, really. And she lives here, in New Hampshire, where she runs her own bakery and café."

"You're summering in New Hampshire? Lucky dog. The city is positively sweltering. Disgusting, really." Joan sighed audibly.

"Yes, it is nice up here," Iris answered, trying to stay on course. "So, my friend, Trish, really knows New England fare. I mean, she is New England fare."

"Uh-huh."

Iris could imagine Joan glancing at her watch or checking her email. Editors were always buried. Iris had to make her pitch fast and strong.

"So what I thought was, why not collaborate with her? I mean, she's perfect. She's got the experience, and we work well together. And her food—well, it's just to die for."

"Right. So you teamed her up with your struggling author?"

"No, no, not my author." She took a deep breath. "I teamed her up with me."

There was a beat of silence on the other end of the line. "I'm afraid I don't follow."

Iris sank onto the bed. "I've been toying with the book idea for a while. So, I thought, why not? I could do this. I mean, I am doing this." Iris swallowed hard. "I'm writing the book. And we've got sample pages, if you'd be willing to take a look."

Joan did not answer right away.

What was Iris doing? Poor Joan probably dealt with wannabe authors all the time. It was no different from the parents who timidly approached Iris at PTA meetings clutching hand-scrawled pages with "*Just the cutest little idea for a picture book! Would you mind?*" Usually about some ordinary fur-ball animal, like a squirrel. Who lived in their attic. Or some equally mundane idea, like the time her sweet elderly neighbor, Mrs. Dooley, flagged her down at the bus stop with a typewritten story about her schnauzer, Otis, who loved to chase his tail. "*Oh, if you could just see him. Once he even caught it!"* And the look on Mrs. Dooley's face: bursting with hope and canine pride. They did not understand that Iris was a nonfiction agent, who could barely connect her own writers with editors in this tough market, and who did not specialize in children's literature or squirrels, and certainly not tail-chasing schnauzers. These painful incidents happened all too often, each time leaving Iris nodding politely, sometimes even feigning false enthusiasm, as she fought the knowledge that if she did not escape quickly she would be forced to stomp this person's dream dead like a bug. And yet here she was, doing the same thing to Joan. Only this time, Iris was Mrs. Dooley.

As the silence stretched painfully between them, Iris decided to grab the bull by the horns. Might as well get trampled trying. "Look, Joan, I know I'm not an actual author. But I know the parent this book is intended for. And Trish knows food. We've been working on these recipes all summer, and they're special. Seasonal, local, healthy fare. And all kid-friendly. It's what every parent I know is craving. No more microwave macaroni. No more hot dogs from the freezer. We're talking fresh, sustainable family dinners where everyone dines and unwinds together. The way we grew up, in our own family kitchens." Finished, Iris collapsed on the bed.

"I see," Joan said slowly, turning the ideas over on her tongue. "Healthy but quick. Getting the family back to the table. Sustainable ingredients." *Please,* Iris thought. *Please ask to see some pages.*

After a pause, Joan spoke. "Tell you what. I'm heading to Long Island next weekend. If you can get me some sample chapters before that, I'll try and take a look."

"Really? Oh, Joan, thank you! This means a lot."

"Just be patient," Joan cautioned. "Most of the team is away right now, and I'm about to take my own two-week hiatus. It's been god-awful here in New York. And I just wrapped a deal with *National Geographic* that about killed me."

"Congratulations," Iris said. "Sounds like you need a break."

"You've no idea," Joan groaned. "Okay, so let's say you get this to me by Friday. I can't promise I'll get to it before I leave town, but I'll try."

Iris bit her lip. Friday? She had Joan's attention now. And she didn't have much time left in New Hampshire with Trish. "Friday it is," she promised.

Twenty-Two

I ris held her last days alone on the farm close. Each morning, she rose before the rest of the house and stepped directly into the swimsuit she'd left on the bedside rug the night before, wrapping her bathrobe tightly about her as she stole downstairs and across the dewy lawn. No longer did she wade in carefully but strode into deeper water, relishing the brisk shock against her skin. Only after she was waterlogged, her limbs heavy with exertion, did she paddle back to shore and return to the kitchen, where she sat in her damp bathrobe at the table and sipped her coffee in peace. Reflecting on the new strength she felt. Counting the days until the kids arrived. And the days she had left alone with Cooper.

Only that particular morning, she was not alone. When she stepped back inside, her feet leaving the faintest of wet prints on the wide plank floors, she spied Millie leaning against the kitchen sink, a teacup clutched in hand. Her expression was neutral, still fogged by the early hour, but she was dressed crisply and her hair was already done.

"Good morning," Millie said as Iris closed the patio door behind her. For once she did not comment on the watery foot-prints.

"Morning, Mom." With the influx of guests and planners, the two had not found themselves alone together since Paul's divorce papers or Cooper's revelations about Leah. And it wasn't as if either had sought the other out. There was too much to say, and yet, it all seemed somewhat pointless to Iris now, a conversation too far past due.

Iris helped herself to a mug in the cupboard and took her usual seat at the table. Millie joined her.

"So, the wedding plans are all set?" It was a feeble attempt at small talk, but one Iris felt she owed her mother. Besides, if she didn't pick the topic, Millie would. And there were plenty of those that she'd rather not discuss.

"I think so," Millie said. "I can't believe it's next weekend." Her voice was as loose as her expression, a rare thing. Iris regarded her closely.

"You all right?"

Millie sighed lightly. "Of course. Just busy. The wedding, the Willetses—thank goodness they went to Maine for a few days. And, well . . ." She did not add Iris and her many pressing troubles, those unwelcome guests she could practically see seated alongside them at the table, each chair filled with an ominous disappointment: Iris's failed marriage to her right. The about-to-be-from-a-broken-home grandchildren to her left.

"I know. I'll be glad when it's all over." Iris looked apologetically at her mother. "Of course, it's been great to be here. And great of you and Dad, to help me through all this."

Millie frowned, expression returning vividly to her face. "Don't be ridiculous, Iris. Of course we're here for you." She regarded Iris more closely. "But since you mention it, what are your plans? You know, when summer ends . . ."

Iris glanced out the window. "I don't know, exactly." It was an honest response, if a less-than-revealing one. "When the wedding's over, I'll go home of course. Paul and I will have to tell the kids." Her voice cracked, just a little. "And we'll figure out the next move from there."

Millie blinked several times, as if this was the wrong answer. "Don't you think . . ." she began, selecting her words cautiously. "Well, what I mean to say is, are you sure about all this? It seems so—I don't know—final." She paused, allowing Iris a chance to fill in the gaps, which she did not, could not, she was so taken aback.

"Mom. Paul sent divorce papers. You saw them. Dad's been working on them with Arthur. I don't think there's any going back."

"Oh, Iris." Millie set her cup down impatiently. "None of this is irretrievable. You are not a sitting duck in the matter. Have you considered that? And the kids, what about those poor kids . . . ?"

Iris put her hands to her eyes. She was tired of feeling so hollow in her mother's presence. "Mom, I know we haven't sat down to really talk about this yet. But I am not a sitting duck. Yes, I was taken aback by all of this in the beginning. But since I've been back here, things have become clearer to me." She braved a look at her mother. "As much as I hated him for doing this, Paul's right. We are not a healthy couple. And we sure aren't a happy couple. In fact, we haven't been for a really long time. You must have known that."

"But you made your choice," Millie interjected, laying her cards and her expectations clearly on the table. *You made your bed, Iris. Now lie in it for all eternity.*

"Is that what you want, Mom? Do you want me to just keep this going, even if it makes us all miserable? Because I used to think I could do that. In fact, that's exactly what I've been doing all these years. But I don't think it's turned out so well. Do you?"

Millie leaned in. "It's not just about you, Iris. It's about the kids."

Which made the tears start. "Of course it is! Which is why I've stayed so long. And fought so hard. You knew Paul and I were in counseling. But do you know for how many years? Do you?" Her voice was high and defensive now.

Millie shrugged sadly, as if it were beside the point.

"Ten years!" Iris sputtered. "First for our difficulty trying to get pregnant. Then for the difficulties that come with being a functional family. And now? He cheated, Mom. Paul cheated on me."

Millie clasped her hands together, twisting her wedding ring. "Iris, men are not as strong as us. Sometimes they make mistakes—stupid ones. Selfish ones. But we have the power to forgive. Forgiveness doesn't make you the weaker sex."

It was the most profound thing Millie had ever said to her.

"Children shouldn't have to suffer from their parents' mistakes."

Iris flinched. "But they are suffering, Mom. Do I want them to grow up thinking it's okay to be with someone who belittles you all the time? Who walks right past you in your own house, like you are invisible? Is that what you want Sadie, Jack, and Lily to think marriage is? Because as awful as I feel about leaving this marriage, I feel far worse imagining them entering one just like it themselves. It's not good. For any of us."

Millie stood abruptly. Either she'd heard too much or there was nothing left to say. But Iris wasn't about to let her scurry away, shaking her head as if something awful were stuck in her ear. "Mom."

Millie set her teacup in the sink with deliberate care. With the same precision, she took a kitchen towel from the cupboard and unfolded it slowly, one corner at a time. Her calmness infuriated Iris.

"Mom, I need you to support me. I'm not asking for you to understand, but I need your support. Dad does," Iris said, her anger rising in her throat. "He may not like what I'm going through, but he doesn't judge me."

"You think I judge you?" Millie cried suddenly.

"No," Iris said, wishing she could take it back. She'd never heard her mother respond so shrilly. "I didn't mean it like that. It's just that you put this pressure on me, like you disapprove of everything I do. Like I'm not good enough or something."

"What's wrong with wanting your children to be their best? You're a mother now. Don't you want that for your own kids?"

"But I don't push them, Mom. I don't hold them at arm's

length and inspect everything they do as if I'm looking for cracks or holes. And I don't pick favorites."

Millie stared back at Iris, her mouth slack. "You think I favored your sister?"

Iris took a small breath. "Whether it was Leah or the farm, I always felt like second best."

Millie stepped back. "I don't believe what I'm hearing."

"Well, what do you expect? It's like I'm not really a part of this family. Take last summer. You didn't tell me about what happened last summer. I had to hear it from Cooper Woods. How do you think that made me feel?"

Millie's voice softened. "Then you know about Leah."

"I do now. But why didn't I hear it from you?"

Millie lowered her eyes, whether in regret or sorrow, Iris couldn't tell. "Iris, I'm sorry. It wasn't something I meant to keep from you."

"But you did!"

Her mother did not answer, but turned on the faucet and stood, waiting for the water to warm. She picked up a cereal bowl and began rinsing it.

"You should have told me."

"I tried. Every time I asked you to come home, there was always an excuse. And things with you and your sister have always been so complicated, I don't know why."

"Because no matter what she does, you always protect her. You always choose Leah!"

With that the bowl slipped from Millie's grip. There was a splintering crash, and she spun around to face Iris. "I had no choice. Leah is not strong like you, Iris. Leah needs more from me. I protect her because I have to. Because I have to protect her from herself!"

Iris recoiled at her mother's expression, as shattered as the broken shard of pottery she still clasped.

It was then Iris noticed her mother's hand, streaked in red.

"Mom, your fingers. You're bleeding."

But Millie was too outraged to hear. Her voice stopped Iris dead in the middle of the kitchen. "Everything I've done is for both of you." Millie swept her arm toward the window, and the greenery beyond it, spots of blood dripping across the counter. "I built all of this for you kids."

"Mom," Iris pleaded, pointing toward her mother's hand.

"Your father and I spent the last forty years cultivating lives for you. And yet you two were so busy fighting, you couldn't look past yourselves to appreciate any of it. Even as adults, you fled the first chance you got. Keeping my grandchildren away from me. Like some kind of punishment." She pointed her bloody finger at Iris. "At least your sister came back. She may be troubled, but she trusted me enough to come home." And then her voice fell, along with her stare, as she noticed her hand. "I'm bleeding." Millie fell back against the sink in disbelief.

"It's okay, Mom." Iris moved quickly, grabbing the towel from the countertop. She took her mother's trembling hand, which still gripped the broken piece of china, in her own. "Let go of the bowl. I need to wrap your finger."

"I'm bleeding," her mother said again, her eyes wide and fearful.

Iris examined the cut, which was long and jagged, but not deep. She ran the faucet, holding her mother's shaking palm beneath the cold flow, watching the stream of pink liquid spill into the basin between them. "It's okay."

But Millie did not answer. She stood back, her arm rigid as Iris wrapped it tightly in a dishcloth and applied pressure.

Iris made herself look up at her mother, whose jaw trembled with effort.

"Make it stop," Millie whispered.

"I'm trying," Iris said softly. "I'm trying to, Mom."

◆　◆　◆

Her mother held the bandaged appendage protectively between them as she made her way about the house and farm stand, working one-handed throughout the day. Her adaptability and refusal to complain only added to Iris's guilt. But that was Iris's own affliction; Millie had not said any more to her on the matter, and instead had pressed forward, determined to dismiss the whole thing. Leah had fussed over their mother, asking Iris repeatedly, "What happened?" To which Millie curtly interjected, "It's nothing. I just dropped a bowl."

Bill had insisted Millie see the doctor. He'd driven the two of them into town, where they stayed for dinner afterward, returning to the house as the peepers were just beginning their evening interlude. Millie retired immediately to the sunroom.

"The doctor said it was just a nasty graze," Bill reassured Iris as she leaned against his bedroom door frame watching his end-of-day ritual, something she took deep comfort from. He took off his watch and set it on the dresser, then emptied the contents of his trouser pockets. A monogrammed handkerchief, which Iris found both old-fashioned and endearing; his wallet; a handful of change. "Your mother needs to slow down with this wedding stuff," he added, shaking his head wearily. "She's taking on too much."

Which made Iris stiffen; was it not her own "stuff" that had caused her mother's injury?

"Your sister is almost settled, at least," he said, bending stiffly to unlace his shoes. "I know your mother worries about her."

It was an opening, and Iris took it.

"Leah's not in great shape, Dad."

He did not reply, but moved his shoes neatly to the side of the dresser. If only he could arrange his children so easily. "I know, honey. We're trying." He, too, was weary from the effort, Iris realized. "Stephen will give her a good life, a stable life," he added. "She's a fortunate girl."

As we all are, Iris thought to herself. And she realized what Stephen represented—a rescuer of sorts, after a long labor of worry.

"What about you?" Bill asked, turning to her in the doorway.

"Me?"

"Yes. I haven't really had a chance to ask after you. Things have been somewhat . . ."

"Crazy," Iris said, finishing the thought for both of them. "I'm fine, Daddy."

Bill regarded her carefully. "You've been spending some time working on the barns, I've noticed. Quite a bit of time, in fact."

Iris's cheeks flushed deeply. It did not matter that she was a grown woman. Under her father's curious gaze, she was forever that knobby-kneed teenager who still found her father's approval essential.

"Yes, I have been spending time up there. I know it must seem strange, considering I've never swung a hammer or really built anything before." She smiled self-consciously.

"Well, there was that birdhouse."

She grinned gratefully. "Yes. The pink birdhouse." It was a Scout project the two had done, for a father-daughter badge. She doubted the Scouts even offered those these days, with the changing structure of modern families. But she remembered it well—she'd banged up most of her fingers with the hammer, and several of her dad's. He'd never complained, though. It had taken them a whole day to complete it. She'd set her heart on painting it pink, and her father had driven thirty miles outside of town to find a hardware store that could mix an all-season pastel oil paint.

Bill pulled a worn cotton button-down from his closet, as close as Bill got to loungewear. "I assume Cooper has taught you a lot, then." It wasn't a question. But in his statement, Iris heard all of her father's curiosities. As well as his concerns.

"It wasn't about Cooper, Dad. I needed a job. Outside of being a wife and a mom."

"You have your work," he reminded her gently.

"Outside of that, too. I needed to tackle something new, something physical. Everything I do requires thinking. And worrying. I just needed to build something." She paused. "And yes, Cooper taught me how."

Her father finished buttoning his shirt, and for the first time looked her directly in the eye.

"You're a big girl. But I guess I'll always see you as my little one."

Iris felt her eyes water. "I know, Dad."

Bill tucked in his shirt and shut the closet door gently, as if the matter were closed. "Arthur's reviewed the papers that Paul sent."

A breath escaped Iris's chest. "Oh. What did he say?"

Bill shrugged. "They're pretty standard; I'll go over it with you later. You'll need to think about property divisions, that sort of thing. The house." He paused. "And of course, the kids. Paul's proposed an equal split."

Iris wrapped her arms around herself. "I see." She had not wanted to read the divorce papers, had not wanted to speak of them even. But she was grateful her father had opened the matter, along with the envelope, for her. Now it was her turn to take over. "That sounds okay. I want the kids to see both of us, to keep things as normal for them as possible."

"Of course."

"Thank you," Iris said quietly. "I'll take a look at them. Are the papers in your study?"

"Another time," Bill said, sparing them both. He went to where Iris stood in the door and rested his hands on her shoulders. "It's been a long day."

Twenty-Three

"Done. *Finito*. Finis!" Trish slapped a thick packet of typed pages onto the café counter with gusto.

"Really? You finished the soup chapter?" Iris fingered the packet and then held it up, impressed.

"Two chapters," Trish corrected her. She placed a cup of coffee before Iris. "I added another on Crock-Pot dinners. Crock-Pots are a busy family's saviors."

"Brilliant!" Iris began to flip through the pages, pausing to ooh over a recipe for slow-cooked beef bourguignon. "I wish all my clients kept your pace. How'd you get all this done so fast?"

"Well, it was smooth sailing—once I got past my little nervous breakdown." She winked at Iris.

"What? Trish, I had no idea this was getting to be too much. Why didn't you tell me?"

Trish waved her hand dismissively. "Please. It was a good excuse to send Wayne and the kids out of my hair for a bit. Besides, it's not like you haven't got enough on your own plate."

Iris studied her carefully. "Are you sure you still want to do this?"

"Are you kidding? This has been one of the best things I've ever done. If you hadn't pushed me into this . . ."

"Pushed? Now you're giving me a complex."

Trish smiled. "Okay—let's say twisted my arm."

"Trish!"

"No, really. I've been meaning to apologize to you."

The sudden serious look on her friend's face caught Iris off guard. "What do you need to apologize for?"

"I've been an ass. Preaching to you all summer, trying to tell you how to get on with things. Maybe I should broaden my own horizons a bit, instead of hassling you so much about broadening yours. It never occurred to me until we started this book."

"Trish, you did not hassle me. You've been the best friend a girl could ask for. Steadfast. Honest."

"Oh, please, I can barely stand the sound of my own voice. Telling you to take better care of yourself. To chase your own dreams . . . I sound like a Disney commercial."

It was true: Trish had stayed on top of Iris about doing all of those things. But in the best of ways. Iris was confused.

"What's this really about?"

Trish paused. "I have to confess something. When you came home all busted up and hurting, my heart went out to you. It really did. But there was a small part of me—deep, deep down— that was sort of relieved. For once, you needed me." She winced as she said it.

"Trish, I've always needed you. We already talked about this. I'm the one who let the friendship slide these past years."

"Yeah, but I'm the one who sort of held a grudge. I think I was jealous."

"Jealous?"

"Because you were the one who got out of here. You went off to college in New York while I stayed home and went to UNH."

"So? You loved that school."

"Yeah, as much as I loved my high school sweetheart. Who I then married and raced home to have kids with. In the very same neighborhood I grew up in!" It was the closest thing to shamefaced Iris had ever seen her friend look. "Ech, I've turned into my mother."

Iris laughed. "Have not."

"But you couldn't be further from Millie. You lived in the city. Had a big, fat career. And still had a family. All while I was here pounding dough back at the homestead."

Now it was Iris's turn to make a face. "Are you kidding? From where I'm standing, you're the one who has it all. A great marriage. A family. Your own business."

"Yeah, but sometimes I wonder. What if I'd been more imaginative? Taken more risks?" She looked at Iris. "Like you did."

Iris was almost too touched to speak. "You know this book never would've happened without you."

"Well, that's true, of course. Seriously, though. I love Wayne and the kids, but sometimes I'd wake up at night and wonder if this was it. If this was as good as it'd ever get. And now, with this crazy book . . ." Her eyes filled with tears.

"Trish."

"You're okay, Iris. You're doing great on your own. I've got no business telling you what to do. Or *who* to do it with."

Iris wiped her own eyes. Here *she'd* been feeling like the loser who'd rolled home empty-handed, in need of Trish's ear and heart, as much as her key lime pie. "Thank you."

Iris reached over and pulled her in for a hug.

"But I'll be honest," Trish said. "Between this job and the kids . . . I don't know how real writers do it. I swear, I need one of those retreats where you escape, alone, to some mountainside cabin for three months where no member of your family is allowed."

Iris laughed. "That's just in the movies. But look at you. You did it anyway."

Trish shrugged humbly. "No big deal. The kids just haven't eaten in two weeks."

"Well, feed them well tonight, because I have some news." Iris tried to temper her own excitement. She was supposed to be the seasoned agent, after all. "I called Joan last night. The culinary publisher I told you about."

Trish raised her eyebrows. "And?"

It was no use. Iris dropped her agent guise like an ugly sweater. "She likes our concept. She's agreed to read it!"

"Holy crap!" Trish squealed, jumping up from her chair.

"But it doesn't mean anything yet," Iris cautioned, pulling her agent hat back on. "There are conditions."

"Such as?"

"Such as, she needs a proposal." Iris winced. "By Friday."

"This Friday?" Trish sputtered. "That's three days away. You never mentioned anything about a proposal!"

"Relax," Iris said. "I'll handle the proposal. It's just a write-up of our concept, with a little marketing insight about our intended audience. No biggie." Though it was a biggie, and the realization of their sudden deadline filled her with her own sense of panic.

Trish tightened her apron strings and took a deep breath. "Okay, Agent Standish. We can do this proposal thing. Or, at least, you can." She looked at Iris firmly. "Right?"

Iris nodded quickly. "Yes. Done it many times."

Trish paused, then leaned in to whisper, "I love this crazy book that you talked me into. And I love you." She leaned closer. "But if you screw up this proposal, don't even think about coming back here for your key lime fix."

"Understood."

Twenty-Four

Iris was driving back to the farm when her phone vibrated in her lap. She looked down and smiled.

"Can I take you to dinner?" Cooper's voice filled the spaces in her mind, pushing away the cookbook, the wedding, and all the other clutter.

Iris glanced at the historic houses as she drove out of the village center, trying to picture the two of them coming into town, like a regular couple on a regular date. "That'd be nice."

"How's seven? I'll come by the house."

Iris flinched. The house. Her mother and father's house. The image of a fresh-scrubbed Cooper knocking on Millie's door to ask permission to take her forty-year-old daughter out for a night on the town flashed in her mind.

"No!" she said. "I mean, why don't I meet you there?" Iris could see it now: Cooper knocks and the whole family flings the door open. Bill in his plaid nightshirt, blinking through his smudged glasses. Leah, scowling over his shoulder. But it was Millie's face that sealed the deal, with its guilt-inspiring force field that only her mother could engulf them in. No, Cooper Woods could not come pick her up at her parents' house. She wouldn't let him anywhere near that door.

"It's no big deal," Cooper said amicably.

Iris would have to spare him. Even if it meant bringing up

the almost-as-awful subject of where they stood. "The thing is, I don't know how my family would feel if they thought we were going out," Iris explained sheepishly. "I haven't exactly told them anything about us yet." She blushed deeply, realizing she was showing her cards. "That is, if there even is an 'us.' Not that we're officially together. But, you know . . ." Well, the whole deck of cards had fallen on the floor now.

"Well, then we definitely need to have dinner," Cooper said, his voice reassuring. "Seven o'clock at the Inn?"

Iris breathed a sigh of relief. "Seven o'clock, it is."

She was just pulling up to the house when the phone vibrated again. She swept it to her ear. "Let me guess, did you change your mind?" she joked.

"Mommy?"

For a second Iris was thrown. "Lily? Is that you, honey?"

"Of course it's me." Lily laughed. "Who else would it be?"

Iris didn't dare say. "No one I'd rather talk to," she allowed truthfully.

"I've got big news," Lily announced.

Iris went along, smiling at Lily's conspiratorial giggle. "You do? What is it?"

"Daddy said we can come up to the farm early! We're coming tomorrow!"

Iris squealed. "That's wonderful, honey. I can't wait!" It was the best kind of surprise.

"Oh, and I finished second place in the swim meet," Lily gushed. "I even got a trophy. It's not as big as Carly Watson's, she placed first. But it's gold."

Iris swiped at her eyes. "Oh, I'm so proud of you! Bring the trophy with you. Your grandparents will love to see it, too."

Sadie was more reserved than her sister when she came on the line next, but Iris was sure she detected a level of excitement in her voice, which was more than she'd heard all summer. "So, what are we going to do up there?" she wanted to know.

"Anything you want," Iris promised her. "We can swim and

take Grandpa's canoe out. I can't wait to show you Aunty Leah's gardens. Oh, and your junior bridesmaid gowns will be in!"

"Cool," Sadie said, and Iris was suddenly so grateful for this one-worded allowance.

There was no mistaking, however, the chilled reserve of Paul's communication.

"So, I guess you know the kids are coming up a few days early," he said. "Is this a good time?"

"Yes, I can't wait." Iris waited for him to continue, wondering suddenly at the changed date. The sooner the better. But was there another reason Paul was sending them up sooner than they'd planned? Like a reason with a name and a face?

Iris pushed the thought away in disgust and tried to focus on the logistics. After all, the kids couldn't exactly deliver themselves to New Hampshire. "And you?" she asked cautiously. "What's the plan?"

Paul's response was abrupt, like a Band-Aid being ripped off. "No plans. As soon as I drop them off, I'm coming back home."

"Of course." It was a stinging reminder, but Iris realized for the first time that she did not want it any other way. The terrain between them had changed. All she needed right now were the kids. She wouldn't wonder what he was doing back at home, alone. Or not.

"Did you receive the papers?" he asked.

Iris thought she heard the smallest tremor in his voice, but his directness left no room for empathy.

"I did, but I haven't looked them over yet. Dad wanted his attorney to review them first."

Paul chuckled. "You mean Arthur Bowen? That guy with the stutter from the golf club?"

Arthur, an old friend of Bill's who led a long-standing and well-respected firm in town, had assisted the family in their legal matters over the years just as happily as he had been to join them for dinner and drinks on any given weekend. Paul would remember him in the unkindest light, of course. Which made

Iris's response easier. "I have to protect myself," she replied curtly, reminding Paul that he was the enemy in all of this. "And the kids, too. We'll get to it when we have a chance."

"Whatever you say, Iris. See you tomorrow." And the line disconnected.

◆ ◆ ◆

The Inn at Hampstead was on the national historic registry, and it was one of Iris's favorite places. As kids, she and Leah had referred to it as the "wedding cake house," because of its expansive white facade and sweeping porches. The old Victorian rested on a hill at the northern end of town, overlooking one of the smaller lakes. Just beyond the Inn, a family-owned vineyard swept out behind it, like a lush green cape. As a child Iris had always imagined herself being married there outdoors among the gardens, instead of in the formal ballroom of the Copley Plaza in Boston, insisted upon by Paul's family, and as she walked up the flagstone path she couldn't help but feel significance in the fact that Cooper had chosen it as the site for their first real date.

The outdoor patio was open for summer dining, and she crossed her fingers, hoping he'd reserved a table for them there.

Iris found Cooper standing by one of the large white columns, just outside the main inn door. But she almost missed him, dressed in a navy sports coat and crisp khaki pants. Seeing her, he stepped forward and took her arm. "You look beautiful."

As they took their seats Iris tried to focus on the shimmering water views. To her surprise her hands trembled a little as she settled her napkin across her lap. Why was she suddenly feeling nervous? She had not hesitated when he leaned her against the truck and kissed her adamantly; she knew intimately the flat plain of his stomach, the curve of his neck where she rested her head when they held each other. But those were private moments, stolen in secret places around the farm. Where she didn't care that her hair was windblown or her fingernails had dirt beneath them. Here, sitting among other crisply dressed couples at the restaurant, she felt suddenly exposed.

When the waiter finished telling them the specials, she glanced shyly over her menu at Cooper.

"What's wrong?" he whispered.

Iris lifted one shoulder. "Nothing. This is perfect. It's just so . . ."

"Official? Like we're on a first date or something?" Cooper asked, as if reading her mind.

"Yes. But in a good way," she added quickly. "It feels like we're 'coming out' or something."

Cooper smiled. "I know. We should've gotten this out of the way a long time ago. Shall we order some wine?"

"Please!" Iris said with a laugh.

Two glasses later, they'd placed their orders, each for the lobster risotto. Iris settled back into her chair as the wine worked its magic.

"It's been quite a summer," she said, studying Cooper across the table. His normally tousled hair was styled close to his head, giving him an even more crisp appearance in the candlelight.

"It has," he agreed. "The best summer I can recall in a long time." He met Iris's gaze. "It's not over yet."

Even in the growing twilight, Iris was sure her blush was apparent. She turned to the water as relief filled her chest, knowing that Cooper felt the same way. And that he didn't want the summer to end, either. But there were certain things they couldn't avoid any longer.

"My kids are coming up," Iris said. "Tomorrow."

"Really? That's great. I didn't realize they'd be here so soon."

"Neither did I," Iris admitted. "But I'm excited. Other than their time at camp, I've never been away from them for more than a night or two before. It's been strange." She looked him in the eyes. "That first week of July, I didn't know what to do with myself. I'm not used to being alone, doing whatever I want, whenever I feel like it. As nice as it was," she added meaningfully.

230 • Hannah McKinnon

"You must've felt like you were missing a limb without them." Which Iris couldn't have described better herself. She smiled, grateful that, despite the fact that he had no children of his own, somehow Cooper seemed to understand.

"But it must've been good for you to have that time, too. To get a handle on things a little," he went on. He adjusted the napkin on his lap. "Splitting up with my ex was the hardest thing I went through. I don't know how people do it with kids." Cooper was treading carefully, but he wasn't shying away from the obvious. It was her chance to be honest with him.

"It's been awful," Iris admitted. "But I haven't exactly been home dealing with it, either. Being up here let me get back to myself in a way I would never have been able to do had I stayed at home." She paused, placing her hands on the table. "But I still have to go back and face the music at some point."

Cooper placed a hand on top of one of hers. "Iris, you do whatever you have to. What you're going through can chew a person up and spit them back out. Give yourself time."

"I know. I just want you to know that I'm really grateful to you." She hoped she was getting through; she didn't want to end what they had. In fact, she couldn't bear the thought of that. Did he understand?

Cooper pulled his hand away gently. "Look, it goes both ways. When Sherry and I divorced I thought I was done with all of this." He opened his arms, gesturing in a motion that circled the two of them. "I didn't think I'd ever feel something like this again."

Iris nodded eagerly.

"But I can't be selfish about it," Cooper continued. "I know what you're about to go through, probably better than you do. And I want you to know that if this is all we have, I'm okay with that."

Iris sat back, sifting through his words. They were not unkind. But she felt the sharp twist of disappointment.

"Besides," he added. "We come from really different places."

Iris laughed. "What are you saying? We both grew up here."

"You know what I mean." He looked out at the lake. "Your family is great. But I don't think your mother would approve of me."

Iris shook her head. "My mother doesn't approve of anyone. But she does like you, Cooper. You've done such great work for them."

"Exactly. I work for them."

"So? You're talented. You preserve history. You should take pride in that."

"I do. I lived differently in Colorado—I had the six-thousand-square-foot mountain house with the view, the cars, the ski condo. And the sixty-hour workweeks that kept me from enjoying any of it. I forgot what was real, living like that."

Iris had known Cooper had worked somehow in finance, but he'd never shared much about it. She hadn't realized that the sort of life he'd left behind was much like the life she lived now, in Boston.

Cooper leaned forward. "I like living simply now, Iris. I like waking up to the lake and working with my hands. And being my own boss. It's a rich life, by my definition. But there aren't any Mercedes parked in my driveway. And while I enjoy a round of golf, I don't plan on joining the club." He looked at her earnestly.

Iris flushed. She'd never felt that way about Cooper, and was flabbergasted that he was made to think she might because of the family she came from. "You can't honestly think that those things are important to me after spending the summer together?"

Cooper looked at her softly. "No, I don't think that. But you live a certain way and raise your family in a certain way in Boston, and while I can appreciate it, it's not something I can offer you. Whatever happens, we need to be realistic."

Iris sat back in her chair, touched. She loved this man for who he was, and for how openly he was offering himself to her. It didn't matter to her what kind of house he lived in, or what kind of car he drove. But he was right. It was a different life. Just as Millie had been hinting.

The waiter arrived with their lobster, which they ate over amicable small talk amid the other diners on the porch. But with each delicate bite of her dinner, Iris realized she could not be realistic. She couldn't help wanting to hang on to this. As she pretended to listen to Cooper talk about a restoration project he was bidding on in town, her mind wandered restlessly. Maybe they were too different. Maybe to him this was never more than a summer romance that he'd think back on fondly over the long winter months. Maybe she was completely delusional.

Dessert came, along with the growing darkness, and afterward they lingered on the porch sipping nightcaps. Cooper pulled his chair around near hers and settled his arm across her shoulders. "So, I guess this is our last night alone," he said.

"There'll be more," Iris replied, leaning over and resting her head on his shoulder. "We'll make time."

Cooper nodded in the growing darkness. "Of course we will."

Iris tried to breathe. The big issues were finally out in the open, at least for the most part. And as grateful as she was to have tied some of the loose ends, she couldn't help but feel the strands were hovering near, swirling in a disconcerting state, fluttering between them. How desperately she wanted to circle back with her nimble hands and tie up each and every one.

Twenty-Five

Lily Bean!" Iris was overcome as her younger daughter streaked across the lawn toward her. "Let me look at you," she cried, holding Lily at arm's length before pulling her in tight again. Lily's nose was densely freckled by summer, her face a tawny peach. Her braids were frayed and blonder than Iris recalled. "Oh, I've missed you."

"And you!" Iris exclaimed, releasing Lily and pulling Jack in. Jack wrapped his arms tightly around Iris's waist and held on. "My beautiful boy," she breathed, kissing his head.

"Okay, okay, Mom." He laughed.

Sadie strode calmly toward her, lips pressed together, but unmistakably pleased.

"Hi, Mom," she said, allowing Iris to pull her in for a hug.

"What did you do to your hair?" Iris asked, instantly regretting the words as soon as they'd popped out. Oh, why did she have to ruin the moment with her big mouth?

"What?" Sadie touched her head, as if trying to remember. "Oh, my haircut. But that was, like, forever ago." *Forever ago.* A time that suddenly presented itself in the form of freckled noses and strange haircuts.

"Well, I love it. It's super cute." It was a sophisticated cut, one she'd expect to see on a teenager. Which, she realized with suddenness, Sadie was, of course. Oh, this was harder than she'd thought.

Behind them the porch screen door slapped shut, followed by a chorus of greetings on the other side. She was glad her family had allowed her to keep the greeting to herself, if only for a moment. "Everyone's inside, waiting for you."

Iris let Sadie go ahead, watching the way she adjusted her messenger bag over her shoulder, tucking her hair carefully behind her ear as she always did, a ritual Iris had watched her perform whenever she dropped her off at the middle school door or at cheer practice. Iris smiled: she would never tire of looking at her children. Their simplest gestures, so familiar and comforting. It was only then she remembered Paul, who was now coming up the walkway.

Don't cross your arms, she reminded herself as he approached with the kids' bags. But her mind blanked. "You made good time," she said inanely.

"Hello, Iris." He stopped just short of her, Lily's pink Hello Kitty duffel dangling precariously from one shoulder. Iris took him in quickly, making mental note of his tan face. But his brow was furrowed. And were those circles under his eyes? She smiled tightly. Not her concern anymore.

"Let me help you with those." She reached forward awkwardly, but Paul shook his head.

"Thanks, I've got it. I'll just leave them on the porch, if that's okay."

They glanced simultaneously up at the porch in question, listening to the flow of laughter through the windows, and suddenly Iris understood. Paul would not be coming inside. "Well, sure. If that makes you more comfortable."

Iris stepped aside, allowing Paul a wide berth. She trailed him up the steps, useless and tentative. Why did she always feel this way in his presence? At the top of the stairs Paul dumped the bags like he was unloading a great burden, then turned, mopping his brow.

"Okay, then."

"Would you like a glass of water? Or maybe to freshen up before the long drive back?" Iris certainly didn't want Paul lingering any longer than necessary. But now here he was, and this was something they were going to have to figure out sooner or later. She supposed he should at least be able to relieve himself without animosity.

"No, thanks. I've got an iced latte in the car."

Iris frowned. Since when had Paul started drinking lattes? He hated coffee. *Not your concern*, she reminded herself. Again.

"Well, I think this is everything," he said, scanning the fallen luggage briskly. He turned to the stairs, pivoting away from her with a rush so intent, it drew her ire.

"Aren't you going to say good-bye?"

Paul paused on the top step, frowning.

"To the kids?" Iris clarified, with emphasis.

"I already did."

Just then the screen door creaked. Millie's voice was unusually neutral, as was her expression. "Hello, Paul."

"Hello, Millie," he said, caught in midescape. He reached to shake her hand with awkward formality. Millie accepted hesitantly.

Iris winced. It was all so weird.

"The kids want a farm tour," Millie said, turning to Iris. "Would you like us to wait for you?"

Iris wasn't sure if this interruption was a rescue offering or a quest to sate Millie's own curiosity about her son-in-law's presence, but she accepted it nonetheless. "Sure. I'll be right in. Would you send the kids out to say good-bye to their father?" *Their father*. Words so heavy on her tongue. Had she ever referred to him as anything but "Daddy" before? She certainly couldn't bring herself to use that term now.

"Have a safe drive, Paul," Millie said coolly. No offer to come inside, no offer of lemonade. At least her mother had made the decision for both of them.

Once more Iris and Paul were left alone, and it occurred to Iris that this was the first official "drop-off." The first baton in the passing-of-the-kids relay. It was suddenly too hot on the porch. But there was one more thing.

"Listen, Paul," she said. She crossed her arms, but hell, she'd allow herself that. There was no easy way to do this. "We need to figure this out."

And there it was again. The weary look, the rolling of the eyes. "Iris, Jesus. Can we just part peaceably?"

A small fire erupted in her chest, but she exhaled deeply. "Hang on. All I'm saying is we need to be able to talk to each other." She gestured inside. "*They* need us to work together. We're still their parents."

Paul sighed. "Of course we are, Iris. What is it you want from me?"

And the fire roared a little hotter. "Damn it, Paul," Iris hissed, stepping down the stairs past him. She indicated for him to follow. There was no way she was going to get into it in front of the family. "I just want to touch base about the kids. Why can't you do that without all this tension?"

Paul threw up his hands. "Because there is no talking to you about anything without tension."

She halted at their car. Correction: his car. "You know what, just forget it. I'm simply hoping for a little exchange here; you know, how the kids are. What they know. How we're planning on working this. Because summer ends in two weeks, Paul. And I'll be coming home."

His eyes widened slightly.

"Did you forget that small fact? It's my house, too. Until we decide what to do next."

Paul stared at the pavement, which suddenly felt unstable beneath Iris's flip-flops, as though it might open up and swallow them both.

"I sent you the papers, Iris."

"Fuck the papers!" She was yelling now. Score one for Paul. At least he'd had the sense to leave the crazy woman who yelled and cursed in her parents' driveway on a perfectly good summer day.

"At some point we have to talk, Paul. Really talk." Desperate, Iris grabbed his hand in her own, which only made Paul flinch. But she didn't let go. "You have to be able to look at me. Don't you think you owe me at least that much?"

Paul's gaze was flat. He'd shut down, she could see it already. Well, what had she expected? She dropped his hand and it swung loosely to his side. Like a puppet's. A hard, wooden-hearted puppet's. "Forget it. I thought maybe we could work this out, for the kids' sake. But if you can't even speak to me, then we are dead in the water. I'll make some calls and find a mediator."

At that Paul looked up. She was speaking his language now. "Iris," he said, pulling the car door open. "We are not getting back together. You have to accept that."

It was a slap in the face. The smug, sweaty bastard actually thought she was trying to get him to take her back.

"Are you kidding?" she sputtered. Now it was her turn to throw up her hands. "Oh, believe me, that is the last thing I want. We are over. So over. And I am fine with that now. In fact, I insist on it. Because you don't deserve me, Paul Whiting. You never have. But I got the best part of you." She jabbed her finger toward the house. "And those three kids are waiting for me inside."

With that, Iris spun on her heels. Toward her mother and father. Toward Leah, and her kids. To where all their misplaced regrets and good intentions awaited her, bound and imperfect, a family album made of glass. But a gift nonetheless.

◆　◆　◆

The kids provided needed entertainment. Lily zealously reconstructed her swim meets, acting out the final strokes of her triumphant races in the confines of the kitchen, bringing tears of laughter to Bill's eyes and a new smoothness to Millie's usually creased brow. Never one to sit out, Leah also jumped in, as if the youthful influx of energy in the house restored some integral part of her. Jack kept bringing in specimens from outdoors: frogs, grasshoppers, once even a mouse, which they all exclaimed over and made elaborate habitats for.

Even Sadie seemed to shed her teenage angst on the farm. Gone, for the moment, were the usual tensions between them. True, Sadie still sequestered herself to moments of solitude, retiring to Leah's hammock, where she rested all but her thumbs as she furiously texted friends back home. But even that was an increasing rarity.

At night, Iris tucked them all in as if they were small children. Jack had the pull-out sofa in the den, while the girls shared the antique four-poster bed in the guest room. It was an old ritual Iris was grateful they allowed her to perform. Perhaps it was the long farm days that tired them, their limbs and minds weary from sun and lake. Or maybe it was the fact that they'd missed their mother in their weeks apart, something Iris herself felt acutely. But there was a profound sweetness to this new evening routine that reminded Iris of their days as babies, and the physical closeness she'd then taken for granted. The way they used to sink against her, already limp with slumber, and how she was free to caress and marvel at them up close. It had been years since Sadie had allowed Iris any kind of proximity like that. Even Lily preferred a quick good night kiss at home, asking her mother to please leave her alone so she could finish her picture book, before turning out her own light. Now, after the sun set each night, she lay beside Jack on the pull-out couch, recounting the day's adventures. Then up the stairs she went, where Iris settled herself between her girls. Sadie to one side of her, with a book. Lily to the other, with her tattered yellow giraffe tucked under her chin. The bed creaked beneath the weight of the three of them, and Iris relished the sound. Sometimes they'd talk about the day; sometimes Iris read aloud to Lily, and Sadie, propped against the pillows beside them, set down her own book obligingly and listened along. It was these final hours that brought her the greatest peace. Just another reason Iris wished this summer would never end.

◆ ◆ ◆

"When can we go out on the boat?" Lily wanted to know one afternoon shortly after they'd arrived. Millie had driven the truck over to the farm stand, and Jack and Lily were busy stacking vegetable crates into the back, having just finished a day of sales.

"Yeah. I want to water-ski," Jack said.

"Well, Grandpa only has the dinghy. But you'd love that, too. How about it, Sadie?" Iris asked.

Sadie hesitated in midcount at the till, furrowing her brow as she wrote down the current dollar amount in hand. "Um, sure." She glanced up at them. "Unless you mean fishing."

"Why else would we take the boat out?" Lily asked.

Sadie rolled her eyes, resuming her count. "Gross. Rain check."

"More fish for me, then," Lily said.

Unlike Jack, who seemed to maintain Swiss neutrality by virtue of both being the sole boy and the middle child, the girls had a more complicated relationship. Sadie was often impatient, perceiving Lily's curiosity and wish to be included as intrusive. Lily was left feeling resentful, especially in the past year, as Iris watched helplessly, ducking in and out in her own attempt to mend their fences.

"It's so good to see the girls working together like this," she told Millie now, as they stood at the tailgate of the truck, watching the kids pack up the stand.

"Of course it is. Hard work is great for kids. It's what I've been trying to tell you for years." Millie was right, of course, and it filled Iris with guilt for staying away. And for inadvertently keeping the kids away from their grandparents and this place, which seemed so right for them all.

"Who's hungry?" Leah strode toward the truck, a bin full of fresh-picked eggplant in her arms. "I vote for eggplant Parmesan tonight."

"With extra cheese!" Jack chimed in. The four of them clambered into the bed of the truck, and Iris noticed the cash bin securely tucked against Sadie's side.

"Want me to take that in the cab for you?" Iris offered.

Sadie shook her head, all business. "I've got it. I still have to input today's profits in the books when we get back."

"When did you learn how to do that?"

"Mom. Please. Grandma showed me this morning."

"You learned all that in one day at the stand?"

Millie raised her eyebrows meaningfully at Iris as they climbed into the cab.

"I know, I know," Iris said. "Spare me the 'I told you so.'"

◆ ◆ ◆

Only one thing had been missing from her life these past few days. As they approached the smokehouse, and the kids' laughter rose up from the truck bed, Iris's tummy fluttered. Cooper was back. His truck was parked out front, though there was no sign of him. Since the kids arrived, Iris had not spoken to him. He'd told her he was taking a few days off on the farm to work on another project across town, and though she appreciated the uninterrupted reunion time, she couldn't help but wonder if it was purposeful on his part. And if so, what it meant for the two of them.

Iris did not ask Millie to stop, nor did Millie offer. Torn, Iris sat up straight for a better look out the window. Ignoring the nervousness that flooded her, just as she ignored the fact that her mother had accelerated, if only slightly.

As they passed, Cooper emerged from the smokehouse,

shading his eyes in the late-day sun. Too late, Iris raised her hand in greeting, wondering if he'd seen her. But it didn't matter. His focus was on the back of the truck, taking in the kids for the first time. As they rolled past, Iris craned her neck to watch out the cab window as Lily raised her hand and waved at the stranger by the smokehouse. As Cooper raised his own and waved back.

◆　◆　◆

After dinner, Iris went up to her room to make the call privately. But Cooper's voice mail picked up. "Hi," she said, "I guess you saw us drive by this afternoon. I didn't realize you'd be here. Anyway, I just wanted to check in." She paused. "I miss you."

Trish, however, wasn't as indecisive. "There's no reason for them to meet," she stated adamantly the next morning. Iris had brought the kids to the café to visit, and they'd made themselves right at home in a booth by the pastry display case. Lily and Jack went to work on their cupcakes as Sadie longingly watched the teenage crowd at a corner table.

"I'm not suggesting you hide Cooper," Trish whispered. "He works on the farm, after all. But until you figure out the next step for you, *and them*," she said, pointing discreetly at the kids, "there is no need. You've got enough on your plate. And so will they."

"I'm not going to introduce them *like that*," Iris said, mildly offended. "Do you think I'm an idiot?"

Trish smiled ruefully. "Only sometimes. But that's beside the point. You know what I mean. Just keep it neutral in their presence. They're here for their aunt's wedding. After that . . ."

Iris grimaced. "The real fun begins."

"Oh, come on." Trish squeezed her hand. "You're going to get through this. You all will." She glanced over at the kids. "It's so good to see them. You are one lucky dog, you know."

"I know. Well, I've gotta run. The girls have a dress fitting. Can you believe the wedding is next week?"

Trish screwed her lips together, her trademark face for deep thought. "How's the bride faring?"

"Okay, I think." It was true. Since the kids had arrived, Leah was like one herself. Kicking the soccer ball around the yard with Lily and Jack, stretching out on the dock with Sadie. Even Millie had seemed more relaxed. Iris was relieved. This time was theirs; it was what she'd come to think of as "the before." "The after," once the four of them returned to their real lives . . . well, that would come soon enough.

She checked her watch and tipped back her coffee. "Fitting time. Let's go, guys."

"Mom, no!" Jack groaned. "I am not going dress shopping. That is so not survivable."

Iris reached across the counter and swiped chocolate frosting off his upper lip. "What? You don't want to spend the day helping me pick out gowns and shoes? I was counting on your great taste."

Jack rolled his eyes.

"Relax, your grandpa is picking you up. He's taking you to the club, to play some golf. Is that 'survivable'?"

Jack breathed a sigh of relief. "Thank you."

"Send me a picture of the girls in those dresses," Trish said.

"Oh, I almost forgot. You and Wayne are coming to the rehearsal dinner at the club on Friday, right?"

Trish grimaced. "Wouldn't miss it for the world."

Iris planted a quick kiss on her cheek before dashing out the door. "I didn't think so."

◆　◆　◆

To their delight, Miss Patty fussed over the girls. She offered each one their own dressing room, and sailed in and out with accessories as if bestowing gifts upon royalty.

As they tried on their junior bridesmaid gowns privately, Iris settled onto the couch between her mother and Leah, who was already fidgeting with her camera, at the ready.

"Is this the first time they're seeing the dresses?" Millie asked.

"Leah sent us a magazine clipping," Iris said, thinking back to the one image of the dress they'd gotten in the mail. But she couldn't remember the details of the gown, so she was just as excited as Lily and Sadie to see the real thing.

"Excuse me," Miss Patty said, appearing with two pink shoe boxes. "What style footwear would you like them in?" She produced a ballet slipper flat from one box, and an open-toe with a sizable heel from the other.

"I can already tell you which one they're going to want," Leah said, smiling knowingly as she lifted the pair of heels out of the box.

"But they have to be able to walk down the aisle," Millie reminded them, ever the voice of reason. "Besides, I think the heels are too old for them."

"But they're so cute!" Leah cooed, running her finger over the tip of the heel, which Iris noticed for the first time was stitched with sequins. "Sadie will freak for these."

"A proven ankle-breaker," Millie cut in, plucking them out of Leah's hands.

"Whose ankle?" Leah demanded.

"Third-grade talent show," Millie replied indignantly, looking at Iris.

"Not my ankle!" Iris said. "What are you talking about?"

"Amanda Breckenworth. Remember? She toppled off the stage like a sack of potatoes. Hasn't walked the same since."

Iris and Leah burst into a fit of laughter.

"You can't be serious," Iris said.

"When was the last time you saw Amanda Breckenworth, anyway?" Leah demanded.

Millie shrugged dismissively. "It's true. Her mother tells me she still hobbles."

Iris held up her hands in mock surrender. "Better make it the ballet flats. Heaven forbid we burden them with a lifelong limp."

Lily swept the curtain aside and twirled out. "Ta-da!"

"Oh, Lils." The bodice was demure, a simple sleeveless shell in cream organza. But the bottom was a full skirt in pale pink that hit just above her knee. Tied around her waist was a delicate celadon ribbon, one of the wedding colors.

"Well," Millie said, coming to stand beside Iris. "Aren't you the belle of the ball."

Lily grinned from ear to ear, unable to contain her pleasure.

"And where's our other belle?" Leah called to the closed peach curtain on the other side of the mirror. "Sadie's is slightly more grown-up," she whispered to Iris. "I hope that's okay."

Sadie emerged from her dressing room with less flair than her little sister, but a grin to rival Lily's. "What do you think?"

Leah whistled. But Iris couldn't speak. The tears were already starting, and she swatted at them quickly, not wanting to embarrass Sadie. *But, just look at her . . .* she thought.

Sadie stood before them in a sleeveless silk dress. The top was a tank style like Lily's, but the skirt was long and straight, flowing like liquid below her knee. It highlighted her slender figure and the small curves that Iris noticed with a pang were starting to emerge.

"Don't move," Leah squealed, grabbing her camera from the couch. "Pictures!"

The kids smiled obligingly for their aunt, who ducked in and out snapping photos like the paparazzi.

But the laughter of the group escaped Iris, who felt transported, as if she were somehow watching this from some cosmic maternal distance. This time she did not roll her eyes when Miss Patty appeared and offered her the box of tissues. In fact, she took a handful as the girls stood in front of the mirror, admiring themselves and each other.

When Leah came to stand beside her, Iris reached for her hand and squeezed it. Hard.

"What is it?" Leah whispered, looking concerned.

The moment had deposited Iris firmly in the memory of

those back-to-school shopping trips, when she and Leah stood side by side in the same kind of mirror. Monkeying around, and laughing too loudly. Being scolded by their mother to "Stand up, stand still. Just stand, will you?" And the fun they'd had.

Iris shook her head, smiling. "Nothing. Just . . . thank you."

Twenty-Six

In the middle of the night Iris was awakened by the creaking of her bed. "Lils?" Iris murmured, still half-asleep. "Is that you?"

"It's me," Leah whispered.

Iris blinked, her eyes straining to focus in the darkness. For a mother, midnight awakenings usually signaled nightmares. Or throw-up. Iris turned over. "What's wrong?"

In reply Leah slid beneath the covers and looped her arm over Iris's side. "I'm sorry."

A lake breeze stirred the curtains. Outside a night owl called in the distance, its cry watery and distant.

"Can we talk?"

Iris glanced at the clock. *One thirty.* "Leah, it's—"

"I know. But I can't sleep."

Iris rolled back over to face her. "Is everything okay?"

Leah let out a breath. "I'm ready to tell you. About last summer."

Iris propped herself up on her elbow and sighed. The importance of her sister's visit weighed on the air between them. "Okay. I'm listening."

"When I came home last summer, it wasn't about the farm. It was to get away."

Iris's voice was still raspy with sleep, and she cleared her throat. "From what?"

"Everything. Myself, mostly." She paused. "I'd been working

at Yellowstone about five months, and I really liked it at first. Every day was something new. New visitors, new locations; it was *great*."

Iris nodded in the dark, remembering how Millie had gone on and on about Leah's national parks job whenever she called. It *had* sounded great, leaving Iris longing for such serene open spaces, trapped as she was by the confines of car-pool schedules and after-school sports. It had seemed a perfect match for her adventurous sister.

"But after a few months, I just felt empty. Like something was missing. There I was working on the trails, guiding people on day hikes and up to their camps. Nothing but wildlife and fields, and these huge blue skies. Iris, you can't believe how blue they were." Her voice trailed at the memory, and Iris lay quietly. "It should've been perfect."

"Maybe you were just homesick," Iris allowed.

"No, it was more than that. Like this itch inside me that I couldn't reach. I was lonely. I was edgy. No matter what I did, I just couldn't seem to shake it. Eventually I let the loneliness get the better of me. And I fell for someone I shouldn't have."

Leah sighed. "His name was Kurt. He'd been up in Alaska running adventure tours for this eco-tourism outfit, and he just reeked of perfection. Conservationist, outdoor adventurer, charmer. The park hired him to train us on backcountry guiding."

"So let me guess, you two hit it off?"

Leah laughed lightly. "No! I couldn't stand the guy at first. I thought he was cocky. Kurt had been all over the world; he spent winters skiing in Europe, and summers rafting in Costa Rica. There was even a rumor he'd been scouted for the Olympic downhill team, but walked away from it to climb Annapurna." Leah turned to Iris, an urgency in her whisper, as if they were still teenagers talking about a boy. "Kurt had this vibe, like he was untouchable, you know?"

Iris nodded. To her, Kurt didn't sound any different from any of Leah's other previous boyfriends. "He was a hotshot."

"And he knew it. So he showed up to train us for backcountry guiding, and everyone was scrambling to sign up. Then they'd come back from his workshops, and they'd be gushing. By the time my boss made me sign up for the last session, Kurt had a gaggle of groupies. I was over it."

"So why the change of heart?" Iris asked.

Leah sighed. "Because once we were out on the trail, I realized why everyone was so smitten. Kurt was . . . amazing." Iris tried to keep an open mind as she waited for Leah to go on. This time she really wanted to understand. "He wasn't just a talented guide; he was a pretty great guy, too. We stayed up late each night talking about our childhoods, all the places he'd been. And the things we wanted to do with our lives. By the time our workshop ended, I found myself not wanting to go back to the lodge. I could've stayed out there on the land with him all summer."

"Is that when you guys got together?"

Leah's tongue clicked in the darkness. "*No*. We were with a group of my colleagues, Iris. Working."

"Sorry. I didn't mean . . ."

Leah rolled away from her. "We didn't hook up until the workshop ended. Kurt had only three days' layover before he had to head out to Yosemite for another gig. We didn't leave each other's side once."

Iris nodded in silence, imagining how easy it would have been. Romantic, even. A young, charismatic guy traveling from park to park, teaching others to save the world. Flying in long enough to shake things up for the staff, then heading off into the sunset. It was something out of a bad romance novel, and yet she got it.

"Did you ever see him again?"

"Once. I flew out to Yosemite, a couple of weeks later, like we'd planned. When I got there, we just picked up where we left off. He took me on this camping trip up in the High Sierra Camps, just the two of us. It was so secluded. We swam naked in the freshwater pools. We couldn't get enough of each other." Leah's voice trembled. "I really thought that this was it. That he was the one."

Iris turned over, studying Leah in the shadows. Her dark hair spilled across the pillowcase, in contrast to the pale oval of her face.

"What happened?" Iris asked, resting her cheek on her pillow.

Leah sniffed. "Kurt had to leave for another job up north. He promised we'd meet up a month later back at Yellowstone, when he got some time off. He even bought the plane ticket." She covered her face in her hands. "But he never came."

Iris lifted herself onto her elbow and cupped Leah's cheek, now damp with tears. "Leah. I had no idea you'd lost someone you loved that much."

"It's not that. It's much worse."

"What then?"

"You're going to hate me, Iris."

"Of course I won't. Just tell me."

Leah looked up at her. "I was pregnant."

A small throb began at the back of Iris's head and she lay down. Leah was pregnant. She'd heard the words. But it wasn't "pregnant" that caused her to suck in her breath. It was the word that came before it: that sneaking past tense.

Leah sat up in the bed. "You see? I knew you wouldn't forgive me. I don't expect you to."

Iris did not answer. Could not answer right away. Leah had been pregnant. And here was Iris, who'd struggled so long to conceive. Who'd fought so hard for her own babies. Instinctively, she ran a hand over the softness of her stomach.

"Please don't judge me," Leah cried.

Iris blinked. "I don't hate you. I just need a second." She rolled away and out of the bed, and padded to the bathroom. She ran the water in the sink and splashed her face, willing herself to feel something. What? Anger? Empathy?

Leah's voice came from the bedroom thick with regret. "I know this is hard for you to hear. But you asked me. All summer you've been asking me."

Iris shut off the water and came back to the bed. But she did not get in.

"Keep going," she said.

Leah was sitting up in bed now, her knees pulled protectively to her chest. "Are you sure?"

Iris sat back on the crumpled window seat cushion and steadied herself. "Keep going."

Leah looked at her warily before beginning again. "I didn't know I was pregnant until I got back to Yellowstone. I didn't want to tell Kurt on the phone. So I decided to wait until he came out. But he kept making excuses, changing the date. Weeks were passing. Finally, I had no choice. I just told him."

Iris waited for her to continue.

Leah's voice caught in her throat. "That's the worst part. He didn't say anything. I just sat there on the phone, saying, 'Kurt? Are you there?' Until he finally answered. And you know the first thing he said?"

"What?" Iris held her breath.

"He asked, 'What makes you so sure it's mine?'"

Iris stood up and went to the bed, pulling Leah against her.

"I was all alone, Iris. I had no one."

Iris did not say that Leah had *her*. That if she'd called, Iris would have flown to wherever she was, no matter the years, no matter the rifts. It was too late for that now.

"After that he stopped returning my calls. I emailed, and left messages with his coworkers, everything. I went crazy, Iris. I really did."

Iris pushed the hair out of her sister's face. "Is that why you came home?"

"I was pregnant. I had nowhere else to go."

It all made sense now. Millie's furtive protectiveness, Leah's shifting facades. Iris imagined her own pregnancies, which had left her both elated and fearful, after years of trying so hard to conceive. But even amid the strain, she'd had Paul and her friends' and family's excitement. Not to mention a petal-pink nursery teeming with baby gifts. She'd crafted the perfect little nest. Imagining Leah, alone at Yellowstone, made her heart ache. She pictured her sharing a dorm room bunk with a bunch of twentysomethings, her only belongings a mountain bike and a knapsack. "It must have been awful."

"I didn't tell anyone at first, I was just so ashamed. Mom and Dad couldn't understand why I'd left Yellowstone, or what I was doing here. Dad was supportive, of course, thinking I was just between jobs. But Mom knew something was up. She never said, but I sensed it."

Iris laughed harshly, as she ran her hands through Leah's hair. "Oh, I can only imagine."

"By then I was almost three months along. I couldn't hide it much longer, but I still wasn't sure what to do. I mean, I thought hard about having this baby, Iris. I really did."

"You don't owe me an explanation."

Leah sat up. "But I feel like I do. I wanted that baby. When I first found out, I actually thought Kurt would be thrilled. Which probably sounds stupid to you."

"No," Iris said quickly.

"Well, it sounds stupid to me now. But if you knew the things Kurt promised . . . I would have had that baby. I would have." Leah paused. "But then he was gone. I had no house, no job. Christ, I was back home, tucked in my childhood bedroom, living with my parents." Leah looked hard at Iris. "I tried to think of a million ways I could do this. But I just couldn't. I'm not like you."

"What does that mean?"

"You're strong, Iris. You can handle things."

"You were in a totally different situation," Iris insisted. "You can't compare a divorce with a child. Who knows what I would have done, if it were me?"

"No." Leah shook her head adamantly. "I thought about you through all of this. Strangely, I probably thought more about you than the baby or myself."

"Why?"

"Because deep down, even though I knew I had plenty of reasons I couldn't make this work, I knew you would've. Somehow, you would've found a way."

Iris sat back against the pillows. "You don't know that," she whispered. "You did what you felt you had to."

"But I always wished I had your strength. I've always been sorry I didn't."

"You can still have your baby. With Stephen. Starting a family with you is all he's talked about since I met him."

Leah pressed a hand to her eyes, shaking her head. "That's the worst part."

"What do you mean?"

"I can't have another baby, Iris. Ever."

Iris sat up, her throat catching.

"After I had the abortion, there were complications. First I had these horrible cramps. But then the fever followed, and I knew something was wrong. Mom drove me to the doctor's and that's when I found out." She looked at Iris, tears spilling down her face. "It wasn't just an infection. I had cervical damage. I can't carry a baby."

Iris was too stunned to answer. As hard as it had always been to imagine Leah as a mother, she'd always assumed she would be someday. When she found the right person. When she found herself.

"Are you sure?" she asked now, unable to give in just yet. "Have you had a second opinion? There are amazing treatments they can offer these days . . ."

"No, we're sure. I've been to three different doctors in New Hampshire and a fertility specialist in Manhattan. Both the cervix and the uterus were lacerated. I'm what they call 'incompetent.'" She laughed grotesquely.

"Leah, there are still ways you can become a mother. A surrogate. Adoption."

Leah nodded wearily. "Yeah, I know. But it's not the same, is it?"

Iris couldn't answer that. "Stephen doesn't know any of this, does he?"

Leah shook her head shamefully. "No. None of it."

Iris lay back down on the bed. So there it was. "God, Leah, you're marrying him in a matter of days. How can you not tell him?"

"I know. I tried. But each time something else always came up. The job at the foundation. The move to Seattle. It was already so complicated."

"But all he talks about is starting a family with you. He wants kids. What are you going to do?"

"It will kill him if I tell him now."

"But what do you think will happen if you wait? Did you think it'd be easier once you were married? At best, he's liable to feel tricked." At this late hour it was a lot to expect of any guy, even Stephen.

Leah's voice thickened with defense. "I told you, I tried. But I knew the second I opened my mouth, everything would change. After all I went through, why not hang on to normal?"

Now look at them, Iris thought. One sister who'd chased *normal* her whole life was ultimately losing it in divorce. And the other, who'd never wanted it, clinging to it by mere threads.

"What about Mom. How much does she know?" Iris thought back to the confrontation in the kitchen, her mother's bloodied hand.

"She knows. The night it all came to a head I was out on the lake. With—"

"Cooper." Iris said the name and her heart skipped. It had to have been the same night.

"How did you know that?" Leah sat up, about to say something more, then stopped. "Of course."

Iris's head spun as it came together. Cooper told her about the night on the boat. But had he known more? "Wait. He never told me about your pregnancy."

"Cooper never knew." Leah turned to look at Iris. "And I don't want him to. Or anyone else for that matter."

"Of course not." But the tiny relief Iris felt over the fact that Cooper had indeed conveyed everything wasn't enough to quell the deep regret she felt for Leah. It was sad enough that she could not bear her own children. But what would that mean to Stephen?

"Dad doesn't know, either. We told him I'd had some female issues and left it at that. He would've been so disappointed, you know? I made Mom promise not to tell him."

Iris wondered at this. What did you do when your child asked you to keep a secret from your spouse? Her mother was strong, fierce even. But had Millie really kept the secret from Bill? It was ironic, when Iris thought about it. Of her two parents, Bill was the patient, forgiving one who'd always listened in earnest and responded with calm. And yet here was Millie, the parent whom Iris had always feared most about disappointing, picking up the pieces for Leah. Asking no questions, guarding her secret. "Does Mom know that you haven't told Stephen?"

"No. It was hard enough for her to deal with everything as it was. We've never discussed it since. Besides, Stephen wasn't in the picture back then. I guess she assumes that he knows now."

Iris closed her eyes. So. At least Millie wasn't guilty of helping Leah keep the secret from Stephen. It was one thing to protect family privacy; another thing entirely to knowingly deceive. More and more, Iris was beginning to understand the gray shadows that motherhood cast.

"You have to tell him. Before the wedding, Leah. It's not too late."

Leah's voice was small, muffled now. "I know." Then, "Iris?"

"Yeah?"

"I'm sorry. For everything."

Iris placed a hand on her sister's shoulder. "Me, too."

Iris leaned against the cool headboard and closed her eyes. Was Leah right? Would she, in fact, have had the baby against all those odds? What if she had never been settled and married? Would she still have wanted a baby so badly that she'd put herself and a new child through a completely different set of struggles? She covered her face with her hands. They were impossible questions.

Leah needed her. Iris wiped her eyes and turned to her sister. "Leah?"

Leah had rolled onto her back, her expression soft with sleep.

Iris slid beneath the covers. She watched her little sister, the images of their pasts playing over and over in her head like a reel of film.

Gently, Iris bent forward and kissed her once. Leah's forehead was damp, like her daughters' in sleep; familiar and earthy. "I forgive you," she whispered.

She would do whatever Leah asked. Not because it was right, but because she had promised to get on board. Never mind that the train was on fire. If Leah wanted them to ride it down the tracks, so they would. Flames and all.

◆ ◆ ◆

Too soon, sunlight spilled through the windows, illuminating the bedroom in a glaring light. Iris blinked, shielding her eyes. She turned over.

The other side of the bed was empty, the covers neatly tucked beneath the pillow. For a moment she wondered if she had only dreamed the previous night. She wished it were so simple.

Twenty-Seven

W ho is that?" Lily asked.

Iris had taken the kids to work the farm stand with her on Monday morning. It was a welcome respite from the house, where Leah's confession still hovered heavily. The weight of the intimacy had left her feeling breathless, though she embraced their newfound closeness. It was a relief when she heard that Leah had gone to Brewster for the day to meet one of her other bridesmaids for lunch, leaving Iris and the kids to run the farm stand. Weekday mornings were the quietest times on the farm. Quiet aside from Lily, who'd been entertaining them with a loud rendition of "The Sound of Music," a song she'd favored since her second-grade musical that spring.

"Damn it, Lily, you made me lose count again," Sadie snapped.

"Language!" Iris warned, glaring at Sadie. "Since when do you talk like that?"

Jack smirked. "Since always."

Sadie shot him a look. "Well, she never shuts up."

"Sadie!" Iris relieved her of the bills and tucked them back into the register. She turned to Lily. "Sweetie, I love listening to you sing."

But Lily wasn't paying attention. Her eyes were fixed on the farm driveway. "Here he comes now," she informed them.

"*Here he comes . . .*" Sadie mimicked under her breath.

Iris resisted the urge to poke her, offering her a warning look instead.

But it was she who needed to be poked when she looked up and realized who their first customer of the day was.

"Cooper! What are you doing here?"

"You know him?" Lily asked.

"Good morning." Cooper smiled broadly at the kids. If he'd heard their little argument, he didn't let on.

"Kids, this is Cooper Woods. He works for your grandmother."

"You're the barn guy," Lily said brightly. She shook his hand vigorously, which delighted him. "I'm Lily." She rolled her eyes. "*That's* Sadie. And that's Jack."

Cooper extended his hand first to Jack, then to Sadie, who shook it dismissively, her attention still focused on the till. "Can I finish counting the cash now?" she groaned.

"*Later*," Iris warned, between her teeth. She turned back to Cooper, somewhat flustered. "I'm glad you came by. How are things?"

Cooper held up a reusable cloth bag he'd filled with peppers and tomatoes. "Good. I'm having a little dinner party tonight. Figured I'd better stock up."

Party? Iris's mind flashed. He hadn't mentioned anything about a party to her. She'd certainly received no invitation.

Lily peered into Cooper's bag, inspecting his produce with a discriminating frown. "The yellow squash is okay," she informed him. "If you put *a lot* of butter on it. But the green squash? Gross!" She made a dramatic gagging face.

"Okay, okay," Iris interrupted, redirecting Lily to some fruit crates that needed stacking. "So. A dinner party."

Cooper nodded, his eyes crinkling with laughter as he watched Lily toss a crate in the air and catch it, returning to her *Sound of Music* rendition.

"What have you got on the menu for your party?" Iris blurted, trying to get his attention. Then, to her instant embarrassment, "And who's coming?"

Which got everyone's attention. It was none of her business of course.

"It's just a little barbecue for my dad. It's his birthday."

"Oh, a birthday!" Iris sputtered. "That's great. That's just amazing." *Amazing?* Now Sadie was staring at her.

"It's just a few neighbors stopping by. Most over the age of sixty," he added with a smile.

"Of course." Iris laughed, dismissing the whole thing with a futile wave of her hand. "Amazing." There she went again.

"Why don't I ring you up?" Sadie intervened. She relieved Cooper of his bag and added up the produce authoritatively, a move so uncharacteristic it was Iris's turn to stare.

"Well, I guess I'll see you around," he said finally. "It was nice to meet you kids."

Iris nodded, wringing her hands. There was so much she wanted to say, but not now. Not with Sadie watching her like that.

"Wait," Lily called after him. "Is that boat yours?"

She pointed to the boat on the trailer, hitched behind Cooper's truck. Until then, Iris hadn't even noticed.

"Yes, it is."

"Cool. Can you take us for a ride in it?"

"Lily!" Jack scolded. But Iris could tell he was wondering the same thing.

Iris tugged gently on Lily's braid. "You can't just invite yourself on someone's boat."

"He works here. So he's not just *someone*," Lily said.

Oh, if you only knew, Iris thought, a sudden stab of guilt hitting her in the middle.

"It's okay," Cooper insisted. "I like a girl with gusto."

"Sorry," Iris said, pulling Lily against her. "We're seven. We get ahead of ourselves sometimes."

"Seven? That's my favorite number," he told Lily, who'd ducked her chin in embarrassment.

Lily brightened. "Really? Mine's eleven. There's this girl in my class who has eleven cats." She wrinkled her nose. "But eleven dogs would be way better."

Cooper chuckled. "Well, I don't have any dogs. Or cats, for that matter. But I do have a boat. And I'd be happy to take you out on the lake. All of you," he added, glancing over Iris's shoulder at the others.

Jack pumped the air. "Cool!"

"You really don't have to," Iris told Cooper. This was already awkward enough, with Cooper on one side of the cash register and her kids on the other, her mother's vegetables between them. Again, Trish's words rang firmly in her ears: *There is no reason for them to interact!*

But of course Cooper couldn't hear them. "It's settled. How about tomorrow?"

◆ ◆ ◆

Tomorrow came too soon. Iris hurried the kids through breakfast, nervously packing totes with towels, sunscreen, and bottles of water.

"Where are you going?" Leah asked.

Iris hadn't yet figured out a way to share this bit of news. She wasn't exactly sure how she felt about it herself. "Out on the lake. Cooper invited the kids on his boat."

Leah raised her eyebrows. "Really?"

But it was Millie who verbalized Iris's most pressing thought. "Is that a good idea?"

Iris sighed, focusing on the cap of sunscreen she was struggling to open. "It's just a boat ride, Mom."

"But, I don't think—"

They were interrupted by Sadie, who sauntered into the kitchen, causing Millie to snap her mouth shut like a small purse.

Iris swallowed.

"Where did you get that suit?"

Sadie lifted one shoulder and breezed past, pretending not to know what all the fuss was about. But there was no getting around the minuscule bathing attire in question. Sadie's black triangle bikini top looked more like two eye patches held together by a mere thread. A short canary-yellow wrap hung loosely across her rear end, which she thrust to the side as she placed a hand on her hip. "What?"

It was an invitation Iris was going to have to accept. A hush settled over the kitchen.

Leah feigned sudden interest in the newspaper.

"I think I'll hit these dishes," Millie announced, turning abruptly to the sink, where she immersed a perfectly clean stack of plates back into the dirty water.

"Sadie." Iris breathed evenly, trying to keep her cool. "I don't know where it came from, but there is no way you are going out in that bathing suit."

"What's the big deal?" Sadie's eyes flashed with defiance as she reached for a coffee mug on the sideboard and dumped in the remains of the pot.

Jack strolled into the kitchen and grabbed an apple from the bowl. One look at the simmering expressions between his mother and Sadie, and he turned on his heel.

"And since when do you drink coffee?" Iris plucked the mug from her hands.

"Dad lets me!" Sadie sputtered, the little girl still in her fighting to hold back tears.

Iris gripped the cup, taking in her thirteen-year-old daughter. The trembling lips, the small bikini-clad bust. It was the most awkward of teenage stages and her heart ached for Sadie. But not enough to hand over the mug. And *certainly* not enough to bend to the bikini.

"You can drink coffee when you go to college," Iris said matter-of-factly, placing the cup back on the shelf.

"Um, is there coffee in that mug?" Millie asked.

But both Iris and Sadie were too entrenched to notice. "Well, I'm not changing," Sadie said, crossing her arms. Her expression was steel.

"Then you're not coming out on the boat." Iris crossed her own arms, then uncrossed them. "Sadie. Honey. You look nice in the suit, but it's just not appropriate. It's too . . ."

"*Slutty?*"

All three women swiveled at the word.

"Sadie Marie Whiting. Don't you ever use that word." Iris paused for effect. "And in your grandmother's house!" It was reaching, but Iris needed all the leverage she could grasp.

Sadie glanced nervously over her shoulder at Millie, as if remembering the ground she was staking was not her own. But she didn't budge.

"Now, go take that suit off!" Iris shouted.

Sadie narrowed her eyes as if she was about to say something truly hateful. Something that would lodge right in her mother's chest. Iris braced herself. But instead Sadie stormed through the kitchen and back upstairs. "Daddy let me wear it all summer!"

Iris remained in the kitchen, hands shaking. "Well, your daddy is an idiot," she muttered.

Leah spoke first. "Well done."

Iris swiped at her brow, which had begun to sweat.

"You had to say it," Millie said. She handed Iris the dish towel that up until then she'd been wringing in her own hands.

Iris mopped her forehead. "Was I ever like that?" she asked, looking at Millie.

Her mother frowned, cocking her head to the side as she recalled. "No," she said finally. She pointed to Leah. "But *you* were."

And just like that the tension fell away. "Me?" Leah squealed, putting a hand innocently to her chest.

"Oh, please. You wore some awful things."

"Like what?"

"Don't you remember that lace underwear set you came home with from the mall one day?" Millie asked her.

"I do not," Leah said defiantly, but she was smiling now, too.

"I remember that!" Iris said, joining in. "It looked like something from the pages of *Playboy*."

Millie closed her eyes, shuddering. "Red, no less."

"Hooker red," Iris clarified.

Leah blushed. "I don't know what you people are talking about."

"I found it in your laundry basket," Millie reminded her. She took a seat at the table, directly across from Leah. "You denied everything, of course."

"Still does," Iris said, unable to resist.

Leah stuck out her tongue.

"But the worst part"—Millie chuckled, pausing to regain her composure—"was when your father found it."

"What?" Leah shrieked. "You never told me that part!"

"Well, of course not. How could I?"

Iris was beside herself at the mere idea of it. "Daddy saw the hooker suit? What'd he say?" She was practically choking on the laughter that rose up in her throat.

"I can't listen to this!" Leah cried, standing up. But Iris grabbed ahold of her arm.

"It was terrible," Millie continued. "I'd thrown it in the back of my closet, fully intending to toss it right in the trash after I confronted you. But then your father stumbled across it when he was getting dressed one morning."

"Oh. My. God." Leah's face was as red as the lingerie in question.

"What did you tell him?" Iris wanted to know.

Millie put a tentative hand to her mouth and winced. "That it was mine."

"You didn't!" the sisters screamed in unison.

"Well, I certainly couldn't tell him it was his fifteen-year-old daughter's!" Millie cried. "Of course, once he saw it, that presented another problem . . ."

"Tell me you did not try it on for Dad!" Leah cried.

"Please," Millie said, adjusting her posture and placing her hands primly in her lap. "I told him the color was simply not me. And that I'd have to return it." She glanced at them sideways. "Though he did look a little disappointed."

"Eeew!" Iris cried, and the three women fell into a fit of giggles.

Just then, there was a loud knock on the door. They all jumped.

Cooper Woods poked his head in. "Sorry," he said, looking at the three of them uncertainly. "I knocked, but I guess you didn't hear me."

Iris leaped up. "Come on in. We're almost ready."

Cooper sat down at the table, looking a little like he'd have been more comfortable waiting outside.

Millie studied him a moment. "So, you're going out on the boat with my grandchildren today?"

Iris grimaced in anticipation of yet another awkward confrontation.

But to her surprise Cooper settled back easily into the Windsor chair. "We are. It's supposed to be a beautiful day. In fact, would you ladies like to join us?"

Disarmed, Millie missed a beat. "Oh. That's very nice of you, but I couldn't. The Willetses are returning from Maine tomorrow, and I need to get the house in order. But thank you."

"Yeah, too much work to do," Leah added, glancing at Iris for confirmation.

"It's just a slow spin around the cove," Cooper said. "I've packed plenty of sandwiches. Some watermelon, and iced tea."

Iris, who still stood on alert in the doorway, was touched. "You did all that?"

Cooper nodded. "Come on," he said again. "There's room for everyone."

As much as the thought of being stuck on a boat between her family and Cooper might have terrified her earlier, the idea was suddenly seeming rather organic. It would be good for all of them to get off the farm for a day, away from the wedding planning and the ghosts of their past.

"Come on, Leah. It'd be fun."

Leah shrugged. "As long as we're not intruding. How about you, Mom?"

"Well." Millie paused, her cheeks still flushed from all the laughter. "The Willetses won't be back until tomorrow. I suppose a little outing wouldn't hurt."

Cooper clapped his hands. "Invite Bill, too," he said. "We'll make it a boating party."

"Party?" Lily skipped into the kitchen, her Hello Kitty bag swung over her shoulder. "Who's having a party?"

Cooper grinned at her. "We are!" he said. "Go get your grandpa."

Twenty-Eight

Cooper was right about the gorgeous day, but for more than the simple reason of the weather. They'd driven to the south edge of town, to the much larger Lake Wapusk, where motorboats were permitted. Bill had seemed delighted at the invitation, and was sporting a pair of faded seersucker swim trunks in the kitchen before the rest of them were even nearly ready to go. Sadie had finally given in and changed into another suit, though she still was not speaking to her mother. Her hot-pink bandeau top was hardly a measurable improvement as far as Iris was concerned, but she wasn't about to pick another battle. Besides, as much as she'd regretted their confrontation in the kitchen, it did have its silver lining. It was probably the first time all summer that Iris, Leah, and her mother had laughed like that together. Probably the first time in years, in fact, and Iris wouldn't have traded that for anything, not even for a Puritanesque one-piece for her stubborn teenager.

Now, as they moved into the lake, Cooper and Bill sat in the captain's chairs, and the rest of them lounged on the cushioned seats in the back. Iris leaned over, letting the water spray her cheeks as they powered out.

"Where are we going?" Jack shouted above the roar of the engine.

"Anywhere you want," Cooper shouted back to him.

Iris smiled, pleased that he was so inclusive of the kids. He wasn't trying too hard. Just being himself provided a much-needed bright spot. Even Millie, in her wide-brimmed straw hat, looked pleased. Iris closed her eyes, leaning against the seat, as the kids oohed and aahed at the old mansions along the shoreline that Leah pointed out to them.

When they reached the middle of the lake, Cooper cut the engine, allowing the boat to rock gently. He hopped to the stern and tossed the anchor in. "Who's up for a swim?"

Jack leaped up. "Looks like it's just you and me," Cooper said to him, tugging off his T-shirt.

Iris studied the freckles running across his tanned shoulders, the same ones she'd traced with her hands just last Saturday after their dinner at the Inn, but which now seemed like a lifetime ago. The recent physical distance between them was disconcerting, and yet in the presence of her family she felt the urge to press her finger to one of those freckles now. Hyperaware of her feelings, she fought the urge to tug his T-shirt right back over his bare chest and cover the man up.

In one swift launch, Cooper was off the boat, followed by Jack, who mimicked his technique.

"Can I go in now?" Lily asked, climbing gingerly up over the seats to the ladder.

"Wait for me," Iris told her, digging through her swim bag. Where was the sunscreen?

"Oh, come on, I just finished second place at swim camp," Lily complained.

"Yeah, Mom. Geez," Leah teased as she made her way to the boat ladder. "I'll take her."

"Okay," Iris said hesitantly, "but stay by her. It's deep out here."

"Dive or cannonball?" Leah asked Lily.

"Definitely cannonball!" Before Iris could object, Lily sprang away from the boat and landed with a small splash. Iris held her breath until she erupted to a chorus of cheers.

"See?" Lily called to her defiantly.

"Good job, baby."

Leah followed suit, diving clear off the back in a clean arc, splitting the surface of the lake with barely a ripple.

"Now it's Mom's turn," Leah called out.

"Yeah! Mom's turn!" Lily echoed.

Great. Iris made her way to the ladder and looked down at the four expectant faces, treading alongside one another. The water looked cold, and she felt utterly exposed standing over them.

"You can do it," Cooper encouraged.

"Mom doesn't cannonball!" Lily laughed loudly.

Had Iris really never cannonballed on a hot summer day with her kids? Why was it that she wasn't the "fun one" more often?

"I do, too!" Iris insisted. "I used to do a mean one." Well— thirty years ago.

Even Sadie looked up from her magazine when she heard that.

Below her, Lily's sunscreened nose wrinkled with skepticism.

That did it. Iris whipped off the sarong she'd tied to her waist. "You asked for it!"

As Iris drew herself up, it all came back to her. The heady anticipation of flight. The feeling of sheer weightlessness as she sprang into the air. The blast of cold water.

"Wow!" Lily shrieked as Iris popped up at the surface. "That was so cool, Mom."

Iris swam up to her, nose to nose. She grinned. "There are lots of things your mom can do."

She tipped her head back, relishing the pull of her limbs as they moved beneath her treading water. Cooper swam over.

"Full of surprises," he whispered.

◆　◆　◆

There was no hunger like that after a swim in cold water. Back on the boat Cooper passed out sandwiches and iced tea. Briefly, Iris worried that he wouldn't have packed enough, having no experience feeding a large family. But she was pleasantly surprised.

There was plenty. And it was good! Chicken salad rolls, fresh melon, an assortment of cheeses and crackers.

"Are there fish out here?" Jack asked, peering curiously into the green lake water.

"Plenty," Cooper said. "I caught a two-footer, just last week."

"Cool!"

"Can we fish?" Lily asked. "Oh, please! I want to catch a two-footer!"

Cooper turned to Iris. "Are you a fisherwoman?"

Oh, how to share the truth? That, for Iris, it was all about the views, a good book, and rocking gently on the lake? If you went home empty-handed, it was all the better.

But she looked down at Lily and smiled nonetheless. "It's great. I used to fish with my dad when I was a kid. Right?"

Bill laughed wholeheartedly. "Iris is our catch-and-release girl," he said. "Sensitive to the plight of the fish."

"In other words, she hates it," Lily stated.

"Hey, I like fishing just fine."

Cooper smirked. "Just not the catching part."

"Or the cleaning and eating parts," Sadie added. Which made everyone laugh.

Iris stood near as Cooper showed Lily how to bait the hook. "You're a real natural," he told her, and Iris felt her insides warm.

"That is so gross," Sadie said, peering over their shoulders. "How can you touch a worm?"

"I'll bait a line for you if you'd like," Cooper offered her.

Sadie shook her head and flopped back down on the seat. "Nope."

"No, *thank you*," Iris prompted, wondering again at the teenager she'd become.

"How about you?" Cooper asked Iris.

"Who, me? The fish hater?"

He winked. "I was just teasing."

"No thanks, I think I'll help Lily," she said.

They spent the afternoon casting their lines with little luck, until Bill finally got a bite. "Go, Grandpa!" Lily shrieked. She was so excited that she dropped her pole on the floor of the boat.

"Careful!" Iris warned as the pole slid beneath their feet, its silver hook flashing dangerously in the sun.

Leah retrieved it. "She's fine, Iris. Relax."

Leah's nonchalance grated on Iris's nerves. Couldn't Leah see how sharp the hooks were? Didn't she realize the line could tangle under their feet?

But there wasn't time to debate those facts. A second later Leah's line tugged as well. "Got one!" she called, and this time Cooper came to stand beside her.

"Reel it in slowly," he warned. "I think it's a big guy."

By then Bill and Lily both brought in their catch, small sunfish that wiggled at the end of the line.

"Can we keep it?" Lily wanted to know.

"You have to kill it first," Sadie said, still lounging behind them on the seat. "Then eat it."

Lily threw her a hurt look.

"Enough," Iris warned her.

"What? It's true."

But Bill was already unhooking the fish. "Too small," he announced, to Iris's relief. She watched as he threw it back in the water, craning her neck to see it pause before zipping away. A small thrill.

"But I think we've got dinner over here," Bill said. They stood back, giving Leah room. Iris watched her sister's hands as the spool whipped beneath them, then caught, as she reeled the fish closer.

"That's right," Cooper instructed. "Give and take. Nice."

"Go, Aunty Leah." Jack whistled.

Even Iris drew closer as Leah worked the line, her expression calm, her tongue poking out the corner of her mouth in concentration. The loose line flew out into the water as the fish ran with it, then went taut as Leah coaxed it back, reeling quickly. Back and forth it went. Iris had to admit, it was a beautiful if fateful dance.

"You've got it," Bill said, leaning over the boat for a closer look.

"Where? I can't see," Lily cried, leaning over the edge of the boat beside him.

Iris reached for her T-shirt, gripping the back.

Leah, who'd remained silent all along, grunted as she reeled the line in one last time.

"It's a giant!" Lily shouted.

Bill leaned over the boat with a net, just as the green speckled bass burst out of the water on Leah's line.

In one deft scoop, the fish was on board, and everyone surrounded it.

"Way to go!" Cooper exclaimed. He clapped Leah on the back, and in the excitement she turned and hugged him hard.

Iris watched, her annoyance growing.

"How big do you think it is?" Bill was already kneeling, examining its size. "It's gotta be at least one and a half feet."

"We're keeping this one, right?" Lily asked excitedly.

"Better believe it," Leah said, wiping her brow. "What do you think, everyone? Dinner tonight?"

Bill clapped his hands. "Absolutely. Cooper, I insist you join us. I've got some vintage pinot that will be a fine accompaniment."

"Sounds great," Cooper said, looking to Iris for approval. But Iris was watching the sleek fish twist and turn on the line, its gills straining for breath. "Put it in the bucket," she said quickly.

"I'll get one," Bill offered. To Iris's relief he emptied one of the bait pails into another, and leaned overboard to fill it with freshwater.

But it was too late. "That's okay, I've got it," Cooper said. She turned as Cooper raised a club and brought it down on the fish with a gut-wrenching thud.

"Mommy!" Lily screamed. She buried her face in Iris's side and began crying.

"Wait," Leah said, rushing to cover the bloodied fish with a towel.

It flopped again, spattering the floor of the boat in blood.

Lily howled into her side, as Iris covered her eyes with her hand. "Make them stop!"

Suddenly Cooper understood. Between them the fish flopped grotesquely beneath the towel.

"Oh, just get it over with," Iris cried, turning Lily away.

Cooper looked stricken.

"Let me." Leah grabbed the small club decidedly from him, and Iris shuddered at the sickening *thwack* that followed.

"It's over, baby," she whispered to Lily.

Cooper came up behind them and crouched by Lily, who still hid her head in Iris's lap. "Lily," he said softly. "I'm so sorry. I didn't mean to upset you like that." He looked up at Iris apologetically. "I should've warned you."

"I didn't know we had to kill it," Lily moaned.

Sadie slid over on the seat and put a hand on her little sister's back. "Lils, the fish either dies a slow death because it can't breathe, or you can end it fast. What they did was actually kinder, if you think about it."

"But I didn't want to kill it."

"I'm sorry, baby," Iris said, trying to sound brave for Lily. "It's over now." She offered Cooper a nod, trying to reassure him that it was okay. But secretly, she was furious.

At herself, for not thinking sooner about how this would go. At Leah, for so blithely relieving Cooper of the club. For the matter-of-fact way she brought it down on the bloody fish. There was so much that a mother wanted to shield her children from.

◆　◆　◆

Back at the docks, Iris lingered with Cooper as he secured the boat.

He climbed out, looking sheepish. "Well, that was a disaster."

"What do you mean? It was a great day, even with the fish incident."

"Right. What's a few years of therapy for poor Lily?"

"It's my own fault. I forgot that her dad hadn't taken her fishing before. Paul used to take Sadie and Jack when they were little." Her voice softened at the memory. "They loved fishing with Paul."

Cooper listened with strained politeness.

"Oh, sorry," Iris said.

Cooper chuckled. "No, no. Next time, let's invite Paul, too!"

Now she was laughing. "You're a sport, Cooper Woods."

Jack shouted to them from the parking lot. "Are you guys coming? I'm hungry for dinner."

Cooper looked to Iris uncertainly. "I wouldn't want to intrude."

"Join us!" Bill called, unwilling to take no for an answer. "I'm going home to get the grill started."

Iris grimaced. "Great. We can grill the fish."

Cooper followed her off the dock, shaking his head. "Maybe you could make Lily spaghetti?"

Twenty-Nine

I ris stood in front of the hallway mirror and took a deep breath, calmer now. It'd been a great day, even in spite of the fish incident. It didn't matter that her hair smelled of lake water or that a sheen of sunscreen still shone on her forehead. It was summer, her kids were here, and she had no place to be but in a chair on the patio with a cold beer.

Downstairs, Sadie had changed into a sundress and was settled on a lounge chair outside. "You look nice, honey," Iris said.

"Why are we having guests for dinner?" Sadie asked.

Iris glanced across the patio, to where Bill and Cooper were opening beers and chatting.

"It's just Cooper. Grandpa wanted to thank him for the boat ride."

"Then why can't he just say *thank you*?" She closed her eyes in exasperation and turned her face to the sun as if the conversation was over.

Iris regarded her sadly. "Huh. I was thinking that that's what you should say to him."

She left Sadie to contemplate this and joined the men. "Wow, you cleaned the fish already?"

Bill headed for the kitchen slider. "Couldn't let it go to waste. Your mother has some fillets of sole in the fridge from the market, so there's plenty of fish for everyone."

"I'm not eating that!" Sadie called over.

Iris took a deep breath. "I'll make pasta for you and Lily," she offered. "You can help."

At which Sadie flopped over on the lounge chair, directing her gaze toward the lake.

"She okay?" Cooper asked.

"She's a teenager. She'll be fine," Iris whispered, reaching for his bottle of beer.

Cooper handed it to her. "Maybe you should talk to her."

"I'm trying," Iris said, taking a deep sip.

"Is there some way we can get away? Just for a night?"

Iris glanced across the patio. "But how? The kids are here, and the wedding's in three days."

"And so is the end of our summer."

Iris's departure had always hovered somewhere around the wedding: a date that had once seemed so far off on the horizon. Too soon Cooper wouldn't be a part of her every day.

Cooper whispered, "I've got that cabin in Vermont."

"Which I'm dying to see. But I worry about leaving the kids. If anything happened, Vermont's not exactly around the corner."

He thought a minute. "I've got a job over in Brewster on Friday morning. How about when I'm finished?"

"That's the night of the rehearsal dinner."

"Right." He ran his hand through his hair.

Iris groaned. How was it that there was already no time left?

"What if we just stay here?"

Iris looked around. "Here?"

"At my place. Tomorrow night. No one needs to know we're there. It's close enough that you can pop back home if you need to."

It was close by and it was his. In other words, it was perfect. She'd come up with an excuse about her book to get away for a night. Trish would help. "Let's do it!" She raised her beer and took a sip. The cold beer slid down her throat nicely, and she passed the bottle back to Cooper, squeezing his hand as she did.

She happened to look over at Sadie, who was studying them.

Instant fury flashed across Sadie's face and she alighted from the lounge chair.

"What's wrong?" Cooper asked, glancing back and forth.

But Iris knew. What an idiot she was!

"Sadie, wait!" Iris went to her.

But Sadie was already plowing through the patio doors, almost knocking Bill aside as he returned with the platter of fish. "I'm going to my room," she said pointedly. "I've lost my appetite."

Iris hurried after her.

She tried the handle to the girls' room, which to her surprise was not locked, despite the slam that had sounded down the stairwell. Sadie turned, a look of contempt on her face. "What do you want?"

Iris drew her gently away from the window to the bed. "Come here."

She balked.

"Sadie, I want to talk."

"I'm not a baby," Sadie said. "You act like I don't know things. Like the fact that you and Leah can't stand each other. Just like you and Daddy. And that you're cozying up with that guy down there."

Iris swallowed. "You mean Cooper?"

Sadie glared back at her. "The handyman," she said through her teeth. It was a blow she dealt matter-of-factly, in the same tone Leah had used when she accused Iris of taking up with the "hired help." As if to further their unwitting alliances, Sadie's lips flushed, the same way her aunt's did when she was angry. For a moment Iris felt she was arguing with her teenage sister again.

"Sadie," Iris began carefully. "Cooper Woods is an old friend from high school, of both Aunty Leah's and mine. He works here, yes. But he's always been a friend."

There was no need to get into specifics.

"Is he Daddy's friend, too?" Sadie asked now. Her eyes were narrow with accusation, and Iris steadied herself to tread carefully. Her job was to reassure, not dole out facts.

"They may have met before, I don't know."

Sadie moved to the dresser, her fingers roaming restlessly over the objects: an old jewelry box, a bottle of perfume. They stopped at a small figurine of a horse that Iris's father had given her as a child. Sadie turned it over in her hand. "Well, he sure seems to like you."

Iris nodded, staring at the floor. "Is this why you're so angry with me?" There was no point in denying it. Had she really been so naive as to think, or hope, that her daughter was not grown-up enough to see the signs? However careful they'd been, however distant, thirteen-year-olds were ripe with hormonal emotions of their own. They practically had radar for that kind of tension.

Sadie didn't answer.

"You're right," Iris said. "Cooper is a good friend." She would not lie. But she would also not burden Sadie with the unnecessary. "The point is . . ." She paused, suddenly out of words. What was the point? That it didn't matter, because Daddy and Mommy weren't together anymore? That Cooper Woods was a question mark, at best? She looked at Sadie, sadness rising up in her chest. Now was not the time to tell her. This was not how she wanted it to be done. Damn, Paul. He should've stuck around and talked to her about this. They should've had a plan before it got to this.

"What, then?" Sadie set the porcelain horse down and turned to her. "What is your point?" Her eyes were steely with suspicion, but behind them Iris saw trepidation. She knew. Somewhere, deep down, she knew things weren't okay with her family.

"The point is, this is what families do. They grow. They change. Sometimes they fight. Mommies and daddies. Aunts and uncles. No different from you and your sister and brother."

"When is Daddy coming up here?"

Here it was. "I don't think he is, honey." Iris waited, then added, "He's busy with work. And it's nice to have time with just us, right?"

Sadie dismissed this. "Do you guys hate each other?"

A plume of sadness rose in Iris's throat. "No, honey. Of course we don't." She paused. "Does it seem like that?"

Sadie looked away. "Sometimes. I don't know. You guys don't laugh or hug each other like Emma's parents."

Emma was Sadie's best friend. Her parents were one of a handful of truly happily married couples she knew. Iris had to admit, comparing them to her and Paul—well, she might as well stamp the divorce papers right here and now.

"Honey, every family is different," she began, then stopped. Sadie deserved more than that. "Listen, your dad and I have some things to figure out. You're right—things aren't the same as they used to be. And I'm so sorry for that."

"Yeah, I've noticed."

"But I don't want you to worry. Nothing has changed about the way Daddy and I love you kids. That will never, ever change. As soon as we get home, we're all going to sit down and talk about it. Together."

Sadie looked over at her then. Gone was the certainty of her anger. Instead, an expression of worry clouded her young face.

"No matter what happens, we're a family. And we love you," Iris said firmly. "Mommy and Daddy. Leah, Grammy, and Grandpa. We all mess up sometimes, but we love one another in and out. And no matter what, we'll always be a family."

Sadie stared past her, to the window, where voices were floating up from the patio. Iris waited for the next question, the question about why her father wasn't here. It was bound to come. And she held her breath, for what seemed an eternity.

"Some family," Sadie muttered finally.

"I know," Iris cried. She parked herself on the edge of the bed, suddenly exhausted. "Families are crazy. Fucking crazy."

"Mom!" Sadie shot her a sideways look.

"I'm sorry. Forget I said that."

There was the tiniest curve at the corner of Sadie's mouth.

Iris fell back onto the blankets. "God, I can't believe I said *fuck*." Perfect. She'd said it twice now.

"Mom. Stop." Sadie was smiling now, giggling behind her hand.

"Sorry." Iris watched as her daughter struggled to compose herself. Her daughter, the almost-adult. "Sades, are you okay? Because whatever happens, I love you. Your whole crazy family loves you. That will never change."

Sadie turned back to the window and rested her forehead against the pane. Her profile was strong and lovely, so much that Iris had to resist the urge to go to her and stroke the hair off her forehead, as she had so many times when Sadie was younger. "I'm hungry," Sadie said finally, steering them unexpectedly to safety.

"You are?" Tears of relief sprang to Iris's eyes and she stood. For a second she restrained herself. But then she surrendered and went to her, pulling Sadie against her and planting a kiss atop her head, which was almost level with her own. "Me, too. Let's go eat."

In the hall Iris almost bumped into Leah. Iris could tell she'd heard. She let Sadie go downstairs ahead of them.

"So, I guess you got an earful."

Leah looked at her sympathetically. "I didn't mean to eavesdrop. I was in my room getting changed."

Iris sighed and leaned against the wall. She'd not discussed any of her feelings about Cooper or Paul, or the kids, with her sister. But Leah had seen plenty.

"For what it's worth, she's a strong girl," Leah began.

Iris tipped her head back against the wall and let out a small laugh. "That's for sure."

"She's going to get through this. You're not the kind of mother who would let her fall through the cracks."

"I know." The late-afternoon light spilled into the hall through the bedroom doorway, illuminating Leah's face with gold. Her concern was palpable. "It's just that there's so much for kids to deal with these days as it is. You know? And here Paul and I are, throwing more crap their way. They're so innocent in all of this. It's just not fair."

"None of it's fair," Leah agreed. "The whole thing really sucks. But you can't change the fact that Paul asked for a divorce. All you can do is be there for them, really be there for them, as it all unfolds." She reached for Iris's upper arm and squeezed it gently. "Those kids are strong and smart."

Iris ducked her head. This sudden show of sisterlyness from Leah was something she was so unused to, and yet something she realized she'd yearned for for so long that Iris feared she'd fall apart if she looked up and met her gaze. She couldn't go downstairs a slobbering mess. Not in front of her kids. Not in front of Cooper. "Thank you."

Leah squeezed her arm one last time and let go. "And in case you didn't already know, your kids have one hell of a head start in surviving this."

Iris looked up. "What's that?"

"You."

Thirty

Iris's heart fluttered in her rib cage as she stood outside Cooper's door holding a box of Trish's cake. Chocolate Sin Cake, Trish had said, winking. Before she could slink out of the bakery with it, Trish had pulled her aside at the counter.

"You're positively glowing," she said.

Iris redened. "Oh, shut up."

"No, you shut up. And you deserve it."

Iris had never been here before. Cooper's place was a traditional A-frame that sat atop a wooded hill, at the end of a long private gravel drive—the perfect getaway cottage. A porch wrapped around the front and sides of the house, overlooking the lake. There were two Adirondack chairs set at the edge of the lawn before it sloped down into a canopy of cedar and weeping willow. It was as if some corner had been turned. Things were calm with Sadie and Leah. Her kids were home with her parents. And here she was.

With the cake in hand and a lump in her throat, Iris knocked.

"Come in!" Cooper called from somewhere inside.

The second she stepped into Cooper's house she felt at home. The rustic space was flooded in late-day sun. She kicked off her flip-flops and followed his voice across the honey-hued pine floors of the living room. The furniture was masculine: craftsman-style. A fieldstone fireplace was flanked by floor-to-ceiling built-ins, which housed more books than even Iris probably owned.

"Back here," Cooper called. She found him in the kitchen, where she was welcomed with the scent of melting butter and garlic.

"No way, are you cooking?"

Cooper turned from the stove and kissed her firmly on the mouth. "Of course I am. Someone important is coming to dinner."

Each burner on the gas range was in use: A skillet of summer corn and red peppers sautéed on one. Pasta boiled in a stainless steel pot. A medley of squash sizzled in butter. And in the corner, a pan of garlic, shallots, and wine reduced. Iris peered into the sink, where a bowl of mussels soaked.

"What are you making? It's divine!"

"Seafood linguine; you said you like mussels, right?"

"They're my favorite." When had she told Cooper that? Touched, Iris wrapped her arm around his waist. "I can't believe you're doing all this for me."

Together they prepared the rest of dinner, passing each other spoons to take tastes from each pan and bumping comfortably against each other in the cozy confines of the kitchen.

Out on the deck, Cooper lit candles and poured wine. Forgetting herself, Iris inhaled the sweet and briny mussels over pasta, slowing only to savor the final bites.

"Leave those," Cooper insisted when she stood to clear the plates. "There's somewhere I want to take you."

Iris followed him down the porch stairs and across the lawn. He took her hand, guiding her toward the woods.

"Where are we going?" Iris was so stuffed she could barely keep up, but the golden end-of-day sun dappled the water ahead of them through the canopy of tree branches, and she felt drawn. She followed Cooper down a rocky path until the tree line met the shore.

Two red kayaks were propped upside down on the rocks. "This one's for you," Cooper said, rolling one over.

They dragged the noses of their kayaks into the water and waded to their knees. Iris positioned hers parallel to the shore and climbed in. It wobbled slightly beneath her. Cooper handed her a paddle. She pushed off from the shallow area and pointed her nose out into the lake. Cooper caught up, and together they headed out into the water. Iris moved into a comfortable rhythm and she relished the pull of the water against her muscles with each stroke. They hugged the rocky shore, paddling past a small family of ducks.

Cooper glided up beside her. "Look. It's you!" He pointed to a clump of marsh grass. There stood a lone egret, preening itself in the fading sun. It flicked its head in their direction as they approached.

She laughed.

When they arrived at the cove, Iris was pleased to find that no one else was there. Cooper paddled into the rocky shoals ahead of her. Hopping out, he grabbed the nose of her kayak and pulled her in where the water wasn't as deep. The plastic sides of the kayak bumped against the rocks, and she climbed out and helped drag them securely onto a spit of sand.

It was then she noticed Cooper's backpack. "What're you up to?" she asked.

"Just a little something to enjoy at the top."

As they had done what seemed like ages ago, they ascended the rocks, zigzagging their way across the steep slope. Once or twice Cooper looked back at her, but Iris didn't need his hand when he reached out. After a summer on the farm, she was stronger and surer.

By the time they reached the top the sun had set, but still stretched its pink fingers over the horizon in a final salute to the day.

"God, I'm going to miss this." Iris settled herself and Cooper kneeled beside her, rummaging through his backpack.

"For you." He handed her two champagne flutes and produced a bottle of Veuve Clicquot.

"Are you kidding? And here I just showed up with one of Trish's cakes and my overnight bag."

Cooper popped the cork. "All you needed was to show up."

They toasted, and even though a late-season breeze had kicked in across the water, Iris was not cold. The champagne sent a warm tingle up her spine, and Cooper pulled her close against him.

"Don't worry, I'm not going to ask you to jump this time," he teased, bumping jovially against her.

Iris stood up, and Cooper's arm fell away. "What are you doing?"

"Something I should've done a long time ago."

"Iris. I was joking around."

"I know." Maybe it was the champagne. Or the crazy pink of the sky. Or the way she felt with Cooper. But before Iris could think of a reason not to, she pulled her T-shirt over her head.

"Whoa, come back here." Cooper hopped to his feet.

Iris didn't answer. She was too busy fumbling with the button of her shorts. She shimmied out of them, spun to face Cooper, and kicked them in his direction. He caught them with his free hand. "Iris. You're crazy."

A gust of wind blew over the rock, and she shrieked.

"Yes, I am!"

Still laughing, Iris scurried to the edge of Chicken Rock. But one look down and her stomach lurched. It was so far down. And so . . . dark.

"Iris, get your tail back here," Cooper called. It would be easy to turn around. To sit back down beside him and finish the bottle of champagne.

But this was summer. Her summer. She flexed her knees. And before she could change her mind, she stepped off.

The wind roared in her ears. It rushed past her and over her. Weightless, she hurtled down toward the water, the glassy dark surface almost opaque beneath her. And then she broke it.

The force of the entry caused her breath to tear from her lungs. When her descent halted, Iris opened her eyes to the green darkness, her chest about to explode. For a second the underwa-

ter world held her, but above there was light. And sky. Iris burst
to the surface.

◆ ◆ ◆

Back at the cabin, Cooper lit the logs in the fieldstone fireplace.
The night had grown chilly and Iris relished the crackle and spit
of the flames after their long paddle home.

"I'm going to dry off," she said. Despite the coziness of his
house and the intoxicant of Cooper's nearness, Iris felt a sudden moment of hesitation. They had already been together
that summer; in the fields, by the lake, in Cooper's truck. They
were passionate moments, but often rushed ones. Suddenly, the
knowledge that they had a whole night together, without threat
of interruption or discovery, made it feel like the first time. Iris
needed a moment to pull herself together. She grabbed her bag
from the couch. "I'll just be a minute."

But Cooper stood up from the fireplace and shook his head.
He took the bag from her hand.

Iris smiled shyly. "But I'm still wet," she whispered as he
pulled her in close.

Cooper shushed her.

"And I smell like the lake."

"You're perfect."

Before Iris could protest further, Cooper placed a finger to
her mouth, silencing her. He traced her upper lip slowly, then her
bottom. She could feel her mouth flush at his touch.

"Cooper."

And then he pressed his own lips against hers, gently at first,
then more hungrily.

Iris stood, helpless. The fire crackled behind her as he slid her
shirt up over her head and drew her closer to the flames. Cooper
began at her neck, moving slowly down to her collarbone. Iris
went limp, sighing with each press of his lips against her bare
skin. He took his time, and desire rose up inside her like a plume
of smoke. It was her turn. She tugged at his shirt, lifting it up and

away, moving her own mouth across his ear, his lips, and down his chest. The heat of the fireplace warmed her bare skin as they reached for each other. They kicked off their shorts, hands moving across each other's bodies with growing urgency. Iris shuddered.

Cooper pulled away gently, studying her expression. "Are you cold?"

She shook her head. *Please, don't stop.*

He reached over for a blanket on the couch and draped it across Iris's shoulders with care. "Better?"

She nodded, reaching for him.

"Wait. I want to look at you."

Iris met his gaze impatiently. She loved how careful Cooper was, but right now she was strung out with desire. Her muscles taut, her breath short.

Iris shuddered as they sank to the floor. For a moment they sat facing each other in the firelight, chest to chest beneath the blanket.

"Iris."

Before he could say anything else, Iris wrapped her arms around his neck and slid herself onto his lap. Cooper surrendered. She encircled his waist with her legs, leaning back over the blanket in front of the fire. Cooper followed, moving over her. Iris felt herself letting go, her body flexing and releasing just as it had earlier on the rock. Like the rush of water she'd felt hours earlier, the fall was like no other she'd had before.

◆　◆　◆

In the morning light, Cooper's hair took on a golden hue. Iris had awakened first, and not wanting daylight to signal the end of their night together, she'd pulled the sheet up over her and pressed herself into the curve of Cooper's back. A moment later, he turned over and reached for her. They lay nose to nose.

Her voice was husky with sleeplessness. "Good morning."

"It is indeed."

He stretched out, and she moved into the space beneath his

arm. Now that she'd tasted what it was like to have Cooper belong to her, she felt more vulnerable than before. It was a pull she no longer felt strong enough to turn from. "Why can't we wake up to each other every day?"

He didn't even pause. "I keep thinking we will. Someday."

Iris closed her eyes. It was all she needed to hear.

Thirty-One

Millie met her at the door. "Have you seen Leah yet?" Millie asked Iris in a low whisper.

The morning of the rehearsal dinner had arrived. Iris had rushed from Cooper's house in the early hours, hoping to beat any of her own family to the kitchen breakfast table. But to her dismay, the driveway was already clogged when she pulled in.

Relieved that her mother seemed to be overlooking the fact that Iris was walking through the door in yesterday's clothes, Iris hurried past her. "Uh, no. She's probably sleeping."

Millie looked at her watch. "I already checked. Her room's empty. And her bed is made."

Odd for Leah, but still not a reason to panic. Iris shrugged. "Maybe she got up early?"

Millie shook her head. "I left a little gift for her on her pillow last night. Grandma's pearl necklace. I thought she'd like it for tonight." Millie paused, her voice wavering. "It's still there. Still wrapped."

Iris glanced warily around the kitchen, teeming with staffers who'd arrived early to set up for tomorrow's ceremony.

From the dining room, Tika waved brightly. "Ladies, I need the bride. We've got some last-minute seating charts to go over."

Millie tapped her pen on her clipboard. "Something's not right."

Iris ducked outside, where the kids were working on breakfast. Iris pecked them each on the head. "Morning, loves. Anybody seen Aunty Leah?" She inspected their sleepy expressions for any sign of curiosity about her night away. But they seemed unfazed.

"Grandma won't let us watch cartoons," Jack mumbled. "The den is full of wedding *stuff*."

"Sorry, buddy. Tomorrow's Aunty Leah's big day. So have you seen her?"

"Uh-uh," Lily answered through a mouthful of bagel.

"What about Uncle Stephen?"

The three of them shook their heads.

Iris poured herself some coffee and it was then she noticed her cell phone on the table. As if on cue, it buzzed.

"That thing woke us up this morning," Sadie grumbled. "You left it in our room last night. Who's calling so much?"

"I did?" Iris never left the kids without having her phone. And of all nights. *Mother of the Year Award.* "I'm sorry, honey, I didn't know I'd left it."

"Well, it's been ringing all morning."

Iris shaded the screen, hoping it was Leah. Maybe it was she who'd been trying to reach Iris, to tell her what was going on. But the screen said *Paul.*

"Who is it?" Sadie asked.

"Nobody," Iris lied, tucking the phone into her back pocket.

The only reason Iris answered Paul's rare calls that summer was the kids. But now they were with her, and frankly she didn't really care what was bothering Paul at the moment.

Millie poked her head through the screen door. "I still can't locate Leah."

"What about the farm?" Jack said.

Millie's eyes brightened. "Of course! I'll bet Leah wanted to run over things with Naomi before they take off for the honeymoon. Will you and the kids go fetch her?"

Which still didn't explain her untouched bed, Iris thought. But Millie was insistent. "Tell Leah that the planners are waiting."

◆ ◆ ◆

The morning dew was already dry on the grassy rise up to the barn. Around them, the birds chirped loudly, and Iris could tell the weather promised a perfect weekend for a wedding.

Just let them be up here, she wished silently, trailing the kids up the hill. But the barn was empty, as was the potting shed. They continued up to the gardens, and Iris scanned the flat acreage ahead for any sign of Leah or Stephen. But the carefully tilled rows were empty, the only inhabitant a stray bunny who scampered into taller grass as they approached.

"Where are they?" Sadie asked, and Iris knew she was beginning to pick up on the strangeness of the bride and groom's absence.

"Probably just went for a walk. You know, to get away from all the fuss," Iris lied.

On the drive ahead there was a low rumble, and they looked up as a truck neared. Iris's heart skipped. Cooper drove into full view and pulled up alongside them.

"You're out early," she said, stepping up to the window. She was aware of how closely Sadie was watching them.

"Good morning." His hair was still rumpled and she resisted the urge to touch it. "Figured I'd drop off some supplies and get out of everyone's way before the big day. I'm sure the last thing the bride and groom want is the hum of a power saw over their string quartet."

Iris wished Sadie would bore of their conversation and give them a minute alone. But she didn't. "Speaking of the bride and groom, you didn't happen to pass either of them this morning, did you?"

"No, sorry. Didn't pass anyone out on the road."

"Give us a ride?" Without waiting for his answer, Iris helped the kids into the back of Cooper's truck.

"Cool!" Jack said, settling himself between some lengths of boards.

Sadie was less game. "What are we doing? Aren't we supposed to be looking for Aunty Leah?"

"We are," Iris said, slamming the tailgate shut. She hurried up to the passenger door and climbed in.

"Long time, no see," Cooper said. Iris all but blushed.

She glanced behind them into the truck bed. Sadie had one eye on them. She kept her voice low, even though she was sure they couldn't hear. "Listen, I think we've got real trouble."

Cooper put the truck in drive. "What's that?"

She'd never told Cooper the truth behind Leah's secret. And there wasn't time to explain it now. "A missing bride. No one's seen either one of them since last night."

Cooper rubbed the bristle on his chin as the truck bumped along the farm road toward the barns. "You think they took off or something?"

"Not together."

They drove down to the house. A floral delivery truck swung in and around them as Iris stepped out.

"Excuse me. I'm supposed to show these to a Mrs. Standish before we deliver them to the club?" the driver asked.

The kids hopped out of the truck and followed Iris to the back of the florist van, whose doors were swung wide. Tissue-stuffed boxes lay open across the back, each teeming with white lilies. Leah's favorite.

A tiny sigh escaped Iris's lips.

"Whoa," Sadie said, squeezing in beside her. "Leah's gonna love these."

"Why don't you kids show the florist inside," Iris said.

For once they listened, and Iris flopped against the van. Cooper came up behind her. "I checked the dock. The canoe's still there. Does anyone else realize they're gone?"

Iris was about to explain the whole story when a lone figure walking up the drive startled them.

She gasped. "Where the hell have you been?"

Leah paused warily. "Out for a walk." Iris noted she was still in her dress from the night before, her eye makeup smudged.

"All night?"

"What makes you say that?" She glanced down, and Iris took in her silver ballet flats, which were scuffed and stained with dirt. Leah laughed nervously. "No, no, I just woke up early and threw this on." She smiled faintly. But Iris wasn't buying it for a second.

"Where's Stephen?" Iris demanded.

Leah glanced around casually, as if expecting him to pop out from behind one of Millie's arborvitae. "Around here somewhere."

"So, you've seen him this morning?" Iris was aware of Cooper shifting uncomfortably behind her.

"Of course I have." She looked around the driveway, as if noticing the slew of vehicles for the first time. "Wow, I guess things are in full swing. Where's Mom?"

The florist returned down the walkway and headed for the rear of the van. Leah alighted, standing on tiptoe to peer inside. "Are those mine?"

"Yes, ma'am. If you're the bride." At which she nodded eagerly. He smiled at her, not seeing the grass stains on the hem of her skirt. The straggly hair, damp with humidity. "Here." He passed her a box of the lilies, which Leah accepted as gently as if he were passing a baby.

"Oh, Iris. Aren't they lovely?" Leah's voice was breathy, and she closed her eyes. The scent of the lilies rose between them on the thick morning air, and for a moment, Iris, too, was intoxicated.

And just like that Leah fluttered up to the house, where Millie met her at the door with a strange look of relief and worry.

The bride was back. She was here and smiling, and eager to attack those darn seating charts. No matter her muddy feet or tear-stained cheeks. Or the tangled hair that Iris was sure had not seen a pillow all night.

Iris turned to Cooper, who shrugged in equal disbelief. He took her hand, but there was no time to commiserate. The sudden crunch of tires on gravel interrupted them. Iris looked up, fully expecting to see Stephen's Saab, another reminder that, despite all evidence to the contrary, the earth rotated according to Leah's pull.

But instead, she stepped back. Dropped Cooper's hand.

"What's the matter?" he asked, craning his neck toward the car that had stopped abruptly.

"It's him."

"Stephen?"

Iris shook her head. "No. My husband."

◆   ◆   ◆

"What did you expect me to do, Iris? You never answer your damned phone." Paul's voice was pleading, desperate. He flopped down on her bed, and Iris scowled at his khaki pants, which were as rumpled as his brow.

"So you just drove up here? On the eve of my sister's wedding?" She kept her distance, standing at the window, where she could focus on the staff setting up in the distant field. The white tent was up, a mystical sail against the sea of rolling green hillside.

"You left me no choice." Paul looked exhausted. Terrible. She wanted him very far away from her, and she moved quickly to the door, hoping he'd take the hint and see himself through it.

"Paul, this is not a good time. Can we do this later?"

"Didn't you get my messages?" he asked.

Iris shook her head. She'd seen his calls from the previous day and ignored them. "I've sort of been busy," she said, glancing impatiently at the window. The kids had not seen their father yet. She'd whisked him inside, too startled to offer any words of explanation to Cooper, who'd just as abruptly excused himself. What was she to say? She'd no idea why he was here.

"Iris, I've made a mistake."

She allowed herself to really look at him for the first time. The hair askew. The smudged glasses. "Have you lost weight?"

"Iris. Are you listening to me?"

She moved forward, reaching for his glasses, a terrible reflex of memory, then caught herself and crossed her arms. Paul's smudged lenses were not hers to worry about anymore.

"Mom?" Lily's voice called up from outside and she strode to the window and peered down.

"What?"

"Can we go for a swim? It's *sooo* hot."

Iris shook her head. "Just a sec, I'll be right down."

"Is that Lily?" Paul peeled himself from the bed and stood, but Iris put her hand up, touching his chest lightly as he moved into it. She looked at it, then up at him. "No," she warned. "Sit down."

Paul frowned. "Why can't I see her?"

"You can. Just not now." She pointed at the bed. "Will you just sit?"

And to her surprise, he obliged.

"Why do I need to sit?" Lily shouted from outside. She'd heard them.

"Not you," Iris shouted back down. This was getting ridiculous. "I meant, wait. I'll be right down."

"So, we can swim?"

"Yes," Iris shouted, frustration rising in her voice. "But wait for me."

She turned to Paul. "Do you see? Do you see how crazy things are right now? This is not a good time."

Paul rose from the bed and moved toward her. He reached both hands out, and Iris stared at them as if they were foreign. She stepped back.

"Iris, I'm trying to tell you." He paused, his eyes watering, and Iris was transported. She'd not seen Paul cry, as far as she could remember. Not since Lily's birth, all those years ago. Some hard rock inside her stomach shifted, and she felt . . . what was it? Sympathy? Regret? She shook her head.

"The papers I sent you. We need to talk."

The rock shifted again. "Damn it, Paul. Can the papers wait one more day? Until after the wedding?"

He took her hands in his own, and she stiffened. "It's not that," he said urgently. "What I'm trying to say is, don't sign them. There's been a mistake."

Iris tugged her hands, but his grip was firm. "What? Some kind of clerical error?"

Paul smiled. Began to laugh, and it unnerved her. "No, Iris. I've made a mistake. I don't want you to sign." He looked at her deeply. "I don't want a divorce."

The thudding in Iris's chest was so loud her ears roared. She pulled her hands away, and this time he let her. She turned to the window. Below, Lily sat patiently, her swim towel across her lap. The tents in the upper field were going up, a glaring white that caused her to shade her eyes.

"Paul. I don't understand."

There was a knock at the door. Without waiting, Millie opened it. Her face froze. She looked from one to the other, and Iris couldn't be sure if it was relief or disgust she was seeing.

"Mom." Iris stood awkwardly between them, as if she were a teen caught hiding a boy in her room. "Paul just showed up."

"I can see that." For once, Millie was speechless.

"And he's just leaving."

"I am?" Paul asked.

"He is?" Millie said.

"Yes." Iris put a firm hand on Paul's back, guiding him toward her mother, whom he gave a wide berth, and through the door. "We'll talk. Later." It felt good to say the words. And even better that she meant them.

He paused undecidedly in the hall. "But when? Where?" he asked.

"Mom? Are you coming?" Now Lily was coming up the stairs herself, having outgrown her patience. "You said we were going swimming." She stopped midway up. "Daddy! What are you doing here?"

"My thoughts exactly," Millie muttered from the doorway.

"Mom. I swear I had no idea," Iris began.

Millie pulled her into the bedroom as Lily raced up the stairs to greet her father. "What's going on?"

"I don't know. He said he had something to tell me." Iris winced. "He's having second thoughts."

Millie considered this, her eyes narrowing. And for a moment Iris feared she would unleash all that Iris herself was considering unleashing.

"Don't worry," Iris reassured her. "I'm showing him out."

But Millie surprised her. "No, don't do that."

"No?"

"I mean, he did drive all the way up here. Maybe you should let him stay."

Iris's jaw dropped. "Stay?" Then, seeing the hopeful look on her mother's face, *"For the wedding?"*

Millie shrugged. "Well, he is family. And he said he wants to talk."

"Mom." Iris held up both hands. "You have got to be kidding."

But there was Lily, laughing in Paul's arms, and Paul looking hopefully over his shoulder at both women.

"I brought a suit," he admitted. "Just in case."

Millie looked at Iris. "How fortunate."

"How presumptuous," Iris said flatly. This whole thing was insane. Had the entire summer somehow escaped Millie?

By now Sadie had also come to the base of the stairs, to see what all the fuss was about. "Daddy!" she shrieked. It was like a regular welcome wagon. There was no mistaking the look on her face. Relief. And something more; something worse, which rolled the rock in Iris's stomach right over. Hope.

"Are you staying for Aunty Leah's wedding?" Lily asked, giving voice to the one question now burning in everyone's mind.

Sadie's gaze darted anxiously between her parents, landing hard on Iris.

"Well," Paul said softly. "That's up to your mom."

"Come on, kids," Millie said, in an attempt to buy them some privacy. "The grown-ups are talking."

"But can you?" Lily pressed. "Wait till you see my dress! It's even got a flower on it."

All eyes were on Iris, burdening her with a weight so intense she couldn't answer any other way. It was the worst answer, the wrong answer. And yet she said it anyway.

"Yes. I suppose Daddy can stay."

The kids erupted in a wave of giddiness that both surprised and touched Iris, and left her feeling guilty for having considered keeping him away from them.

When she looked at Paul, there it was again: the desperate shimmer in his eyes. What was happening to him?

"But he has to go back tomorrow. Right after the wedding." Iris couldn't let this run away with her. She shot Paul a look of warning. She was giving this one inch for the kids. It would not turn into a mile.

"Yes," he said, nodding in agreement. "It's just a quick visit. I have to get back for work."

Iris squeezed past them all, the celebratory air sticking in her chest. Millie was one step ahead. When they reached the bottom of the stairs, Iris leaned against the banister, the reality of what she'd just done sinking in.

"It was the right thing to do," Millie assured her.

Iris groaned. "Really? For whom?"

Millie gestured in the direction of the kitchen, where the wedding preparations had reached full momentum. Where

Leah, now freshly showered, and changed, stood at the island. Still bleary-eyed, but present. Beside her Stephen was radiating enough eagerness for both of them.

"Stephen just arrived. Look how happy he looks. What a couple."

Iris watched, feeling as if the whole house were on a seesaw. Before her, the kitchen rising high into the impossibly white clouds, the clattering of pots and pans and pre-wedding chatter chiming their arrival into the heavens. Behind her, the sound of Paul and the kids thumping down the stairs, returning her to earth with a resounding thud. And in the middle, at the crux, Iris and Leah wavered, unsure of whether to hang on tight for another sweeping rise into the skies or leap off to their escape as they touched ground once more.

Beside her, Millie's words filled her ear, a muffled interruption. "You did the right thing," she said again. "For all of us."

◆ ◆ ◆

Iris's heart pounded in her chest as she half ran, half walked the distance between the house and barn. She'd made her escape at lunch, leaving the kids with Paul, who had not stopped throwing her pointed looks of pleading and remorse. Looks she'd tried to dodge all morning, happily accepting last-minute wedding chores, however small, to avoid him. She was furious at Paul for pushing through a door she'd worked so hard to close these past few weeks.

And Cooper! He'd practically vaporized from the driveway when Paul arrived. By the time she took her bewildered eyes off the wreck that was her soon-to-be ex-husband, Cooper's tailgate was already disappearing down the road. And he'd not answered her texts since.

Once more, she pulled her phone from her pocket and scanned the bars. No service. "Damn it," she muttered. Roaming left, then right, with her hand held high overhead, Iris scurried up and down the lawn, toward higher ground by the barns, eventually landing herself by the potting shed. Pressed up against the siding they'd been working on, she was finally able to achieve one bar of service. She dialed Cooper.

"Hello?" his voice was breaking up, but to her relief he'd finally answered.

"Thank God," she breathed. "I need to explain." There was no reply, and at first she feared he'd hung up. "Cooper?"

"I'm here," he said.

Iris tipped her head back against the wooden siding. "I wish that were the case."

"Iris, you don't owe me an explanation."

"But I do," she insisted. "I had no idea Paul was coming, really. I can't believe he's here."

"It's okay, Iris. Really." His voice was even, seemingly free of anger or any of the other things she'd worried about. But now she wasn't so sure that was a good thing. Shouldn't it bother him?

"He's not supposed to be here, Cooper."

"But he is. And it's probably best that you take some time and figure that out."

She didn't have time. And she certainly didn't need to figure things out. Paul had done that already for them, back in June. Leaving her to spend the summer doing just that, by herself. She was sick and tired of being expected to figure it out.

"Cooper. I know what I want. And it's not Paul."

There was a pause on the line. "Then you need to share that with him."

"I am," she said, somewhat defensively. "I mean, I will. But I want you to know that first."

"That's nice to hear," Cooper said. "Thank you." Was that relief in his voice? Or was she just projecting her own hopes onto him?

"Okay." She didn't know what else to say. "I guess I'll see you tonight, at the rehearsal dinner."

"About that . . ." Cooper said.

"You are coming, right?"

He sighed. "I don't think it's such a good idea."

"Cooper, don't let Paul keep you away. You were invited. You're a guest, regardless of what crazy stuff is going on with my family."

"Iris, let's be honest. I'm not just a guest. And now that Paul is here, well, it just doesn't seem respectful."

"To Paul?" A new swell of resentment rose up. Paul had thrust himself on all of them, ruining everything, just when she was finally feeling happy. Why should any of them be concerned about being respectful to him?

"Why don't I wait and come tomorrow for the wedding? Bigger crowd, lots going on. I think that makes more sense, don't you?"

Iris shook her head. "Please, Cooper. I want you there tonight. For me."

Finally, he relented. "Okay. But for the record, I don't think it's a good idea."

"It'll be fine," Iris insisted. "We're all grown-ups."

"Just don't seat me next to the guy, okay?"

They were both laughing now. But she didn't feel relief; his words hung in the air. Just because she'd gotten her way didn't mean it was a good idea.

◆ ◆ ◆

Back at the house, Iris whisked through the kitchen, only to be stopped dead in her tracks in the living room. Paul, who was seated alone on the couch, jumped up. "There you are."

But Millie, who flew out of the kitchen as if on cue, beat him to her.

"Where have you been?" she asked, frantic. "We've got to be at the club in one hour. Everyone's upstairs getting ready. The kids need to get dressed now!"

Relieved at the diversion, Iris threw Paul a look of faux apology and hurried up the stairs behind her mother.

Jack emerged from her bathroom, dressed in a crisp white shirt and a red striped tie. "Oh, honey. You look so handsome!"

The girls were also dressed. Sadie had on a little too much makeup, but Iris didn't say anything. She helped Lily tie the bow on her dress and sent them downstairs to wait. "Don't go outside. And don't eat anything!"

Quickly, Iris showered and blew out her hair. She slipped into her dress and did her makeup. In the hallway she paused only long enough to tug on her heels.

Millie was summoning them from downstairs. "They're pulling the cars around. I've got the kids."

Apparently only Iris and Leah were left. Iris went to her door. "You ready?"

Leah sat at her vanity, brushing her hair. She turned around. "God, you look stunning," Iris said. There was no trace of the puffy eyes or hollow expression Iris had witnessed that morning. Iris watched in awe as her sister expertly swept her hair back into a chignon.

"Thank you." Leah held up the string of their grandmother's pearls. "Can you help me put them on?"

She'd found them after all. "This was sweet of Mom." Iris paused. "She left them on your bed last night."

"I didn't come home."

"I know. What happened?"

Leah sighed. "I couldn't sleep. I just kept thinking about what you said. That Stephen needs to know."

Iris secured the clasp. "And?"

"And I don't know what to do. It will break his heart. All Stephen wants is to start a family."

Iris sat down beside her. "There is never going to be a good time, Leah. You have to tell him."

Leah shook her head. "I can't."

Even though Iris had the sense she was pushing too hard, she couldn't let it go. There was still time to do the right thing. "Leah, it's not fair. You've got to tell him the truth."

The bedroom door opened. Stephen stood in his cream linen suit, as handsome as Iris had ever seen him. A look of uncertainty clouded his face.

"Tell me what?"

Thirty-Two

The country club drive was lit up like something out of a fairy tale. To her chagrin, Iris had ended up in the back of the Willetses' car.

"Oh, will you look at that," Adele purred as they rolled down the twinkling cobblestone drive. All the pear trees lining the country club entrance were draped in tiny white lights, and between them rows of luminarias flickered against the glowing purple sky.

Iris had to admit it was magical. But she couldn't focus on the beauty of the night. She was too shaken by the image of Leah's distraught expression when they both turned to see Stephen. He'd heard too much. Stephen had stood in the doorway for what seemed an eternity before either Iris or Leah recovered.

"What does Iris want you to tell me?" he'd asked again.

Leah had been the first to respond, rushing over and silencing him with a kiss. "Oh, nothing," she'd said breezily. "Now scoot out of here and let me get dressed, honey. We can't be late to our own rehearsal!"

He'd relented, but not before he locked eyes with Iris, who'd excused herself quickly from the room, heart pounding in her chest. Just how much he'd heard was unclear. If only Iris hadn't brought it up to begin with.

Ahead, her parents' BMW rolled to a stop in front of the large double doors, and the valet helped her family out of the car. First Millie, who stood on the bottom of the granite steps in a knee-length powder-blue dress. She touched her signature pearls and accepted Bill's arm as he rounded the front of the car. Then the back doors opened, and Stephen stepped out. Standing in the circular drive, Stephen looked tanned and handsome, and Iris held her breath as he reached one hand into the car. Leah emerged. Like the perfect plastic wedding cake topper, the elegant bride and groom stood staring up at the clubhouse, arms around each other. *Just stay that way*, Iris willed them.

By the time Iris climbed the stairs to the club, her family had already moved inside. Music met her at the open doors. She hurried underneath the crystal chandelier and across the foyer. In the dining room a small brass band was set up in the bay window, and guests mingled among the tables. Anxiously, she scanned the room, locating Millie with a group of women she recognized from the garden club, and her father over at the bar. To her relief, Leah and Stephen were posing by the fireplace, smiling for pictures. Maybe Leah had worked her magic once more and he'd let it go. Maybe things were fine after all.

"Can we get Shirley Temples?" Lily appeared at her side and began tugging on her arm excitedly. Paul was right behind her.

"Just one!" Iris called as Lily took off across the dance floor.

Sadie and Jack followed, but Paul did not. "What a setup," he mused. Iris had to agree, but she wasn't about to say so to him. "Can I get you a drink?" Paul asked, looking at her more carefully. "Hey, you cleaned up well."

She ignored the half compliment. "Yes, actually. I'll have a—"

"Dry martini, stuffed olives. Our usual."

"Usual?"

Paul chuckled. "Iris, come on. We've been married for sixteen years."

She tried to ignore the shiver that accompanied that observation. Of course they had been. But the way he'd said it. As if they would be for sixteen *more*. And come to think of it, she couldn't remember ever truly liking that drink. It was Paul's favorite.

"Wait," Iris said. "Make mine a beer."

Paul turned, eyebrows raised. "A beer?"

"Yes. Sparkling ale, actually."

"Since when do you like *sparkling ale*?" he asked, the words clipped on his tongue.

"Since always, if you'd ever asked."

"A beer it is, then." Paul shook his head, but left her, as she'd hoped he would. Suddenly the room seemed stuffy, and she tugged at her shoulder strap.

"Yoo-hoo. Iris!" She turned to see a petite blond woman making a rapid approach. "Look at *youuuuu*!"

"Bitsy Hartmoore."

Bitsy, a childhood classmate, clapped her hands as if she and Iris were long-lost friends. Though friends, they'd never really been. While Bitsy had never managed to fully penetrate the more popular crowd, she'd spent her high school years circling them like a shark, snapping up thankless positions like class treasurer and pep rally leader, any measure to keep her abreast of the gossip, which she had always more than generously shared.

"Bitsy Hartmoore-Greene, now!" she gushed, holding up her left hand, which was nearly swallowed by the golf-ball-sized diamond on her ring finger. Bitsy kissed Iris on both cheeks, twice. "Wonderful to see you."

"Wonderful," Iris echoed hollowly, glancing again at the door. She didn't feel like making small talk with the likes of Bitsy, who still appeared to be a size zero in both dress size and personality.

Bitsy waved her left hand again. "We're just so excited for your little sis. Our popular girl, wasn't she? We didn't think she'd *ever* settle down!"

Iris nodded vaguely, wondering at Bitsy's use of *we*. As if they'd commiserated over Leah over the years. As if they'd ever commiserated on anything, period.

"Yes." Iris laughed stiffly. "Well, you know. People *change*."

"If you say so." Bitsy lowered her voice. "Speaking of, I heard there are some little *changes* in your life, too." She raised what was left of her overly plucked eyebrows, hopefully.

And then Paul appeared with Iris's beer.

Again, Iris craned her neck toward the ballroom doors, hoping to be rescued by Millie or interrupted by a wayward relative. Anything to pluck her from this little huddle of her least favorite people. As if on cue, Trish appeared in the main doors.

"Trish!" Iris waved.

Trish, spotting them, gave Iris a conservative wave back. And a sharp flick of her head in the opposite direction.

And she realized why. Right behind Trish, filling the doorway, was Cooper. Looking more handsome than she'd ever seen him, in a charcoal-gray suit and rugby-striped tie. He paused, glancing around the room, giving Iris's little group just enough time to spot him before he spotted them.

"Oh, look. If it isn't Cooper Woods," Bitsy announced with a little too much pleasure. She bumped Iris suggestively with her bony elbow. "See? Over there."

If they'd been back in elementary school, Iris would've kicked her right in the shin. Something she wasn't necessarily above doing now.

Paul's brow furrowed as he glanced from Cooper to Bitsy to Iris, trying to decode the signals. "Someone you know?"

"Nobody special," Bitsy interjected. Then, giggling, "Just our high school homecoming king! Right, Iris?" And there was that bony elbow again.

Iris forced a smile just as Cooper found her in the crowd. Their eyes locked as he took in Paul, then Bitsy and her wishy-washy husband, who both waved, to her dismay. Would he feel obligated to come over? Iris closed her eyes, feeling herself begin to wobble in her heels. Not now. Not with Bitsy Hartmoore-Greene as witness.

But when she opened them, to her relief, Trish had taken Cooper by the arm and was whisking him across the room, to a table of high school classmates. Bitsy took off after them.

Iris took a long swig of her beer, willing her ankles to stop shaking and her heart to stop pounding. Paul leaned closer, whispering in her ear. "I'm glad I'm here," he said.

◆ ◆ ◆

They got through dinner, which everyone said was delicious, though Iris was too fidgety to taste any of it. She'd tried to focus on the kids, but they kept running off to play with distant cousins they'd reacquainted themselves with. Though Stephen remained reserved, Leah blushed and giggled in all the right places as toasts were given, each growing more colorful as the drinks were poured and the night rolled on. Iris, having not eaten much, found herself feeling a bit tipsy, which interestingly enough had an inverse effect on her ability to walk in her high heels. As she strode across the dance floor, Trish pulled her into a small group of old friends. "Finally!" Trish said, her expression flushed and full of questions. "Didn't realize you'd have two dates tonight!" She gestured toward Paul. "*What* is going on?"

"Long story," Iris shouted over the music. "But don't worry, he's leaving tomorrow."

"Which one?" Trish teased.

When Iris didn't laugh, Trish grabbed her by the hand. "Come on, let's dance."

Their old high school favorites coursed through the ballroom: Madonna, Bon Jovi, Springsteen. Before long, she'd forgotten Paul, who remained seated at the table, watching impatiently. And for a moment she'd almost forgotten her worries about Cooper, whom she'd been able to keep tabs on across the room all night, as he talked among old friends. So far no awkward paths had been crossed. The music picked up, and the floor thickened. When "Dancing Queen" came on, Iris allowed herself to be propelled into the center of the group, delighted to find Leah right there with the rest of them. "What a night!" Leah cried, throwing her arms around Iris's neck. Iris was nearing drunk now, she realized. She looked down at her feet, which she suddenly realized were bare. Where had she tossed her shoes?

Longingly, Iris scanned the room. Where was Cooper now? When she felt a hand on her shoulder, she turned, heart leaping. But it was only Stephen's best man, who reintroduced himself as Sully, Stephen's college roommate. "Figured I'd better come clean with my moves, before the big day tomorrow," he joked, offering his hand.

Iris laughed. Sully was a flirt, and a cute one at that. As he'd warned, he wasn't the smoothest, but he was a clown, and they danced together as the music turned to classics and the DJ spun "Twist and Shout," which got everyone up on their feet, even Iris's parents, who were clearly having a good time. Leah shrieked playfully as Sully tugged her into the center and, with hands on her hips, got down, mimicking his exaggerated twist. "Come on, man!" Sully called to Stephen, who stood watching from the bar. But Stephen just shook his head.

"If this is the rehearsal dinner, I can't wait for the reception!" Trish appeared at her arm with shots of tequila and passed her one.

Iris declined, putting up her hands. "I've had too much."

"What's one more?" Trish nodded toward the dance floor, where Sadie and Lily were bopping around with Leah and some of her bridesmaids. Jack was dancing nearby with Millie. Paul watched idly from their table. "Put Paul's visit to good use. Let him be on kid duty for the night," Trish said.

Iris laughed. "What the hell." They clinked their tiny glasses and Iris tipped her shot down, a warm fire smoldering instantly in her tummy.

Looking around, as the music pulsed through the floor, Iris realized that right at this moment everyone she'd ever loved was under this one roof. Her kids, her parents, her sister. Trish,

Cooper. And even Paul. All of the people who made up the bedrock of her life were right here. It might never happen again. A wave of sadness rushed up, the kind of wave to which the old Iris would have succumbed. But the new Iris pushed back. No, she would not fret over the passing moment. If she'd learned anything that summer it was that all you ever had was right now. And right now felt pretty damn good.

Just as everyone was flushed with exertion, the DJ spun an oldie. The room slowed, and the melodic notes of "Moon River" washed over the guests. Iris swiped at her brow; she needed a drink of water and some air. Pushing her way to the bar, she felt someone's eyes on her. Leaning against the French doors was Cooper.

"I thought I'd never get you off that dance floor," he said as she glided past him and out onto the balcony. The night air was crisp and welcoming, and she leaned against the iron railing, trying to catch her breath.

"Not a dancing guy?" she asked playfully.

Cooper smiled. "I can be coerced. Just didn't think it was our night." He nodded over his shoulder, toward the ballroom inside.

Hard as it was to keep her distance, she really did appreciate Cooper's discretion.

"Wouldn't want to give good ol' Bitsy any more to gossip about than she already has," Cooper whispered, stepping closer.

"Bitsy can go to hell." And with a quick glance over their shoulders, Iris pressed her lips against his. They tasted faintly of beer, which she found terribly intoxicating. "I miss you."

Instead of pulling away, Cooper wrapped both arms around her waist and pulled her firmly against him. They kissed once, then again. Long, desperate kisses, until Iris couldn't breathe.

"We can't," she whispered, pressing her forehead to his. "Not here."

"I know, I'm sorry." Cooper stepped away. Resting his hands on the railing, he looked up at the sky, his back to her. "Look, there's something I have to tell you."

A sense of dread washed over her. "What is it?"

Cooper paused. "Remember what I said to you at the restaurant that night?"

Iris's head swam, rewinding through the roller-coaster images of the past week. Paul's unexpected arrival, the spilling of Leah's secret. Her reunion with her kids. And finally, back to the porch of the Inn at Hampstead, where she and Cooper had shared their first real date. Where he'd warned her that things would only get more complicated before they got easier again. But it was what he'd said last that had struck hardest.

"When you said that if this was only a summer thing, that that would be enough?"

Cooper flinched. "Yeah. Forget it. Forget all of what I said."

"You didn't mean it?"

He turned around, facing her. "I wanted to mean it, for your sake. I didn't want to put any pressure on you. But after this past week apart, I take it all back. Iris, I want more than just this summer."

Iris's chest swelled. So.

"I know you're going through a lot. And I know you need time. But I'm not going anywhere. Okay?"

Iris nodded, her eyes filling in the darkness. "Okay."

Cooper stepped closer, pressed his lips against her forehead. "And I want more." With that, he stepped back inside, leaving her alone on the balcony.

Iris sank onto the stone bench, overwhelmed. She turned to the sweeping view, all stars and shadows. Then back to the view inside. Dizzy, she rested her forehead on the railing and laughed, a loud and crazy laugh that erupted from her tummy. *Cooper wants more.*

Behind her came the sound of footsteps once more, crossing the patio to her. She grinned, closing her eyes. What more could he say to her now?

But it was Paul. "I've been wanting to get you alone all night," he said, out of breath.

Iris flinched.

"Iris. I want you back."

Iris closed her eyes. "Paul, not now."

"No, you need to listen." He grabbed both her hands with his own, which were clammy. "I'm sorry for everything I've done, Iris. I know I screwed up."

Iris withdrew her hands sharply. "Screwed up? Is that what you call it?"

"Iris, please. We'll do whatever it takes. A vacation. That gardening shed you've been wanting me to build. Whatever you want."

Iris was stunned. "A trip? A shed? You think that's going to erase everything you put this family through?" She moved away from him, toward the doorway. Inside was everything that mattered. And out here on the porch, she realized she felt almost nothing. No real hatred. No desire to go back to what they once were.

"Iris, I'm sorry about what happened. And about how I hurt you." He paused. "She didn't mean anything."

Iris turned around. For the first time she felt almost sorry for him. "That's the thing, Paul. She doesn't mean anything to me anymore, either."

◆　◆　◆

Back inside, Iris's head buzzed. She couldn't believe Paul. She couldn't believe his selfishness or his stupidity. But for the first time, she felt no anger. Nor resentment. She smiled, realizing what it was that she was feeling. It was relief.

"Mom!" Jack loped over. "Grandma needs you. It's time for Aunty Leah and Uncle Stephen's speech. She's been looking all over."

Iris checked her watch. Eleven p.m. already? "Sorry, buddy. I was just out on the porch."

Jack shook his head. "No, she can't find *them*."

Iris scanned the dance floor and the bar. She found Trish and Naomi waiting by the ladies' room.

"Maybe they snuck off for some private time," Naomi joked, winking.

That was something the old Leah would have done, but Iris knew better. She hurried to the ladies' room and peeked under the stalls.

"They can't be far," Trish said when Iris came out empty-handed. But Iris had a bad feeling.

"Would you check the porches?" she asked her friend. She left the ballroom again, passing once more beneath the giant chandelier. So much had happened since she'd crossed beneath it just a few hours ago. The front steps of the club were empty, save for a couple of groomsmen sharing cigars in the doorway. "Hey, guys, any of you seen the happy couple?"

They shook their heads in unison, returning to their cheerful banter.

Millie found her in the foyer, tapping her watch for emphasis. "The elderly guests are tired. We really need to get started on speeches."

As a last resort, Iris headed up the main staircase. The hall was dim, only the light from the gold sconces illuminating her way along the mahogany-paneled corridor. All of the doors she tried were locked, and she was about to give up when she heard the muffled sound of voices.

"Leah?" Iris moved toward the end of the hall, stopping outside a door labeled "Powder Room."

But it was a man's voice that came from the other side. "You're not listening to me."

"Please, it doesn't have to be like this."

It was Stephen and Leah.

Iris stepped back, unsure of whether to get out of there or announce her presence.

Stephen's voice grew adamant. "I mean it. If you don't tell them, I will. It's off."

Before she could decide what to do, the door opened abruptly. Iris jumped back as Stephen stepped out. He glanced at her briefly, startled. Then smoothed his jacket and headed quickly down the hall, away from her. A small cry came from inside.

"Leah?" Iris rushed inside the bathroom. "What's going on?"

"Iris." Leah stood before the mirror, staring at her reflection. Nervously, she dabbed her eyes. "I was . . . uh . . . just washing up."

"What's Stephen talking about? What is he going to tell everyone?"

Leah forced a small smile. "Oh, that. It's nothing, really. We're just having a little disagreement." She lifted one shoulder unconvincingly, still dabbing at her smeared mascara.

"Oh, God. Did he hear us back at the house?"

Leah shook her head. "Don't worry, Iris. It's just a little cold feet."

"Leah, I was right outside the door. I heard you guys."

Leah looked away. Why couldn't she be honest? "Does he know?"

"Iris, please," Leah said, sniffing. She examined herself once more in the mirror. Smoothed her hair, as if it were the only thing askew. "I imagine they're waiting for us downstairs."

"Well, yeah. Mom's practically put out a search party."

Leah nodded, snapping back to business. "I'll be right down."

"But shouldn't we find Stephen first? He looked pretty upset."

Leah shook her head. "He's fine. I'll meet him down there." She pulled a compact from her purse.

Iris glanced worriedly down the empty hall. She couldn't imagine he'd have returned to the festivities below with a false smile. Not after what he'd just said. "Look, everyone down there can wait. Why don't you find Stephen and settle things first?"

Leah looked at her sharply. "Like I said, he'll come around." She pressed the powder roughly to her cheeks, her hand shaking as she did. "Tell Mom I'll just be a minute."

Iris couldn't leave her like this. "Leah."

"Go!" Leah's eyes flashed angrily in the mirror. She herself seemed taken aback. "I'm sorry," she said, turning to Iris. She placed her trembling hands on Iris's shoulders. "It's been a stressful day. Just let me finish up here, and I'll meet you in the ballroom. Okay?"

"All right," Iris relented. Reluctantly, she made her way down the hall and back downstairs, her head swimming all the way. Leah's false smile could mask only so much. This time, Iris wasn't so sure she could fool everyone else.

"Did you find her?" Millie wanted to know the second she returned to their table.

"Yes, she's freshening up." Iris looked around the ballroom. The dance floor was empty. The women, having pulled off their heels, were now rubbing their feet; the men were lounging in their chairs, scraping forks across half-eaten dessert plates. Iris couldn't locate Stephen anywhere among them.

Lily joined them, flopping in Iris's lap like a rag doll, just as she used to do when she was little and in need of a nap. "You tired, baby?" Iris kissed the side of her head, one eye still on the door.

"No way." Lily yawned. "I'm just gonna close my eyes a minute." And she lay her head on Iris's chest.

"Sugar crash," Jack informed her, plopping down in the seat beside them. "She ate three pieces of cake."

"Did not," Lily mumbled sleepily.

Iris was relieved for the weight of her children against her, for the way it normalized her even in stressful moments. But she couldn't ignore the nerve-racking fact that neither Stephen nor Leah had yet appeared.

"I thought you said she was coming," Millie whispered tersely across the table. She'd begun to twist her wedding rings.

"Mom. Do you want to go check on her for yourself?"

"I will!" Lily said, popping up to full attention.

Iris shook her head. But Lily was off her lap and already headed across the ballroom. She looked to Sadie, who rose dutifully. "I know, I know. I'll keep an eye on her."

Bill, stifling a yawn, patted Millie's hand the way he always did to smooth his wife's demeanor. "And speaking of . . ." said Bill.

Iris followed his gaze to Stephen, who was making his way across the dance floor. Alone.

Desperately, Iris searched the ballroom. As Stephen approached the DJ the sounds of the ballroom roared in her ears. Spoons clanked in coffee cups. Conversation rolled melodically. Was she the only one who noticed him?

With a sharp swish, the music was shut off. Everyone turned.

"Excuse me." Stephen cleared his throat, staring uncomfortably at the microphone in his hand. For the first time, Iris noticed Adele and Lance, who stood behind him like sentinels to an oncoming storm. Iris watched helplessly as Adele dabbed at her eyes. All of Leah's worst nightmares were coming true. He'd told them.

"Thank you for coming this evening." Stephen paused, his voice cracking.

Iris reached across the table. "Dad."

"I'm afraid I have an announcement to make," Stephen continued.

All three kids appeared at Iris's side. "Where is she?" she asked them urgently. "Did you find Aunty Leah?"

Sadie shook her head. "She wasn't up there." Then she narrowed her eyes as she sensed the uncertain cloud hovering over the ballroom. "Is something wrong?"

Lily leaned against Iris, twirling her finger. "Lils, did you see her?"

But Stephen's voice pulled her attention away. "We appreciate how far some of you have come, and how much love you've brought with you. We are very grateful for that, indeed." He paused. "Unfortunately . . ." Stephen looked back at Adele, who Iris could now see was crying. Confirming her worst fears, Lance placed a hand on his son's shoulder and urged him on.

"What's the matter?" Jack asked. Glancing from Stephen to his grandparents, who now stood beside the table, looking as if they were about to be swept over by a terrible wind.

"Mommy," Lily whispered.

"Not now," Iris said, one eye on her parents, the other on Stephen, still trying to pull himself together at the microphone.

Lily, who was still playing with her finger, scratched Iris's arm.

"I said not now," she snapped. It was then she saw what Lily was playing with. She grabbed her daughter's hand, holding it still.

"Where did you get that?"

Lily covered the diamond ring protectively.

"Tell me!" Iris gripped her hand, tugging the engagement ring off her little index finger.

"Aunty Leah gave it to me," Lily whimpered. "Just now." The diamond glittered ominously in Iris's palm.

"Dad!" Her chair toppled behind her when she stood.

At the sound of the crash, Stephen stopped and turned in Iris's direction. The guests stirred uneasily, glancing back and forth between Stephen and the maid of honor.

But it was too late. From the grand foyer came another interruption: the urgent clatter of footsteps. The doors to the ballroom burst open. And this time they all turned, to a young man who stood shaking in the doorway. His server's jacket hung from one shoulder at a grotesque angle.

"There's a woman at the bottom of the pool," he cried. "Someone call 911."

Thirty-Three

A t first, she thought she was at the lake. The sun had the soft buttery glow of early morning, and she turned her face toward it. All around her was the reassuring throng of peepers. She relished this, their steady hopeful chirrup. Though there was something strangely mechanical about the rhythm of their song. What was it?

Iris turned her face back to the sun. If she could just stretch out, maybe she'd nod off again. But the stiffness in her limbs nagged, pulling her toward consciousness. And she startled, awakening in the vinyl hospital room chair. Wishing she had not.

Before her, the monitors on the machines throbbed. *Beep, beep, beep.* Iris squinted as the ventilator swished beside her. An IV pole stood sentinel, and her eyes traced the slow drip of fluid, to the long narrow tube, to the arm connected to it all.

Leah.

Iris lurched from the chair. "How is she?"

Millie was pulled up close to the bedside, hunched over the small form tucked beneath the white sheet. She did not turn around. "The same."

Iris stood behind her, peering down at her sister. A ventilator tube had been taped to her open mouth, her full lips pale and stretched around it. But aside from the clear tubes crisscrossing her face, Leah looked strangely peaceful. Iris reached for her, running her fingers across Leah's forehead.

"Oh, sis." Leah's chestnut hair was splayed across the pillowcase. Wavy and free like a mermaid's, underwater. And at that thought Iris's stomach flew up into her mouth.

◆ ◆ ◆

When she finished vomiting, Iris braced herself at the tiny bathroom sink. One cheek was creased from the vinyl chair, where she'd spent the night. Her eyes were sunken. She glanced at her watch: 7:25 a.m. They'd been in the ICU since last night, when Leah was transferred from Emergency.

At first, Stephen had been the only one allowed in the ward with Leah. For two hours, they'd all sat in the ER waiting area, the Willetses slumped against one side of the room, the Standishes on the other. Even in their shared grief, a line had been drawn. It did not matter that Stephen had not had the chance to utter the words of his impending announcement at the rehearsal dinner. They were no longer a family about to be joined, and neither would they share in their grief. Now there was blame to place. And though Iris felt it resting heavily across her shoulders, her mother had aimed hers at the Willetses. Who were they to show up, here, now?

And so Iris had sat between her parents, knees shaking. Braced for an eruption. Readying herself to intervene. But in the end, no words had been spoken. Instead, an orderly had been sent to deliver the news that Leah was still unconscious but was being transferred upstairs. When they'd been told that they could finally see her, they'd pushed past the Willetses and through the swinging doors without looking back. They'd seen no sign of Stephen, or his family, since.

Now, back at the bedside, Iris placed a hand on Millie's shoulder. Her mother shuddered beneath her touch, bristling.

"Sorry, I didn't mean to startle you. I'm going to the cafeteria for coffee. Want some?"

The shake of her head was so minute, at first Iris wasn't sure her mother had heard. "How about tea? Or a muffin?"

Millie waved her away.

"I'm back." Bill entered the room, looking about a thousand years older. His arms were filled. He carried an overnight bag, its mouth gaping, as if it were about to spit out its contents, and the old floral blanket Iris recognized from Leah's bedroom at home. He stood, lost in the middle of the room, holding Leah's things as if for dear life.

"Here, Daddy, let me help you."

Iris arranged the quilt across Leah's still legs, glad for a job. Its flowers looked faded and small under the harsh ultraviolet lighting.

"I brought this, too." Bill pulled a tiny picture frame from the duffel bag. He set it on the table beside Leah, whom Iris noticed he avoided looking at.

It was a silver framed photo of Leah and Stephen standing on the farmhouse porch, their arms around each other.

For the first time Millie looked up. Fury clouded the exhaustion in her eyes. "How could you?" she cried.

Bill froze, eyes darting from his wife to the picture in question. "What?"

"Mom. It's just a picture."

Millie leaped from her chair and plucked the frame off the table.

"What were you thinking?" she cried, her face crumpling. It was the most responsive Iris had seen from her mother since the fateful moment the country club doors had burst open last night. Since the gasping crowd had gathered at the edge of the pool, where staff had already pulled Leah from the twinkling blue water and up onto the concrete patio. Since they'd stood at the curb as the ambulance pulled away, Stephen ghost-stricken in the back with his unconscious bride-not-to-be.

"Mom, it's okay," Iris said, reaching for the picture.

But Millie hurled the frame across the room, where it struck the wall and fell to the floor in a tiny splintering crash.

"He almost killed her!" she screamed.

Iris turned to the bed, for a crazy moment fearful her mother would awaken Leah. Then instantly hopeful that she would. Her gaze turned to her father, whose pallid face filled with anguish, the sorrow spilling from behind his glasses. "I-I'm sorry," he stammered. "I didn't mean . . ."

"Dad," she said, but Bill lifted one hand and went out into the hall.

"He's only trying to help," Iris told her mother, who'd already resumed her watch at Leah's side, returning to her own coma of singular concentration and grief.

Iris cleaned up the glass and tucked the photo into her pants pocket without looking at it. Out in the corridor, she found her father slumped in a chair. "Come on, Daddy. We need to eat something." As they descended in the elevator, Iris kept one hand pressed to her pocket, feeling the folded edge of the picture within. A gesture that came too late, as if she could somehow protect the torn remnants of what remained.

◆　◆　◆

She had no cell service, but a young nurse had shown her to a private phone in the ICU waiting area. A corner room with carpet and curtains, and real upholstered furniture. Iris wondered at its plushness; as if it could somehow cushion its occupants from their pain, or at least muffle the sound of their suffering to those outside.

"The kids are doing okay," Paul reassured her on the phone. "They woke up a little bit ago. They want to see Leah."

"They can't," Iris said. "Not yet."

This morning she was grateful for Paul. For taking care of the kids, for the natural way their conversation flowed back and forth. Free of strife, focused instead on logistics. She realized with a pang that she still needed him. And he was there.

"I almost forgot," he added. "Trish called. Said she's got a ton of food to bring over to the house." Iris had a vague recollection of Trish and Wayne bundling the distraught kids and Paul into their car last night, insisting that Iris go ahead with the others to the hospital.

"So, what's the latest word over there?" Paul asked now.

Over there. The sterile land of hospital monitors and plastic tubes. All morning, Iris had watched nurses come in and out, hovering around various machines, making notes in charts. When the doctor, a man who seemed far too young to deal with so much, arrived on morning rounds, she and her parents had huddled, speechless, as he spoke. Holding their collective breath for the good news. Or the bad. But neither had come.

"The doctor said it's still too early to know anything for sure. The good news is that they don't think she was in the water very long. But her system was full of sedatives. They pumped her stomach twice last night, once they'd stabilized her," she told Paul.

Paul paused. "So, it was an overdose?"

Iris nodded stiffly, and though there was no way he could see this, her silence was affirmation enough.

The doctor had told them Leah had suffered a lack of oxygen, and that they weren't sure what effect that would have on her neurological functioning. There were no hard-and-fast rules with brain injuries. And that's when Iris realized it. Her sister was not going to die from an overdose. Or drowning. Or even a broken heart. In fact, there was hope that she would come out of the coma. But what state she'd be in when she awoke, well, that was a very different story. After listening to the worst-case scenario of possible side effects from lack of oxygen, she could not help but think that perhaps it was still a death of sorts.

"Paul. It's not just the coma. She's really sick."

The words flashed in Iris's brain, the same words that the doctors had used when they met with her family this morning: Suicide attempt. Overdose. Depression. A doctor from the psychiatric unit had been invited to join them. Her words were like scissors, slashing through the summer and all of the silence, a visceral cut that felled them all, but somehow also freed them from their helpless inertia. *Finally.*

"Even when she wakes up, she's going to be hospitalized for a while."

Paul sighed deeply on the other end. "I'm sorry, Iris. What about you?" he asked. "What can I bring you from home?"

Iris couldn't say. She was still in her heels and rumpled dress from last night. Her toes were covered in blisters, and her back ached. But aside from Leah, all she could think about was everyone else back at the house. The kids, sequestered on the farm. The confused relatives and guests stuck at the inn, probably scrambling to find flights out a day early. And the cast here; Millie, hunched over the bed. Her father, wandering aimlessly through the hospital corridors. But mostly, Leah.

"Dad brought some stuff for Leah, but Mom's the one I'm starting to worry about. Could you maybe pull together a bag for her? Trish or Naomi can help."

"Of course. But what about you? Tell me where I can find your flip-flops and some fresh clothes. And what you feel like eating."

As soon as the words were out of his mouth, Iris doubled over. She didn't deserve comfy shoes or fresh clothes, or even Trish's homemade food. While Leah had had a deft hand in the fallout, it was she, Iris, who had dealt the final blow. Pressing Leah to tell Stephen at the eleventh hour as, unbeknownst to them, the man stood in the doorway behind them. Now, leaning against the ICU phone cubicle, she covered her face. "Why didn't I just stay out of it?" she cried.

Paul would not know what she was talking about. But it didn't stop him. "That's it, I'm coming," he said.

"Okay." Her voice was small, but her relief was not. Paul was coming to take care of her, and for the first time in a long time, she realized she wanted him to.

Thirty-Four

The plate of food beside Millie was untouched. She'd frowned at Bill, who'd eagerly finished off one of the sandwiches that Paul had delivered from Trish, along with fruit salad and fresh coffee. Millie had acknowledged them only once, turning to scowl as Bill wiped the crumbs from his button-down shirt. As if his appetite was some form of weakness. As though her refusal of nourishment and comfort was a purer vigil, her self-sacrifice evidence of the depth of her devotion to their daughter.

"She's so angry," Iris whispered to Paul as they convened in the hallway, out of earshot.

"Wouldn't we be?" His question caught her off guard, both in the use of *we* and in its context. Thus far she'd viewed Leah's hospitalization from the lens of sister and daughter. It had not yet occurred to her to imagine what it would be like as a mother.

"You need to eat, too." Paul held up the uneaten half of her sandwich, which he'd carried into the hall for her. He held it to her mouth, a gesture too intimate. But one that she accepted timidly. "Good girl. Have another bite."

The egg salad on her tongue was so reminiscent of her childhood lunches that tears sprang to Iris's eyes.

"Oh, Paul. When is she going to wake up?"

He wrapped his arms around her, and without thought, Iris fell against him. She buried her face in the crook of his neck and breathed. There it was. His familiar smell. The way she fit, just so; a hug like an old glove stretched to her size. "I'm here," he whispered. "We're going to get through this."

This was not the Paul who'd served her divorce papers, not the same man she'd spent the last few weeks hating. It would be so easy to surrender, to let him take her home with the kids. Who would blame her? Given the confusion swirling around them in the harsh glare of the hospital corridor: The beeping of monitors in the room behind them. The anguish of her parents. And Leah, laid out before them like a portrait of all the grief and wonder they'd shared as a family all these years.

Iris did not know how long she cried in Paul's embrace. But suddenly she sensed him there. Her awareness of Cooper Woods was visceral, even with her eyes still closed. She recognized the purposeful strikes of his footsteps coming down the hall, louder even than the pounding of her heart. Then, a sudden pause. Her skin prickled. She looked up just in time to see Cooper standing at the nurses' station, a large bouquet of yellow flowers in his hand. And the way that hand fell to his side when he saw them together, like a soft exhale.

"Cooper." Instantly Iris pulled away from Paul, a stab of guilt overcoming her. "You're here."

"I don't want to disturb your family," he said, approaching uncertainly. "I just wanted to bring these."

He came closer, holding the flowers stiffly between them. "For Leah."

"Thank you, they're beautiful." Their hands brushed as Iris relieved him of the bouquet. "I'm glad you came." He was like sunlight in the hospital hallway, a reminder of how long she'd been cramped inside. How desperately she wanted to touch him, to follow him back outside, into the green summer day.

"How is she?" His eyes were full of concern. And something else.

"We're still waiting for her to wake up." Iris's voice cracked, telling him this, after their summer together. He'd been through so much with her family; he understood her fears better than anyone. Certainly better than Paul.

"Will you let me know when she does?" He glanced briefly over her shoulder at Paul, whom Iris could feel standing his ground behind them. But it was Cooper she wanted to reassure. "Yes! Of course. Do you want to come in?"

Cooper nodded toward the nurses' station. "They said family only. Besides, I don't want to intrude."

Iris shook her head. "Not at all. You're like family." She meant it, and she wanted him to believe her. But Cooper turned to go.

"Please give your folks my best, okay?"

Iris had to fight herself to keep from reaching for him.

"Tell your dad I'll keep an eye on things at the farm. Whatever he needs, just let me know."

Iris heard the implication. Whatever her *father* needed; not she.

"Cooper, wait." There was so much she wanted to say. Oh, why was Paul still standing there?

Cooper turned back to look at her one last time, and his eyes, so like the shoals of the lake, filled her with sadness. She could follow him down the hallway. There were so many things she needed to tell him. But whether it was the pull of her family, in the room behind her, or Paul, still watching them, something held her back. As she stood facing Cooper under the fluorescent glow of the hospital lights, Iris could feel their summer seeping away as surely as if a rainstorm had opened up overhead and was washing them clean. Clean of their lust and their happiness and all that they'd shared, which suddenly, given the context, seemed very small and selfish. Maybe Millie was right; family was all that mattered.

And Cooper Woods was not family.

Cooper broke her silence. "Take care, okay?" And then he turned and headed down the hall, taking the light and the breath out of her chest.

Helplessly, she watched him go, her eyes fixed on the back of his checkered shirt. Looking past the young nurse who was rushing toward her. Then the other. Followed by an orderly, pushing some kind of cart. Iris moved to the side as they brushed past, her eyes still locked on Cooper's retreating figure.

There was a scuffle in the doorway behind her. Then she realized.

"Iris." It was Paul.

Then Millie, whose voice reached her, rising over the sudden din in the hallway. "Where's the doctor? We need him now!"

Sprinting to Leah's door, Iris froze on the threshold. Her parents had been pushed aside. And through the group of nurses and orderlies who swept efficiently around the bed, Iris saw Leah.

Sitting up. Blinking. Holding out her hands, as if to shield herself from all the commotion.

Thirty-Five

Lily galloped down the corridor, a pink homemade card flapping in her hand. Sadie, Jack, and Paul followed quickly behind.

"Aunty Leah's awake!" Lily sang, hopping from one foot to the other. Iris swept her into a hug, breathing her in, feeling the life rolling back into her limbs.

It had been two days since Leah had regained consciousness. Remarkably, she was doing well, the doctors insisted. Though to Iris, it seemed they were being generous. Mostly, Leah had slept. Each time filled Iris with fear that she would not awaken again. But she did, for longer periods each time. And she'd begun to speak, though her speech was somewhat garbled and inconsistent. What was most relieving to Iris was that she seemed to understand everything they said to her. She followed commands, could identify everyone in her family, and knew the date. What she did not seem to remember was the night of her "accident," as Millie insisted they call it. It was as though she'd awakened unsure of how she'd gotten there, but had accepted it. She was even beginning to eat and drink on her own. The "accident" was something she would recover from in time. Though time was exactly what they were looking at.

"Yes, baby, Leah's awake," Iris told Lily happily. "Though she's still pretty tired."

They approached Leah's bed hand in hand. Leah was resting on her side, eyes closed.

"Is she sleeping again?" Lily wondered loudly.

Leah's eyelids fluttered. She looked around, her gaze finding them. "Kids," she whispered. Her voice was rough and unused, and Lily leaned hard against Iris.

"It's okay. Leah, the kids are here to see you. They wanted to say hi."

Leah smiled slowly, her lips cracked at the edges.

"Hi," Lily said in a small voice.

Leah mouthed "hi" back to her.

Jack only stared. Sadie took a step closer. "How do you feel?" she asked shyly.

Leah looked dreamily at all three of them, as if wondering herself. "Tired," she whispered. She tried sitting up, and Iris reached to help her, adjusting the pillows behind her head.

"That's better, now you can see everyone." Iris turned to the kids expectantly. "Want to show Aunty Leah the special picture you made?"

They stared back, unsure. Sadie elbowed Lily. "Show her."

"Here. This is for you." Lily dropped the card lightly on Leah's chest, taking a quick step back.

Leah blinked at it before reaching gingerly to pick it up. Her movements were cumbersome and slow, and Iris could see her tiring already.

"Oh," she said as Iris held it up before her. "Beautiful."

"How about I hang this up for you?" Iris offered cheerfully. Her voice sounded false and loud in the small room, and she realized she was making too much effort for all of them. "I'll get some tape from the nurses' station."

She left the kids for a moment, nodding encouragingly at them.

When she came back with the tape, they were in the same position, shoulder to shoulder, staring at Leah. Who had already fallen back into a quiet slumber, her face relaxed on the pillow.

"She's sleeping again!" Lily said worriedly.

"It's okay, honey." Iris handed her the picture and helped her tape it to Leah's bedside table, where she'd see it when she awoke. Hopeful she'd remember the kids' visit when she did. "She's probably going to rest a lot the next few days. She'll get better, though."

Lily glanced back at the doorway. "Can we go home now?"

◆ ◆ ◆

"How'd they do?" Paul asked as they followed the kids to the elevator.

"Good, considering. But it's scary for them. She's not the Leah they're used to."

"She will be," Paul said, punching the down button. Instead of finding his take-charge attitude reassuring, Iris found herself prickling.

"Well, yes. We hope. But you heard the doctor last night. She's going to need rehabilitation. The specialists have to come in and do their assessments—there's still so much we don't know."

"Iris." Paul put his hands on her shoulders, as if he were trying to calm a small child. "We know. But try to be positive, okay?"

He punched the button impatiently again, and Iris felt herself deflating in the old way she used to. She *was* positive. She was just realistic, too. This was her sister. Who could blame her?

The doors opened. While they waited for the elevator to empty, it was not lost on Iris that this was the same elevator Cooper had entered alone days before. And here they were, crowding into it now. The five of them, looking like the perfect family again.

◆ ◆ ◆

Back at the farm, Iris awoke from a nap on the couch to find Paul standing in front of her, holding out a plate of spaghetti. "Why don't you go to bed, after you eat something?" he said. "You look awful."

"Gee, thanks."

"No, you know what I mean. You need sleep."

She'd slept little to none in the last couple of days. Right now her bed sounded so good. She wrapped the afghan blanket more tightly around herself and sat up. "Okay. I think I will." She accepted the plate gratefully. "But what about the kids?"

"I'll put them to bed before I head back to the B and B. I called work and told them I'd be staying a few more days. If that's okay with you."

Was it? Sure, things were crazy right now, and Iris could use help. The kids needed their father, too. But what did it mean if she let him stay longer, if she let him continue to take care of them all? "I don't know what's going to happen next with Leah, or how long it'll take."

"I know. Which is why I'll stay. And when things settle, I figured I'd bring the kids home. You can stay up here as long as you feel you need to." He looked at her meaningfully. "And come home whenever you're ready."

At the mention of home, her insides fluttered. What was home, for any of them, anymore? She looked around her childhood family room now, wondering when Leah would be able to return to the farm. No matter how hard Iris tried, she couldn't picture Leah staying here through fall, alone on the farm. Trying to recover, sitting on this couch where Iris now sat. Looking out at the lake, waiting for her life to start again.

Just as she couldn't picture herself staying here, either. Struggling to start over with the kids. The mere thought of trying to move them away from their friends and their school back in Massachusetts seemed an impossibility. Not to mention moving them away from their father. But the alternative no longer felt right, either. She put the half-eaten bowl of spaghetti on the coffee table.

"You're right, I need sleep." Iris stood, the afghan dragging on the floor behind her. When Paul lifted it and draped it around her shoulders, Iris stiffened.

"I'll clean up the kitchen and get the kids organized for the night. Why don't you head up to bed?"

"Okay." Iris started up the stairs, her eyes trained on each step. What was she doing? Paul was only trying to make things work, something she'd found comfort in earlier. Maybe if she tried harder, too. She looked down at him from the steps. "Thanks, again, for dinner. And for taking care of the kids. I don't know what I'd do right now if you weren't here for them."

Upstairs she did not climb into bed so much as fall. She was too tired to contemplate tomorrow; today was already so full. Leah was awake. Paul had the children. And here, thank God, was her pillow. Check, check, check.

◆ ◆ ◆

Iris stopped at the nurses' station to sign in.

"Going to see our favorite girl?" the young male nurse asked.

He was handsome, no older than his early twenties, and Iris had to laugh at the fact that even in her weakened state Leah had apparently charmed him. "Yes," she said. "How's she doing today?"

"She's been busy with her fan club. Physical therapy, then speech therapy. The counselor. Though I think they're all done by now." He glanced down at a schedule. "Yep, looks like you're her first 'fun' visitor today. Aside from her husband, of course."

Iris blinked. "Excuse me?"

The orderly looked up from his paperwork. "Mr. Willets. Your sister's husband."

"Fiancé. I mean . . . ex-fiancé." Iris shook her head. What Stephen was, at this point, didn't really matter. "Where did you say he was?"

After the first night in the ER, Millie had barred the hospital from allowing the Willetses access to Leah. Demanded that only family be allowed into Leah's room. Given the fact that Leah was on suicide watch, the psychiatrist on call had agreed that it was best. An assigned social worker had enforced the request. Even though Iris had heard how angry the Willetses were with this measure, she'd had to agree with Millie on this one.

Without access to Leah, as far as Iris knew, Stephen had flown back to Seattle with his parents. Since then, the only concern she had for Stephen Willets was what she would say if Leah asked after him. Which, by some miracle, she had not yet done. Now Iris's heart skipped a beat.

The nurse frowned and looked at his notes more carefully. "I'm sorry. I assumed Mr. Willets was your sister's husband. Since he's been staying with her."

◆   ◆   ◆

Iris raced down the hall and halted in the doorway. "I thought you went back to Seattle."

Stephen spun around, his eyes wide but unapologetic. "Iris."

"What are you doing here?" she demanded.

"I couldn't leave her. Not like this." He motioned to Leah, who was sleeping. But Iris couldn't take her eyes off Stephen. He looked haggard, his shirt rumpled and his hair askew.

"Oh, I see. But you could leave her at the altar."

Stephen winced. "Iris, please. Now is not the time."

"You're right. I think I'll come back later. With the social worker." She tugged her purse firmly over her shoulder.

"Don't!" Stephen's voice was firm, but his expression crumpled with worry. "Please, don't. She needs me."

She paused, her hands shaking.

"She needs all of us."

Iris had never been able to conjure the same rage that Millie held to so tightly, but she'd not exactly held Stephen blameless. You could hardly assign all the responsibility to a bride at the bottom of a pool.

"Please," Stephen begged. "I know you hate me. But you have to listen."

Iris turned, her eyes on the linoleum floor. "I don't hate you," she whispered. "I hate what's happened to her. That she could just try to leave us like that," she choked. And there it was. The admission that, despite all the other antagonists in her story, it came down to Leah's choice to try to end her life. To decide to leave them all.

"I know. It's all I think about, every minute." Stephen stood wearily and pulled an adjacent chair over. "Come sit."

Reluctantly, Iris joined him.

Stephen let out a long breath and took Leah's hand in his own. She stirred, but slept on. "I heard you and Leah talking before the rehearsal dinner."

Iris closed her eyes. It was a talk they had to have.

"Stephen, I tried to get her to tell you. But it wasn't my news to share."

Stephen shook his head, silencing her. "I'd known that she was keeping something from me all summer. Suddenly she didn't want to go home to Seattle. And then she changed her mind about working for the foundation, something my parents worked so hard to include her in. She just wasn't herself."

"She had a change of heart about those things, Stephen. But she still loved you."

"I know. And I could accept those changes. But starting a family was everything. She and I talked about it all the time." He turned to look at Iris. "You need to know something: it wasn't that Leah couldn't have children. It was that she lied to me, again and again, whenever I tried to ask her what was bothering her this summer. It was that I had to find out, by accident, by overhearing the two of you."

Iris leaned forward, listening. "I'm so sorry you had to learn about it like that."

"She should've told me about the baby and about what she went through last summer. Because I could've helped her somehow. I wanted to help her. But Leah didn't feel she could trust me with the truth. And in keeping those secrets, she kept a part of herself from me. That was the betrayal I couldn't get past."

Iris nodded. Here was the only other person, beside herself, who truly understood how complicated Leah was. "I'm sorry she lied to you about something so important. But still—I just don't see how you could leave her at the altar."

Stephen stood. "I didn't leave her at the altar!"

"You were going to!" Iris cried. "You were standing there with a microphone in your hand and your grim-faced parents behind you. I know what you were planning to say. The only reason you didn't is because Leah beat you to it—she threw herself into that pool before you had to make your announcement." Now she was crying.

"No, Iris. Even to this day I don't know what I was going to say," Stephen said, his own eyes filling with tears now. "I wasn't in my right mind. I felt like she'd already left me. I'd felt it all summer long. And that was the final blow." He wiped his nose with his sleeve. "Leah doesn't let people in. And I couldn't stand up before all the people who love us and pretend that I was going to spend the rest of my life with someone who doesn't love me enough to let me in."

Iris put her hand on Stephen's arm. She knew. She'd spent her whole life trying to get Leah to let her in.

"She loves you, Stephen. She may not know how to let people in, but she loves you."

Stephen nodded, covering his face with his hands. He took a few ragged breaths.

"She looks better today, don't you think?" Iris asked. Leah's cheeks were rosy, a more vibrant color than the ashen hue they'd been. Briefly, Iris wondered if it was something about Stephen's presence.

"She's never looked more beautiful." There was protectiveness in Stephen's voice, which Iris drew comfort from.

A nurse came in and did a quick check of vitals. "Mr. Willets, would you like me to have them send in a cot again tonight?"

He glanced quickly at Iris, nervously, then nodded to the nurse. "Yes, that'd be great." He stood up. "I can help you with it."

"No, no," the nurse said, shooing him away. "You stay with your bride. We know the drill."

Iris studied him as Stephen walked to the window, arms crossed uncomfortably.

"So you've been sleeping here?"

He nodded.

"For how long?"

"I haven't left yet."

Iris looked around the tiny room, at the bed, the one chair. The bedside table crowded with pictures, cards, and flowers.

"But how? I haven't seen you. And my mother said—"

"Your mother meant well. But she was wrong." He turned to face her. "Leah needs me."

He walked around the bed, to Leah's pillow. Touched her hair.

"So you mean to tell me you've been hiding out here since the first night?"

Stephen sighed. "Yes. But please don't share that with Millie. I don't want to upset her, because that will only upset Leah. I didn't want to fight her on this, but I will if I have to." His voice softened as he looked back at Leah. "Whatever she needs."

"So you've talked to her about this?" Iris nodded toward Leah, who stirred in the bed. "And she's known you've been here all along?"

"Yes, of course. We wanted to keep it between us. She needs peace."

Iris sat back in the chair, taking it all in. So that was why Leah had not asked after Stephen yet. She hadn't had to. "How'd you do it? Leah never said a thing."

"When your family visited, I stayed on the cardiac floor, below." He shrugged. "My mom brought me clothes, and I ate in the cafeteria."

Iris's jaw dropped. "Your parents are still here, too?"

He looked at her sheepishly. "Just my mom. She thought it was the right thing to do."

So Adele was in on it. But instead of drawing ire, the move

filled Iris with a new appreciation. "So your mother has gone into hiding somewhere in town, and you've pretty much camped out in the cardiac center for a week?"

"Pretty much." He smiled roughly, rubbing the overgrowth on his chin. "Though I don't recommend trying to bathe yourself from a restroom sink. Not very thorough."

Iris squeezed her nose with one hand, playfully. "Now that you mention it." But the relief of their easy banter was quickly overshadowed by concern. "Stephen, I'm amazed you did this. Really." She paused, struggling for the right words. "But what does all this mean?"

"Mean?" The confusion on his face was genuine.

"Leah couldn't handle you leaving again. She's got a long recovery ahead of her."

"I wouldn't do that to her," Stephen said. He turned back to Leah and swiped at his eyes. For the first time Iris saw the spill of tears, running down his cheeks. "You have to believe me, I wouldn't do that."

Iris rested a hand on his back. "I want to believe you." She had all the answers he had to give. For now it would have to be enough.

Thirty-Six

Iris awoke to a buzzing sound. She glanced at the clock. Nine thirty. Had she really slept through the night?

Her phone buzzed again on the nightstand, and she reached to silence it. *Two messages.* Her heart jumped. Had Cooper finally called?

The first was Trish, checking in to see how Leah was. Impatiently, Iris hit Delete. She'd call her back. The next was a number she did not recognize. From out of state.

"Iris!" It was Joan, her editor, and at first Iris's heart fell in disappointment. Cooper hadn't called.

"I finished the proposal, and I went ahead and shared it with the marketing and business team." Joan paused, and Iris's stomach flip-flopped at the realization that this was the call she'd been waiting for. She held her breath, pressing the phone tighter against her ear. "There are a few questions about format, and we really need to rethink the title, but I have to tell you . . . they loved it! I've put together some numbers for you. Call me. It's a go!"

Iris squealed. Phone in hand, she leaped up, both feet straddling the twisted blankets beneath her, and began jumping up and down on the bed. "Oh my God! Oh my God! We did it!" An energy raw with happiness coursed through her like a bolt, and she jumped until she was afraid the bed would break.

She had to call Trish! She had to go downstairs and tell the kids! And her parents! But first, she wanted to tell Cooper.

She grabbed her phone. His number was at the top of her screen, under Favorites. All she had to do was hit Call. But instead, Iris set the phone down on her bedside table and covered her face with her hands.

◆ ◆ ◆

Iris navigated the Rover up the wooded drive. She'd taken a chance on finding him here at home. Cooper had not been to the farm all week, and she couldn't go another day without seeing him. Buoyed by the joy of sharing her news with her family and Trish, who'd about blown out her right eardrum on the phone, Iris had decided to make the first move.

She hopped out and looked around the small clearing. Overhead a red-tailed hawk circled. A small breeze stirred the pines. She climbed the wooden steps to his porch and took a deep breath before knocking.

"Cooper?" There was no sound of footsteps inside, and for a moment she felt something akin to relief. She went to the porch railing and leaned out, looking down the hillside through the dense pines.

She was about to give up when she heard the crackling of twigs from the woods. Cooper emerged from the trees, a bundle of kindling under his arm. Before she could call his name he looked up and saw her.

Iris lifted her hand, a small gesture for all the big things she'd come to see him about. He nodded as if he'd been expecting her.

◆ ◆ ◆

"So, how is she?" The teakettle sputtered on the gas stove, and Cooper dropped tea bags into two blue mugs, his back to her. He wore a few days' growth of stubble on his face. Iris watched quietly, wondering if this would be the last cup of tea she'd share with him.

"They're going to transfer her to a rehabilitation center in Keene soon. Millie's over there doing the paperwork now."

Cooper turned to really look at her for the first time. His eyes didn't crinkle in the corners, like usual. "So, she's got a bit of a road ahead of her."

"Yeah, she does." Iris paused. "Her fine motor skills are coming along. Her speech is almost back to normal. But there's still the mental health part of recovery that she's got to tackle."

Cooper filled the mugs with steaming water and brought one to her. "Still. It's a miracle, really, when you think about it."

"Pretty much." Iris couldn't let herself flash back to the edge of the country club pool, because if she did she would lose it.

As if reading her mind, Cooper put a hand on her back and guided her into the living room. "How're you holding up?"

Had anyone else asked her that? "Okay. It's been pretty crazy." She took a sip of the hot tea and settled herself onto the couch. "But I did get some good news."

"Oh?" He looked at her hopefully.

"The cookbook that Trish and I have been slaving over all summer?" She couldn't hide her grin. "It's getting published!"

Cooper smiled, a moment too late. Had he been expecting her to say something else? But he stood and hugged her tightly, whispering congratulations. "I knew you had it in you. That's fantastic! So what's next?"

"Trish and I have a lot of editing to do. When that's done, we're going to New York to meet with the publisher, sometime this fall." Just the mention of fall shifted the air between them. Reminding Iris of why she'd really come.

"So now I know a famous writer," Cooper teased.

"I wouldn't go that far. A writer, at least." She shook her head. "It's been quite a summer."

"How are the kids?"

"Good. They're still here. And so is Paul."

Cooper's expression remained even. "You need all the help you can get. I can't imagine."

"I wanted to call you."

"Iris, don't. I'm fine."

"Well, I'm not." She ran a hand through her hair, looking around them. At the wooden mantel on the fieldstone fireplace. At the knotted pine floors, a gleaming honey against the gray day outside. Everything in this cabin emanated warmth and peace, like Cooper himself. So unlike the chaos of the farm these last few days. So unlike her own home, brimming with tension, back in Massachusetts.

"Cooper, I don't know what to do anymore." Iris stood and began pacing the room.

"About?"

"How can you ask that? Us, of course."

"Oh." He stared into his mug.

"Haven't you wondered? I mean, I can barely sleep. Eat. Or think."

"It's all I think about, Iris."

Iris felt a tightening across her shoulders. She had to ferry them to some kind of decision; she had to be honest. "When I came here in July, my marriage was over. That hasn't changed."

Cooper waited, listening.

"It was Paul who brought it on. But as hard as it was to face at first, he was right. And so I came up here to heal. To move forward."

She went to the window, searching for words. "But now, after everything that's happened, it's changed the way I see things. And suddenly Paul is back, and he wants us to work through this."

"Is that what you want?"

"No! I want *us*, Cooper. I want us to have a chance. I think we'd be good. I know we would."

Cooper's eyes held her own. "But?"

"But then I look at Sadie and Lily and Jack. They have so much ahead of them. And I can't help but wonder how much I'd derail that if I let my family go. It kills me to think about what this would do to them; the shuffling back and forth between two homes. The fact that they are either with their dad or with their mom, but never have access to both at the same time. And I think kids need that; I really do."

Cooper watched quietly as she went on, her voice as rapid as her pacing.

"It's so unfair to the kids. What if Lily gets sick, and she's at her dad's? What if she wants me in the middle of the night?" She paused, imagining the scene in her mind. "And the split—who gets the weekends? Who gets Christmas?" She was rambling now, a stream of all her domestic fears pouring out into Cooper's quiet living room. "Forget about the holidays, what about the little things: like making sure they have healthy lunches packed for school each day? And that Jack does his homework. And who's monitoring their friends, and social media, and making sure they're okay? This whole separate-parenting thing: God, how does it even work?" She stopped in front of the fireplace, a wild look on her face.

Cooper, who'd been patiently waiting for her to finish, stood. "Iris. These are the things I was talking about that night at the inn. Splitting up was the hardest thing I ever went through, and I don't even have kids." He approached her carefully. "These are not small decisions. And as much as I wish I could help, I can't make them for you." He reached for her hands, but instead she fell against him, burying her face in his neck.

"Before, it was easier. It was Paul's decision, and somehow that made it different. Now, it's all on me. If I choose not to get back together, then I'm the one pulling the trigger. I can't imagine putting the girls and Jack through that. It just seems so selfish."

"I know. Hearing you say it like that . . ." He pulled back, looking at her. "It's why I've stayed away, Iris. Because someday, when things got tough, which they would, you'd resent me. I don't want to saddle you with that kind of regret. Too much is at stake."

Iris nodded appreciatively. But it didn't make it easier. "I don't want to stay in an unhappy marriage, Coop. I know people divorce, and kids get through it. But this feels like I have to choose between the kids' happiness and ours."

Cooper looked pained. "I have to say this, Iris."

"What?"

"Paul cheated on you. He had a woman like you, a beautiful, intelligent, strong woman. And he cheated. He doesn't deserve you back—he never did in the first place."

Iris felt her insides give. It was what she wanted: Cooper was fighting for her.

Cooper looked at her searchingly. "Iris, I love you. But whether you end up with me or not, you deserve a happy ending. Paul can't give you that."

Tears formed in her eyes. "I can't find the 'happy' in any of it. Someone ends up hurting." She went to the window. The clouds had darkened the sky to a steely gray that reminded her of winter. She shivered. "Tell me what to do."

Cooper came to stand beside her. "I'll do whatever you need me to."

Iris put her hands to her eyes. She felt as if she might fly apart into a million pieces right there. "I feel so damn alone."

"You're not alone," Cooper whispered, pulling her back against him. "Every night I sit on that porch thinking about you." He pointed outside to the wooden deck overlooking the pines. "And every day I stand at that stove imagining making you breakfast." He pointed to the kitchen behind them, where they'd done just that.

Iris looked up at him. "I want that, too. You have no idea how much." She swallowed back her tears. "Every night I lie in bed, and my limbs ache. They just ache to be held."

Cooper squeezed her harder. "Iris, before this summer, I didn't think I'd ever fall in love again. Not like this." He laughed sadly. "You made me feel like a teenager. Like we were two crazy kids with nothing ahead of us but a long, hot summer. You made me feel so alive."

"Me, too."

"But we aren't teenagers anymore. We've got grown-up lives and responsibilities. And I never expected you to turn your back on all that."

"Oh, Cooper. I'm sorry. I've made such a mess of things."

"Hold on a minute." He sat back, his hands on her shoulders. "I wouldn't trade this summer for anything. No matter how it . . . ends."

The word shifted in the air between them, ushering Iris to the heart of the matter. "I don't think there's any other way," she said, her eyes brimming. "I tell myself that this is the right thing to do. I have to go home."

Cooper's blue eyes clouded, and he blinked as she said it. "With Paul? Is that what you want?"

She shook her head. "Paul and I aren't in love; it's too late for us. But I think I have to stay in this marriage for the kids. I just want them to have a happy childhood. To feel loved."

"What about you?"

"I had my chance. Right?" She put a hand to his cheek. "I had this summer. I'll just have to take it with me."

Cooper sat down on the couch. "All right," he whispered. "If that's what you want."

"Do you understand?" she asked, her voice breaking. "Do you know how hard this is for me? That it goes against every grain of my being?" She looked into his eyes, which were glistening now.

"You're an amazing woman, Iris. I wouldn't expect any less from you."

There, he'd said it. He'd freed her to go, though going was the last thing she wanted to do.

Cooper stood and jammed his hands awkwardly in his pockets, just the way he'd done on that first morning back in July when they'd bumped into each other at the farm stand. "It's probably the right thing to do."

"Is it?"

He forced a small smile. "Every night your kids will have you."

"I know," she cried. "But every night when I close my eyes, it'll be you I see."

And as suddenly as it was said, Cooper moved to the door. Iris hesitated, her heart pounding in her chest. It was the worst decision, and the right one. Her head spun at the realization that she'd done it. It was over, and if she'd meant what she said, then it was time for her to go home.

Cooper did not open the door but stood there, beside her, as she paused on the threshold. Gentleman though he was, he would not be the one to open the door that would let her walk out of his life.

Iris turned, one last time, and brushed his cheek with her lips. He inhaled softly.

She kissed his face lightly, trailing her lips across the stubble on his jaw. "I love you, Cooper Woods." She kissed his eyes, his forehead. Until her mouth found his, and she pressed against them with her whole being.

Cooper wrapped his arms tightly around her waist, his mouth opening to accept her. To taste her, one last time.

And when she thought she would either burst or cry out, she turned away, pushed through the screen door, and hurried down the stairs. She did not look up at the porch as she pulled away. Vision blurred by tears, she navigated the gravel drive roughly. It wasn't until she reached the main road that she stopped, rested her head on the steering wheel, and wept.

Thirty-Seven

Leah was sitting up in a chair working with the speech thera-pist when Iris arrived the next morning.

"How's she doing?" Iris asked when the therapist came out.

"Remarkable, considering." She glanced at her notes. "I'm going to refer her for continued assistance at the rehabilitation center, but I think they'll discharge her shortly thereafter." She smiled at Iris. "Like I said, she's doing great."

At least one of us is, Iris thought as she returned to Leah's room. She hadn't slept at all the night before, and her stomach felt queasy.

"Come here," Leah said, patting the bed. "I want to talk to you."

Iris waited as Leah tried to scoot over to make room for her. "Take your time," she said, reaching to help.

But Leah waved her hand away. "I've got it."

The therapist was right. Leah was doing remarkably well, and Iris had to stop fussing over her.

"So you're busting out of here, I hear?"

Leah smiled. "Yeah, tomorrow."

Leah had been given the thumbs-up to be transferred to the rehabilitation center the next morning. She'd have access to all the help she needed, from the occupational therapy room to daily sessions with the in-house counselor. It was a relief to all of them.

"Mom and Dad are over at the center now, checking things out," Iris told her.

Leah rolled her eyes. "Great, you know what that means."

"Millie will have instilled the fear of God in the staff before you even arrive. And your roommate, if you have one, will have been displaced from the room. Which will have been completely rearranged and redecorated, of course."

Leah laughed. "And they'll all hate me before I even arrive."

"Nah, you'll win them over the second they meet you. Like you always do." Iris squeezed her sister's hand. "Remember how Mom used to 'visit' Girl Scout camp before our session each summer?"

"Oh, God. The gym schedule was totally revamped to make way for performing arts. And the junk food cereal was pulled from the mess-hall shelves."

"Don't forget the time she suggested that the boys' camp be moved across the lake!"

Leah shook her head, giggling. "Remember we pretended not to know her on visiting weekend? We were so afraid the other kids would tease us."

Iris grinned. "She always knew how to ruin stuff."

"But she meant well," Leah added in their mother's defense.

"And she still does." They sat for a minute, recalling their mother's interferences with fondness.

"Listen, I need to tell you something," Leah said. She looked at Iris with an intensity that Iris could tell was hard to muster.

"Are you tired? Maybe I should go and let you rest."

Leah shook her head. "It's about Stephen."

"I already know. Did he tell you we 'bumped' into each other?"

"Yeah. That's what I want to talk to you about. I don't want you to be mad at him."

"I'm not mad," Iris reassured her, and Leah shot her a skeptical look. "Not anymore. We were just worried about you."

"I know," Leah said. "But I'm the one who made those choices." She lowered her voice. "From keeping a secret to—"

Iris interjected. "You were hurting, Leah. I wish I'd known how much. I should've done more to help you."

"No," Leah interrupted. "Don't say that. You were there for me, just like Mom and Dad were. You were all just trying to protect me." She shook her head ruefully. "From myself."

Iris leaned against the pillows, allowing herself to think back over things she'd tried to forget. "Mom and I didn't agree. She wanted to let things go, and leave things up to you to handle. But I pushed you to tell Stephen about the pregnancy. On the eve of your wedding, no less. It wasn't my place."

"You were trying to protect me from this." She held her hands out, indicating the sterile hospital room around them. "Maybe if I'd listened, I wouldn't be here now."

"So you're not upset with me?"

Leah sat up and wrapped her thin arms around her. "How could I be?"

"What do you want to happen next? What can I do to help?"

"Listen, Stephen and I have talked. A lot." She paused. "We've made a decision."

"About?" Iris asked warily.

"We want to work things out." Leah beamed as she said it, but Iris couldn't help but be skeptical.

"Are you ready for that? I mean . . ."

"Yes. I am. Which is why I want you to tell Mom for me."

Iris laughed out loud. "Excuse me? Were you not listening to everything we just said about summer camp?"

"Seriously, Iris. She has to know. He wants to stay, and I want her to let him." She blinked. "I need him."

"Okay. But why me?"

"Because she listens to you. You're the good one. The one with 'her head on straight.'"

"I wouldn't go that far."

"No, it's true. She'll take it better coming from you. You're always so good at rationalizing things. If only you'd gone to law school, like she wanted." She smiled teasingly. "Really, will you do this one thing for me?"

Iris hesitated. "Okay. But what do you want me to tell her exactly?"

"Tell her that we've decided to stay in Hampstead. Stephen thinks he can work from the East Coast. When I get better we'll find a place together near the farm." She sank back against her pillows, stifling a yawn. "I'm not saying it's going to be easy. But somehow, I think we're all going to be okay."

So, they were staying after all. It was the best news Iris could've hoped for her. Leah would get to stay at the farm, doing what she loved. And Stephen would be with her, doing what he loved, if from a distance. "I'm happy for you, Leah. You deserve this."

Iris watched as Leah's eyelids began to flutter. It was still hard to see her vibrant sister worn out by a mere conversation. "I'll tell Mom."

"You too, Iris. You're going to be okay, too."

"I know."

Leah opened her eyes. "No, you don't. I saw you this summer. I know how messed up I was with my own shit, but I saw you." She yawned again, her words coming more slowly. "You were the old Iris."

"Old?" Iris forced a laugh.

"The happy Iris. Like when we were kids."

Iris looked out the window. "I don't think I was ever *that* happy as a kid. Not compared to you, at least."

"Sure you were."

"No, that would be you." Iris let out a nervous laugh. "The popular one, the champion swimmer. No matter what I did, you always came along and did it better."

Leah turned to her. "Why do you think I tried so hard? How do you think I won all those ribbons?"

Iris sighed, the old jealousies of it creeping back. "Honestly, I have no idea."

"I was just trying to keep up with you."

Iris stared back at her sister, a blank look on her face.

"Come on, you must've known. You were the good one. I may

have been the loud, exciting one, but that was your shadow I was always chasing." Leah adjusted the blankets and closed her eyes again. "You deserve to be happy, Iris. Just let yourself."

Iris stiffened slightly on the bed. "Listen, you'd better get some rest. Besides, I should probably head back to the farm. Paul's been with the kids all week. I think they're getting ready to go home soon."

Leah gave a small nod against her pillow, eyes still closed. "What about you?" she murmured.

Iris wavered. Although she'd come to a decision at Cooper's, she was still not at peace with it. "I think maybe I should go home with them."

Leah didn't answer at first, and Iris wondered if perhaps she'd fallen asleep. After a minute she got up and quietly fetched her purse. But as she paused at the bed, Leah's hand found her own.

Her voice was a mere whisper before she gave in to sleep. "You are home."

Thirty-Eight

The next afternoon Iris stood by her own bed, in her child-hood room. She gazed at the suitcase and bags strewn across its quilted surface and shook her head. How had she acquired so much stuff?

"This is pretty," Trish said, handing her a coral silk scarf. It was the one she'd bought in town, in her fit of defiance. Along with the two pairs of heels, which she held up now. She examined the soles of the black pair, which Leah had scuffed up that crazy night in the bar. Even her shoes retained the scars of the summer.

"You take these," Iris said, thrusting them at Trish.

"What do you mean? You rocked these heels."

Iris frowned. "Where am I going to wear those back at home? Soccer? A Girl Scouts meeting?"

"Well, aside from the fact I couldn't jam my size-eleven feet into these to begin with, you are not tossing these out. You find a place to wear them. They're part of the new you!"

Trish was smiling, but Iris wasn't so sure that bringing the new her home was such a good idea. "They make me feel guilty."

"That's crap." Trish dangled the black heels between them. "How can a pair of shoes make you feel guilty?"

"I don't know. I bought them when I was mad. When I was trying to turn into someone else. They just feel illicit somehow, coming home with me."

"Illicit my ass. You mean sexy. And there is nothing wrong

with sexy, Iris. You could use a little more sexy. Now pack these in that suitcase before I rap you over the head with them."

Iris gave in and tucked them under her mom jeans, which had so far escaped Trish's attention. Until now.

"These, however, should be burned!" Trish plucked out the pair of Iris's saggy old jeans. Before Iris could snatch them away, she tossed them over her shoulder to the garbage can in the corner.

"Stop, I can wear those in the garden," Iris objected.

Trish narrowed her eyes. "Oh, I see. I get it now."

"Get what?"

"You're going to go home and revert right back to your old ways. As if this summer never happened."

Iris stared at her suitcase.

"Isn't that right?" Trish pressed.

"Well, how else do I go home? It's not like I'm gonna make a scrapbook on Shutterfly and tote it to Back to School Night. 'Look, Ainsley Perry. Here's a photo of my sister causing a bar brawl! Here's a picture of the divorce papers I never went through with! And *here's* my summer boyfriend, the man I slept with while my no-longer-to-be-divorced-from husband was home watching my kids!'" Iris forced a small laugh, but inside she felt like she might throw up.

Trish did not laugh. Instead she sat down on the bed, studying Iris in a way that made her want to crawl into the suitcase. "Is that how you really feel about your summer?"

"No. I don't know. How should you feel about a summer that you love, but that never should have happened?"

Trish listened quietly. "Here's what I think. I think that this summer was forced on you. Paul started it. Hell, he sent you divorce papers. And you were simply reeling in his wake. You were brave to come up here on your own. If you ask me, I think you found beauty at the bottom of a toilet bowl. You survived it. And so what if you've got a pair of sexy shoes to show for it?"

Iris listened in disbelief. She'd been so busy worrying about the kids, about Leah, about Cooper. She'd forgotten that this summer had originally started out as a time when she needed to be worried about herself. And that it had been not only a forgivable indulgence but a necessary one.

"Don't you feel guilty for a second." Trish pointed her finger right under Iris's nose, then pinched it.

"What am I going to do without you?" Iris leaned over and hugged her.

"You won't have to find out. You're coming back to visit me. Every month!"

"Trish, I don't know if that's such a good idea . . ."

Trish held up her hand. "Fine. Then I will visit you until the dust settles. But you'll be back."

Iris smiled sadly; somehow, someday, of course she would.

Together they finished packing, tossing all her stuff into the suitcase. The faded red swimsuit. The designer denim, right on top of the mom jeans Iris confiscated from the trash can. As Iris contemplated the items before her, she realized that each piece told a part of the story. And she didn't have to choose between them. Yes, she was a mother, who fell behind on coloring her hair, and sometimes forgot to brush her teeth. But she was also still a desirable woman, who, as Trish insisted, could rock a pair of heels. And, more meaningfully, fall down in the tall grass under the stars with a man who had fallen in love with her. She would not be ashamed of any of it, each layer of her in all its complex glory.

Back downstairs, Trish hugged and kissed them all, reserving a cool handshake for Paul, whom Iris understood she would never really forgive. But that was part of landscape of friendship.

"I'll see you in New York in two weeks," Iris promised.

Trish leaned out her car window before tearing off. "Wearing those heels!"

◆　◆　◆

Back upstairs, Iris found the kids had packed themselves with more speed and efficiency than their mother had done. "I'm ready, Mom!" Lily announced, dragging her Hello Kitty duffel bag out into the hallway. Iris was almost disappointed to see how eager they were to go home.

Millie was down in the kitchen, feverishly packing turkey sandwiches and slicing up fruit, which she bundled into small bags for each of them. "I put extra mayonnaise on Sadie's, butter on Jack's, and nothing on Lily's," she said breathlessly. "Just the way they like them." She did not look up at Iris, who'd stopped beside her at the kitchen island.

"That's great, Mom. Thanks."

"And I added a little of that basil cream cheese you like so much on yours."

"Sounds delicious," Iris said, watching her mother's deft hands, which had begun to shake.

"But I'm not sure about Paul. Does he like whole wheat or white?"

Iris reached with both hands across the expanse of countertop and very gently placed them over her mother's. For the first time Millie looked up, her eyes a watery gray.

"Mom, thank you. For everything."

Millie nodded brusquely, returning her gaze purposefully to the food. "I just want to send you off full. Can't drive home on an empty stomach."

Iris circled the island and opened her arms. And to her surprise Millie fell into them. "Oh, Iris. I just don't know."

Iris held her, nodding in silent agreement. "She's doing great, Mom," she said, taking a deep breath. "Leah's going to be fine."

Millie stepped back to look at Iris. "Leah? Of course she is." She reached for a piece of Iris's stray hair and tucked it behind her ear, an uncharacteristically tender gesture. "I was talking about you."

"Oh." It was Iris's turn to hold back tears. "Well, I'm still sort of working on that one."

The mudroom door swung open and Bill poked his head in. "The kids are waiting, ready to go."

Outside the afternoon light was the hue of an early peach, yellow and succulent. The late-August sun hung over the rocks on the other side of the lake, glazing the green edges of leaves and the tips of the grass in gold. It was Iris's favorite time of day, in her favorite season.

"You going to follow us, then?" Paul called to her. He stood awkwardly by the car, his door open. They'd not spoken about next steps yet. Paul and Iris had only discussed some of the practical travel details the night before, at the kitchen counter, long after everyone had gone to bed. The easy details. He'd told her that the kids were ready to go home, and she'd agreed.

He'd heard about her cookbook deal, of course. But this was the first time he'd mentioned it to her alone. "So, you're really going to do this book thing, huh?"

Iris had bristled a little. "Yes, of course I am. We worked hard at it."

"I'm sure you did."

She'd waited for the other shoe to drop, silent.

"But?"

Paul looked surprised. "No buts. I'm just wondering what you'll do next."

"Next? You mean after it's published?" She hadn't thought past the glory of this book, but somewhere deep down she was pretty sure there would be another. Was certain, in fact.

"This was a nice little diversion for you this summer. But now you're coming back home, and you've got the kids and a house to run." He looked at her. "Right?"

Diversion? Iris was stunned. Not only at his lack of enthusiasm or pride in her accomplishment but at his complete lack of understanding about what this book represented for her. And about her!

"I hadn't thought that far ahead," she allowed, trying to keep her disappointment at bay. She would not lose it this early on.

Surely he hadn't meant to make her book sound so trivial. Paul was just being practical. Just inquiring.

But there was more. "I've been thinking. If you want to work that bad, you should approach the agency about getting your old job back," he told her. "The firm's doing well, but we've got to buckle down. There's the home equity line. And the driveway needs repaving. Every dollar helps."

And there it was. The dollars and sense that Paul coffered at every turn. Iris could've kicked herself; had one summer away really made her expect something different? Iris had walked out of the kitchen and gone to bed perplexed and angry.

Now, standing in the driveway, Paul waited uncertainly for her reply.

"Yes," she said finally, around a giant lump in her throat. "I'll follow you home." She gestured to the walkway, where her father was approaching with her bags. Paul lurched forward to assist.

"Thanks, Bill. Let me help." Paul relieved Bill of the bags, but then halted, frowning. "Geez, Iris, what have you got in here?"

She shrugged. "Just the stuff I brought with me. And a few new things I bought in town this summer."

He sighed. "New clothes. How much did you spend?"

"What it cost. I needed those things. And I *liked* them."

Trish's face flashed in her mind as Iris watched Paul impatiently jam the bags into the trunk of the car, but she pushed it away.

She focused instead on the kids, who were hugging their grandmother good-bye.

"Don't worry, Grandma," Jack said, peeking into his lunch bag. "We'll eat our sandwiches before we have dessert."

Millie enveloped him in one last hug. "Oh, go ahead and eat the brownie first." She looked at Iris, smiling. "Life is short."

Iris watched as the kids settled themselves into the back of their father's car. "If Lily bugs me, I'm riding with you," Sadie warned her mother.

"You keep your dad company," Iris said, closing the door and leaning into the open window. She had chosen them. She would follow Paul home, but she needed this last ride to herself.

Before ducking into the car himself, Paul thanked her parents. For what, Iris wasn't sure. For not throwing him out? For giving him a second chance?

"I'll be behind you," Iris told him. "After I make a few last good-byes."

Whether he understood or not, Paul did not press. Instead he offered a short "Drive safe."

And then they were gone.

Millie, who had never liked good-byes, pecked Iris quickly on the cheek and scurried back inside. Only Bill stood in the driveway, watching as Iris put the last of her things in the Rover.

"You know you can always come back when you want to," he told her.

"I know, Daddy." And then she hugged him good-bye. "You're so good to me."

Bill chuckled softly in her ear as they hugged, his voice warm and comforting. "Take your time," he told her.

"I will."

He held the car door as she stepped in. "Just remember one thing, for your old man, all right?"

"What's that?"

"There's more than one road leading home."

Thirty-Nine

The gravel crunched beneath her tires as she pulled away from the house and up onto the dirt driveway leading out of the farm. The red barn loomed before her, and Iris scanned the grassy hillside. There was no sign of him.

She left the engine running. The barn was empty, the sliding door swung wide open as if expecting her. Inside, the air was cool and dark. Dust motes floated lazily on the sun shafts that spilled through the paned windows. Iris stood on the threshold, letting her eyes roam across the barn's expanse, past the horse stalls in the rear. Over the dents she'd made with the shovel that first afternoon, still fresh on the old stall door. And above, to the beams that she'd helped restore during those long, hard early days. She studied the evenly spaced chestnut beams running across the ceiling, each so square and solid. It seemed years ago that Cooper had first passed her a hammer, joking that she'd best put that arm to use. And even longer ago that he'd held her, pressing his lips to her forehead, in this very spot as the whole summer stilled outside the windows.

When would she be back here? She could not imagine letting time pass, as she had before, without returning. No, the kids had had their first real taste of the farm and the lake. They'd be eager to return. And someday, so would she.

It had been a good summer. One that had shaped each of them in a way that would stay with them. Despite its pain, she wouldn't have changed any of it. Like the beams she'd supported in the barn ceiling that summer, it came down to sistering. "You've got to sister the beams, Iris," Cooper had explained. "You don't need to tear down the old ones. It's part of the history. All it needs is to be sistered."

"Good-bye, barn," Iris said out loud. She walked to the center of the dirt floor and looked up at their work, craning her neck to take it all in. As if under a cathedral, she turned in a slow circle. Then another, a little faster until the beams spun lazily overhead. The same dizziness that had filled her limbs when Cooper kissed her began to alter her balance, and soon the whole barn flew past. The stalls, walls, and open door tumbled by as she spun, until suddenly a dark figure filled the doorway.

Iris halted, swaying on unsteady legs, and stumbled forward. "Cooper?"

The figure stepped forward and Iris blinked.

It was Ernesto. "Sorry, Iris. Didn't mean to scare you."

She stood, trying to catch her balance. "You didn't."

He pointed to a pile of wood stacked in the corner, left over from her barn project with Cooper. "Your mother asked me to clean up. That okay?"

Iris watched as Ernesto dragged the leftover plywood and timbers and carried them outside to his truck. He was cleaning up. Tossing out the debris of her summer project. Salvaging the good remnants. It was time to go.

Iris retrieved her tool belt from the corner, the weight of it heavy in her hands. She looked at the engraving: *Iris, Summer 2015*

"Are you sure Cooper doesn't want any of this?" she asked.

Ernesto paused. "Mr. Cooper finished his work here. He is done."

Iris shook her head. "But—the smokehouse. It's not complete."

Ernesto shook his head. "He quit. Gave the job to me to finish. Mr. Cooper went to Vermont."

Iris's voice caught. "Cooper quit? Do you know when?"

Ernesto shrugged. "This morning."

◆ ◆ ◆

Iris navigated the hilly roads of Hampstead carefully. The evergreen trees were dense along the lakefront outside her window, and the terrain rose and fell around her. But she scarcely noticed the views. Cooper had left before she did.

By the time she pulled onto Route 7, Iris's throat was tight. It didn't surprise her. She'd not slept well, and she was probably well on her way to catching a cold. As the signs for Interstate 91 began to dot the roadside, her nose began to run and she had to reach over and fumble in the glove box for a wadded-up tissue.

Suddenly Iris's phone chimed in her purse, and she plucked it out, her heart stopping. Was it him?

Instead, *Paul* flashed across her screen. "Yes? Hello?"

"Hi, Mommy." It was Lily. "We're stopping for doughnuts. Do you want to meet us?"

Iris blinked, her vision suddenly blurred, and she realized her eyes were welling.

"You guys go ahead. I'll meet you at home, honey."

The tears began to stream down her cheeks, a steady flow that caused her to let go of the wheel for a second to swipe them away.

"Mommy, are you there?" The final sign for Interstate 91 loomed before her, and for a moment Iris hesitated: which way was home, east or west? Her mind blanked in confusion. At the last second, Iris swerved left onto the western entrance, nearly sideswiping a car pulling up the entrance ramp beside her. The car blared its horn and she slowed, letting it pass. "I'm here!" She shook her head, willing clarity. What was the matter with her?

Iris checked her side mirror carefully this time and merged onto the highway. Forty-two miles to Boston, the big green sign read. She leaned back in her seat, breathing hard. "Honey, I better go. I love you. I'll see you at home."

Home. Where her bedroom, with its antique canopy bed,

probably unmade since she'd left it, awaited her. Where she'd unpack her bags and look around, wondering where to begin. All of it right back where she'd left it, nothing having changed. But *she* had changed.

The first few miles went by quickly enough, but the tears did not abate. If anything they fell faster, and before she knew it Iris was crying openly, her chest racking with each sob. What was happening?

She wondered what Leah was doing right now, even thought of calling her. But no, it was her first day at the rehab center. She was probably exhausted. Iris knew she had several grueling weeks of therapy to get through. But at least she had Stephen.

What did Iris have? As soon as she wrapped up that "cute little project" that was her book, what next? She shuddered. It was the end of summer, which suddenly felt like the end of *her*.

Iris gripped the steering wheel and fought to catch her breath. "Boston 30 Miles," the next sign said. But Iris did not think she'd make it another second. Up ahead, a rest stop loomed on her right and Iris flipped her signal on and swerved into the exit lane. "Gas. Food. Lodging." Her vision blurred as she followed the signs. She had to get out of the car. To get air. But just as the exit ramp roared up on her right, her eyes rested on another sign.

"91 East to Vermont."

She gasped. What was it her father said about roads leading home? Reflexively, Iris flicked off her turning signal. Sailing past the rest stop exit ramp, she leaned back into her seat and steered straight.

The tears stopped.

◆　◆　◆

For the next twenty miles Iris did not think. She scarcely breathed. But somehow the car continued in its lane. She did not have a plan and she would not allow herself to try to think of one.

Iris knew Cooper's cabin was just off Route 7, in the village of Stowe. She did not know the exact address. Or whether it was listed under his name or his father's. But she did have an idea of where the little roadside café was. The café that he stopped at each time he made the trip. The very place he'd wanted to take her when he'd invited her to make the lumber run all those weeks ago. She checked the clock. It was already one thirty. Past lunch. Hell, Cooper had left Hampstead that morning, according to Ernesto. He would've beaten her to Vermont at least two hours ago, if he'd stopped by the café at all. But it was all she had to go on, and so she went.

Miles later, she entered Stowe village and slowed the car, craning her neck as she passed through downtown. A bookstore. A ski shop. An inn, and a hardware store. Once the village fell away, she pulled into the lot of a stately white New England church and rolled down her window. Up here the air was crisp, the sky an impossible blue. She could swear she almost smelled fall coming.

Cooper had said the café was just on the outskirts of town, but she didn't know which end, or its name. So far she hadn't passed anything, but she was well outside of the village center now. She picked up her phone, intending to Google Stowe eateries, but of course she had no service. Frustrated, she tossed the phone back on the passenger seat.

Ahead, a sharp curve took her around a large outcropping of rocky hillside. On the other side of the road a silver trail of river snaked through a gully. The road straightened, dotted with only a few clapboard houses and inns, and she followed it another mile. She was just about to give up when a small red house caught her attention up ahead. There was a sign in front covered in white lights. "Andy's Café." This had to be it.

Cooper's truck was not parked in the small gravel lot. Iris's heart sank, but it was quickly followed by a surge of anger at herself. What had she been expecting? She had no idea if this was the right place. Or if Cooper was even in town, for sure. It dawned on her that this might be a big mistake.

Iris did not know how long she sat outside Andy's. She stared numbly at the twinkly white lights that adorned the hand-painted sign. Even in her haze of confusion, its charm was not lost on her. The little café was barely larger than one of Millie's potting sheds, and yet it had old barn siding and transom windows with teeming flower boxes. A copper gooseneck lantern hung over the front door. Lily would've thought the place magical, the stuff of fairies.

When her stomach began to rumble, Iris realized she'd been stewing in the car for over thirty minutes. At the very least she needed to eat something. Stiffly, Iris got out of the car and stretched. The chalkboard sign by the front listed crème fraîche pancakes as today's breakfast special. Mouth watering, she hoped they'd still serve them.

They did. When she'd dragged the last forkful of fluffy pancake through the puddle of maple syrup on her plate, Iris was stuffed. It was time to go home. Paul and the kids would be wondering. Paul would probably be impatient; what reason did she have for delaying her return? She'd suddenly decided to go antiquing in Vermont? Iris closed her eyes and rubbed her temples.

"Is that all, ma'am?" The waitress was about Millie's age, though soft around the edges and quick with a smile. Iris was half tempted to ask her to drive her home. She was suddenly exhausted.

"Yes, thank you."

"Why don't I get you another cup of coffee, hon. Would you like that?"

Iris nodded, her eyes still closed. Yes, she should ask this nice lady to drive her home. She'd probably stay below the speed limit and keep the radio turned to something soft, so Iris could sleep. She might even come in and make them all dinner when they arrived home.

The bell above the door jingled again.

"Would you like cream in that coffee, honey?"

"Better make that a decaf, Mary."

Iris's eyes flew open at the sound of his voice. Cooper Woods stood across from her.

His eyes were glassy with emotion, but his voice was steady. "Caffeine makes her talk too fast," he said. "Though I love the sound of her voice." He sat down across from her. "But then again, she talks so much it's hard to get a word in, anyway."

"Decaf it is." Mary disappeared, leaving Iris floundering for words.

"What are you doing here?" Iris sputtered.

"Me?" Cooper laughed.

Iris flushed deeply, the reality of what she'd done rushing at her. He was here. And so was she.

"Iris, what are you doing here? Is everything okay?"

"Yes," she sputtered. "Now it is." She composed herself and looked him in the eyes. "I want to have lunch here with you next week."

Cooper's brow furrowed. "Next week?"

"Yes." She was grinning—it was all making sense now.

"I don't understand. I thought you were going home."

"I am going home. I have to. But I want to have lunch with you next week. And the week after that. And the next one, too."

Cooper studied her carefully, his head cocked to one side. The corner of his mouth lifted in the beginning of a smile. "Are you saying what I think you're saying?"

Iris couldn't help it. She laughed, with joy and nervousness and relief. "This can work. My marriage is over; I know that for sure now. Hell, I knew it before you and I even began." She paused, looking at him in earnest. "So, I have to go home and get through that. But as I do, I want you in my life, Cooper."

The look on his face wasn't exactly what she'd been hoping for. The smile disappeared, and Cooper glanced to the door, and back at her. "Iris, you don't owe me any promises. I'm so glad you're here, but after everything you said at my cabin . . ."

She reached across the table, knocking the saltshaker over,

and grabbed his hand. "I'm not making you a promise. I'm making a lunch date. Every week, until I figure things out. However long it takes."

"Are you sure about this?" His voice was soft, uncertain.

Iris squeezed his hand. "Cooper, this summer I came home. Not just home to my parents' farm or to my crazy family. But home to myself. And I'm not leaving that ever again."

"What about Paul? And the kids?"

"It's going to be hard. But it's not fair to the kids, or even to Paul, to pretend. I don't want to raise a family in a house full of sadness."

Iris looked out the window at the maple trees across the main road. Already, the edges of the leaves were hued in the yellow of fall. "If anything, Leah made me realize life is too short." She paused and took a deep breath. "My kids will always come first, but that doesn't have to mean I come last."

Cooper listened intently, his eyes moving over her face as she spoke. When she finished he blinked and sat back in his chair. He was still holding her hand.

Mary returned with their coffees, and set one cup in front of Iris and the other before Cooper. "One decaf, one regular. Anything else?"

"The menu, please," Cooper said finally. His eyes still on Iris.

"You don't want your regular, hon?" Mary asked.

Cooper shook his head, grinning in that boyish way that made Iris's breath catch in her chest. "I think I'd better try something new this time. It seems we'll be coming here a lot more often."

Forty

The postcard showed a bird's-eye view of the farm's north field, dappled orange with fat round squash. Leah's dreamy script covered the back in one sweeping sentence. *"Come pick a pumpkin!"*

Fall had spread through New England, tracing the leaves in gold and tickling the fresh-mown lawns with its detritus. Each morning the air was crisp, the scent of wood smoke thick, as Iris wrapped her neck with one of Millie's pilfered woolen scarves before walking Samson.

Now, as she stood at the counter in her kitchen, Iris set the postcard down and looked outside. Sadie stood at the mailbox, her skinny long legs once browned by the summer sun now covered in denim, like two navy toothpicks. From here, she looked so grown-up. Beside her, Jack bent over a mud puddle, dragging a stick through the water. He dropped it for a rock, which he tossed into the puddle. Iris watched as Sadie jumped back, scolding him. Lily laughed and brandished the muddy stick, and began chasing them both. The kids were okay.

It had been a long couple of months back home. Iris was thankful the kids were happily settled into their new classes at school; the routine had ferried them through the rougher days. Paul, to her dismay, had been more surprised than she'd imagined when she came home late that August afternoon to tell him it was over.

There were long October nights when Iris cried, alone under her sheets, wondering if this was all a terrible mistake. But when she stood at her window and looked up at the rich constellations dotting the darkness, she felt something lift. Remembering the sky over Hampstead Lake. The person she'd returned to that summer. And the family still awaiting her there. And then she knew they'd get through, somehow.

They'd agreed easily to joint custody, and were cognizant of allowing the kids access to them both whenever they wished. For now, Iris and the kids remained in the house. The advance for the new book had given her some cushioning, at least for the present. It wouldn't hit store bookshelves for another year. In the meantime, she had taken on two new authors, turning Paul's den into her own office, and while the work was still young, she felt promise.

As for Cooper, she kept her promise about lunch. Sometimes twice a week, sometimes once every other. They spoke on the phone before bed every night, his voice in her ear as crisp as the fall air.

In the beginning, Iris had worried so much about dividing herself, about the going back and forth, and what it meant both for herself and for the kids. But she was learning that those were only places; she already had what she needed inside. And what was missing, Cooper was gently filling in. With each word, each whisper, each touch.

Now, Iris ran her finger over the orange pumpkins on the postcard once more, and glanced up at the wall clock. The bus was coming. No time for a coat. She raced outside and down the driveway, her breath coming in short white puffs.

"Is that for me?" Lily asked, grabbing the postcard from her hand.

"The pumpkins," Iris huffed, doubling over. "They're ready."

Jack frowned. "For what?"

"Aunty Leah says the pumpkins are ready to pick. Who wants to go to the farm this weekend?"

◆ ◆ ◆

As the school bus doors slapped shut, Iris tucked the postcard back in her vest pocket. She waved heartily as the bus heaved itself back onto the road, and away. Lily's grinning face growing smaller in the window.

In the end, it was not about Paul or Cooper, or even the new book with Trish. It was something her father had said. The words were murky now, as time tends to make things, but the sentiment remained visceral. Bill Standish had warned her about roads. The winding and the scenic, the ones that rose up over craggy hilltops and vanished down the other side. It was something that coursed inside her, a lane that led her away and back again to what mattered most. More than one road led home. It was all right to change course, as long as she kept her compass pointed in the right direction. And for the first time in a long time, Iris knew the way.

ACKNOWLEDGMENTS

In keeping with the metaphor of "sistering," I am so thankful for all the "sisters" in my life. To those girls with whom I laugh, cry, walk my dogs, throw together recipes, share my bike, carpool . . . you know when to show up with a bottle of wine, and never question the chicken feathers in the backseat. Jennifer, Jen, Sarah, Jamie, Alexander, Dawn, Amy C., Becky, Amy R., and all the rest: you know who you are. May you also know how fiercely I love each and every one of you.

I must thank the incredibly talented and always effervescent MacKenzie Fraser Bub, of Trident Media, who first got her hands on these pages and left no room for guessing in her enthusiasm for this story. You remained steadfastly on board, from first read to completion—always checking in. I'm so grateful for our partnership. And I love that you tote a hammer in that sleek handbag! Thank you.

Thank you to my amazing editor, Megan Reid, at Emily Bestler Books, who fell in love with these sisters and eagerly took the reins. I remain in awe of your expedience, your sharp ear, and your belief in Iris. You're a sister at heart yourself; I knew that this story was in competent hands from the moment we met. Working with you has been pure joy.

To Emily Bestler, who leads a powerhouse team at Emily Bestler Books, of Simon & Schuster. I am ever grateful for your kind words, which were both generous and immensely meaning-ful to me as a writer. I am honored to be on your team.

Family is everything. And families make good stories. To my parents, Marlene and Barry, who first taught me the love of a good book. To my brothers, Jesse and Josh, who survived the shared stories of our childhood that delight my own children today. To my grandmother Marjorie, the real storyteller of the family, whose ebullient voice still rises in my memories. And to my grandfather Seth, who still delights in a good dog tale. Most of all to my own family: to Jason, Grace, and Finley. You are the reasons I do what I do every day. You are my reasons for everything.

The Lake Season

Hannah McKinnon

A Readers Club Guide

EMILY
BESTLER
BOOKS

AP
READERS
CLUB

Introduction

Iris and Leah Standish have never quite seen eye to eye. As sisters growing up on Hampstead Lake, Iris would carefully dip her toe in the water as Leah dove in headfirst. In high school, Iris focused quietly on her studies as Leah threw herself into the social scene. Twenty years later, Iris has a big house in the suburbs with her lawyer husband and three children as Leah bounds back from her cross-country adventures with a successful and charming fiancée on her arm. But behind Iris' picture perfect life is a crumbling marriage, and Leah's bright plans for her fairy-tale wedding are threaded with doubt, and a dark secret.

It only takes one hot, New England summer to unravel everything that Iris and Leah think they know about each other. For despite their incongruent paths, the Standish sisters both find themselves back in their childhood home, dangerously close to losing everything. *The Lake Season* is a stunning testament to the intricate and sometimes tenuous bonds of sisterhood and family.

Questions and Topics for Discussion

1. What does Leah's postcard—"Please Come"—say about the current state of her and Iris's relationship? Why does Iris say yes to such an enigmatic missive?

2. Iris finds solace in her friendship with Trish, who tells her to "embrace the dirt," in both the garden and her life. What do you think she means by this? Does Iris follow her advice?

3. Not only does Iris have to navigate her sisterhood with Leah, she also has to foster one between her daughters, Sadie and Lily. What complications echo between the two relationships? How

are our identities formed by our siblings? And how much can a parent really intervene?

4. Leah scoffs at Iris's notion that a life can be reduced to chapters. Who do you think is right here? Why?

5. At the dress fitting, Iris catches a troubling glimpse of Leah staring blankly in the mirror and smearing ChapStick on her lips. Discuss Leah's undercurrent of mental illness throughout the narrative. Why do you think Millie and Leah feel the need to be so secretive? Especially when it comes to Iris?

6. Iris's high school crush, Cooper Woods, is an unexpected source of comfort. He also teaches her about "sistering," a woodworking trick in which a new beam is installed to support an old beam. How does this tie into the themes that resonate throughout the novel?

7. Why do you think Leah panics when she senses that Cooper and Iris are developing romantic feelings for each other? How does it reconfigure the social order of their relationship? Discuss the jealousies at play.

8. At the Hampstead Brewery, Trish suggests that Iris "stayed away long enough to *make* it hard to come back." Do you agree with Trish? Is Iris partially responsible for her family's emotional distance? What are the consequences implicit in returning home?

9. As Cooper and Iris get closer, Iris realizes she can't move forward until she figures out what she wants. Leah also has great difficulty facing herself, as evidenced by her nervous breakdown and near drowning. Why do you think this is such a difficult task? How do we get stuck in the trenches of adulthood?

10. When Leah finally opens up about her relationship with Kurt in Yellowstone, Iris is taken aback to hear that Leah considers her

to be the stronger sister. Cooper and Trish echo this sentiment. Why can't Iris see herself this way? How do our self-perceptions differ from those around us?

11. Discuss Iris's official transition from literary agent to cookbook author. How does this signal a definitive shift in her life approach? What is different about the two roles?

12. Stephen is heartbroken to hear that Leah has lied to him about her pregnancy and subsequent medical condition. Discuss the role that trust plays throughout the narrative. Where and when is it most essential, especially for Iris and Leah?

13. As Iris prepares to begin a new phase of her life, her father reminds her that there is "more than one road leading home." How does this affect her decision to follow Cooper, instead of Paul?

Tips to Enhance Your Book Club

1. Hampstead Lake figures prominently in the narrative as a source of peace and comfort. Take a relaxing group trip to your local watering hole, whether it's the beach, lake, or local pool.

2. Despite their differences, Leah and Iris are both big believers in the curative powers of a good martini. Host a martini night and open up about your own best sibling stories—the good and the bad! In honor of Trish and Iris's new farm-to-table cookbook, patronize your local farmer's market and cook up a fresh dish to go with those drinks.

3. Check out another incredible sister story from Emily Bestler Books, Jodi Picoult's *My Sister's Keeper*. Or rent the feature film, starring Cameron Diaz.